Hood Wife, Good Wife

CYNTHIA MARCANO

Urban House Publishing

Publisher's Note: This is a work of fiction. Names, characters, places, and incidents are a product of the author's imagination. Locales and public names are sometimes used for atmospheric purposes. Any resemblance to actual people, living or dead, or to businesses, companies, events, institutions, or locales is completely coincidental.

Book Layout ©2022 House of Cynthia Designs
Copyright © 2022
First Edition 2022 – Hood Wife, Good Wife
Author: Cynthia Marcano, Indian Spice
Library of Congress Control Number:
ISBN-13:

For My Sister Delma

The epitome of a ride or die &, praying wife.
You are both His, and his, beauty and beast.

PROLOGUE

Elijah

ending over the sink, I took in a mouth full of water and rinsed before spitting it out. I splashed cold water on my face hoping to revive myself and clear my foggy head. My thoughts were fuzzy and only bits and snatches of when, where, why, and with whom were making sense to me. I reached for a nearby white towel stacked neatly in the corner of the hotel vanity, wishing the room would stop spinning. After patting my face dry, I stood tall and looked at my reflection in the large mirror. I couldn't tell you why, but shame washed over me, and deep down inside I knew no amount of soap and water could cleanse me of the filth.

Stumbling nude back into the bedroom of my hotel suite, I looked around before collapsing onto the corner of the king-sized bed. Through a slit of the drawn curtains, I could see the moonlight reflecting off the Delaware River. It was still the middle of the night. That brought me a measure of relief. I had a few more hours to sober up. My head was pounding like crazy, and the sight of some leftover room service made my stomach churn. A few bottles of brown liquor and empty glasses littered the room. A flashback of whiskey burning my chest surfaced.

I laid back in the dark and placed my arm over my eyes, focusing on getting my head straight. This was exactly why I was never suited to be the party guy. I couldn't hang and I knew it. But my fam and my boys insisted we do my bachelor party big. After turning down a boy's trip to Vegas, I could only agree to a small bachelor party in a Philly hotel. I should have stuck to a football game or something because this hangover wasn't worth the misery, I was now in.

It didn't take long before I dozed off. I began dreaming of Tianna, my fiancée. In a few weeks, we'd be married. I couldn't deny I was anxious for the honeymoon. Ever since she'd recommitted her life to God, she'd remained celibate and insisted that we wait to be intimate,

5

although we'd already been sexually active as teens. That eventually led to her miscarrying our baby and not a topic of discussion we brought up. All that mattered now was that I loved that woman, and she was worth waiting for. I'd never pressure her.

But that was in reality. In my dreams, she was pleasuring me like a champ and my body was reacting as if it was real. I didn't want to wake up. I reached down wanting to slide my hands into her luxuriously long hair, but I kept my arms still not wanting to risk the possibility of disturbing the dream. I pictured my future wife loving on me, and my heart and blood started racing. Tianna was fine and only got better with age. Tall and slender with just enough curve in all the places brown women were often naturally well endowed.

As if she felt my love and desire for her, she began to increase her pleasuring and after a while, I couldn't hold on any longer and released. I couldn't remember the last time I had had a wet dream. I slept so deeply after that. A few hours later I woke up to the smell of freshly brewed coffee and the sun shining through the large windows. I sat up and saw the curtains had been opened and the room tidied up. All of the empty bottles and cups had been placed in the trash. By the cup of fresh coffee that had been set by my watch, was a note with feminine handwriting, a few hundred-dollar bills beneath it.

Your secret is safe with me. Please do the same for me. I wish you and your girl a happy life together.

My hands got sweaty, and I looked around the room frantically. Whoever had been there was now gone. I opened the door and heard the ding of elevator doors. I ran down the hallway wrapped in a white bedsheet, but I had gotten there too late. I slammed on the closed elevator doors. "Shit!"

I rushed back to the room and downed some coffee. I tried remembering what happened the night before. Slowly memories began to resurface before they all began to rush back to me in an avalanche. As anxious as I had been to remember the details of the night, the desire to forget was two-fold. Shame filled me like hot air in a balloon. Flashbacks of me and that woman pounded my memory, but the image of her face was a blur. One thing I knew for sure, however, was that my dream hadn't been a dream at all. And it wasn't Tianna that had pleasured me. Not during and definitely not the few times before it.

I showered and changed not knowing how to go home and face my fiancée. I loved her with all of my heart. Had I been sober, I would have never cheated on her. After years of being apart, when I finally saw her again, I did everything in my power to get her back. I would never risk losing her again. It was a piss poor excuse, but it was my truth. I decided right then and there that I would take that secret to the grave. Some unknown woman, that meant nothing to me, wasn't worth hurting Tianna. I made a promise to myself to never get that drunk again. I'd marry the love of my life. I'd be a father to her son Justin Junior, who I already loved as my own. I'd spend the rest of my life making Tianna the happiest woman in the world.

ONE

Tianna

One Year Later

T he sound of thunder startled me into action. I jumped over a puddle that had gathered at the entrance of the school's side door and ran into the dark toward my car as fast as my flats allowed. I quickly unlocked the driver-side door, tossed my bag and wet coat on the passenger's side, and jumped in. The steady rain hadn't eased since it had begun overnight.

I took a second to catch my breath before I slid the key into the ignition and turned, bringing the car to life. I snapped my seatbelt in and turned on the radio. I'd missed the five-o'clock traffic jam mix, so I played my Amerie CD instead. I drove out the parking lot slowly, Camden's streets in no condition to be raced down. The potholes were like freaking craters.

At the red light, I was hypnotized by my windshield wipers moving back and forth rhythmically. In sync. Their steady swish lulled me into a trance. Movement on the street corner snatched my attention. A group of young women were yelling and moving fast. I peeked through my passenger side window, but the streetlight was out, intentionally damaged by the local drug dealers that had occupied the street corner day and night.

When the light changed, I eased off the brake only to slam on them when a young woman fell against my hood, a rowdy crowd surrounding her. As my wipers cleared the rain, I saw a young woman yelling, anger etched into every feature of her baby face. She cocked her fist back before hammering it into a petite girl's face that had fallen onto my car. Coming from behind her another young wearing a baseball cap took her turn and kicked the girl in the stomach. When the thin girl knelt forward clutching her stomach, she caught another kick to her face. Before I knew it, the angry mob began pounding down on her without restraint.

It enraged me. I slammed my palm on my horn and held it down. The loud, long and obnoxious noise made them all jump back. The young woman that was being jumped, rose and looked at me. It wasn't an intentional stare. She was dazed, confused, and stumbling with blood running down her face. For a split moment, I recognized her. Memories of my best friend Bianca engulfed me. I missed Bianca's crazy self.

Bianca was my sister from another mister. I would give my life for hers and her for mine. As if the enemy had read my thoughts, one of the mob members took a fist full of hair from the Bianca look-alike, spun her around, and smashed her face into the hood of my car before they all began another round of assault.

I immediately took my seatbelt off and exited my car, not caring about the rain. I yelled for them to stop. The angry mob turned to me, vulgarity and threats being hurled at me, but I couldn't bring myself to care about my own welfare. I pushed my way into the crowd in an attempt to shield her from the onslaught. A blow to the back of my head knocked me forward and onto the young woman I was trying to save. I covered her body with mine, taking on every kick and punch. I felt my head get yanked back by my hair so viciously, I thought my neck had snapped.

Soon after, I was thrown down to the ground. I felt a swift kick to the abdomen. Then another to my face. The world began to spin briefly before I was able to gain some clarity of vision. I looked up and saw the young woman's head being bashed into my car. I forced myself to my feet. They were going to kill her if they continued this vicious assault. I stood to my feet and stumbled my way forward. The sound of a gun firing multiple times had the gang of girls fleeing in all directions. I made it to the battered young lady and caught her, just as she was about to pass out. I lifted her as best I could, allowing her to rest her weight on me.

I drove in a mad rush to Cooper Hospital, illegally parking my car in front of the emergency room doors, and ran in screaming for help before I collapsed to the ground, exhausted. The young lady had seized while I drove, and looked on helplessly. I didn't know if she was even still alive. An attendant calmly crouched down before me and began asking me a bunch of questions about myself. I shook my head at her. "Not me. Please. There's a young lady in my car." I could hardly get the words out as pain began to rip through my midsection. I turned to the side and vomited.

I wiped my mouth on my sleeve and when she began asking questions again, it irked me. Why was this woman not understanding me? I pointed toward my car. "Go help her!" I yelled.

"Someone is already helping her," she assured me evenly. "I need you to answer some questions for me, ok?"

I nodded. My mouth began to water, and I suddenly felt like I had been sitting in a sauna, I had gotten so hot. Sweat beaded above my brows and my stomach convulsed. I turned to vomit again then promptly passed out on the cold tiled ER floor.

I woke up as I was being placed in a hospital bed. I heard a woman's voice close by but had trouble making out what she was saying. A few minutes later she stepped into my line of vision and smiled at me.

"Welcome back, Ms. Townsend."

"Mrs.," I responded groggily. "I'm married."

"Well at least that makes one of us," she joked, a slight accent as she fixed the intravenous tube flowing from the monitor to my hand. She was an exotic-looking brown woman with a wide nose and mouth and eyes so hazel they'd practically glowed goldenly. I stared at her a little confused. She must've noticed. She smiled as she continued her ministrations. "I'm originally from Australia. My very white father fell in love with my Aboriginal mother and here I am as a result."

I broke eye contact and slowly turned my head away from her. Had I not had a million things fighting for mental attention I would have been embarrassed. But I wasn't. Instead, I changed the subject. "I'd like to call my husband."

She tucked the wire under my blanket, working as she talked. "The emergency contact information in your wallet has already been notified. Is that your husband?"

Relief washed over me. "Yes." I was so glad El had convinced me to do that. He didn't like that I worked in Camden but respected my decision to go where I felt led.

The nurse's face sobered. "I need you to just take it easy for me for a little bit. You went through a rough ordeal today."

Suddenly the memories of being pounded on with fists and feet rushed to the surface. I kept seeing the Bianca look-alike falling like she was Rocky after fighting the Russian the first time. I shook my head at the reference. My over-active imagination and my brother, Abe's, obsession with martial arts and fighting movies were screwing with my head. More than anything right now I just wanted to know she was ok. "Where's the girl I brought to the ER? Is she ok?" I was beginning to panic remembering her convulsing in the back seat of my car.

"Sabrina was taken into emergency surgery. Are you any relation to her?"

I shook my head.

"Then that's all I can tell you."

This time she stopped fiddling with tubes and blankets and monitors and looked directly at me bright-eyed and smiling. "The doctor will be in shortly. Get some rest." Then she sauntered out.

That was easy for her to say. She hadn't just witnessed and experienced what I just had. My heart was beginning to race recollecting all I'd seen and heard. The shouts and vulgarities. The sound of her little body being broken. My throat constricted but I held back the tears.

I began to pray and sing a hymn quietly to myself. My body felt like it had gotten run over, reversed, and run over again. I just wanted to be home with the two loves of my life.

Justin Junior was probably driving El up a wall. I smiled at the thought. It wasn't long before my husband was at my bedside, his worry evident in his furrowed brow. "Ti, baby. Thank God you're ok." He took in every inch of my battered face and bruised arms and I saw rage fill his eyes. "Who did this to you?"

His nostrils flared and I could see he was angry on my behalf. El was not a violent man, but he'd erupt when driven to the point. I lowered my head not wanting to see him so upset. "I was at a red light and a group of girls jumped a girl and slammed her onto my car. They all began to punch and kick her so I jumped out to help her. I managed to shield her for a minute before they jumped me and then went back to her."

"Ti, that was dangerous. They could have killed you!" El raised his voice and it angered me. What did he expect me to do? Just watch a young girl get beaten to death?

"They almost killed her! I couldn't just sit there and watch!"

El paced back and forth rubbing his head in disbelief. "Of course, you wouldn't do that," he said his voice now calm and sad. "You're too good a person. But sometimes I wish you'd let someone else be the good Samaritan and you stay out of it."

"She reminded me of Bianca and I reacted."

Elijah looked at me, his eyes tender. I know you miss her. And from the insane amount of times, she calls you, I can assume she misses you too. I'm about to disconnect the phone so I can get some of that quality time with you."

I smiled at his words.

"But Ti, it wasn't Bianca. Camden is a dangerous city. You can't just go getting in fights that aren't yours. I already worry about you enough working there."

I sobered seeing how concerned he was. That man loved me and I loved him. I felt bad for making him worry. When I first got the job offer to teach art in Camden City public schools he was dead set against it but my heart was set so he supported my decision. I know that took a lot for him to think of me first. And here I wasn't even thinking about him or Justin when I jumped out of that car. I instantly felt guilty. They could have lost me forever. I called over to Eli. "Come here." He came to me and sat beside me on the bed. I intertwined my hand in his and he began to caress it. "You are right. I'm sorry. I'll be more careful from now on."

Elijah nodded and brushed aside a large strand of hair that had been loosened when someone had pulled my hair. "Get some rest, baby. We don't need to talk about this now."

I laid my head down on the pillow just as the doctor walked in, the nurse trailing behind her. "How are you feeling?"

"I've been better," I admitted. No sense in pretending otherwise.

She nodded in understanding. "That's understandable and I'm afraid I have some news that will be hard to hear," she said and look over at El then back at me. "I'm not sure you'd want me to share it aloud."

"Oh, that is my husband Elijah. You can say anything in front of him."

The doctor nodded again. "Very well. Mr. and Mrs. Townsend, I am so sorry to tell you that your son didn't survive."

Elijah and I looked at each other confused. "Doctor, what are you talking about?" I panicked and yanked on Elijah's arm. "Where is Justin? Where is he?"

Elijah looked back and forth between the doctor and me, even more confused. "Ti, JJ is with your brother. Safe and sound. I don't know what the hell she is talking about." He looked at the doctor, his glare demanding an explanation. "Ma'am, our son is home safe. What are you talking about?"

The doctor looked at the nurse puzzled then back at me. I wanted to run home and hold Justin just to prove to her she was wrong. I was both relieved and angry. Justin was safe but my heart had exploded inside of my chest. "Doctor, it is extremely incompetent of you to come into my room and deliver news meant for another patient. My son was not with me when I was assaulted."

She inhaled deeply, exhaled then met my glare full on. "Mrs. Townsend, I assure you I am not incompetent and I wish I were wrong, but I am not." She paused. I wanted to jump out of the damn bed and yank her tongue out of her mouth. "I am going to assume that you were unaware that you were pregnant. My apologies. I figured with you already being at least sixteen or seventeen weeks pregnant that you knew."

Had she sprouted wings and flown away, I would not have been more shocked by her words. I couldn't process the information, although she'd spoken in plain English. Elijah must have suffered the same disbelief. He, however, could speak. "Wait. What do you mean, pregnant?"

"While your wife was unconscious, we ran some imaging to assess for fractures. That was how we found the fetus and estimated how far along she was. An ultrasound confirmed it. As well as no fetal heart rate."

"Seven, seventeen weeks?" I forced the words out, my voice hoarse from astonishment. "That is impossible. I haven't had my cycle this month yet, but I know I bled last month or…" I paused. I couldn't remember my last cycle. My thoughts were racing like bumpers cars, smashing into each other and not going anywhere. Had it been that long since I'd had a period and hadn't even noticed?

I was beginning to hyperventilate and my heart was speeding. I looked over at Elijah. He looked at me in expectation of an answer. I tried to speak but couldn't and shook my head, tears gathering in my eyes.

His glare softened and he squeezed my hand gently. "It's ok, Ti. Calm down. Just breathe." I nodded furiously, as tears rushed down my face, exhaling slowly. It was how I'd learn to cope with the panic attacks that had begun to plague me in recent years; slow, deep breaths. After a few minutes, I calmed down.

"You ok now?" El stood to his feet and I couldn't read him. For the first time since reconnecting, I couldn't pick up his energy. Maybe I was just too overwhelmed.

I nodded quickly as a child would still fighting to hold back the tears. A baby I didn't even know existed was here and snatched away in a split second and yet I still felt his loss as if I'd loved him for a thousand years. I exhaled noisily through my nose hoping to release all that was building up inside. I had to endure for a little longer. I needed to know all I could about my son.

My son.

"Doctor, please continue with your news."

Elijah turned to me in shock. "Ti." He shook his head. "Don't."

A tear escaped but still I pressed on. I trained my attention on the doctor. "Please tell me the cause of death of my baby. You said it was a boy, correct?"

The doctor nodded appearing uncomfortable, but her discomfort was nothing in comparison to my anguish. After a few moments, she slipped back into the mindset of a professional, lifted her chin, and crossed her hands in front of her. "It is hard to tell but the most likely cause is blunt force trauma to your abdomen."

How had my day turned into such a mess of agony? Guilt consumed me whole. I was suddenly drowning in a sea of pain physically, emotionally, mentally, and spiritually. Where was God? Did he not see that all I had tried to do was save a young woman? Why was I the one being punished for being a good person? I stopped myself from traveling down that road. I exhaled slowly again. I had to take all of this in one mouthful at a time or I'd choke on my guilt and carelessness. I swallowed the lump in my throat and forced myself to speak. "And what happens next?"

"Tianna." Elijah's voice trembled in hurt and anger, an unspoken request to stop but I could not. I refused to lower myself in a pit of despair. I had lived there so many times and escaping it got harder every time. I couldn't dwell here so I pressed forward. "Doctor, please tell me what happens next."

She hesitated but continued. "There are several options, but I recommend a dilation and evacuation procedure. But you don't need to decide that right now."

Elijah walked out of the room quietly. I buried my grief and sorrow deeply, wiping away the tears brusquely. At my request, the doctor explained the procedure and I decided to proceed with her recommendation. The days afterward were a blur. The evacuation left me empty of my son, my hope in humanity, and my trust in myself. I was an empty vessel with a hole in it.

TWO
Micah

My fingers were beginning to cramp from signing my name a hundred times, but I hadn't cared. I was the new owner of another real estate investment and this would be my most lucrative acquisition yet. Old man Carlos had finally decided to sell me his lot of properties after asking him for years. At a damn good price too. He was getting too old to maintain it all and his bum ass sons were lazy as hell so they weren't any help. How could a real man just sit on his ass all day and leach off their Pops?

I shook my head at my thoughts and just kept on signing. After closing on the properties, I hugged Mr. Rivera and joked he could finally move his wife back to Puerto Rico and enjoy retirement. His smile seemed sad as he shrugged. I could only imagine he hated parting with his livelihood after so many years. He'd rented his properties so long it must have been a part of him. I'd met him when my mom had rented from him years before and even then I could see how much hard work he had put into his business. He'd been a good landlord and had inspired me to be as well.

I got into my car and sighed in relief. I was twenty-seven years old and I already owned an apartment building, a duplex, and had just added four rowhomes with, lots to my growing empire. The drug game had gotten me my start-up money but I wasn't nobody's fool. While these dudes were out here pimping out their rides and buying name-brand this and that, I kept my profile humble and stacked all my dough. As soon as I had saved enough and the opportunity presented itself, I slowly left that hustle behind for a safer one.

On the way to my mom's, I stopped by Lou's and got her a Panzarotti. Crackhead Fred was in there talking his shit as usual. He was always going on and on about the world coming to an end and famine and all this real crazy apocalyptic type shit. I bought him a cheesesteak. He looked like he hadn't eaten in a while. It was the least I could do after having been his main pusher for so long. Sometimes I felt bad knowing the drugs I sold him contributed to his current state of misfortune. Other times I was fully convinced he was a grown man and decided to use drugs all on his own. If it wasn't me, it would've been someone else supplying him. I didn't introduce or force him to use dope so why should I feel bad?

I handed him his food and walked out with my mom's. I pulled up in front of my apartment building, where my mom lived rent-free and parked. As I got out of the car, I spotted Sharmayne walking quickly down the street toward me. From the second I had first laid eyes on her I knew I wanted her to be mine. A while back I'd seen her at a bus stop down the street and offered her a ride. She looked at me like I was crazy and then gave me her back. I suppose that was some creepy-type shit of me to ask a perfect stranger to get in my car, but I lost myself in her womanly figure and mocha skin. I laughed thinking about how perverted I must have seemed to her back then.

Funny how life had a way of making new opportunities when you weren't expecting them. It wasn't six months later when she contacted me inquiring about an ad on Craigslist about a vacant apartment I was renting in my building. When she came to see it in person, she had had no idea I was the same bozo who had offered her a ride months before, and I surely didn't tell her, especially since she was pushing a baby stroller this time.

At the sight of her motherhood, I checked myself and kept our interaction strictly professional. I just assumed she had a man. Despite having better applicants, I rented her the apartment anyway. Since then, I had seen no baby daddies or anyone except for her mom coming and going.

I walked up the steps of my building slowly and took my time unlocking the main entrance door. Once inside, I checked my mom's mailbox and sorted through it purposely stalling just so I could run into my tenant. A minute later, she walked in and did the same.

"Good afternoon," I said to her. I don't know why she always made me so nervous. I was a grown-ass man, not some young dude.

"Hey," she said as she stuffed her mail in her backpack. "Have a good day," she continued before she walked toward the stairs.

Maybe it was the rush of my business savvy paying off or just perhaps her big round apple, but I stepped out of myself and made a move. "Sharmayne. Hold up a sec."

She stopped at the bottom step and turned toward me. "Yeah? What's up?"

I felt like the biggest man on the planet and I knew I had a lot to offer the right woman, so I took a chance. "Maybe I can take you out to eat sometime this week."

She seemed nonchalant by my invitation. "I'm not really dating right now. I have so much going on with work and my daughter. I'm studying for my finals and trying to pick up extra shifts whenever I can. And plus, my mom won't babysit Jaya, unless I'm at work."

She shut me down fully and completely. I could tell she was well seasoned at turning men down. "It's cool. No worries." I waved and walked toward my mom's door. Although she turned a brother down, and I admit that shit stung a little, I was too hype about the new venture that I bounced back from rejection in no time. Once she saw what I had to offer, she'd change her mind. In the meantime, my mom would be the only woman I would be taking care of and that was cool. For now.

THREE
Sharmayne

To say I was shocked that Micah had asked me out would be a lie. Ever since he'd offered me a ride from the bus stop and I'd rented an apartment from him because it was the only one I could afford, I knew he liked me. I just pretended not to notice or remember who he was. Truth was, I didn't really pay him any attention in any way. He was nice and all, but I had dreams for myself and my daughter, and Micah did not fit into that picture. At this point in my life, no man did. I could do bad all by myself. I was on my way to being an attorney come hell or high water. The last thing I needed was some drug dealer turned landlord just to hide his illegal gains, dragging me down. Nah. I was good. I was born and raised in Camden but this sure as hell wasn't my final destination.

I ran up the flight of steps and walked to my door. I could hear the Dora The Explorer theme song on full blast. I shook my head. I had asked my mom over and over again to limit the amount of time Jaya was watching TV. I had spent money on books and learning toys for that very purpose. I refused for my daughter to be a couch potato, or not knowing anything, like these little rugrats from the hood. I needed her to be prepared to be on the same educational level as the other children she'd eventually attend school with, in a much better neighborhood. Those parents could afford daycare and get a jumpstart on learning for their kids. I could not. But I'd do the best I could for my baby and her future.

I unlocked the door and tossed my bag on the dusty recliner my neighbor had thrown out. It wasn't exactly 'another man's treasure' but it was better than nothing. I lowered the volume on the television and tossed the remote by my bag. How Jaya was asleep in her playpen with all that noise I'd never understand. If I so much as laid her in her crib after falling asleep on me, she'd scream like a banshee. I looked down at her sleeping peacefully. I tucked the blanket around her tightly and watched her. She was so beautiful and innocent. I'd change my whole world just to make sure she'd have a safe one to grow up in. And I had.

I walked into the kitchen and grabbed a glass out of the cupboard, filled it up, and downed some water. The weather was beginning to warm up and I purposely would speed walk my trek home from the bus stop to get some exercise in. I had let myself go once I found out I was pregnant. I didn't know what activities were safe or weren't during pregnancy so I just stopped doing almost everything altogether. A little dramatic it seemed, but if anything, it was ignorance. My mom wasn't exactly a person to ask for motherly advice or the role model I wanted to emulate. But I suppose I could have had worse. If it weren't for her, I wouldn't have been able to maintain school and work.

I called out to her. "Mom. I'm home early." I flicked the light on in my bedroom, sat on the corner of my bed, and removed my shoes. Being a waitress sucked but the tips could be good if you knew how to treat the customers right. I removed my socks and massaged the aches away. I was given a few hours break before I had to return to cover the late-night shift call-out instead of the evening hours I usually worked. With Jaya asleep, I could get a nap in before working another eight hours.

I went in search of my mom to let her know that I'd be working another shift and to deliver a message from my Aunt Vicky. "Mom!" I checked her bedroom and nothing. I heard movement in the bathroom and knocked on the door. "Mom, I'm home. Oh, and I saw Aunt Vicky and she wanted me to tell you that her phone got cut off so she can't call you."

"Oh, oh, oh, kay," she replied her words slurred.

She sounded weird but she had her days where she seemed to be in a different world. "I have to go back to work tonight. The new girl already called out. I'm covering her shift."

She groaned a response before I heard a crash within.

"Mom! You ok?" I tried to open the door but it was locked. "Mom, open the door!" I jiggled the knob as if it would just magically unlock itself. I ran to my bedroom and searched for my tweezers. I quickly found them and picked the bathroom door lock. My mom was passed out on the floor, the shelf above her hanging on by a nail and all the toiletries it housed scattered on the floor.

I quickly knelt before her unconscious body trying to wake her. "Mom? Mom?" When she didn't respond I began to panic. I patted her face but nothing. I shook her again. Still nothing. I leaned over and put my ear to her chest. I heard her heartbeat and it seemed slow, but what did I know about normal heartbeats? I felt her breath on my neck and suddenly she coughed and moaned. The air went back into my lungs and I sat back on my haunches a bit relieved. She wasn't dead, but something was wrong.

"Mom? Mom?" She moaned again in response before she spoke.

She turned the little attention she could muster toward me. "Hey, baby. Whatcha doin' home so early?" The words muffled and slow, made me stop and stare at her.

I heard something fall to the floor by my knees. I casually looked down to investigate, and that's when I saw it. It rocked my world on its axis. A syringe sat nestled between the toilet and my knee. When I took the time to look around, I saw a spoon and an empty baggie, white powder remnants in it. A scene from when I was thirteen crashed into my consciousness. It had been the first time I had ever seen my mom shoot up. I didn't understand it then but knew it was wrong. I knew exactly what it was now and it infuriated me.

She'd been clean and sober for so long I searched my memories to see where she'd relapsed. It was a pointless search. I was so worried about my own business and Jaya, I didn't give my mom much thought. That sounded selfish but I had to be. No one was gonna take care of me or my baby. My mom was a grown-ass woman who could take care of herself. The fact that she chose drugs instead of her children when she was young was one thing. My brother, Kyle, and I had been in and out of foster care more times than I cared to count. I'd long since moved past that and forgiven her.

But I would never forgive her for putting my daughter's safety at risk. I could only imagine how many times she had been high while she was supposed to be caring for Jaya. Did my baby go hungry? Did she sit in a dirty diaper for hours? Was she just roaming around the apartment alone crying?

On and on my mind went until my rage boiled over. I went into the kitchen and grabbed a cup. I went back into the bathroom, filled it with water, and tossed it in my mom's face. She came to but barely conscious. "Hey, baby," she said smiling, high as a kite. I had no idea how long she'd sailing.

"Get up."

"Baby, what's wrong?" I could hardly understand what she was saying. She was trying to stand but could not grasp any bearings on her mind or body. I helped her to her feet and into her bedroom. She fell into her bed groaning. I stormed into the kitchen and grabbed some trash bags. I began stuffing all her clothes and belongings into them.

I closed the door behind me and set all her shit by the front door. Once she sobered up she had to go. I called my supervisor and told him I had a family emergency and couldn't cover the night shift or my shift for the next few days. He was agitated but he'd have to get over it. In one minute, my entire life, plans, and goals had come to a complete halt. Without my mom's help, I had no one to babysit. How would I work without a babysitter? Not working meant no money. And with my mom helping with some of the bills, I would need a second job just to maintain this shitty lifestyle.

I thought about calling my old boss to see if I could get my old job back but I quickly trashed the thought. I needed to continue to move forward no matter how impossible it seemed to reach my goals. There was nothing for me in my past.

Jaya began to cry. I prepared a bottle before I picked her up and snuggled my nose into her neck. Together we lay in my bed. As she drank her milk, I soothed back her curly hair and promised that I would find a way to make her proud and keep her safe. No matter what.

FOUR

Tianna

In the elevator on my way up to see Sabrina, I squeezed tightly on the stuffed bear that I had gotten for her. The get-well balloon floated above my head where my thoughts had been. I don't know what possessed me to go to the hospital to visit a complete stranger but something inside of me longed to see that something positive came out of this tragic ordeal. I needed to see that Sabrina was on the mend.

Once I got to her room, I knocked softly before entering the opened door. The beeping from monitors crashed with the sound from the television. An older woman looked up from her crossword puzzle book, her stare questioning. I looked over to the bed quickly to see Sabrina staring at me and immediately introduced myself.

"Hello. I'm sorry. I don't mean to interrupt. My name is Christianna Townsend."

Before I could finish my prepared speech, the woman sitting down, rose from her chair, quickly sat her book down in her place, and walked over to me. "Mrs. Townsend. Yes. It's so good to put a face to a name. I'm Tracy, Sabrina's grandmother. Please, come on in."

I handed her the stuffed animal and balloon before I wiped my sweaty palms on my thighs and took a small step deeper into the room. Tracy sat the bear on the windowsill and dragged a chair over gesturing for me to take a seat. Reluctantly I did as to not seem rude. I could feel Sabrina's glare burning a hole in my profile so I casually turned to her and smiled. "Hi, Sabrina." She stared but said nothing then turned toward the window.

"Sabrina Monroe. I know you heard Mrs. Townsend say hello to you. You better show her some respect."

Sabrina turned back toward me smirked more than smiled. I raised my eyebrow surprised by her little attitude but before I could even think of how to process any of it, her grandmother spoke. "Little girl, don't you make me finish the hurting they put on you."

Sabrina turned toward the window ignoring both her grandmother and me. No words. No expression. Just silence. I'd made a mistake in coming. I hadn't expected such animosity from the person I'd helped. "I really can't stay," I said ready to remove myself from the awkwardness.

Tracy looked at me sorrowfully. "Well, thank you so much for all you have done for Sabrina. I can't even think of what could have happened had you not been there."

I rose to my feet and smiled as genuinely as I could muster. I fought back the urge to cry on behalf of the son I'd lost. It would only embitter me toward a young girl. I remember how hard my life had been as a young girl and the abuse my body endured. My heart instantly went out toward Sabrina. She was lucky to have a caring grandmother. "I did what any decent human would have. You don't need to thank me." I looked over at the patient bandaged up and body ravaged but at least she had lived to heal and see another day. Not everyone had had that privilege. "Goodbye, Sabrina. I pray for a swift recovery and full healing. Hopefully, you'll be back out soon and enjoying the summer's warm weather in a few weeks."

She let out a humorless harrumph and shook her head, essentially dismissing my words as nonsense. "Sabrina!" Tracy looked at her granddaughter then at me mortified. "I'm so sorry about this Mrs. Townsend."

I raised my hands signaling that I was not offended. "Please call me Tianna, and it's ok. Sabrina has been through a lot and I am probably just a reminder of a brutal day. I should have called and gotten permission first. So please, forgive the intrusion."

"Mrs. Townse— Tianna, it was no intrusion. My family is grateful for you. Truly. You're in my prayers, young lady."

I said my goodbyes to that sweet woman and sat in my car questioning my life and decisions and heart. The 'What If' game tortured me. I played out scenario after scenario wondering what I could have done to save both Sabrina and my son. It was a fruitless task. No matter what outrageous scenario I could think of, nothing could change what had already happened. I started the car and kept my mind pre-occupied with errands.

Abe was picking up Justin from school and taking him straight to Karate class for me so I decided to take advantage of a few hours alone with El.

When I got home I made him his favorite dinner of *arroz blanco y pollo guisado*. After learning how to cook some basic and soul dishes from Bianca, *Mami* had taught me to cook Puerto Rican dishes as well. She had said it was important to keep our traditions and culture alive and carried on. Although I had been born and raised in the states and was only half Hispanic, my mother said a drop of Puerto Rican made you *Boricua* whether you wanted to be or not.

My cooking lessons had taken a handful of trial and errors before it was even edible and then a few more tries to make it delicious. But it had been worth it. The look on Eli's face every time I prepared it, always made me feel like I was doing something right.

As the music played in the background, I lit some candles and poured us some wine. As I was setting the table, he walked in, his face worn, frown lines situated across his forehead. He was surprised to see me in the kitchen. "Hey, beautiful. What's all this?" He asked as he set his briefcase down on the island.

I approached him, wrapped my arms around his middle, and kissed his neck. "Your favorite dinner and my favorite wine."

He moaned at my affection and brought me in closer, holding me tight. "Oh yeah? Bianca's in town and made fried chicken?" He stretched his neck pretending to search behind me for her.

I wanted to laugh but I played my part and feigned offense. With my mouth gaped open I tried to remove myself from his brace but he just held me tight and nuzzled my neck, his chuckle drowning there.

"Smart-ass," I replied then laughed.

"You know I'm just teasing. That crazy woman can fry a mean chicken, but it doesn't compare to chicken stew." He kissed me on the nose, then pecked my lips before he loosened his grip. "Where's Champ?"

"Abe took him to karate class then they were getting pizza and watching Yu-Gi-Ball."

Elijah removed his suit jacket and hung it on the back of the chair as he chuckled. "Yu-Gi-Ball? I think you meant Yu-Gi-Oh or Dragon Ball Z, Babe."

I flicked my hand in his direction as I reached for wine glasses. "Whatever. Same difference."

"Oh yeah? Don't let Abe hear you say that." El sat at the table and loosened his tie.

"Oh please. Me, scared of a grown-ass man still watching cartoons and playing video games?"

"No. You should be scared of his black belt in Brazilian Jujitsu."

"Oh please. Nothing a frying pan upside his head won't fix."

El chuckled. "Why are Puerto Rican women so violent? I'm scared you're turning into your mother."

The nerve of that man. I poured a glass of wine and walked it over to the table. "You are lucky I love you and am a pacifist." I kissed his head and handed him the glass.

"You keep this one and I'll have a beer instead."

While I walked over to the refrigerator for the beer, he walked over to the cupboard and turned on the small radio I had mounted underneath. He popped on a Boyz II Men CD and walked over to me. "May I have this dance?"

I blushed and slipped my hand into his. He pulled me close as the quartet crooned about love-making. El kissed my neck slowly and began to intensify. I longed to get lost in paradise with my husband. We rarely had alone time and every opportunity was special to me. He cleared the kitchen island, grabbed me by my waist, and sat me on it. We began to undress each other and kiss passionately.

He went for my pants when I pulled my lips away from his hastily and stopped him.

"What's wrong?" He asked breathlessly.

Reality crashed into me. It hadn't even been a week since my pregnancy was terminated and I needed to heal. I tried to get the words out but my mouth refused to obey. I looked at El and understanding registered in his eyes and he nodded before he wiped his lips and stepped back. The disappointment there made me want to cry. I had caused that pain. I buttoned up my top and slipped off the kitchen island as he gathered himself.

I fetched some dishes and served dinner. We sat quietly and ate dinner for a while before El placed his hand over mine and smiled. "I forgot to ask how was your day."

I could tell he was trying to be gentle with me and I didn't deserve it but my love for him grew deeper in a seemingly small gesture. I contemplated not telling him about Sabrina, but dishonesty and harboring secrets from my husband was not how I wanted to repay his love toward me and I knew he wouldn't like it but I'd hoped he'd understand.

"I went to the hospital to see Sabrina."

He was quiet for a moment before he met my gaze. He seemed more tired than bothered. "How is she?"

"She's on the mend." That was true enough.

"Did she know why she was assaulted?" I could see the wheels turning in Elijah's head trying to make some sense of our loss. I shook my head and watched him deflate. "Did she say anything at all?"

I braced myself for what I had to share next. "No. She wasn't exactly happy to see me."

"What does that mean?"

"She was rather rude. Didn't say two words to me."

"Rude?" His tone grew rigid. "Rude?" He asked again appalled.

I stood and began to clear the dishes. "She's a young girl that's been through a rough time, Eli."

"That doesn't give her the right to be rude. And to you of all people. Does she even know—"

I abruptly turned toward him and cut him off. "Don't." Tears began to gather in my eyes before I blinked them away and began to wash the dishes.

I felt El wrap his arms around me and it was all it took for me to break down. I turned and buried my face in his shoulder and sobbed. He lifted me into his arms and carried me to the couch. He sat beside me and soothed my back as I cried. "I love you, Ti. We're gonna get through this."

If Elijah said it, I believed it. He was my rock steady. I fell asleep in my husband's arms half hurt and half hope.

FIVE

Sharmayne

S eeing Micah's car parked out front, I knocked on his mother's door hoping to talk to him. The rent wasn't due for a few more days but I was short a hundred and fifty dollars and I needed an extension. The worry of being evicted gnawed at me. I didn't have any place else to go and I refused to take Jaya to a shelter. Mrs. Payne, Micah's mom, answered the door and eyed me real funny. I had been living in the building for a year and had never spoken to her although I'd seen her a bunch of times.

"Good afternoon Mrs. Payne. I don't mean to bother you. I'm Sharmayne Little. I live on the second floor-"

"You Felicia's daughter."

Caught off guard that she knew my mother by name, I lost my train of thought and fumbled my words. "Uh. Um. Yes. Felicia is my mother. I didn't know you two knew each other." After several awkward moments of silence and no response from her, I remembered why I was standing at this woman's door fidgety. "I'm sorry, but is Micah here." I pointed toward the main door that led to the street. "I thought I saw his car outside."

"He's in the shower," she said scowling.

"When he's done could you ask him to stop by my apartment?" Her brow went up an inch and at her reaction, I stopped talking. It dawned on me quickly that this heifer thought I had intentions with her son. I straightened my shoulders ready to tell her about herself when she cocked her head to the side and crossed her arms. "Where is sweet baby Jaya? Where did you leave the baby?"

The accusation and concern in her tone knocked me upside the head. I didn't want to respond to her nosey ass but I couldn't back down from her. I didn't care if she was my elder. Respect was earned not given. "With all due respect, I don't see how that is any of your concern."

"If I call DYFS, I'm sure they'll make it their concern."

Oh no that bitch didn't. My nostrils flared and I wanted to knock her in her big ass nose. From the moment I found out I was pregnant, I had completely changed my life for Jaya. I would never intentionally bring harm to my child. She was the most precious thing to me in the world. Hell, I put my mom out for her welfare. Yet, truth be told she was alone upstairs asleep, and I knew that would qualify as child endangerment. I didn't regret it though because if I had to choose between leaving her upstairs for a few minutes alone in the safety of her crib while she was asleep or bringing her to a drug dealer's apartment to beg for a favor, I'd make the same decision all over again.

Without another word, I walked away from Mrs. Payne-in-the-ass and took the steps to the second floor, two by two. I wanted to slam my door, but I didn't want to wake Jaya. I sank onto the couch and buried my face in my hands. What the hell was I going to do?

I closed my eyes and exhaled slowly mustering up the courage to call Alonzo, my former employer and caregiver. I hadn't been in contact with him for a long time, but I knew he would help. Unfortunately, not from the kindness in his heart. Refusing to cry at what I was about to do, I decided to shower while Jaya was asleep. Admittedly I was also trying to buy myself some time to think of another solution before resorting to my last one.

I spent most of my shower stressing about money, studying, and Jah-Jah that I'd sunk into a deeper state of hopelessness and had settled on calling my former sugar daddy rather than avoiding him. As I got dressed, I thought about what I'd say to him. We didn't exactly part on good terms, and he'd tried to contact me a few times since I'd left. I'd seen him once since then, but he didn't see me. I hid until he was out of sight. I'd known him long enough to know that he harbored resentment toward me leaving suddenly and without explanation.

At fifteen years old, he took me in when my mom had gotten caught up in one of her stints of drug abuse and was never around. My brother, Kyle, began hanging out at my Aunt Vicky's with my cousin Robby and together started running the streets at fourteen. Soon after Kyle got locked up for drug possession charges and I was alone. Alonzo fed me, clothed me, and protected me for years. And when I was old enough, he gave me a job and made sure I was always good. It wasn't until I had turned eighteen that the nature of our relationship changed. His favor required favors given in return. I was too blinded by the lavish lifestyle I didn't care what was I doing to maintain it. Until I got pregnant. Then I just bounced on him.

I thought about explaining that I got pregnant and wanted a better life for my daughter but my gut was as anxious now as it was then to keep that information from Alonzo. He was not a safe man for children to be around. I knew that then and I knew it even more so now. The more I thought about it, the more I was convinced that under no circumstances could he know about Jaya's existence. But I needed money to take care of Jah-Jah. I could not move her into a shelter. The thought of it boosted my courage to put my shaky plan into action.

I set the comb down, walked over to the phone, and dialed Alonzo's number. Half of me was hoping it was disconnected. When it began to ring my heart started pounding so loudly inside of my chest I thought I could hear it.

"Hello."

My heart sank. It was crazy that after such a long time of not hearing his voice, it still affected me. I wanted to hang up but Jaya's diaper stack only had a dozen or so of diapers left so I steeled my nerves. "Hey, Ace."

"Do my ears deceive me or am I speaking with Ms. Sham—"

"Yes, it's me. "I cut Ace off before he could voice the name he'd given me. "I know we haven't seen each other in a long time but time is irrelevant when two people have a connection." I rolled my eyes at my own bullshit but I had to play nice if this was going to work.

Ace laughed loud and long and I had to keep myself composed. "I give it to you Shar. You still know how to run game girl."

"It's not game. I just speak what others won't. You know that."

"Maybe, maybe. Now, why don't you tell me why you really calling 'cause I know it ain't just to shoot the shit." His voice hardened a little and I knew to immediately stop trying to manipulate him with my words and just be blunt.

"My mom…" I didn't know how to finish what I wanted to say. My mom had fucked up big time, but I didn't need to broadcast that to the world. "I need help paying my bills."

"You asking me for money?" He interjected quickly.

"No. Of course not. I wouldn't dare. I wanted to see if you had any work available."

His tone softened. "Ah. You want your old job back, is that it?" His cat and mouse games had always grated on my nerves but I knew what to expect and shouldn't have been surprised.

"No, not that job. But I can waitress or wash dishes or something like that."

He was quiet for a long minute before he spoke again. "Nah. I don't need none of that. But come get this money. You can borrow what you need until you straight."

I shook off the nerves and accepted a deal with the devil. "I'll be there tomorrow morning. And as soon as I can, I will pay back every dime plus interest."

"Nah, Shar. A favor for a favor."

Fear washed over me and suddenly I realized I'd made a big mistake in calling him. But the fact remained that my situation was looking like hell and I had to choose which of the two hellish roads laid at my feet wouldn't consume my baby, even if it consumed me. "What kind of favor?"

"We can discuss it tomorrow. Face to face."

Jaya woke and I rushed Alonzo off the phone promising to discuss it further in the morning. I didn't want him to hear her crying in the background. Over my dead body would I ever allow my two worlds to intertwine. Alonzo was poison and Jaya was life.

I walked into my bedroom and she was sitting up, cranky with tears in her eyes. When she saw me, her face lit up and she stood up holding on to the crib for support. As I got closer she raised her arms in expectation for me to pick her up and I did. I felt a twinge of guilt. She seemed relieved to see me and I couldn't help but wonder about the extent of my mother's negligence. Anger began to turn into rage and I refused to be an angry black woman with mommy issues so I looked at Jaya and made a silly face. She giggled and the sound was addictive. I needed to hear it over and over again.

A few minutes later, a knock on my door disrupted our bonding. It caught me off guard. Nobody knew where I lived, let alone had the right to invite themselves over, so I already knew it was someone I didn't want to entertain. I tried to sit Jaya in her crib so I could see who the hell was knocking but she had a full-blown tantrum. Again, I wondered if my mom had kept her locked up in the crib all day. Rather than keep adding fuel to that fire, I sat Jaya in her walker and walked toward the door.

. I opened it anxious to see if maybe I
with him in regards to the rent. As soon
:side him, I tossed that hope right in the
·r in their faces but I wouldn't give his
1ving a reason to be rude. "Hey." I
ny presence.
)pped by and needed me to come up. Is
roken that needs to be fixed?"
ny head. "No. The apartment is fine.
ugh."
:hat case what did you need to see me
and rolled her eyes with her smart-ass
.d forth between us confused. "Can
g on?"
between us, as neither one of us jumped
up to say anything. She began gurgling and practically ran me over
trying to go outside the doorway in her walker. I pulled the walker
back and tried to push her back inside but she was insistent on getting
through babbling loud and happily. She raised her arms wanting to be
held but it wasn't me that she was trying to get to.

I looked to Mrs. Payne who was all smiles and joy looking at Jaya.
The woman was practically gushing. "Hey precious. How are you,
baby girl?"

Jaya began to jump up and down in excitement, babbling as if she
were responding. I removed her up from the walker and held her
wondering why she seemed to like the woman that was threatening to
have her taken from me when she leaped out of my arms and into Mrs.
Payne's. I wanted to snatch my baby back but Mrs. Payne quickly
nuzzled her in her arms. Jaya grabbed her face and began kissing her
cheeks.

"Mom, what is going on?" Micah asked because I sure couldn't
form the words. At least, not as tactfully as he had.

Mrs. Payne held Jaya close as she spoke. "Every now and then I
would check in on Felicia. A few times Felicia—" She abruptly stopped
talking and eyed me quickly. "A few times Felicia needed a break so I
would feed the baby and put her sleep so Felicia could rest.

33

My jaw hung open at the revelation. I had so many mixed emotions and questions I didn't know where to begin. Micah seemed none the wiser and just smiled at his mom. "Dang, Mom. I had no clue you knew Sharmayne's mom."

"I knew her in high school. I hadn't seen her since I quit school until she moved in here." Mrs. Payne looked down at Jaya, kissed her on her head, and handed her back to me. "I came to check in on her. I haven't seen her in a few days. Is she here?"

I was so stuck on stupid with all that I'd just learned I hesitated before I responded. Yet once I replied, my agitation was clear. "No. My mother is not here. She doesn't live here anymore. Now, I gotta go." I took a step back to close the door before Micah held it open, concern on his face.

"Woah now. We didn't come up here to cause drama, Shar. You came and knocked on her door looking for me and she delivered the message. That's why I'm here. My mom asked if she could come with me so she could just introduce herself. That's all. Now, I don't know what is going on between you two but there's some obvious tension here."

I raised my hand to get him to stop being the voice of reason. I already had enough on my plate to think about and the last thing I needed was a feud with my landlord's mom, not to mention my neighbor. "I have nothing against Mrs. Payne. I have a lot on my plate and it's time for Jaya's bath. And as far as me knocking on your door, please pretend it never happened. Everything is fine now." As patiently as I could, I waited for them to respond with an understanding and farewell, but Micah wouldn't leave well enough alone.

"Well, if you need something, please just ask."

I hit him with a fake smile so good, he smiled back and waved goodbye. Mrs. Payne looked at me intently before I thought I saw remorse in her eyes, and she too turned and walked toward the stairwell.

Once I closed the door, I exhaled and leaned against it. I'm glad that was over although I was left with a mountain of questions. But above all my thoughts the one that hovered above them all was how long and to what extent was Mrs. Payne caring for Jaya? The more I thought about it, the more I was convinced that it had been for a very long time.

SIX

Tianna

With a basket of laundry under my arm, I walked past the living room toward the laundry nook, minding my business just as Elijah was ending a phone call.

"I love you too. I can't wait to see you either."

I stopped dead in my tracks and listened. He paused. I assume to listen to the response of whoever was on the other side of the call. He then continued, "No. She doesn't know yet. Don't worry about that. I'll let her know soon. I just have to find the right time, that's all."

At this point, I realized I had two choices and needed to decide quickly which path to take. Snatch the phone and then snatch him up by his throat, or be still and allow him to keep lengthening the rope which he'd use to hang himself. I set the laundry basket down on the couch and become a captive audience to Elijah's suicide. I was never a violent person and I wouldn't start now.

"Ok, goodbye."

I took a step forward ready to interrogate El but halted when he began talking again.

"Hey, before you go, make sure you wear that thing I like." He laughed softly. "Oh, you get a new one? You gonna model it for me?"

Elijah had chosen violence that day. I balled up my fist ready to jump on his back and pound on his head.

"That's what I'm talking about, baby. Ok. I'll see you this weekend. Oh, one more thing. Ti is standing behind me listening and probably ready to beat my ass. I'm gonna tell her that I'm just kidding before she stabs me." Elijah turned around with a stupid grin on his face. With my heart rate slowly getting back to normal, I looked at him like he was an idiot and unclenched my fist.

"Go ahead and keep playing games. You gonna find yourself with a frying pan upside your head." I picked up the basket of laundry, annoyed but relieved.

El grabbed me from behind and held me tight, rocking me from side to side and kissing my neck. "Woman, you know I don't have eyes for anybody but you. Not even that fine new receptionist Matthew hired."

I elbowed him in the gut. "Watch yourself, Elijah Townsend. I still got a little fire burning from your childish prank. Don't get yourself burned."

He kissed me on the cheek before he released his grip. "Never baby. You are the only one for me. But since you're already in a great mood, I mind as well tell you the news."

I almost chuckled at his sarcastic remark but didn't want to encourage him. "Can't wait to hear it."

"That was actually my mom on the phone. She wants to visit."

I picked up the bottle of detergent and put it in the basket before I situated it against my hip. "I would have preferred you had a girlfriend," I said as I walked away. I heard him chuckling behind me.

"She's not that bad!" He yelled as I kept walking.

Of course, he thought his mother was a saint. She birthed him and had made him her everything. True momma's boy. Well up until she sent him to live with his father after she found out I was pregnant with his baby when we were teenagers. Funny how I rarely thought about Elijah's mom, Marvette. A lot of hurtful memories were tied to her. I found it strange when Elijah told me that his mother had also been pregnant back then and hadn't told him. The hypocrisy of her shaming me for being a pregnant teenager by the boy that was my best friend and lover and her, a grown-ass woman pregnant by Lord knows who.

But I chose to stop Elijah when he began to fill me in on her story. I still grieved the baby I lost when I fell down the bleachers at school after running away from her hateful and shameful words toward me. Although that had been years ago, I knew a part of me resented her because while I lost my baby, she birthed hers. Tyler Mackenzie also known as Mac, was the shining bright light of their lives.

Elijah doted on his younger brother. Once or twice a year, he would fly out to Florida where she had moved, to visit them. I never accepted the invitation and El never made a fuss. He knew as much as I did that his witch of a mother didn't want me there just as much as I didn't want to be there. I hadn't seen her since my wedding, where I'd met Mac for the first and last time. He was an adorable kid but all I could wonder about was what my child would have looked like at the same age. It was awkward and I was relieved that Mac didn't live nearby and be a constant reminder of what I'd lost.

I began loading the laundry into the washer when Elijah walked in and leaned against the doorway. "So?"

"So what?" I knew he was asking for my blessing, but my flesh was screaming and having a tantrum.

"Come on Ti. You know exactly what."

"You don't need my permission for your mother to visit your house." I added the detergent and closed the washer lid. Stepping to the side, I bent down and swung open the dryer door. After pulling a towel free, it still felt damp to the touch so I tossed it back in and started the dryer all over again. I could feel Elijah watching me carefully.

"It's our house Ti, and I'm not asking for permission. You know that."

I loved my husband with all of my heart and for his well-being and to make him happy I'd endure many things if need be. Including his mother. "I will be a kind and gracious host to your family." I curtsied for effect.

"Our family."

"Don't push it, Mr. Townsend."

Elijah pushed off from the doorway, chuckled, and pulled me toward him. "Oh, I'm pushing alright. What's the chances I can sit you on this dryer and we can make it shake?"

I raised an eyebrow intrigued. "Very good I'd say."

Elijah didn't waste time and plopped me on top of the dryer and began kissing me like a mad man. I began to shimmy my pants down, as he did, until we heard a small voice.

"Mommy, what are you doing up there?"

"Shit!" El whispered forcefully as he pulled his pants up. "Hey, Champ."

Justin Junior looked at us baffled then turned to El. "Daddy what are you doing?"

I chuckled and turned away mortified. El secretly squeezed my thigh for laughing at him then cleared his throat. "Mommy said she wanted to ride the rocket."

I quickly slapped El's arm "Elijah!"

He hid his amusement and bent down to eye level with JJ. "Mommy just needed to relax a little bit but sitting on the dryer was a very bad idea. I don't want you trying that, ok Champ?"

JJ shrugged his shoulders the least bit interested. "Yes, Daddy. Can we go to Karate class now?"

"We still have a few minutes. I'm gonna take Mommy upstairs. You stay down here. Whatever you do, don't come upstairs—"

I slapped El on the arm again as JJ nodded and walked into the living room.

"What?" he asked annoyed. "Woman I know you ain't sending me outside like this." He looked at the bulge in his pants and I couldn't help but crack up.

"You'll survive." I hopped down off the dryer and fixed my clothes once I heard the TV blaring.

"Alright. But there's a bunch of single moms already eyeing me up in Karate class. Don't blame me if they think I'm happy to see them."

El had a point. Bias aside, my husband was fine. There'd been a few times I caught women eyeing him and I reveled in it because he rarely noticed. And if he did, he would kiss me or whisper it in my ear like we were girlfriends sharing a secret. He was my lover and best friend. I trusted him more than anyone else on earth and I knew he'd never betray me. But since he liked being a smart ass, I obliged him. "You're right." I crossed my arms and nodded thoughtfully. "Let me write a note that says 'out of order' and stick it on your—"

"What? Oh! Woman, you done lost yo damn mind. Ain't nothing out of order around here. Matter of fact, get yo ass back on that dryer! I'll show you real quick how everything is fully functioning."

"Like within two minutes?" I rolled my eyes at him knowing I had hit a nerve but not wanting to laugh outright.

El stopped and stared at me appalled then without a word, picked me up and tossed me over his shoulder. I burst into laughter at his antics. He was overdramatic sometimes and I loved it. He knew how to make me cry tears of laughter, love, and joy.

"JJ, stay down here Champ!"

All the way up the stairs I laughed at El's King Kong madness. When we got to the bedroom, he didn't give me a chance to argue and began savagely making love to me as if he were thirsty and I was water. I got lost in my husband and he in me. The only one complaining was JJ for being very late to karate practice.

38

SEVEN
Sharmayne

I woke up early the next morning and got me and Jaya ready. I picked up my younger cousin, Lenora, so she could sit at the playground with the baby, that way I could keep an eye on them from across the street at Ace's place. Once I got there I was all set to make up an excuse why I couldn't stay long. I wanted to hear what he needed, get the money he promised, and bounce within ten minutes. I mean, how long would it take for him to ask for a so-called favor?

I was nervous as hell but I played it cool. I knocked and one of his underlings answered the door, a game controller in his hand. I'd never seen him before. Granted I hadn't been around in years so I wasn't surprised he had taken in a few new people to do his bidding.

"I'm here to see Alonzo." The dude pinched his brows together confused. "Ace. I'm here to see Ace. Could you tell him Sharmayne is waiting outside?"

"Yeah. He said you'd be coming. He said for you to go to the backyard."

I panicked a little bit. I didn't want to step foot in Ace's house, let alone go all the way to the backyard. I wouldn't be able to keep an eye on Jah-Jah and I sure as hell didn't know what to expect when I got back there.

I looked back at Lenora putting Jah-Jah on the slide and quickly darted inside. The faster I got this done and over with, the faster I could get back to the girls. The inside of the house hadn't changed much. Still dark, with the dark curtains drawn. The smell of weed smacked you in the face as soon as you entered.

His cousin Wesley was sitting on the couch, yelling at the TV as he played the video game. Two dudes were sitting at a table eating and debating something, yelling over each other. I didn't make eye contact with anyone and walked to the backyard quickly. I exhaled deeply before I opened the screen door and stepped outside. Ace was sitting in the same beat-up recliner he had had for years and refused to replace. Except now it was on the patio instead of in the living room.

"Good morning," I said trying to steel my nerves.

He looked up from his newspaper and removed the cigar from his mouth. Ace was a handsome light-skinned man in his late twenties by now but he was raised by his older father, the original owner of the recliner, so he grew up as an old soul. Very disciplined and old-fashioned in many ways. Yet, growing up in Camden had also instilled in him hustling in a way his grandfather could never relate to.

While they both sold women and their services, Ace added guns, drugs, and several legal ventures to his empire. His father didn't trust banks or the law so he kept his money hidden in that recliner until the day before he died when he confessed it to Ace. I'd never told Ace that I'd walked in on their conversation and accidentally overheard part of it before I walked right back down the hall and into my bedroom. From that point on I simply stayed away from the recliner.

"Well if it isn't Ms. Sham—" he paused then continued, "my bad, Ms. Sharmayne. I didn't think you'd show." He set the cigar in an ashtray beside him and folded the newspaper before placing it on the side table.

"I'd said I'd come, and here I am."

He smiled and nodded. "Here you are." He waved me over and I cringed within. I didn't want to get any closer to this man. My feet felt like they had hundred pounds weights holding them down, but I took one step at a time and closed the gap between us.

"Listen, I have to be somewhere in an hour and I gotta catch the bus, so I can't stay long." *Just tell me what you want and give me the money so I can get the hell up out of here.*

'Take a seat, baby girl. You got time. Let's catch up. I haven't seen you in a minute." Ace pointed to a small leather loveseat near the recliner that had seen better days. Sitting beside it was a large pit bull chained to an exposed brick wall. I eyed the dog and the couch, hesitating before I made my feet move. As soon as I got near, the dog stood on all legs, growled then barked as I got closer. I ignored him as he was no immediate threat but sat on the end of the couch farthest from the dog. Ace commanded the dog to sit and shut up. He barked a few more times before he obeyed. Ace then turned to me calmly. "So. Where you been?"

Ace sat back in his chair as if it were his throne and gave me his undivided attention. When I lived here, I had never been scared of Ace. He had been my provider and protector. But I also knew what he was capable of and that made him a very dangerous man. Now that I was no longer under his protection, the knowledge of his past actions had put a fear in me I'd never known. I could feel the heat of his scrutiny under his gaze and I had to be very careful with my words. If he ever found out about the secret I was hiding from him, he'd probably kill me.

"School." That's all I offered.

"I remember. Did you get your degree?"

"Yes."

"What kind of degree Ms. Education?"

"Law," I said confidently.

He just stared at me not seeming to care one way or another. Made me wonder why bother asking at all, but I'd known him long enough to know he was just setting me up. The more information I provided, the more he'd play me like a game of chess, so I remained quiet. He smiled and picked up his cigar. "Do you remember my father?"

Of course, I did. I'm the one who helped feed and clean him up at the end of his life when he couldn't do much for himself. Ace knew that but I played nice and nodded my head.

"It's been almost three years since he's been gone." He brought the cigar to his lips and inhaled. Ace hadn't changed a bit with his mind games.

Truthfully, I had never thought about his father or his death after I'd left. He wasn't a very nice man and died painfully. Punishment for all the women he had used and abused. I had run away shortly after.

While Big Al was a memory forgotten, the timeframe of when I had run away was often at the forefront of my mind. Each day that passed the consequences of harboring my secret grew. Some days I didn't care. Other days I wondered what would happen if Ace found out about Jah-Jah. I watched him exhale the puff of smoke but said nothing in response. He eyed me for a few moments then put the cigar out.

He sat forward and intertwined his hands, resting his elbows on his lap. "So let's get down to business. You needed money."

"And you wanted a favor."

Ace nodded once before he stood and walked behind the pit bull chained down. He fed it something then pulled the dog by the collar, moving him aside. Underneath the dog, was a hidden hatch door. Ace pulled the lever, put his hand inside, and pulled free a stack of money, followed by a gun. I froze in place.

He walked over to me, tossed the stack of money into my lap then walked behind me. "That's two grand."

My hands trembled as I picked it up. "I don't need—"

I felt a pop to the back of my head that jolted me forward before he pulled me back by my throat, cocked the gun, and put it to my temple.

"You think I'm stupid Sharmayne?" He whispered in my ear, and I could hear the contempt in his voice. "You think just because I didn't come find you and end your worthless life that you pulled that shit off? Nah, Bitch. I just been biding my time waiting for the right opportunity. And ain't that just my luck that rather having to go find you, you bring your little stank, raggedy-ass right to me instead."

Hot tears began stinging my eyes and I curse myself for coming here. What the hell was I thinking? I wanted to run and take Jah-Jah far away from here. I hated this city and this life. I hated that my mom was a dope-fiend and wasn't a better mother. I hated that my dad was a coward and left us. Never even bothered to want or care for his own children. But most of all I hated myself for putting Jah-Jah in a place where she too could end up in foster care. No, I wasn't a drug user or a bad mom but in the end what did that matter if Jah-Jah ended up exactly as I had?

I found the courage to speak between my fear and tears. "Ace, I'm sorry I left. I'm sorry." Snot was running down my nose but I was too afraid to move and wipe it and have my head blown off.

He released me, uncocked the gun, and crouched down before me meeting me eye to eye. "I don't give a fuck that you ran away. Where's my fucking money?" The rage in his eyes and tightened expression made me sit back. I had only ever seen him this angry once, right before he beat a man to death for taking a bigger cut from a deal than was negotiated. I was afraid to speak and didn't know what he was talking about. He set the gun down, grabbed me by my hair, and punched me in the eye a few times. "Answer me! Where is my money?" His rage exploded. He tossed me to the ground. In both shock and fear, I pressed my palm to my eye which was now throbbing.

I shook my head quickly. "I don't know what you are talking about," I cried. "I left with just the money I had saved up. That's it. I swear!" I pleaded.

He kicked me in the stomach, then kicked me in the mouth before he picked up the gun and walked back to his recliner. "Bitch, stop playing with me. Tell me where my money is or I'll kill you and that little girl."

My head snapped up immediately, my glare meeting his. I don't know how he knew about Jaya but it didn't matter at this point. I crawled over to him and begged him to leave her out of it. "Ace, I swear I didn't take any money from you. I swear. I would never. Please don't hurt Jaya. I'll do anything." My lips were swelling. I tasted the rancidness of blood on my tongue and could hardly speak but I had to try.

He grabbed me by my hair and shoved the gun to my lips. He lowered his voice but his fury was still on high. "Sharmayne, I will make you eat a mothafuckin' bullet if you don't tell me where my father's money is in the next five seconds."

My eyes opened wide. I had no idea where his father's money was. I inadvertently looked at the recliner and he followed my line of vision. Immediately I regretted it. He popped me in my eye with the butt of the gun. "Bitch, I knew you took my money."

I fell back and shook my head vehemently. "I didn't. I swear I didn't." I repeated it over and over again, but he refused to hear me.

Ace sat back in his recliner and placed the gun on his lap. He picked up his cigar, lit it again, and puffed a few times before he spoke again. "Next week, some people are coming into town. Some associates of mine. You are gonna dance for them. You are gonna do whatever they want you to do for them. And every dollar you earn comes to me. You gonna pay me back every red cent you owe me, plus three years of interest and pain and suffering. The two grand I'm giving you right now is to buy some suitable clothes to hoe yourself in. You look like shit. You paying me back all of that money too. You will continue to dance and hoe until it's all paid back and in return, you and your brat live another day. Are these terms fair Shampagne?" He laughed and puffed his cigar again.

I shook my head, got to my feet, and ran out of the house. Once I got outside, I ran to the park but Lenora and Jah-Jah weren't there. The world was spinning and I was feeling drained and dizzy. I could hardly see as my second eye was beginning to swell too. I shook it off and searched the playground for the girls but they weren't there either. Fear gripped me and I wanted to vomit. Where was my child?

I heard someone calling out my name. I looked to see Lenora waving at me from the corner store. I ran toward her needing to make sure Jah-Jah was in the stroller safe and sound. As I got closer to her, the smile on her face diminished, giving way to a look of terror.

"Oh my God! What happened to you?" I ignored her and quickly got to the stroller examining my daughter. She smiled at me as she sucked on a lollipop. I exhaled then snatched the stroller from Lenora's grip. Quickly I rushed down the street practically running, ready to pass out. My adrenaline was pumping and all I could focus on was putting distance between Jah-Jah and Ace. For now, that was what mattered most.

EIGHT

Tianna

The last bell of the school day rang and I dismissed my students. I walked around the classroom putting away paint, paper, and brushes. High schoolers were just as messy with art supplies as kids were. I emptied a few leftover containers of dirtied water into the waste basin and carried it to the sink covered in paint. I made a mental note to dock the culprits some points on their assignment for not cleaning up properly.

Coach Edelson tapped on the opened door. "Need some help?" He was carrying his messenger bag and wore a baseball cap as always.

"No, thanks," I said as I poured the water down the sink. "Thanks though. On your way to practice?"

"Making these boys run laps today."

"Don't hurt yourself." I set the basin down and winked at him. John Edelson was only ten years older than I was, but he'd grayed early so every chance I got, I teased him and called him old.

"Oh! You got jokes!" He chuckled and tapped the door once more. "Have a good one! Be safe now." He waved and headed toward the gym.

Ever since I'd been beaten by the traffic light at the corner of the school, a few of the teachers had made similar comments to me. I wasn't offended. They were just being concerned and I appreciated that. I'd noticed more police presence when arriving and leaving school. El had asked me to not stay late anymore and I obliged him. A group of the teachers began walking out in pairs for their peace of mind. I neither sought nor avoided that but understood why they did. Especially the teachers that weren't raised in an urban area.

I instead chose to begin parking by the athletic fields. The constant after-school activities ensured that I was never alone and always surrounded by witnesses. As I approached my car I immediately noticed that my car looked lopsided. When I was close enough I saw that two of my tires had been completely slashed. I looked around to see if whoever had slashed my tires had still been around but everyone seemed occupied in their tasks and not paying the least bit of attention to me.

I heard snickering and looked across the street. A group of girls were laughing obnoxiously. "Having car trouble?" One yelled at me and the others cackled at her taunting. I instantly recognized her as one of my attackers.

Anger rose in me. I began to march across the street when one of the girls stopped laughing. "You better think real good before you cross this street. You don't think those tires got sliced up with fingernails, do you?" She pulled out a switchblade and I wanted to shove it down her throat. Then I saw a petite girl with big curly hair step forward, her arm in a cast. The sight of Sabrina immediately halted my steps.

"Sabrina?" I saw a vacancy in her eyes that disturbed me.

Visibly angry she yelled. "Stop calling me by name! You don't know me." I didn't understand what was happening. She pointed to my tires. "That's for getting in my business. Next time you'll lose more than two tires."

The group of girls with her began to encourage her just as the girl that had slammed Sabrina's head onto my car hood put her fist out offering a congratulatory pound that Sabrina returned as she laughed too.

What the hell was going on? Sabrina looked at me and smiled. "Hey, y'all! Guess what? She lost her baby too! Whoever kicked her dumb ass in the stomach made her lose her baby!" She began to cackle so loud and genuinely that I felt sick to my stomach. They joined in on her taunting.

Sabrina shook her head at me. "You got to be real dumb to get in a fight when you pregnant, and can't even fight. Look at you just sitting there crying and looking stupid. Your baby dead and that's your dumb ass fault. Nobody told you to try and save me. I was getting initiated, and you made it worse with your nosey self."

"Bri, don't explain nothin' to her! You in now so none of that don't even matter no more. You took that beat down like a true Fremont Street Femme. You ain't gotta tell nobody nothin'. Ya here me?"

Sabrina nodded and began walking away with the crowd as they joked and laughed at my expense and the loss of my innocent baby.

Fury bubbled over as had my tears. I had had enough. I walked back to my car, unlocked the club lock from the steering wheel, and pulled one part free from the other. I slammed my car door shut with my foot. Carrying a piece of the metal rods in each hand, I went after them.

I made it to the corner when I felt someone grab me from behind. I swung and nearly caught Coach Edelson in his chin. Had I made contact, I would have shattered his jaw. He looked at me as if I were crazy and maybe I had temporarily lost my mind because all I could think of was hurting those responsible for my baby's death. I began my march back to get my justice when he wrapped me up from behind and pinned my arms against my sides. I thrashed about, my adrenaline giving me strength I hardly knew I possessed.

"Christianna, calm down! You won't solve anything this way! Calm down!"

"Let! Go! Of! Me!" I screamed and began kicking and flailing my legs trying to get loose. "They killed my baby! Those bitches murdered my child!"

Before I knew it, I was lying on the ground, Coach Edelson holding and talking me down. "It's ok. We'll get you justice. But not like this Christianna. Not like this. Let go of the weapons and calm down. "

I stopped fighting him and broke down sobbing. "They killed my baby," I whimpered over and over again, a steady stream of tears soaking my face. "My baby boy is gone."

I don't know how long I sat on the ground crying before Coach walked me to my car where I tried to gather myself together. I cleaned my face and just stared out the window out onto the athletic fields. The crowd that had gathered had now dispersed and went back to their business. I didn't even care that I had caused a scene. If I had to do it again, I would have grabbed the club first and gone off on each and every one of them.

The tears began again as I played Sabrina's words over in my mind. I lost my child helping a girl who volunteered herself to get beat up as initiation to a gang. Although I had clearly heard her words, my mind could not wrap itself around them. She brought that on herself, and I dared to try and save her. Sabrina was right. I was a true dumb-ass. I buried my face in my hands and wept.

"Baby."

I felt an arm on my shoulder and looked up to see El. I jumped out of the car and into his arms and cried on his shoulder. "They killed our baby Elijah. We gotta go make them pay. They killed our son." He pulled me back and looked into my eyes and I could see he was concerned and confused but once I could explain everything that happened, he would see it just like I did. Those bitches had to pay for what they did. "We're going to make them pay, right?"

He offered me a sad smile and nodded. "Let's get you home."

I resisted a little. "Ok, but they have to pay first. Right? They went that way." I pointed in the direction of the park. "They are probably hanging outside. If we look we can find them." I insisted.

Elijah's demeanor changed. "Ti, let's get you home first. We can talk about it at home," he whispered forcefully trying to get me to cooperate.

"I don't want to go home," I replied angrily and yanked my arm out of his hand. "Let go of me."

He rubbed his forehead, and I could see the vein on his forehead beginning to throb. "Stop making a scene. Let's go home and put Jay to bed and then we can discuss this like adults."

I stepped into his face and with everything in me let him know how disgusted I felt with him. "If you don't want justice for the murder of our child, and want to go home and pretend it doesn't matter, then go. I'm going to make the people who killed my baby pay!" I pushed him back not wanting to even be near him.

He grabbed my arms, brought his face to mine, and yelled in my face, "You killed our baby Tianna! You did!" He shoved me away and cursed out into the sky. "Now get in the damn car!" He angrily walked over to his car and got in.

All of the air rushed out of my lungs, and I could hardly breathe. Coach Edelson walked over to me and held my arm walking me to my husband's car. "Go home Christianna. Please get some rest. You've been through a lot today."

I nodded and thanked him for his help before I got into my husband's car and rode all the way home in silence.

NINE

Elijah

The silence was killing me but I feared I'd say something just as equally ugly as I had already done so I stayed quiet. The truth was, I was angry. Not just about today. A part of me resented Ti for what had happened to our son and if I was honest with myself my heart did blame her more than those dumb young girls who don't know better. My brain told me to stop and consider the fact that she didn't know she was pregnant and deserved grace. My heart argued she should have been more in tune with her body. How could she not know she was pregnant? My brain reminded me that a woman's body is complex and goes through changes constantly.

On and on my heart and brain battled each other. Most days the world saw my brain in control. Many times, when I was alone, I allowed my heart to rule. Tianna miscarried several times. Every time I thought about it, I ached for our loss. Everyone always considered the mother more than the father. I could understand that to a degree, but that didn't make the grief any less real.

Tianna had Justin Junior and although I loved him as if he were my own, it didn't satisfy the yearning for my own flesh and blood. I used to dream of having a son to teach basketball to or go fishing with. All that corny, cliché shit. It didn't matter what it was as long as I was able to carry on my lineage and namesake.

After a year I bargained with God and agreed that I would settle for a daughter. A princess I could spoil and protect. And I wish one of those little horny teenage boys dared tried to disrespect my baby…I laughed picturing myself holding a rifle. Yeah, that was overdramatic, but Daddy had to make a statement even if it embarrassed her. It was a dad's job to embarrass his daughter in front of the boys trying to get in her pants. They'd think I was crazy and think twice before doing something stupid.

49

That too slowly faded from my daydreams. Tianna and I had been married for a few years and I had accepted that Justin Junior would be our only child. I had even become content in that. She and I could retire early and still enjoy our younger years after Champ was out on his own. We were saving a good amount of money. With Jay being so close to Tianna's family and his grandmother on his father's side, there was no shortage of babysitters.

I had a good and content life until I lost all I'd forgotten that I had wanted in an instant. The insatiable yearning of being a father swept over me like a tidal wave and I was trying my damndest to break the surface and breathe, but my grief weighed me down and I was drowning in sorrow. A part of me resented my wife. I needed someone to blame and whether it was fair or not, I blamed her. I didn't know how not to.

Today all the loathing and resentment surfaced and boiled over. It was as if I finally broke the surface and could release my anguish and breathe. How sad that it was at the expense of my wife's feelings. I knew she carried the heavyweight of guilt on her shoulders. There were days she hadn't gotten out of bed riddled in pain and self-loathing. I knew it full well and in one moment of emotional explosion, my need to breathe superseded her need to try and lift herself.

I felt like a failure. What kind of husband put his wife through more anguish to relieve his own? And not just any wife, but a good wife that never really meant harm and was just being a good person and Godly woman trying to save a young girl. I probably would have done the same if I were in her shoes. What kind of husband?

A human husband. It wasn't an excuse, and I wasn't dismissing her hurt. I knew I had to ask for her forgiveness. In fact, a better husband wouldn't have been afraid to be vulnerable and honest to his lover and best friend. There was a time and a place to have a conversation with her and express my pain. And it definitely was not tonight in front of her co-workers and in the middle of a Camden City neighborhood.

Yeah, I couldn't stop being human, but I had a lot to learn about dealing with my emotions rather than bottling them up until I exploded. For now, though, I had hurt her enough and chose to remain quiet, the sight of her tears tormenting me. It was a punishment I had to endure until I could fix this.

TEN

Micah

The houses I had bought from Mr. Rivera had needed more work than I had anticipated and I regretted not negotiating the price a bit better but what was done was done and there's nothing left to do but get to fixing them. Unlike Mr. Rivera, my plan wasn't to be just a landlord. I wanted to buy houses and flip them for sale until I could have enough money to purchase nicer buildings and homes I could rent outside of the hood. I'd learned the hard way I couldn't have anything nice in Camden. The residents tore my apartments up and security deposits barely covered the damages, so I had decided that fixing and reselling was the better hustle. The market had been good for it too.

I stopped by the first house we were working on and checked in on the crew. My boy, Mendez, had told me his Pops and Uncles could do any kind of labor and would need to be paid under the table due to their illegal status in the States. That meant more money in my pocket at the end of the day, so I hired them and was glad I did. The dudes were workhorses and did more in a shorter amount of time than the contractors I hired for my building two years back. And they did the job right. They had almost finished patching up the walls and had measured the square footage to see how much paint they needed so they could start painting. Not wanting them to halt progress, I volunteered to go buy the paint and offered to buy them all lunch. Needless to say, I was happy to treat and in exchange, they were grateful and put in that much more effort. A win-win situation.

On my way to the home repair store, I stopped at my Mom's. Figured I'd get her something to eat too while I was in the neighborhood. After walking all the way inside the building and not finding her home, I remembered she had a doctor's appointment and cursed myself for being so absent-minded. I really needed to stop smoking so much damn weed and start focusing on shit. I laughed at myself and locked her door before heading back to my car.

I pulled off and waited at the stop sign when I saw a woman with a stroller walking fast and not paying attention before she crossed the street. She looked like she was high on something, and I shook my head sadly at a young mother with a baby wasting her life on drugs. As she got closer I realized it was Sharmayne and the sight of her knocked me back a bit. I'd never seen her looking crazy like that before. Her hair was everywhere and her clothes were disheveled. When she finally crossed, I peeped her face and saw one of her eyes had been swollen shut. She was practically stumbling and looked like she was about ready to collapse.

I turned around to reverse and check on her but there was a car behind me blocking me. He began to honk his horn when I hadn't moved. I waved him around me. "Go around!" He sat there like a jackass not doing a damn thing so I honked back, stuck my arm out of my window, and motioned for him to go around. "Move!" I yelled loudly. He finally sped around me cussing me out in Spanish. I gave him the finger and quickly reversed back into the parking spot I was in, not giving a shit about his tirade. *Asshole.* I jumped out of the car now irritated even more than before and caught up to Shar just as she was about to climb the steps.

"Sharmayne?" I touched her shoulder and she jumped back scared, her fists ready to swing on me. I put my hands up quickly to show her I wasn't a threat. "Whoa, whoa, whoa. It's just me baby girl. It's just me, Micah."

She shook her head frantically and grabbed the baby out of the stroller, leaving it at the bottom of the stairs while she tried to go up. She made it up two steps and stumbled back. I caught her and the baby just in time, otherwise, she would've fell straight cracked her head right on the cement sidewalk.

"Let go of me!" She began trying to wrestle out of my grip and covering up Jaya as if I was gonna hurt her or the baby. That stung a little. I had never before been a threat to her or her daughter but I tried to let the offense slide. She was obviously not right mentally and the bruising on her face was proof enough that she was probably delirious. Someone had really beat her bad and I had no idea how she had even still been conscious.

"Shar, I'm not gonna hurt you. Relax. I'm trying to help you!"

"Get off of me!" Now she was sobbing.

I set her down carefully on the step and unlocked the door for her. There was no use in trying to rationalize with her. She wasn't trying to hear me.

She tried to get up but couldn't. Her sobbing grew louder. She looked so pitiful. and my heart went out to her. I wanted to help her but she wouldn't let me near, so I grabbed the stroller and took it upstairs, setting it by her door. When I got back downstairs, she was still crying, holding the baby for dear life. I don't know why I did it, but I took the baby from her. She began to claw at me but could barely raise a fist. I took the baby upstairs sat her in the stroller and rushed back down.

By the time I had returned, Sharmayne had made it to the landing where the mailboxes were. She crawled to the stairs threatening to kill me if I hurt her baby. I rushed down to her, picked her up, and carried her up the stairs. "I'm not gonna hurt you or your baby woman. Calm down." I didn't know if it was the sudden movement or because she couldn't hold on any longer, but she passed out in my arms.

I panicked and got her upstairs quickly. Searching through her pockets I found a stack of money and her keys. I wasn't the smartest man alive but I knew wherever that money came from was trouble and I wanted no part of it. I put the money back where I found it and used her keys to unlock the door.

I was sure I was breaking all kinds of tenant laws but I was even more sure if Shar would have been conscious she would have wanted her daughter to be safe inside of their apartment. I laid Shar on the couch and picked up the baby from the stroller when she began to cry. She screamed even louder afraid of me. I tried to calm her but she refused no matter how much I shushed her. I was beginning to get a headache. A baby's screeching cry was enough to drive a man insane. I was rocking and walking back and forth with her hoping anything would work, but she only screamed until she was almost hoarse.

"Mike?"

I turned and breathed a sigh of relief. My mom was standing in the opened doorway looking puzzled. She looked inside and saw Shar laying on the couch and I saw panic fill her eyes. "What happened?' she asked. She waved me over not wanting to enter the apartment and took the baby from my arms. Jaya looked at her and continued crying but the howling had ceased. My mom grabbed a bottle from the stroller still sitting in the hallway and began trying to feed Jaya. She refused the bottle so my mother coddled her and soothed her back until she quieted, only her sniffles remaining.

"There, there, beautiful. It's ok. It's ok." My mom rocked her up and down walking back and forth down the hallway until she fell asleep. With the wad of money I had found in Shar's pocket and not knowing what kind of trouble she was in, I didn't dare call an ambulance. It was risky but with nobody to care for Jaya she would have been taken into child welfare services and I couldn't let that happen.

It took some convincing but my Mom finally came into the apartment agreeing to help me figure some shit out. That was when I realized how up until that point in my life I really hadn't ever cared about what happened to someone other than my mom or myself and with all this drama, I damn sure didn't know if caring was even worth the trouble.

ELEVEN

Shamayne

My head was pounding so badly it felt like it was being used for drum practice. I tried to open my eyes but those hurt too. I felt fear but didn't know why until suddenly memories of Ace beating me for believing I stole his father's money rose to the surface and my heart began to pound as hard as my head. Where was Jaya? I pushed myself up and tried to focus but could only see out of one eye. "Jaya!" I tried to scream but my throat was dry, my cry barely above a whisper.

"Lay back down."

I recognized her voice instantly and it brought me no comfort. If anything, it made me want to leap out of the bed in a single bound like I was Superwoman. "Where is my daughter and why are you here? I told you, you aren't allowed here anymore." I tried to stand again, but my body ached so badly I wondered if Ace had been wearing workboots with metal plates.

"Jaya is downstairs with Kendra. She is fine but you are not. I won't be here long. Whether you like it or not, I am your mother. Now cut the shit and rest."

My mother was known for her foul mouth, so it didn't surprise me she was lacking in bedside manner, but she didn't scare me. "Who the hell is Kendra? And I didn't ask for your help. And none of this would have happened if not for 'my mother' so the only one that needs to cut the shit is you. I didn't need you then and I don't need you now."

Her humorless chuckle irritated me. "Kendra is your landlord's mother and you are just like your damn father. Stubborn and stupid."

It was wrong to hate anyone, especially your mother but I found myself letting the hate fill me drip by drip. Some days like a running faucet. This moment like an opened fire hydrant. "Get out," I said passively. I didn't have the energy to waste on her. I pulled the blanket off me so I could get up and go get my daughter.

I heard water being poured and suddenly felt arms behind me sitting me forward. "Drink some of this water and take these pain pills then lay your ass back down. Cut out the foolishness. I'll be gone soon enough."

I stopped and stared at her. I'd only sat up and was already exhausted and ready to collapse. I took the glass from her and took the medication before I laid back down. "You leave tomorrow, and I want my daughter back before then." She didn't respond but just sat there staring at me. I turned away from her and dozed off.

I woke up the next morning to an empty bedroom. My bladder was begging me to get up and relieve myself so I got up as quickly and painlessly as I could. The pounding in my head downgraded to a mild headache. I managed to get up and make it to the bathroom without too much hassle. I made good use of the trip and brushed my teeth. I ran the shower and took a seat on the toilet seat to catch my breath before I undressed and got in.

The hot shower felt good on my sore muscles, and I wished I had a shower chair so I could sit in the tub for a long while. After a few minutes, I felt my energy starting to wane so I lathered and rinsed but couldn't finish washing my hair. I barely had enough strength to stand, so I quickly rinsed the shampoo out and got out. The mirror was fogged from the steam, and I wiped it to see my reflection. Seeing my face bruised and beaten angered me. Wrapping a towel around me, I practically dragged myself out of the bathroom not wanting to face myself a moment longer.

I heard my mom in the kitchen and smelled coffee brewing. My stomach grumbled in reaction. I couldn't remember the last time I had eaten. "I'd like some. Sugar and cream," I said loud enough for her to hear me before I retreated into my bedroom. I grabbed a long tee shirt, too weary to put on pajama pants, and slipped the tee over my head. As much as I didn't want to, I picked up the comb so I could untangle my hair. My tight curls would get knotted up if I neglected to at least run a comb through it.

Sitting at the edge of my bed, I looked out my window into the sunlight. I lifted my arm, raising the comb, and felt soreness in my ribs from where Ace had kicked me.

"Damn it!" I cursed having hair and brought my arm back down. I attempted to do it again with my left arm doing the most work but all I managed to do was get the comb stuck in my hair. I let my arms rest beside me, and left the comb in my hair. I was too tired and too sore to deal with it. If I woke up with matted curls, so be it.

I felt the comb being pulled from my hair and then being used properly. I turned back and saw Micah. Startled, I tried to get up and put distance between us. "What are you doing here?"

"I'm sorry. I didn't mean to scare you. My Mom asked me to bring you your breakfast. I thought you knew I was coming."

"How would I have known that?" I was discreetly looking around my bedroom for something to use as a weapon.

"Your Mom, I guess."

"Where is she?"

He looked completely baffled. "Who? Your mom? " His brow spiked, and he shrugged his shoulders almost annoyed. "I don't know," he said like I was dumb for asking him. Maybe I was. "Listen. I came in here to tell you there was coffee and food in the kitchen. I saw you struggling with the comb. I was trying to help you out but it's whatever. I don't know how to brush a female's hair anyway."

"Bring me back my baby." I didn't need his help for anything else.

He set the comb down and walked out of the room. I heard the front door close and felt my shoulders relax. I tied my hair up and dragged myself to the kitchen. Micah had poured me a cup of coffee and plated up some eggs, toast, and home fries. I went on a momentary guilt trip before I brushed that off. Men weren't to be trusted no matter how much they claimed to be helping.

After I picked at my breakfast, I took some pain meds and waited for Micah to bring Jah-Jah upstairs. It wasn't long before I heard a knock on the door. I was expecting Micah, but instead, it was Kendra. Jah-Jah saw me, and her face lit up. Her deep dimpled smile, inherited from her father, made my heart melt. She began kicking her legs and jumped into my arms. I squeezed her tight and flooded her face with kisses. She got too excited and accidentally bumped her head into my face and I nearly lost control of her from the pain.

Kendra braced us both for support before she took Jah-Jah from me so I could sit down on the couch. I tried to shake it off fast so she wouldn't want to stick around. "I'm fine," I assured her. "But thank you. And thank you for staying with Jah-Jah."

"It's no problem. She's a sweet baby." Kendra put Jah-Jah in her walker, and I was relieved. Truth was I needed a few minutes for this blinding pain to subside. She hesitated before walking out. "Do you want to just lie down for a bit? She's about due to eat, and I love feeding her. I pureed her some yams and chicken. She loves it."

A tinge of jealousy mixed with being weirded out surfaced. Why was this woman going above and beyond for a baby that was not hers, nor even related to her?

"You don't have to do that, but thank you."

I couldn't read her blank expression. "You're welcome. Take care."

She was about to close the door when I called out to her. "Oh! Mrs. Payne!"

She faced me. "Could you tell Micah, that I have my rent money? I forgot to give it to him when he was here earlier." She nodded and walked out.

After she closed the door I rested my head on the couch and closed my eyes hoping the pulsating in my black eye would stop. It took longer than I had hoped but it managed to go away almost completely. I was picking up the toys Jah-Jah had thrown out about when Micah knocked.

He handed me a bag and skipped the formalities. "My mom sent this for that baby." I peeked inside the bag and saw a container with presumably yams and chicken, a small, opened package of diapers, and a change of clothes. I felt shameful being jealous of a woman who was clearly, loving on my child. "Tell your mother I said thank you. She is very good with Jah-Jah."

Micah nodded but didn't speak.

"Please come in. I have the rent money right here." I moved aside and held the door open.

"Nah, I'm good right here."

I knew he was upset about this morning but oh well. How could he fault me for being leery of men I don't really know being inside my apartment without my knowledge? "Suit yourself," I responded.

I left the door open and took a few steps to the couch where I had seen my jacket. I picked it up and searched the pocket. Not finding it, I searched the other pocket. "Where in the hell is this money?" I checked the pockets again. I peeked out the door. "Hold on. I'm looking for it. I put it here, but it must have fallen out of my pocket." I didn't wait for Micah's reply but instead searched the couch, then the floor, but still didn't find it.

I sat down on the couch feeling defeated. I had been so out of it walking home I could have dropped that money anywhere. Angry tears brimmed my eyes. All of the mess I had gone through and for what? I was in a worse situation than before; no rent money, no clothes money, and I still had to pay Ace back all of that cash plus some. I was so overwhelmed, I tried to hold back the tears, but they overflowed.

"Shar, you good?"

I looked up to see Micah standing above me. I quickly wiped the tears away and stood up. "Uh, yeah. Sorry. I thought I had the money in my pocket, but I must have hid it and forgot where. It's been a rough couple of days."

He looked back and forth between my jacket and me. He hesitated but pointed at the jacket. "Is that the jacket you were wearing when I found you outside?"

He'd found me outside? The memory was fuzzy but somehow felt accurate. "I'm sorry but my memory is a little shaky. Thank you for helping me. And yeah. That was the jacket I wore a few days ago."

He nodded. "When I carried you upstairs and was looking for your house keys, I found the stack in there, but I put it back."

The fact that he said it was a stack, confirmed he wasn't lying, and I believed he didn't take it. Why confess he even saw it, if he was the one who stole it? Nah, Micah didn't take it. And I didn't lose it after all. That meant just one thing. My darling mother Felicia stole it and as sure as I was standing there, she was flying high somewhere.

I sat down and screamed into my jacket. Why did my mother have to be a junkie? Why did she have to ruin my life every chance she got?

"Yo Shar? What's wrong?"

Micah sat beside me, and I had no choice but to be real with him. "That was my rent money and I'm pretty sure it was stolen. But I'm gonna pay you as soon as I can." I got a little frantic. I couldn't get evicted on top of everything else.

"Who do you think stole it?" He asked matter-of-factly.

"That doesn't matter." No matter how messed up my mom was, I couldn't bring myself to drag her name through the mud to strangers.

Micah looked down at his hands and then back up at me. "Spoken like a true junkie's kid. Trust me I know and can speak from experience."

Strangely I wasn't the slightest bit offended by his reference about me. If anything I was surprised he'd confessed something so personal, and it was a small sort of comfort. "Your dad?"

He shook his head, and I couldn't have been more shocked at the revelation. "My mom has been clean for fifteen years." He seemed sad but proud at the same time.

I would have never guessed Kendra was a former user.

"Listen, this is my fault. I'm the one that found your mom down the street and had her come take care of you. If I hadn't done that, she wouldn't have been here or stolen your money, so consider your rent paid for the month. And we don't ever need to bring this up again."

My heart sank to my stomach. I was relieved and scared at the same time. "And what do I have to do in return? I'm not going to have sex with you so you can forget that!" If he thought for one second that I was a hoe, he was dead wrong.

Micah stood up without warning. His tone was even but his words spoke volumes. "What is wrong with you? I don't want nothing in return. I was just righting my wrong. Take care Shar." Micah walked out of my apartment without a second thought. Me, on the other hand, I replayed that conversation over in my head a thousand times. When had I become so cynical and bitter? I recognized I was wrong in assuming he wanted something in return but I couldn't find the means to feel sorry about it. Life had more Ace's than Micah's running around and I wasn't about to let my guard down for the one who was only possibly different. I wasn't always right but I also hadn't forgotten that Micah was a street nigga just as Ace was.

TWELVE
Tianna

Friday had arrived faster than any other Friday in my entire life. I usually looked forward to the weekend, but El's mom had arrived this morning, and I had been dreading attending the pizza and bowling night El had planned. I had promised to go and be a supportive wife but of course, that was before a lot of ugliness had sprouted between he and I. We hadn't said more than a few words to each other since my breakdown in the school parking lot.

I missed my husband but at the same time, he wasn't who I had known him to be lately, and I didn't want to be around this cold version of him. It was very clear that he felt the same toward me for he hadn't so much as been in the same room with me for more than a minute or two before he made himself scarce. We pretty much avoided each other. Until the day of our plans had arrived way too fast, God help me.

After setting aside the art piece intended to distract me but didn't, I ran up the basement stairs for the ringing telephone. "Hello," I answered out of breath.

"Mrs. Townsend?"

"Yes, this is she."

"It's Detective Shearer from the Camden City Police Department. I am calling you to update you on your case."

"Good afternoon, Detective Shearer. Yes, please, I've been waiting." I had filed a police report for my assault resulting in the loss of my son.

"We found Sabrina and she corroborated your story. She admitted that she was assaulted by a group of girls. She also confirmed that you voluntarily involved yourself in the altercation. However, after that point, her story is a little different. She claims that she is very grateful for you trying to save her and because of you she survived. She has no reason to wish you harm and your claim that she is at fault is false. She

61

claims that you went to the hospital to see her and that she and her grandmother thanked you in person."

"Yes, I did go to the hospital and her grandmother was very kind but—"

"We spoke with her grandmother as well and she has given a statement stating the same. She also included in her statement that Sabrina has been home recuperating and couldn't have been the person who threatened you outside of the school."

My heart sank. How could people be so cruel and dishonest? There had to be another lead to follow. "Did Sabrina tell you who the girls were? They are a gang of girls. Mickle something or other. I wouldn't lie!"

"Mrs. Townsend, I didn't accuse you of lying. And Sabrina said she couldn't accurately identify any of her assailants because they hit from her behind and she didn't get a look at their faces."

"That's bullshit!" I yelled. "She is one of them! I saw her with them!" I began to cry out of anger. "There were witnesses! Coach. Coach Edelson was there. You can ask him!" I pleaded.

Detective Shearer went quiet for a moment. "Ok. I will follow up with Coach Edelson but unless we have some solid evidence, it doesn't look like we have anything further to go on. I will keep you informed if anything new turns up."

I thanked him and dried my tears as I hung up the phone. When I turned, I saw El and Jay staring at me. "Mommy, why are you crying?"

"I'm ok, handsome. Don't worry about it. Let's get ready for pizza and bowling." I ignored the look of disdain on El's face and got Jay and me ready.

An hour later, I walked to El's car and thought about sitting in the back but that seemed petty, and I wasn't about to start being petty. He unlocked the doors and I helped Jay get buckled in before I got in the car. The last time I had been in El's car was the day he had picked me up from work after my meltdown. I had a quick flashback of him screaming in my face and the silent ride home afterward. I wondered if he had the same trigger because he quickly turned on the car radio distracting me from the thoughts that would have taken me down a path I didn't want to walk.

Hip hop started blaring through the speakers at deafening levels, but I didn't make a fuss although it was annoyingly loud. I had no intentions of arguing with El. Instead, I looked out the window at the passing scenery. After a minute I realized I wasn't as unbothered as I thought I was and turned the volume down because I couldn't take it anymore, only to hear Jay rapping at the top of his lungs. "Now, I ain't saying she a gold digger. But she ain't messing with no broke niggas. Go head girl, go head get down."

My head snapped back quickly. "Justin Saunders Junior! What did you just say?" Jay was steady bopping to Kanye West without a care in the world and I wanted to snatch him up.

"I'm just singing the song, Mommy."

"That is not a very nice word, and you shouldn't say it! As a matter of fact, you shouldn't even be listening to this song at all!"

Jay chuckled innocently. "Mommy, I can say nigga. I'm black. That's what Daddy said."

I slowly turned my gaze to El who was doing a poor job of hiding his amusement. He kept his eyes on the road but addressed me with an icy tone. "Don't look at me like that. That's not how it happened. Champ overheard a conversation, and I may have said that during the conversation, but I did not give him permission to say that."

I sat there waiting for the part of the story where El had a chat with Jay about not using that word at all, but instead, I got El purposely trying to rile me.

"Although, technically, Champ is right."

"Seriously?" I wanted to knock the stupid smirk off his face.

"Hey, Champ."

"Yeah, Daddy."

"You're too young to talk like that, ok?"

"But Daddy you said—"

"Justin."

"Ok, Daddy."

I shook my head at the nonsense between father and son. It sometimes felt like raising two kids. The song ended and I was glad for it until the next one came on and Jay was back to bopping.

"I'll take you to the Candy Shop. I'll let you lick the lolli—"

El quickly turned off the radio.

"Hey! Daddy, I like that song!"

I sat in silence just letting the ridiculousness play on without saying a word. I didn't need more aggression piled on all that I had yet to release.

"Champ, that's not a song you should be singing either."

"Why?" I could feel Jay pouting behind me. "It's about candy and I want to go to the candy shop too. They have lollipops!"

El scratched his forehead and held in his laughter, "Candy rots your teeth, Champ."

"When I turn ten years old, I'm gonna say that word all the time and I'm gonna go to the candy shop every day," Jay whispered to himself.

El let out a chuckle but quickly reeled it back in, then shook his head smiling.

A few minutes later we pulled into the Playdrome Bowling Alley parking lot, and I really did not want to get out of the car. El got out first and let out an anxious Jay that had already jumped out of his seatbelt. After stalling for too long, El knocked on the window and gave me a stern look. I smiled pleasantly and held up one finger requesting his patience. I closed my eyes and prayed.

Lord, please guard my mind, my body, and my tongue. Especially my tongue. Amen.

El rolled his eyes and waited for me to get out of the car before he locked the doors and turned on the car alarm. "That was overdramatic. She's not that bad."

I remained quiet. *Get behind me Satan.*

Marvette and Mac hadn't arrived yet, so we rented a lane and got our shoes. Jay was like a pig in shit and couldn't keep still with all of the lights and blaring noises of billiards, video games, and bowling balls crashing into pins.

"Hey, handsome. Let's go find you a bowling ball." I put my hands on his shoulders and tickled him. He giggled then ran toward the rack of bowling balls.

"I want this one." He tried to pick it up but couldn't.

When I caught up to him, I opened my eyes wide at his choice. The holes were the size of fists. "Umm, Jay, that one is too big for you. That's Hulk's bowling ball, so you can't use that one."

His eyes got so wide. "Whoa! The Incredible Hulk bowls here? That is so cool!"

"Yeah, sure." Technically that was sarcasm and not intended to deceive my child, so I let it slide and refocused. "How about this one?"

"It's pink," Jay complained.

"But it's your size. See you put your fingers in here like this—"

"Mommy, I don't want that one."

I surrendered my quest to convince him and spent ten more minutes finding a suitable, non-pink ball. On the way back to the lane, I saw El hugging a kid. I looked and saw Marvette pleased as punch, watching her sons embrace each other. My palms began to sweat. *Just two hours, Ti. You can do this.*

Jay pulled my hand and brought me back to the present. "Mommy, is that Mac, Daddy's brother?"

"Yeah, baby."

"So, is he my uncle like Uncle Abe?"

"Yeah. Sorta." I hadn't expected Jay to think of anything like that and his question caught me completely off guard. "Let's go say hello, ok?"

He nodded carrying his bowling ball proudly to El. "Daddy, look! I found a cool ball. And it's not pink."

El beamed at him. "Good job Champ!" El took the bowling ball from him and held it. "Come say hi to my mother and brother." Jay looked at them suspiciously. *That's right baby. Be on guard.*

Mac stepped and touched the bowling bowl. "That's a cool ball. I want to get a ball too." He turned back to Marvette. "Mom, can I go find a ball?" Mac was only eight years old and carried himself like a well-behaved young man. I could almost guarantee he wasn't rapping 50 Cent in his mother's car.

Marvette nodded to him and smiled. "Yes. Please don't walk off too far. Stay where I can see you."

Mac nodded his head before his attention got snatched away by Jay. In an instant, the boy had run halfway down the bowling alley and was yelling and waving like he had no home training, just to get Mac's attention. It would have been the perfect time for the floor to swallow me whole.

Marvette eyed Jay sternly then back at Mac, who hadn't budged from the spot like a well-trained dog. Not that Mac was a dog. He was actually a sweet and kind kid. On that, I could not judge Marvette. She had raised two kind young men.

El didn't seem to notice Marvette's silent command to Mac to stay put and he laughed it off. "Come on Mac. Let's go see what Champ found."

Mac looked at his mother and she nodded ever so slightly before he walked beside Elijah who put an arm around his shoulder and chatted with him as they walked together. I was now alone with the barracuda, but I would make the best of it.

"Marvette, it's good to see you. How are you?" I approached her intending to hug her, but she crossed her arms in front of her, holding on to her purse for dear life. *Ok, then.*

"I am well, thank you."

I waited for more but got only silence. *Other than your son being an ass lately, I'm well too. Thanks for asking.*

I laughed to myself wondering if I'd be talking to myself the entire weekend. Probably and that was ok. I inadvertently met her gaze, and she was eyeing me strangely. She probably thought I was crazy smiling at nothing. I sobered and attempted small talk again. "So, did you get your shoes and find a ball?"

"I'm just going to watch. I'm not fond of wearing shoes other people sweat in." She looked down at my feet then back up at me and raised her eyebrows quickly before she rolled her eyes.

The witch hadn't even been in my presence for ten minutes and had already eyed my son like she had beef and just tried to play me for wearing bowling shoes. This was going to be a long-ass weekend. "Suit yourself," I replied and sat down at the monitor and entered our names for scoring.

The boys came back with a ball that Jay couldn't stop talking about. Mac quietly unzipped a backpack that had been sitting on the plastic bucket chair and removed a crisp pair of bowling shoes. I refrained from rolling my eyes. People bought bowling shoes all the time. It wasn't a big deal.

Where I attempted to ignore it, El had to shine a light on it. "Mac, you got your own bowling shoes. Are you a bowler, or in a league?"

"No." He shook his head. "I've never bowled before."

Good Lord, that woman was strange. I stood up and changed the subject. "Who wants pizza? Or maybe some chicken fingers and fries?"

Jay raised his hand excitedly. "I want pizza Mommy! And a soda!"

"You got it handsome. Mac would you like pizza and a soda too?"

He looked over at his mother and she replied for him. "I can purchase his food. But thank you for the offer."

El jumped in. "Mom, no way. This is our treat."

Marvette looked like she was about to argue back but held her tongue. "Thank you, Elijah. Mac can have pizza, but we don't drink soda. Juice is fine and bottled water so I can dilute it. Otherwise, it's too much sugar."

"Mom, Mac can go one time having a soda or undiluted juice. It's not going to kill him."

She scrunched up her face before she caved in and agreed. "Ok, but just today. And I mean that." Elijah kissed her on the cheek roughly and the witch managed to crack a smile. I was sure somewhere a pig flew away from a farm.

"So, Mac, pizza or chicken fingers?"

"Pizza," he said excitedly, and I could see the eight-year-old peeking through.

"Ok, so I'll just get two pies and a few pitchers of soda." El walked off like the father and son of the year. He hadn't even bothered to ask me what I wanted.

Marvette took a seat close by and watched as I gathered the boys to show them the basic techniques of bowling that I knew, which granted were only two. Throw it down the lane. Aim for the pins. "Who wants to learn how to bowl?"

Jay raised his hand, stretching it high. "I do! I do! Uncle Mac, do you want to learn how to bowl?"

Mac looked at Jay surprised before Marvette interjected her tone oozing offense. "Young man, my son is most certainly not your uncle." She rolled her eyes and said barely above a whisper, "Or your daddy for that matter."

My nostrils flared and wanted to throw her down the lane and knock her into some pins but Jay in his innocence questioned her rather than being offended. "But why not? Mommy's brother is my uncle so that means that daddy's brother is my uncle too. That's what mommy said."

Marvette looked at me with her mouth gaped open. "Well, first of all, little boys shouldn't talk back, but I'm not surprised you do. Mommy doesn't seem to teach you as she should."

"Mommy knows lots of things. She knows how to paint and how to pick a bowling ball. She knows who bowls here. Uncle Mac, Mommy said the Incredible Hulk bowls here. We saw his bowling ball over there!"

Marvette pursed her lips and shook her head.

I was beginning to get a headache and I was not about to explain anything to that woman, so I took my son from out of her warpath rather than engage in it. It was only for the weekend I reminded myself.

"Ok, let's learn bowling," I took the boys onto the wooden floor to demonstrate. "Don't pass the red line, here. Don't roll it into the gutter." I pointed as I showed them where to stand and how to hold the bowling ball. They put their little fingers in the holes and complained it was weird, so I showed them the hold-it-with-both-hands-and-swing-it-between-your-legs method and they preferred that technique.

A few minutes later, we got started and both boys and I guttered our turns. El returned with the drinks and bowled his turn, knocking down nine. The boys began jumping up and down in excitement and asked El to show them how to bowl because apparently, I hadn't done a good enough job. He guided them each to the lane during the turns and showed them arrows and how to aim. After a few tries, the boys were hitting a pin or two, while El was getting strikes and spares like they were on sale a dime a dozen. Showoff.

"Mommy! Daddy is the best bowler ever!" Jay could hardly contain himself.

The pizza arrived and I grabbed some plates ready to serve. The boys were enraptured in El's bowling skills, so I attempted to be courteous to my mother-in-law. "Marvette, how many slices would you like?"

"You didn't wash your hands. I can serve my own pizza. Thank you."

I looked down at my hands, then back up at her, and had the urge to slap a slice across her face. I checked myself though just as El and the boys ran toward us, the boys happy about the pizza. Jay went to grab a slice and El stopped him.

"Whoa, Champ. We gotta go wash our hands first."

Marvette chuckled under her breath, and I wanted to sit mother and son down beside each other and do a flying round kick or whatever Abe told me it was called but I pasted a smile on my face and volunteered to take the boys to the restroom to wash up.

"I got it," El said. "These are men now. They can't go into the lady's room."

Jay and Mac agreed. "Mommy, you go to the girl's bathroom, and we go to the boy's bathroom. Right Daddy?"

"Right, Champ."

All the machismo permeating the air threatened to choke me but rather than be annoyed I just agreed with my son. "Good thinking."

There was a short line for the women's room so by the time I was done, the boys had already gone back to our lane. I wasn't in a rush to get back to Cruella DeVille so I took my time, taking in all of the other bowlers.

I was a few feet away from our lane when I saw her, stopping me dead in my tracks. Her hair was out and wild as I had always seen it and her arm in a sling. To think she used to remind me of Bianca was a joke. Bianca was crazy but she was never cruel.

My adrenaline began to rush and before I knew what I was doing, I grabbed a souvenir wooden bowling pin displayed on the registration counter and headed toward her lane. Still, a few feet away, she looked up and caught eye contact with me. She tapped the girl beside her and pointed at me. They began to laugh. "What you think you gonna do with that bowling pin?"

By now, the other girls in her group had all turned toward me. They began to taunt me, but I kept advancing.

"She stalking us and shit!"

Sabrina laughed. "Nah, she just mad 'cause her dumb ass tried to press charges for assault and she don't got no proof. Even my grandma making her look stupid and crazy."

"Word?" The girl that had slammed Sabrina's face into the hood of my car was the only one not laughing. She stared at me with such hatred in her eyes, I could feel it down to my soul and I recognized it because it's exactly how I felt about her. She was the one that kicked me in my stomach. She's the one that deserved the wrath even more than Sabrina had."

I aimed the bowling pin at her. "It was you."

She was sitting on the top of the bucket seat chair with her feet on the seat, leaning forward with her hands casually folded between her knees. She sat up and pointed at herself mocking me. "Oh, you want me?" She got down from the chair and stood tall. She removed her jacket, and her girls began encouraging her to 'beat my ass.' "So, you losing your baby wasn't enough? You tryna lose your life too?"

Never in my life had I been a violent person. Never in my life had I been in fights. Never in my life had I lost complete control of myself and given in to such rage and hatred. Yet, none of that mattered. I didn't give that girl another chance to say a thing before I fired the bowling pin at her with all my might. She dodged it. As I was about to charge her, I felt a small hand grab mine and I shoved it away.

I ran toward her, and she ran out of the lane and up to the landing where there was open space. "Come on bitch!" All of her friends ran up behind her egging her on.

"Beat her ass, Tay!"

I walked back around the chairs and ran toward her with tunnel vision before someone grabbed me from behind and pinned my arms against my sides. I kicked and struggled trying to get free but couldn't. I got dragged away and was brought down to the ground.

Now out of breath, I stopped struggling and sat on the floor, angry tears streaming down my face. I looked and saw Elijah with his hands on his hips catching his breath. Behind him Marvette stood, the boys standing in front of her, her hand on Mac's shoulder. She looked down at me sitting on a grungy carpet, a pile of anger, hate, and tears. I didn't care. Who was she to judge me?

Then I glanced upon my son. Jay was crying and he looked at me with terror in his eyes. All of the anger washed away and all I wanted was to shield him from all he had seen. I waved him over to me to assure him everything was ok. "Come here, baby." He walked forward until he reached Elijah, stuffed his hand in his father's, then hid behind him where I couldn't see him.

It must have been his hand I pushed away. My son was scared of me, and it broke me down more than I already had been. I looked around and saw people staring at me sitting there looking crazy and I couldn't wrap my mind around how I'd gotten to this place of insanity. Everyone that meant the world to me was distant from in either heart or space, while people who brought misery I couldn't escape.

I got up off the floor and headed to the restroom, only to be stopped by an employee. I looked at her name tag. Joyce, Assistant Manager, raised a hand, stopping me. "Ma'am, are you the woman that started an altercation?"

Out of the corner of my eye, I saw Sabrina and crew back in their lane watching. I tried to walk around the Assistant Manager and head to the restroom, but she sidestepped me.

"Fighting and throwing pins are not allowed. I need you to leave now before I call the police."

I didn't have to look to know where the roar of laughter came from. The pent-up frustration was being provoked again.

Elijah came up beside me and held my elbow, a silent warning to contain myself. "That's not necessary. We are leaving," he responded on my behalf.

Silently, I walked to the glass entrance doors, exited the bowling alley, and waited for El. The night air breezed in cooling my flushed skin. I don't think I had ever been so angry in all of my life. Not even toward the man that had molested me as a child. Yes, I detested my mother's brother, but he hadn't killed my child and he was rotting in jail for his crimes.

As I waited, my emotions dipped and dived. Anger, sadness, confusion, determination to overcome, and denial took turns pulling my thoughts. I wish I had refused to be a supportive wife and come bowling. Had I stayed home, none of this would have happened. I was beginning to think that the more I aimed to be good to others, the more it backfired in my face.

I heard Jay and waited for them to exit the bowling alley. "Daddy, I don't want to leave. What about the pizza and where's Mommy?"

"We gotta go Champ. We'll go get pizza somewhere else. Mommy has got to be outside."

I pushed up from against the wall so they could see me but halted when I heard Marvette speak.

"Elijah, before we go out, I need to speak with you."

"Mom, its ok. We can have dinner somewhere else. Let's not make this a big deal, please."

"I most certainly will make this a big deal. I do not wish to take Mackenzie anywhere with Christianna behaving as she did. And what is that about her losing a baby?"

"What are you talking about Mom?"

"After I went to the restroom to wash my hands, I saw Christianna holding a bowling pin ready to attack those young ladies. I could tell they were riff-raff but they seemed to be minors. Your wife should know better than to assault a minor. Then one of them mentioned Christianna losing a baby. Are they referring to a recent pregnancy or her teenage one because for Pete's sake, can't that woman even do her duty as your wife and bear you a child? Then again, I always said that first child wasn't yours."

Elijah paused. "Boys go sit there for a minute while I talk to Mom."

"Ok. Daddy. Come on Uncle Mac, let's go look at that video game." Jay's excitement returned and I was glad that children bounced back quickly. But just like, it was snatched away.

"Justin honey, Mackenzie is not your uncle. Please don't say that anymore sweetie."

"Ok, Grandmom. I'm sorry." He sounded so sad and I had to force myself to stay put.

"Grandmom?" I could hear the outrage in Marvette's tone.

"Hurry along boys," Elijah said, his voice eerily even and I knew him well enough to know that was not a good thing. There was silence for a few moments before Elijah spoke again presumably waiting for the boys to be out of earshot. While the boys walked away, I took a step closer to make sure I heard every word.

"First, the child that Tianna lost when she was a teenager was my child whether you choose to accept that or not, and we will never bring that up again. Secondly, my wife is a good woman, so before you judge her know that those 'minors' and 'young ladies' assaulted her while she trying to be a good Samaritan. They beat her so badly and viciously, they killed our child that she was carrying."

Marvette quickly interjected. "Elijah, I didn't know, but that is beside the point."

Elijah cut her off and continued. "Beside the point? You as a mother, how could you not even understand the love of a mother? Who could blame her for her grief and despair? Those minors get to walk away without punishment while we are left with a loss. And rather than them showing my wife remorse and respect, they taunt and threaten her."

"Elijah, don't question the love I have for my sons. I have made sacrifices you will never know of and love you and Mac both with everything in me."

"I don't doubt that because I know what it is to love your son. How? Because Justin is my son. My son. You don't need to like it, but don't ever chastise him for being an innocent child wanting to form bonds with the people who are supposed to love him. If you don't want my son to call you grandmom, that is fine. Then none of my children will ever give you that privilege because he as much mine as any biological children Tianna and I will have."

"Elijah Townsend, don't you dare speak to your mother that way."

"I am a grown man. I am not the teenager you sent away to live with his dad to try and control my life. Tianna is my wife and there is nothing you can ever do to change that. You don't need to accept, but you need to respect it, and her. Just as I expect her to respect you as my mother. But I'll be damned if either one of you is going to try and control who and how I love. Now I am going to take my family home. I will go to your hotel room tomorrow so that I can spend time with you and my brother. And I am taking Justin with me to spend time with his uncle. Yes, his uncle. If he is not welcome, then I am not welcomed."

All I heard was silence and I wanted to step out of the shadows and see the look on Marvette's face, but what did it matter? Elijah had put her in her place and left her speechless. That was good enough for me.

"Of course, you are both welcome to come. Don't be ridiculous Elijah."

"Good. Boys! Let's go!"

Elijah walked out the door and stopped when he saw me standing there. He stared at me, and I could see the ice and fire in his eyes. I wanted to bury myself in his arms, but I feared he'd reject me. Or maybe it was my pride that kept me from him, but I stood rooted there a big old mess of emotions.

Jay and Mac walked out talking about the video game, Marvette right behind them. Elijah heard them and waited for Jay to reach him before he grabbed the top of his head and shook it playfully as he always did. "Let's go get some pizza Champ. Where do you want to go?" I moved aside waiting for them to file out when Elijah reached for my hand, intertwining it with his and without saying a word, walked his family to the car, treated us to pizza at King of Pizza while reminding me that no matter what we went through, I was his queen.

THIRTEEN
Shawayne

I was already running late and the last thing I needed was Ace finding another reason to add to the amount of money I now owed him, or worst, putting his hands on me. The click-clacking of my heels on the polished floor of the Crowne Plaza in Cherry Hill increased as I sped up my pace. I reached the elevator doors just as they were opening. Relieved I wouldn't have to wait, I clumsily rushed in only to run into a wall of chest and polo shirt rather than the elevator. He grabbed my arms to steady me from losing my balance. I hadn't worn stilettos in a while and I was out of practice. Between embarrassment and my bruised face, I didn't dare look up into his face.

"Whoa. You ok?"

"Yes. I'm sorry about that. I'm in a rush. My apologies."

"No worries," he replied as I finally walked into the elevator. It was only then that I noticed a young boy in a soccer uniform trailing behind him. "C'mon Champ," he called out to the boy urging him to catch up, too busy kicking his foot in the air pretending to fight karate. "Eeee-yah! Ee-yah!"

With distance now between us I looked up and caught a glimpse of the man's face waiting impatiently for his son. Mortification set in and I leaned forward pushing the button repeatedly hoping to speed up the closing doors. Once I was alone in the elevator, I leaned against the wall and expelled a noisy breath.

I'd only met him twice before, but I recognized Ace's nephew without question. He was the same age as Ace and Ace had had a love for him but they ran in different circles and hadn't been close since they were teenagers. I was surprised to see Elijah here and not someone Ace would usually invite to one of his gatherings. Especially with a child. But what did I know? I hadn't been in Ace's life for a long time and I had no idea what he was up to or who he associated with.

I began to panic a little. Who else would be at this party? I wanted to get off the elevator, run away and forget I'd made one of the biggest mistakes of my life going to Ace for help but I had no place to run to. I got off the elevator and self-consciously looked at my reflection in the large mirror in the hallway. The makeup had done a decent job of covering up the bruising on my face and luckily, the swelling had gone down a lot but my left eye was still smaller than my right. If anyone gave me more than a passing glance, they would easily notice that my face had been used as a punching bag.

I was more concerned that Ace's associates would think they too had the right to put their hands on me. I snuck into the ice machine room, peeking out to make sure no one was coming before I pulled up my skirt. I felt for my switchblade tucked into my garter belt. Still secured snug to my thigh, I lowered my skirt and rushed to the suite. I knocked on the door and evened my breathing.

Huggie, Ace's homie and muscle, answered the door, his massive, sloppy frame taking up most of the entrance. He lifted his chin as a salute but said nothing else as I walked in. He closed the door behind me, and I entered the lion's den. A bar to my immediate left was stocked with alcohol, a woman wearing just was a man's tie was bartending. I averted my eyes from her bare breasts and stepped further inside.

In front of me, the open suite was divided into a dining area and a sitting area. The dining table was covered in an assortment of fast food that made my stomach churn. I saw men sitting on two couches being served drinks by another topless woman and I beelined in search of the bathroom. I waited a minute before a man stepped out zipping up his pants and avoided his gaze.

I stepped into the bathroom and locked the door behind me. I took off my jacket and checked my makeup again. I closed my eyes and cleared my mind reminding myself that this was not who I was or ever would be. I was doing what I had to do to stay alive and not leave my daughter in this fucked up world alone. I would never feel shame for protecting her by whatever means necessary. I'd endure this, so she wouldn't have to.

I removed the knife from the garter and stuffed it in my jacket pocket. No more stalling. I was as ready as I was going to be and wanted to get this done and over with. I stepped out of the bathroom and placed my jacket on the chair at the end of the bar. I wasn't topless, but my top was sheer and left nothing to the imagination.

I looked around and Huggie read my mind. "It's over there," he said nodding in the direction of the dining area. "Ace will be here in five minutes. You already late. You better hurry up."

I picked up on his warning and appreciated the heads up, but I wouldn't mistake that for kindness. If push came to shove, Huggie would kill everyone in this room for Ace and not think twice about it. His loyalty to his boss and savior ran deep.

Just like me, Ace had taken Huggie in off the street and under his wing when he had run away from foster care at sixteen years old. Huggie could barely read and write but he could kill a man with one solid blow to his head and that was what Ace truly cared about. Huggie had never done anything to hurt me, but he certainly wasn't someone I could consider a friend or depend on for help. Nevertheless, he was right, and I needed to do what I came to do.

I reached into my bag and pulled out the large summer hat I had bought last year. I had to make do with what I had since I couldn't afford to buy anything new. I placed the hat on my head and took out a CD of mixed songs. I found the light switch and dimmed them a little bit. The men quieted down, and I knew I had had their attention now. From that point on I knew all eyes would be on me and it was showtime.

I sashayed to the radio and popped in the CD pulling the hat low hiding my face. To the spectators, they probably thought it was theatrics but in reality, I was nervous and felt shameful. I would do it because I had to, but I didn't want to entertain a room full of strange men. I hadn't stripped in so long, hiding my face for a while helped me find my rhythm.

The Asian-inspired beat for Dip It Low began to play and I matched the chords with my hips. As the song played on, I had incorporated some of the choreography from the seductive music video into my dance and added a few more sexually explicit ones. I began to get lost in the song forgetting I was wearing a hat until I snapped my head back and it flew off my head, my braided hair flying free

The men began encouraging me to take off more. My hands shook as I snapped my sheer top open savagely baring my breasts increasing their enthusiasm and my shame. I dared to look at my audience and nearly crashed to the floor when I saw Micah watching me quietly, unlike his counterparts who'd begun throwing money at me, yelling for me to expose every inch of myself.

Micah walked out of the room, sipping on a drink, no longer watching me. I blocked him out of my mind. I needed to earn all of this money to pay Ace back and I didn't have the luxury of being ashamed in front of my landlord.

By the end of two songs, I was tired, perspiring, and fully nude. I picked up my money and placed it in my hat walking out of the spotlight. I let the CD play and headed for the bathroom to gather myself but was cut off by Ace's cousin Wesley. "Ace wants you."

I nodded breathlessly. "Let me get myself together for a minute. I'll be right there."

Wesley shook his head and inadvertently peeked at my hat. I intentionally looked down at my hat full of money and let out a humorless laugh. Ace really didn't trust me. I extended my hand before me. "Lead the way." He smirked and pushed me ahead of him.

I spun and pushed him back. "Don't put your nasty hands on me."

"Nasty? You the hoe out here naked, shaking your ass for a few dollars." Wesley laughed. "Walk your black ass on before Ace beats you again."

I felt rage begin to bubble up inside of me but remembered where I was, and with who. Ace or Huggie could kill me right here and now and I'd be able to do nothing to stop it. I silenced my tongue and did as told. I had to weave through bodies as several more people had arrived since I had begun dancing. When I got to the bar, Ace had been laughing at something one of his colleagues had said. He smiled at me and looked happy to see me. I'd known him well enough to know he didn't give two shits about me and all he saw were dollar signs.

"Champagne, Champagne. You haven't lost your touch." He gave me a soft hand clap then caressed my right breast.

I endured the objectification but didn't let him see me break stride although inside I was rebelling. "You needed to see me?" I asked politely, not daring to embarrass him in front of his guests.

He knew me well too, and my penchant for being passive-aggressive. I saw his lip twitch in anger before he masked it with a wide, menacing grin. Straight white teeth and a deep dimple in his left cheek. The prettiest smile I'd ever seen belonged to the ugliest person I'd ever known. "Can I offer the lady a drink?" He turned to the bartender before I could respond. "Lotti! Get Champagne whatever she wants!"

Lotti smiled and nodded waiting for me to order a drink. "I'll have a bottle of water, please. And Lotti, I'll open it myself, thank you." Ace had taught me never to let my guard down when entertaining. At all costs avoid accepting drinks from men I didn't know and trust and if I had to, order an unopened bottled water that couldn't have been tampered with. Dancers were always being drugged and raped by accepting drinks from their clients.

Ace chuckled. "You were a good student Champagne. What a waste of my time, though." He sobered and I could see his anger peeking through itching to be set free. "Put that money on this bar and go fix yourself up," he demanded, grin gone as he turned his back to me and dismissed me.

"I'd like to count it first," I said as if I had some control over the situation.

He spun back around on the stool and quickly snatched the hat from me. "Bitch, I said go clean yourself up. You don't need to count my money. This ain't nothing but chump change anyway."

I had collected it all off the floor and knew I had had nearly a grand. It was just a small dent, but a dent, nevertheless. I looked in the hat once more before he dumped it on the bar. "Lotti put this away." He tossed the hat back in my face and gave me his back again.

Lotti nodded and collected the bills, put them in a tip jar, and stored it beneath the bar. I walked away and found my clothes. I spent twenty minutes in the bathroom before someone began to knock and turn the knob furiously. "Other people are waiting out here!"

I put on my hat and stepped out not making eye contact with anyone. I stayed in the corner sipping my water. Several men had approached me. I played it politely but let them feel my disinterest. A few minutes later, Ace addressed the room of about twenty men. Some wore suits. Some wore casual clothes. They all gave Ace their full attention.

"It is always a pleasure to gather with like-minded men to discuss business. But all work and no fun makes Ace a dull boy. So tonight, I planned a little something to help all of us remember to enjoy life. To the victor goes the spoils, right? Or some shit like that." Ace laughed and then men joined him. Bunch of sapsuckers kissing his ass.

A bunch of women filed out from the bedroom and lined up in front of the couches. All of them dressed in lingerie and heels. The men began to whistle and yell out obscenities. In response, the women laughed, waved, and winked flirtatiously.

"Fellas, I got some high-stakes poker set-up over here for those who like the thrill of luck and chance." Ace pointed to a poker table that had been set up by the bar. "And right here," he gestured to the women, "I have an auction for those who prefer a sure thing." He laughed and some of the men began to bark out loud like dogs. "Who would y'all like to see auctioned first?"

The men began to call out the colors of the lingerie the woman were wearing or pointing to them, and Ace laughed, enjoying every moment of his perversion. "I want the stripper!" Someone yelled.

Ace raised an eyebrow. "The stripper?" He puckered his lips and nodded as if he was intrigued. "That's Champagne, and she's just not anybody. She's special. Y'all boys sure y'all can afford her?"

My heart plummeted to my stomach. I had never agreed to be auctioned off. I was not a prostitute and had only ever danced while working for Ace. Suddenly his words rang in my head. *'You will do whatever they ask you to do.'* More and more I began to despise this man.

The men began to chant my name like juveniles. Ace motioned me over with a tilt of his head. I forced my feet to move before he publicly beat me. He could auction me off if he wanted to, but I wasn't sleeping with nobody. I stood beside him while the men watched. I felt like meat at a meat market.

He smacked my ass the rubbed his hands together. "Yeah, fellas. She ripe for the picking. Umm." He perused my body with his eyes surveying me like he was hungry and I was a full course meal. "Champagne likes to play wild horse and wants to see who can tame her."

The hair on my body stood on end. Ace practically gave the men full permission to rape and take what they wanted. The more I fought them, the more they'd think I wanted it. They began to call out to me trying to get my attention but I looked past all of them. What kind of man thought it was a turn-on to take a woman against her will?

"The bidding starts at three thousand."

An old man in a business suit in the back raised his hand and I wanted to vomit.

"Four thousand," said the man that had exited the bathroom earlier.

"Five." The older man in the suit responded casually.

Ace chuckled. "We have five. Bry, six?" he asked the other bidder.

"Nah. She ain't worth all that." A few of the men sitting near him laughed and high-fived him, in agreement.

"I assure you, Bryan, that Champagne is worth much more. Trust me. I don't give that praise to just anyone." All the men began to hoot and go wild. Ace had a reputation for only sleeping with women who were sexually superior to most. He'd prided himself in sleeping with women who supposedly knew how to truly please a man.

"Six," said a new bidder. A white guy dressed in a hoodie and jeans.

"Best six grand you'd ever spend Mighty Matt," Ace joked. "Give those computers a rest and let Champagne hack you instead."

Mighty Matt turned ten shades redder, and if I had to have my choice, I would opt for him. I could probably talk my way out of sex with his nerdy ass.

"Seven," Bryan called out. "Aint no way I'm letting some white dude, have all that."

Ace clapped and laughed out loud continuing to pull their puppet strings and them not even realizing it. "I hear you, Bry! A black queen needs a black king!"

"Ten thousand," came a quiet voice from the back. Everyone went quiet and turned to see who had outbid them all.

"Well, well, well. The real estate mogul came to play today. The black Donald Trump got ten k to spend on a woman?"

Micah walked forward and dropped money on the nearby coffee table that had been pushed to the side. "Ten grand."

Ace gave Huggie a nod. He walked over to the table and verified the amount and gave Ace the ok. Ace smiled wide. "Ten thousand going once, going twice, sold to Mike Trump. And make sure you enjoy every dime worth." Ace hadn't even let anyone else try to top the bid.

Micah looked at me and motioned for me to come to him. Of all the men there, he was the last one I wanted to leave with. I walked over to the bar and grabbed my jacket. I slide my arms in and discreetly felt for my blade. It was still in the pocket. He walked to the door and opened it waiting for me to walk out first. I glanced at his serious expression on the way out.

His eyes met mine and all I saw was exasperation rather than lust. But then again, I wasn't exactly in the right state of mind to make a sound judgment. My heart was racing, and I wanted to escape all of this. I wanted to get home to Jaya. Make sure Lenora got home safely after babysitting and I wanted to leave this life behind again, but this time forever.

Micah didn't speak as we walked to the elevator. While inside, he stood in front of me quietly not acknowledging me at all. When the doors opened, he walked out, and I followed like a puppy dog. He opened the passenger side car door for me before he walked around to his side, still silent.

On the ride, he turned on the radio and switched the music to a rap CD. I had never heard any of the songs and the voice wasn't familiar to me either. "Who is this?"

"Mobb Deep," he replied his eyes focused on the road.

More silence but I found that I didn't mind the quiet. In fact, I preferred it. It had stopped raining, but you could hear the wet tires against wet pavement between songs and it soothed me. I had no idea where we were going until he got off the highway and took the exit that led to my neighborhood. A few minutes later he turned down my block and parked the car in front of my building. As he had done earlier, He came to the passenger side and opened my door. He left it open, not waiting for me to get out before he walked up the stairs and unlocked the front door. I jumped out of the car trying to catch up to him. He was very mistaken if he thought he was coming to my apartment.

I made it up the stairs and he closed the door behind me. As I was about to let him know the deal, he walked toward his mother's apartment without saying a word to me.

"I'm not going to your mother's place, and you are not coming to mine!" And I meant that shit. I don't care how much money he paid to have sex with me.

Micah didn't even turn around. "Good night, Sharmayne."

I heard his mother's door open, close then bolt shut.

My mouth dropped open. I felt cheaper than I had dancing for money. I walked up the steps embarrassed and wanted to crawl under a rock. More than ever, I wanted to succeed in life and leave this hell hole. I made it home and settled in after getting Lenora into a cab and called me when she made it home. After I showered, I picked up my books and got back to studying for my bar exam. I reminded myself again that I was the only person I could truly depend on, and I refused to let myself down again.

FOURTEEN

Micah

The last of the new appliances arrived and were installed. I had to get some used ones rather than new ones I was planning on putting in the house after unexpectedly spending ten thousand dollars I was saving to fix up the next house. I wasn't stressing it though. With the amount of money, I had saved on labor I was still in a good place financially for renovations. With the plan I had thought out, I would end up better than before, so long as my second part of the plan to sell my house went smoothly.

The next day my mom came by and cleaned up the empty house. She vacuumed the carpet and went grocery shopping. The Mendez brothers helped me move my furniture in. By the weekend, I had set up the bedrooms and had completely moved out of my bigger house into the smaller onr. The Mendez brothers began the small renovations needed on that house so I could put it up for sale. It was in Collingswood and would sell for a great price. The profit I made would go into renovations and purchasing another fixer-upper.

I showered and headed for my building to finally go talk to Sharmayne. I hadn't seen her since the night at the Crowne Plaza. We had some things we needed to discuss whether she wanted to or not. I knocked on her door, admittedly a bit nervous.

She answered the door, Jaya on her hip and a highlighter clenched between her teeth. Without saying a word, she walked away, leaving it open, assumingly an invitation to enter, so I did. I shut the door behind me and followed her inside. She put Jaya in her playpen stepped away, returned with a bottle then handed it to her. The baby put the bottle in her mouth and tilted her head back comically guzzling it down.

Shar went back into the kitchen and sat at the small table in front of a notebook and textbooks as if I weren't even there. I followed her and leaned against the entrance. "You just gonna act like I'm not here?"

She didn't say a word and pretended to be reading. Even flipped a page for good measure. I didn't know whether to laugh or snatch her up and make her listen for once. The woman was so damn stubborn and irritating as hell, but I couldn't stay away from her and with every passing day, I just wanted to take care of her more and more. Jaya too.

I hadn't told Shar but the days the baby was at my Mom's I was there too doing my part. At first, my mom wasn't with it, but I had already decided to try and win this woman, and that included her daughter. Word around the street got back to me and I know Ace was the one that beat her. It infuriated me but I had left that violent and illegal life behind and instead approached the situation the best way I knew how. I knew she'd be at the party and what would happen. I had experienced my fair share of Ace's meetings. I didn't know about the auction, and I planned on playing poker just to keep an eye on her. It didn't matter how I got her out of there safely. All that mattered was that I had. But what was the point of keeping her safe for a day rather than long term?

"We need to talk?"

"I'm not having sex with you. I will pay you back a little at a time when I get the money." She didn't even have the decency to face me as she talked her shit.

"Why do you keep saying that to me? I don't want you to pay me back Sharmayne. And I didn't come here to have sex with you. What is wrong with your mean ass?"

She swung around fire in her eyes. "Mean? I am not mean. I am just tired of sorry-ass men thinking they can do whatever they want and get away with it because they have money and carry guns. I am not scared of you, and I didn't ask for your help. So, if you came here looking to threaten me, you can get in line. Ace already done did that and I survived."

Her phone rang and she grabbed the receiver off the cordless phone. "Hello," she answered still frustrated from her rant. After a few moments, she gave me her back and tried to whisper. "How is that possible? Between the auction money and the dancing, I shouldn't owe you that much Ace." She walked out of the kitchen just as the baby began to fuss and was listening as she tried to quiet the baby down. "This has nothing to do with my daughter. Leave her out of it."

Watching her pace back and forth nervously and trying to hush the baby fueled something in me. I picked Jaya up out of her playpen and quieted her down. She began to fuss with my gold chain, and I let her so long as she didn't put it in her mouth. I listened and watch, Shar like a hawk picking up every infliction in her tone and taking in every word she said. She was scared and I knew Ace was threatening her.

She rushed to the window and peeked through the blinds. "Don't. I'll do another meeting or work it off at the club, just leave Jaya out of it."

Seeing her so scared pissed me off. What kind of coward threatened a woman and her baby for money especially when he had plenty? I knew right then and there I would have to speed up my plan.

Sharmayne hung up the phone and came and grabbed Jaya from me. "Thank you. I got her. You have to go now."

"Sharmayne, let me help you."

"I don't need your help. What I need is for you to leave."

"How did Ace threaten you? Tell me. You don't have to be afraid of me."

"Leave!" She yelled.

Just then a few bullets came through the window, glass crashing everywhere. I dove over her and Jaya bringing them down to the floor and covering them with my body, her screams in my ear. After a moment, when the crashing sound and screeching tires ceased, I got off her fighting me to make sure Jaya was ok. The baby was crying from being scared but wasn't physically hurt.

"Get your stuff. You can't stay here anymore."

"You can just evict me! That wasn't my fault!"

"Sharmayne, shut up and get you and Jaya's shit! It's not safe here!"

I startled her and she quieted but nodded her head and quickly packed Jaya's baby bag and some clothes in a trash bag. I went out and checked outside before I brought her and the baby out. I drove them to my renovated house.

"Where are we?"

"This is my house. I just finished fixing it. There is a spare bedroom. You and Jaya can stay here for a while."

She shook her head no. "I can't."

"You have somewhere else to stay?"

She shook her head no.

"Then stop arguing with me." I took them inside and showed them around. The entire time she held onto Jaya like someone was going to jump out and scare them, but I understood. She settled in her bedroom and closed the door. I ordered some Chinese food and knocked on her door to invite her to eat. She denied the request.

Over the next few days, it was more of the same. She barricaded herself in her bedroom and would only come out to prepare food and bottles for the baby. I never once saw her take anything for herself. On my way out of the bathroom freshly showered, I ran into her in the hallway. She looked pale. "You don't look so good. You ok?"

She nodded and I heard her stomach growl. Her face turned red and she put a hand to her stomach as if that would stop the grumbling.

"Where's Jaya?"

"She's asleep. I was just going to go wash out her bottles."

I picked Sharmayne up and tossed her over my shoulder. She kicked and screamed her weakened state not helping her resistance. I carried her to the kitchen and sat her at the table. "Sit there and don't move."

"Who the hell do you think you are? You think just because you paid all that money and I'm staying here that you can tell me what to do? Well, you can't! I am a grown-ass woman and can do whatever the hell I want!"

I quietly watched her have her tantrum and waited for her to say her piece before I responded. "Don't move woman."

I opened the refrigerator and took out a carton of eggs and made her a Western Omelet with cheese. It was the only thing I knew how to cook. I slide the plate in front of her with a fork. She looked at me like I had lost my damn mind. I popped the toast out of the toaster and buttered it for her. The utensils clinked as I slid them on the table beside the eggs then sat down across from her waiting to eat it.

"It's getting cold. What you waiting on? Eat it." She didn't budge. "Fine, I'll eat it. I reached for the plate and she snatched it closer to her. She picked up the fork and tasted a small amount. "Well?"

She eyed me but didn't say anything. One bite led to two then three, and before I knew it she was fucking it up like she had been starving. I kicked myself for not having made her eat sooner but from now I'd make sure she was well fed. After she ate, she asked for something to drink and I pointed to the refrigerator. She shook her head, got up, and washed the dishes she used and the ones I had cooked with. Heading for the door, she tried to leave the kitchen without getting a drink.

I gently got up from my seat and blocked the door, not allowing her to pass. "Weren't you thirsty?"

"I'm ok," she said looking past my shoulder, her back to the kitchen.

"There's some juice and soda in the fridge. Some bottled waters too."

"I'm good," she reiterated still avoiding eye contact.

I grabbed her hand. When she tried to pull it back, I gripped it tighter. I walked her to the refrigerator like a child that needed to be taught a lesson. "Whatever is in this house is yours too. You can go anywhere you want, take anything you want, and have anything you want, Shar. Do you understand me?"

She looked up at the ceiling as if she were that stubborn and wayward child. I tilted her chin down and she smacked my hand away. I did it again and caught her hand the second time. She finally looked at me, ready to snap.

I shook my head at her and smiled. "Damn, woman. You such a pain in the ass. It ain't that serious. I took her hand, opened the fridge door, and forced her to grab a bottled water before I closed it. "See? It ain't that hard."

She snatched her hand away, marched out of the kitchen with the water, and rushed up the stairs. I laughed knowing I pissed her off, but she'd get over it soon enough. In the meantime, I had to go pay Ace a visit. It was time he understood that Sharmayne and Jaya were off-limits. I didn't care if Jaya was his daughter or not.

FIFTEEN
Tianna

O bsessed was probably the most accurate description of my foolishness, but I just didn't know how to let this go and a week had passed since I had taken matters into my own hands. Detective Shearer had called me to update me on my case and with no further leads and my voluntary decision to get involved in the altercation, he closed the case. Camden City had dozens of numerous open cases of murder and other violent crimes needing the manpower to investigate. My little old complaint wasn't worthy of their attention. Justice for my son wasn't a priority to them.

To me, however, I couldn't let my son's death be in vain and if they wouldn't find evidence against Sabrina and company, then I would. Every day I arrived at work early and left a few minutes later just to try and catch the gang of girls together again. Maybe if I could show Detective Shearer a photo of Sabrina keeping company with the assailants, he would have something to go on. Put a crack in her story. What victim would consort with their enemy?

Taking a quick bite of my chicken caesar wrap, I set it back down in the container and focused on my surroundings. It was a beautiful spring day and a perfect day for delinquents to be outside starting trouble. I sipped my flavored water and kept vigilant. From my rearview mirror, I saw Coach Edelson approaching my car and I had half a mind to start the car and pull off. I wasn't in the mood for anyone's pity or lecture.

Instead, I keep my guard up for the girls and only looked to the passenger side when he spoke. I turned to see his forearms leaning comfortably on the lowered window and his forehead resting against the top of the door. "So, this is going to be an everyday thing, huh?"

"What is exactly?" I asked as I turned away and looked out the front windshield.

"C'mon Christianna. You know exactly what."

"I'm sitting in my car enjoying my lunch, John. Is that against school policy now?"

"Forget school policy. A few faculty members may have said a few things and I tried to put it to rest but they aren't stupid, and neither am I. You are asking for trouble sitting out here, looking for trouble. Literally."

"I'm just eating lunch in my car, John. No big deal."

I heard my car door open and looked at John like he was crazy when he sat in my passenger seat. "Fine. I'll have lunch here too," he said matter of fact before he picked up the other half of my wrap and took a bite.

I had to pause and take in what I had just seen. No, the hell he hadn't just sat his black ass in my car without permission and eaten my food. "You aren't invited, I'm pretty sure this is considered trespassing and did you just bite into my lunch?"

"I sure did. The way I see it if I got to sit my black ass out here during my lunch break to keep you from losing your job and being arrested for assault, the least you can do is feed a brotha."

I rolled my eyes and shook my head at him. I didn't have the energy to explain what was none of his business anyway. I grabbed the half of my lunch that he hadn't touched, and finished it, just to keep from having to talk to him. After a little bit of silence and no sign of Sabrina, I rolled up my windows ready to call it quits until after school.

"Oh, we done for the day? Cool. You know this was actually a nice peaceful lunch. Thank you."

I just stared at John as if he had no sense then exited my car. I wasn't going to entertain the nonsense and let him believe it was welcome. It wasn't and I wasn't the jovial person he had come to befriend. At least not when it came to this.

After school, I did what had become my normal routine and drove around the adjacent streets searching for evidence before heading for the highway to go home. I spotted three girls and quickly pulled over. I reached into the backseat of my car and snatched my camera out of the bag. I was an amateur at best, but I zoomed in as much as I could and snapped a few photos. None of them were Sabrina and I wasn't even sure if they were connected but I'd collect all the evidence now and sort through it later. I planned to look for matching faces from my previous photos and start a trail of crumbs that led to the loaf.

For today, these pictures would have to be enough as no one else had been around. Anxious to study the photos I went immediately home. When I pulled into the driveway, I saw Elijah was already home and I instinctively felt comfort just knowing he was near. He was a huge part of my peace when I weathered storms. He didn't have to do anything but be himself. Half the time he hadn't realized how he'd steadied me when I felt like I was riding a rollercoaster.

I walked into a dimly lit house and heard *Gotta Be* by Jagged Edge playing softly in the background with Elijah singing along to it, a rose in hand. It was our high school sweetheart song. I set my purse and camera down confused but tickled. "Babe, what's going on?"

"You know I gotta beeeee," El belted out off-key. I'd heard a man in love would be willing to make a fool of himself just to see her smile. While most people would have thought he was being foolish, I was blushing like a teen getting attention from her secret crush.

I covered my mouth to hide my laughter because the truth was he sounded horrific, but I didn't interrupt and instead watched him like an adoring fan. I suppose wives could be foolishly in love too. El strolled over to me and handed me the rose still butchering one of my favorite songs ever.

"Cause I will always love you so…"

I smelled the single rose then caressed my cheek with it. "I love you," I said and I meant it with every fiber in my being. He looked at me with deep love in his beautiful brown eyes. That was all we needed to let Jagged Edge finish the song without El's help as his lips were too busy serenading mine.

After he kissed me like he meant it, he trailed the kisses to my cheek, down my neck then back up to her ear. "Runaway with me Mrs. Townsend," he whispered.

"Any day Mr. Townsend," I replied lost in our intimacy. He pulled back slowly from our sensual embrace and spun me before we began to slow dance. "Where is Jay?"

"With your mom," Elijah mumbled between kisses on my neck.

"What time is he coming back?"

Elijah moved my hair off my shoulder and explored the other side of my neck. "Later."

"How much later, though?" I asked rubbing his back, half enjoying his tenderness. I had an irrational fear that my child would one day walk in on mommy's bare ass in the air and see things a child should never see their parents doing. I was a grown woman and was still grossed out by the idea of my parents having sex. "And who's bringing him home?" I continued my interrogation.

"Focus wife."

I had to stop being so anal and remember I trusted that El knew me well enough to plan a romantic night and take care of all the details so I wouldn't have to worry. He led me to the dining room and I relaxed and gave into the moment. A beautiful dinner was set up and I was happy I didn't have to cook it. I was even happier that I knew he ordered the food and that I wouldn't need to clean the kitchen later. I really got into it. I kicked off my shoes and sampled the asparagus after he poured me a glass of wine.

"Dig in baby," he said before pouring himself a glass. "I already blessed it."

"You prayed over the food before I got here El?" My husband could be strange sometimes.

"Damn right. I was planning on having you already naked before we got in here to eat and I thought it would be disrespectful to God to pray for what I was about to eat what was on and off the table."

I choked on my wine.

"Woman, we grown. God made us and He made sex. Ain't nothing wrong with a husband that wants to enjoy the wife God created for him."

"Ok, Preacher Townsend. Be half paying attention during Sunday service but know every scripture about sex. Ready to preach a whole sermon about it."

He stared at me blankly then chuckled so hard. "You right. You right. But God ain't finished with me yet so don't be judging me, woman. You vowed to honor and obey me. You better watch what you say."

I tossed an asparagus spear at him and he caught it with his mouth, then winked as he chewed it. "You next. Hurry up and eat. Build up your strength. You gonna need it preacher's wife."

I couldn't help myself and burst into laughter. "You get on my nerves," I said amused by his nonsense.

He winked then beamed his one in a million smile my way. It roped my heart and lassoed me in every time he graced me with it. After all of these years, I still thought Elijah was fine and he could create butterflies in my stomach. And he was mine. I was one lucky woman.

After dinner, he made good on his promise and made love to me so sweetly. I couldn't remember the last time we had been so tender with one another.

He began to kiss me again. "Round two. I'm warmed up now. You better hold on to something, girl."

I cracked-up. Elijah was the worst at smooth-talking but he made up for it in other ways. I kissed him passionately and stopped when I thought I heard a knock on the door. Elijah had been too busy to notice. I went back to kissing and then heard it again. This time he had too. We waited and heard the knock, but louder this time.

Elijah dropped his forehead onto my chest. "Why? Why? Why?"

I rubbed his head then kissed it, as I laughed. "You know you gotta go answer the door, 'cause I sure ain't."

He jumped up from the bed frustrated and slipped some pajama pants on. "I bet you, it's somebody from your family. Every time I get near your vagina, it's like their senses start tingling. Instead of Spiderman, Cockblockaman."

I got out of the bed, trying to hold in my laughter. El was only half-joking. I slipped into one of Elijah's tees and followed him to the stairs. Another knock on the door, this time harder, had him jogging down the steps.

"Ok, ok. Damn." I went halfway down the stairs and peeked to see who had been at the door. El unlocked it and swung it open. "Abe. What a surprise," El said sarcastically. He looked back at me and I shrugged and tried not to laugh as I took the rest of the steps down.

"Hey bro. What are you doing here?" I asked.

"I came to drop Jay off. Pop got home not feeling well and *Mami* done diagnosed him with the Bird Flu. I had stopped by for my laundry and she told me since I ain't married and therefore ain't doin' nothing important I could drive Jay home. He sitting in the car. Y'all was taking forever and didn't answer the phone when I called." Abe looked at us and laughed. "Looks like y'all was doing something important married people do though."

"Man, I'm trying," El pouted. "I turned off the ringer so we wouldn't be interrupted. Why don't you be a good uncle and take Champ for the night."

Abe shook his head and curled his lip. "No can do. I got a date and I got kick-boxing early in the morning." He whistled for Jay before he turned back to El. "And Bro, what the hell? I am a very good uncle. That's my little dude. Right Jay-Jay?" Abe yelled back at the car.

Rather than hear the sound of my son praising the uncle he worshipped, I heard the simultaneous noise of glass shattering, tires screeching and my son screaming. Before I could understand what was happening, Abe was at his car opening the door. He looked around frantically calling out to Jay.

"Mommy! Daddy!" Jay was crying out from my car instead.

Elijah ran to my car and flung the door open. Just then I noticed an orange glow from within my car and the faint odor of something burning. I began to advance to the car. "Jay! Jay!"

Elijah pulled him out of my back seat and yelled at me to stay back as he cradled our terrified son crying out for me. When Elijah got back to me he handed Jay off to me quickly. "It's a flare! Call the fire department! Now! I'm gonna get the fire extinguisher!"

I nodded quickly and turned to make sure my brother was ok but all I saw was his back as he chased the car down that had shot a flare into my back window. I ran into the house, Jay gripped onto me for dear life, still weeping. I soothed his back then set on him the table. He refused to loosen his hold on me.

"Jay, baby. I need you to let go. Let me look at you. Are you ok?"

He let go and nodded, still sobbing. I looked him over relieved he was safe and sound. After I got him down off the table I called 911. Elijah hadn't put a dent in the fire with our small extinguisher and it began to blaze higher. Neighbors began to circle my driveway. I stayed indoors soothing Jay. He'd stopped weeping but the sniffling continued as he laid his head on my lap and I rubbed his head. What the hell were people thinking. *Why would someone intentionally shoot a flare into my—*

Before I finished my thought, I had a very good idea who would and why. A minute later Abe walked into the living room out of breath. "Is Jay, ok?"

At the sound of his voice, Jay jumped from my lap and ran into his uncle's arms. "Uncle Abe they burned mommy's car!" The tears began again.

Abe hugged him then set him down. "It's ok Jay. You're ok and Mommy is ok, right?" Jay used the back of his hand to wipe the tears away, nodding in agreement. "Right. I know you were scared bud, but they're gone now. I promise that won't happen again, ok? Let me talk to mommy in the kitchen for a few minutes. You good in here?"

Jay nodded again as he walked back over to the couch and reached for the remote. "I'm gonna watch TV."

"I'll bring you some popcorn."

"No mommy. I don't want popcorn."

My heart broke a little. Jay never turned down popcorn. I walked behind Abe into the kitchen. "Before firefighters start asking questions. I didn't catch up to the car, but I cut through your neighbor's backyard when I saw them make a left turn at the corner. I got a glimpse as they just passed me on the next block over as I ran out into the street. I couldn't get a look at the plate but I saw a few girls. Teens. Maybe in their early twenties. At the least the driver was. Car was a dark Honda sedan."

"Did you see a girl with big curly hair like Bianca's?"

Abe shook his head. "Nah. The driver was a brown skin girl with dark hair. It was pushed back in a ponytail."

I wondered if it was Tay.

"But now that I think about it, I did see a girl running down the street with wild hair like Bianca's. I ran past her when I was chasing the car but she was running in the opposite direction—"

I left Abe talking and ran outside past the firefighters and gathered crowd and looked down the street in both directions but saw no one. Abe caught up to me, outside barefoot with nothing on but a tee.

"Ti, what's going on?"

I shook my head and marched back inside the house ignoring everyone who had tried to grab my attention, Abe right on my heels. I headed straight to my camera. I turned it on. "Do you recognize any of these girls?" I asked as I held up the camera for him to see the small preview screen.

He studied the picture then shook his head. "No."

I took the stairs up two by two and ran into my bedroom. I snatched my laptop off the nightstand and hurried back to Abe. I opened the folder on my computer where I'd stored all the pictures of the girls I'd taken. "How about any of these?"

Abe looked at me strangely. "Ti, what is going on. Who are these girls?"

I shoved the laptop closer to his face impatiently. "Do you recognize any of them?" I asked forcefully.

He took the laptop from me and sat down perusing the pictures. After a minute or two. He pointed at a girl. "Maybe her," he said shaking his head unsure.

I looked at the photo. The girl resembled Tay. It made me wonder if perhaps they were related to each other. "The girl driving looked like her?"

"Yeah, but I can't be sure it was her. The car was going fast."

"Anyone else look familiar?"

"No Ti. I told you it all happened fast. What in the hell is going on and why do you have all these pics?"

"Yes, Tianna. What is going on?" El stood with his hands on hips like an upset father wanting answers. "A damn flare was shot into your car where our son was. The Fire Department suspects some teens out being mischievous, but they're wrong aren't they?"

I rushed over to El with my laptop relieved we finally had a lead. "It was Sabrina. Look." I held up the laptop and rushed through what Abe had shared, my surveillance, and my theory that it was all connected. "They must have followed me home after school! I'm going to call Detective Shearer." El rubbed his forehead, looked down at his feet, and shook his head. "Why are you so quiet? El, we have proof. And now that they burned up my car, we have even more to charge them with! Don't you understand that we finally got them?"

He snapped his gaze to mine. "Got them? We ain't got shit but a burned up car and a scared little boy that could have been killed!" He raised his voice and I jumped back.

Abe stepped forward trying to be the voice of reason to deescalate the situation. "Yo, El man. I know you're mad. But calm down bro."

"Don't tell me to calm down in my own damn house!"

Abe raised his hands and stepped back. "You are absolutely right. My bad. I'm out."

I rushed to Abe's side, tugged on his arm, and urged him not to go. "Abe, no. Wait, wait, wait. I need you to tell me everything you saw. Whether you think it's important or not. Please."

Removing my gripped hands off his arms, he shook me off him annoyed. "Tianna, what in the hell is going on? Why are you acting crazy like this?"

"Yeah, Tianna. Tell your brother what the hell is going on because that's who and what is the priority." El walked out of the kitchen without a backward glance. "Come on Champ! Let's go watch a movie in my room."

That hurt my heart a little. A huge part of me wanted to rush up the stairs behind them and be with my family, but another part of me needed to do what I needed to do to get justice for the member of our family that didn't have a voice or a choice and never would. I hoped El would one day understand that.

I turned to Abe and urged him again. "Please baby brother."

He exhaled a noisy breath. "Ti, I don't know. El is pissed and although I don't know why I do know he's not the type of guy that would get pissed over nothing. I'm not getting involved in whatever y'all got going on."

I looked up at the ceiling and let my shoulders fall. I didn't want to but I knew I had to tell Abe everything that happened with Sabrina. I sat him down and explained in detail. He listened carefully and only when I described how they beat me and me losing the baby did I see any emotion play across his face.

"I'm pretty sure they must have followed me home today. That's why I need you to try and remember every detail."

Abe's brow furrowed in the middle, as he gazed at me confused. "Ti, do you really not see why El is upset?"

"Do you not really see why I need to find them and have them pay for what they've done? They killed one and nearly killed my other one!"

Abe abruptly stood to his feet. "Let it go Tianna."

I stood up just as fast. "Let it go? Did you not just hear everything I told you?"

"Every word. But do you not see how you keep poking a dangerous bear rather than just letting it go back into its cave?" Abe's expression softened. "Sis, focus on your family. They are more important than revenge."

At that moment I accepted that no one would ever understand why I couldn't let the bear I crossed paths with ever just 'go back in its cave' and resolved that I was going to fight this battle alone, but no matter what, I was determined to fight it.

SIXTEEN

Micah

2 Weeks Later

Multiple offers came in for my house and I sold it quickly. The following month, the first house I flipped made an even bigger profit. I thought selling drugs had been an easy hustle, but profiting from real estate was the real deal. Who the hell would want to stand out on a corner and deal all day and night? Who would even want to run a whole set and worry about police raids, jail, or even death? The higher you rose in the drug game, the bigger target you had on your back.

Nah. I was good making paper, flipping houses. I was good at it. But the biggest benefit was my peace of mind. I went to bed every night without stressing about the streets. Lately, I had been coming home every night and seeing Shar hard at work studying for her bar exam. Yesterday, she was walking around in a pair of tights looking like wifey. She had taken her hair out of her braids and it had been a wild mess of afro and curls. I wanted to put my fingers in it, pull her head back, and kiss her.

But I didn't. Instead, I had taken my ass a shower and headed to my bedroom, after a long day helping the Mendez boys do some roofing, then focused on the budget for the rest of the renovations. Despite having all that taking up a good majority of my mental space, there was one thing that nudged everything to the side. Ace.

I had decided when and how to approach him. Truth was that nigga was crazy underneath all that polished surface he presented to the world. I had come to the conclusion that no matter how I went about it, it would only end up one way and that was alright by me. I just needed to make sure I had had all my ducks in a row first.

Throughout the week, I had taken my mom grocery shopping and told her to stockpile. She asked why, but I just told her I'd be busy with renovations and wouldn't be available to take her again so soon. I did the same with Tianna. Of course, her stubborn ass fought me way harder. I hid some of the baby's diapers so she'd have no choice but to come with me. On the ride there she told me she knew I'd hidden the diapers and if I'd gone through all of that then she figured she'd come. I just shook my head at her. The woman insisted on giving me a hard time.

I stockpiled our house like we were hibernating for the winter.

"You are so overdramatic. We can leave food for the rest of Camden County you know."

"I want to make sure you and Jah Jah gonna be alright for a while."

Her brows furrowed. "What's that mean?"

"That means I takes care of mine!" I joked it off to avoid the conversation. "I'm practicing for when I get a wifey and a mini-me."

She rolled her eyes before she cracked a smile.

"Ah. So she does smile."

She looked at me blushing then quickly turned her face and changed the subject. For ten minutes she talked about learning how to make baby food for Jaya like my mom had and I could tell she was trying hard to keep me from flirting with her. I had no intention of letting her but I didn't force it. She'd let her guard down on her terms and I was a patient man. I'd get into her heart one smile and omelet at a time. But I knew a big obstacle stood in my way and I got back to making sure Shar and Jaya had everything they needed.

It wasn't until Friday evening that I drove to Ace's place and knocked on his door. A young female answered the door and eyed me up and down. "Well, hello. Can I help you?" She asked still eyeing me flirtatiously.

"Yeah, I have a business meeting with Ace."

"Come in." She moved aside and held the door open as I walked onto the porch. I waited for her to step fully into the house before I had. She closed the door behind me and touched my ass as she stepped around me and walked through the main door. "Excuse me. I just needed to get around you."

I stepped away from her and gave her a look. "Next time you can just ask me to move aside first." Even if I weren't interested in

Sharmayne, this woman was not someone I would entertain. I didn't want anything connected to Ace or this house connected to me.

She shrugged her shoulders essentially dismissing my reprimand just further proving she was nothing but trouble. She led the way to the dining room where Ace was cutting into a steak. He stuffed a forkful into his mouth before sipping his drink. Knife and fork in hand again, he waved me over.

"Black Donald Trump. How you doing? Come in, come in." He pointed to the chair beside his. "Join me for dinner. Danae, serve Mr. Trump some steak and potatoes. And bring some more of those shrimp."

I motioned for Danae to not trouble herself. "No thank you. I already ate."

"You sure brother? Danae is a little on the ugly side but that bitch can cook!"

I looked over at her quickly and was surprised to see her smiling as if Ace had just told her she won Ms. America. He leaned toward me as if he was about to whisper but lowered his voice just a little but still loud enough for her to hear. "She a little loose in the legs too. Bitch was giving away my merchandise for free so I had to give her some other gainful employment before I killed her ass. It's amazing how you will learn another person's talents once you threaten to take away the air they breathe. I had no idea her little hoe ass knew how to cook this good. I'da had her in here a long time ago. But all's good that end's good. Ain't it Danae?"

She nodded at Ace but this time she looked frightened and headed into the kitchen returning immediately with a plate full of shrimp. I watched him devour several before he acknowledged me again.

"So, Mike, what's up? You said you had a business deal you wanted to discuss with me."

I nodded. "It's about Sharmayne."

Ace set his knife and fork down before he sipped his drink, looking at me over his glass. "Sharmayne?" He picked up his fork again and pierced a few pieces of broccoli and stuffed those in his mouth. "Did she not give you what you paid for? He asked as he chewed. "I don't do refunds. But I will make her give you your money's worth."

I shook my head. "Nothing like that."

Ace stopped chewing and set his utensil down, finished chewing, picked up his napkin, and sat back in his chair as he wiped his mouth. "So what exactly can I help you with then Micah?"

I immediately noticed the change in his demeanor. Ace was no master of disguise, nor would he ever be good at poker. He gave away all his feelings in his expression. But I would say that he was extremely intelligent and could read a situation accurately with only a few words spoken. He already knew I had a thing for Sharmayne and he didn't approve. But that was not my concern.

"I know you are a businessman and I have a proposal for you. A very more than fair one. I believe Sharmayne still owes you some money. I want to pay off what she owes you, plus give you an additional five thousand."

Ace crossed his hands in front of him. "In exchange for?"

"Her debt is wiped clean. She owes you nothing else and you leave her alone and let her live her life with her daughter." There wasn't any sense in beating around the bush.

He cocked his head to the side and raised an eyebrow seemingly intrigued by my offer. But I knew him well enough to know he played hardball and would no doubt counteroffer.

"And why would I allow Sharmayne to just run off with my daughter? I wouldn't be a good father to my baby girl if I did that now would I? Leaving her without a father." Ace kept his eyes on me and raised his glass. Danae rushed over to him and refilled his cup.

So the bastard knew Jaya was his after all. I had to check everything in me not to grab him by his throat. "Jaya has a father." I shouldn't have said it but I couldn't back down now.

The unexpected laughter caught me by surprise but I masked all of my emotions and only spoke the words I needed to. Nothing more. Nothing less.

"That little bitch done put you under her spell." Ace laughed again. "She really was my best student. Let me guess. She sat you down in a chair and gave you a lap dance. Rode you like a horse."

My anger began to bubble over and I had to take control back. I opened my backpack and put two stacks of purple bands on the table. "Here is four grand. The other four are outside and you'll get that once I walk out of here alive. Do we have a deal?"

Ace eyed the money then eyed me, a residual smirk present on his thin lips. He eyed Danae and motioned to another room with his eyes.

100

I had no idea what that meant but I knew it couldn't be good. "I'll tell you what. I will consider Shar's debt paid in full and I accept your bonus. You can have the little bitch. But my daughter is not for sale." I began to rise from my seat when Ace put his hand up to still me. "Hold on brother. I ain't finished yet."

Ace looked to his left and smiled before he picked up the bands and tossed them across the room. I followed the trajectory to see Huggie standing close by, catching each band. He handed them to Danae who quickly disappeared with the money.

"As I was saying. My daughter is not for sale but I will allow her to grow up with her mother for a few more years before I introduce myself. I don't like babies. But my princess is gonna meet her daddy soon enough."

"I can't promise you that. That's Sharmayne's decision."

I could see Ace's anger and he didn't even try to mask it. He slammed his closed fist on the table causing all the dinnerware to rattle. "That's my daughter! Sharmayne can't tell me nothing!"

I rose from my chair ready to swing if he so much as thought as putting his hands on me. "Like I said. That's Sharmayne's decision."

He tossed his napkin onto his plate and rose from his chair and began to leave the room as he spoke, not even looking at me. "This conversation is over. You can have your whore. I will come for my daughter when I am ready. Huggie, see Mr. Trump out and get my money. He is allowed to leave here alive after that. And only after that."

"Yes, Ace."

I followed Huggie outside then led the way to the four thousand I hid in a brown paper bag that I shoved in a nearby bush. I looked around before I pulled the bag free. I opened the bag, and put my hand in it slipping the brass knuckles I'd hidden in the bag on first. I tossed him the bag with the other hand and put my hand behind my back.

Huggie caught it and tossed it back. "Open it and take it out. Then hand it to me."

Damn it. He was smarter than I thought. I did what he asked and braced myself but I'd be damned if I was going out without a fight. Just as I suspected, as soon as I handed him the money, he punched me with left across my jaw. I swung and caught him on the chin with the knuckles. He staggered but stayed upright. I don't know how that hadn't knocked him out but he recovered quickly and grabbed me by the collar, head bunted me then swung again.

His fists were like hammers and every time he hit me, I'd lose vision and focus. I hit him an uppercut and he stumbled back for just a second before he grabbed me, spun me around, wrapped both arms around me, and squeezed. I couldn't escape his grip and tried to head bunt him but he didn't ease up even after I made contact with his rockhard head. I finally understood why they called him Huggie. I screamed in pain as he cracked my ribs.

"Stop struggling Brownie and he'll let go."

In agonizing pain, I heard a woman's voice but couldn't make out who had stepped in front of me and blindfolded me before I passed out.

SEVENTEEN
Sharmayne

Micah was usually home by now and when he hadn't arrived I packaged up dinner and put it in the refrigerator. My plan to show him gratitude for all he'd done for me and Jaya and me by cooking him dinner had gone down the drain. Well technically he could just warm it up and eat it but I had hoped to surprise him with it all on the table.

I had a mental picture of Micah eating the food and me watching him enjoy every bite of it. I checked myself. That was too close to looking like a couple and I wasn't going there. The only person I was interested in was Lady Justice.

I sat next to Jaya on the floor and smothered her with kisses. She pushed my face away only interested in the remote control. Micah had bought her a bunch of toys and all she wanted was the remote. I kissed her again and she got irritated. She pushed me away again and fussed loudly keeping her focus on the remote. It only made me want to laugh and bother her more, but I had too much studying to do.

After an hour or so Jaya began to fuss and I knew she was getting cranky. I bathed her and laid beside her on the bed as she drank her bottle. She was asleep in twenty minutes. I laid her in the crib and went back downstairs to grab my books. I heard a soft knock on the door and looked at the time. It was nearly ten o'clock and no one ever came to visit Micah other than his mother and I doubted she would be out this late.

I waited and heard it again. It almost sounded like someone was knocking in slow motion. I went to the window and looked out but didn't see anyone. I heard the knock again and pressed my head against the window to get a better look to see Micah sitting down, his legs sprawled out in front of him. I recognized his work boots and rushed to open the door.

He collapsed inside and I caught the back of his head before he crashed landed on the floor. He was half-conscious and when I tried to move him he roared in pain, clutching his side. I released him afraid I'd cause pain. He was blindfolded and his face swollen and beaten.

"Micah! What happened?"

"911. My ribs," he uttered before he passed out. I ran to the phone and called for an ambulance before calling Kendra. Micah had come to before the ambulance arrived. He was trying to tell me something but I couldn't understand his muttering. The ambulance arrived and his moans began again.

They asked me questions and I told them that he uttered asking for an ambulance and said ribs before he went unconscious.

"Possible fractured ribs," one of the EMTs reported to the other after she finished talking to me. Together they loaded him on the gurney, his cries of pain tearing me up. I wanted to go with him but I couldn't just leave Jaya.

I ran up to the EMT before they pulled off. "Which hospital?"

"Cooper," she said. I called Kendra back to update and she said she was on her way.

All night I waited for word but who I was to Micah that anyone would update me? The next morning I lost the courage to call the hospital and decided to stay in my place. No one owed me any updates. Nevertheless, I found myself distracted from my studies wondering about Micah. In the evening I called Kendra and she answered. I inquired about Micah but she wasn't very forthcoming with details. I couldn't blame her. I was just his roommate and it was right not to spread her son's business.

"Micah is being released tomorrow. He'll be coming here to stay with me for a while until he's better."

A tinge of sadness spread through my chest but I pushed it down deep. "Ok. Well, if you need anything let me know. Maybe I can take you some of his pajamas or something."

"No, that's ok. He has clothes here but thank you. How's your precious baby girl doing?"

"She took her first steps a few days."

"Yeah, Micah told me. That's wonderful. A late walker but some babies just want to take their time. No sense in rushing to go nowhere."

I forced a smile. Older women always thought they knew better than everybody. My baby was developing normally, no matter what Kendra thought.

"And how are you doing?"

I snapped back to the present surprised she asked, but I appreciated her manners. "I am well. My exam is in a few weeks, so I am studying full time."

"That's good. I'm sure your mom would be proud."

I didn't respond to that. "Well, again if you and Micah need anything, please just let me know. He has been extremely kind and generous to me and Jaya and if in any way I can return the favor, I will do my best."

"Thank you, Sharmayne."

I hung up the phone feeling sad. I refused to accept that I missed Micah. I did not have the luxury to miss anyone. I put away my books and went to my bedroom. Jaya and I played patty cake for a while before she was engrossed in trying to shove her finger up my nostril for twenty minutes. After a while, she got bored and climbed on top of me, and fell asleep on my chest. For an hour I just held her. She was the most important thing in my life and I needed to remember that. I loved Jaya with everything in me and I couldn't let her down.

It did me good to have spent those hours just being in her world and her presence. It put me right back on track. All that missing Micah and being sad was a distraction I couldn't afford. I was extremely grateful for all he had done for me and I would return the favor one day. For now, I would cook and clean to contribute as much as I could. But none of that required having feelings for Micah. That was simply too high a price to pay.

The following day, I studied for a while before my mind began to wander again. "Damn, Micah." I reminded myself of Jaya's future and my pep talk. *Get it together girl.* I started re-reading my notes from the top of the page and after ten minutes was lost in my thoughts again.

I slammed my notebook down and refused to do this to myself. "I need a distraction." I looked at Jaya who had been holding on to the couch as she walked back and forth alongside it. "How about we turn on some music?" I asked her. She looked at me and laughed showing me the few pearly whites she had.

I turned on the television and surfed to the Music Choice channels and choose the R&B station. Sean Paul's catchy song We Be Burnin' filled the living room. Jaya began to bounce up and down uncontrollably. I cracked up at her dancing. "Go Jah! Go Jah! Go Jah!" She chuckled and continued bopping up and down until she fell on her butt. She rolled over crawled back to the couch and started all over again.

"You burning over there little girl?" I laughed and walked over to her and held her hands so we could dance together. We bopped together and she loved it. I swooped her up and tickled her neck, pretending to eat her up. She loved when I did. She laughed so hard her whole body shook. "Come on. Let's go to the kitchen so we can be burnin'. You want some cookies, little girl?" I knew she had no idea what I was talking but I'd read it was good to talk to babies. It helped develop their motor and language skills.

I put Jaya down on the floor and fired up the computer Micah rarely used and searched for some cookie recipes on the internet. "Jaya, chocolate chip or sugar?" I yelled out over the music.

"Peanut butter sounds good."

I jumped up from the chair and spun around. Micah was standing behind me, Kendra helping him walk. I picked up the remote, turning the TV off silencing the noise. The house was suddenly quiet with only Jaya's baby talk filling the silence as Kendra helped Micah take a seat on the couch. Soon his groan overpowered Jah's gurgles.

"What are you doing here?"

Micah opened his eyes surprised. "No, I meant, your mom, Kendra, said that you would be recuperating at her house. Not that you aren't supposed to be here. This is your house. Of course, you can be here." Micah looked at me and smiled, rendering me quiet. I had been shooting off at the mouth and didn't know how to stop.

"He's hardheaded and refused to go to my house."

"Mom, I'll be fine here. Besides, I missed Jaya. Hey beautiful," he called out to her. She crawled to the couch in between his legs and tried to climb onto his lap. "Dada."

I nearly died of embarrassment but was not nearly as affected as Micah. Never had I ever seen a brown skin man turn red. He blushed and chuckled. "Somebody set her up here on my lap." He beamed down at Jaya that was steady using her pudgy feet to try and climb up his leg and gripping his pants to help pull herself up.

"No," Kendra and I both said at the same time. Micah waved us both off.

"She's gonna hurt you." It wouldn't be intentional, but Jah-Jah using him as a jungle gym would cause him pain. I picked her up and held her. He seemed so disappointed, so I aimed to make him feel loved. "Jah-Jah blow Micah a kiss," I said to her. She puckered her lips and put her chubby hand to her mouth and kissed it.

Kendra melted and laughed. Micah looked like he won the lottery he was so smitten. I put Jaya in her playpen with a few toys and stood out of Kendra's way as she settled Micah in.

"Do you need anything?" I asked.

"My peanut butter cookies."

I smiled and an hour later brought him some warm cookies and a glass of milk. "I've never made them before so proceed with caution." He took a bite and made a face. Shocked I grabbed a cookie and tasted it. It tasted fine and when I looked at him to question him, he was chewing a mouthful, a stupid smirk on his face. He winked then sipped his milk, teasing me..

"They're good," he finally said, four cookies later. "Thank you."

It felt good being the one on the other side of need. I was glad I could help him at least a little. Kendra stayed around for the rest of the day and I stayed out of their way, confining myself to my bedroom. I heard them struggling coming up the stairs and went out to offer my help.

"Sharmayne, could you go into Mike's bedroom and just make sure his sheets are pulled back so I can get him in bed?"

"Mom, I don't need you helping me up the stairs. And I don't need anybody tucking me in bed. I am a grown man. I'm ok."

I did as Kendra asked and stepped aside when he stepped into his bedroom. It was weird that I had been living in this house for a while and had never been in Micah's room.

"Is there anything I can get you?" I asked.

"Yes. A glass of water if you could. Micah needs to take his pain medication in an hour. I promised my auntie I'd stop by today to check in on her so I can't stay to make sure he takes it."

"Mom, I am not a little boy. Please go take care of Auntie Rose. She needs you more than I do."

"Boy, hush your mouth." Kendra ignored him and turned her attention to me. "I forgot the bottle downstairs. If you could just make sure he gets it. I gotta go. It's already late."

"No worries Kendra. I'll make sure he's good before I settle back into my room for the night."

"Thank you Sharmayne."

"Oh, now y'all the best of friends when it's time to gang up on me huh?"

I gave him the stink eye and followed Kendra downstairs. She began to hand me the bottle of pain medication then stopped. "These are addictive. Don't leave the bottle in his bedroom. Just give him the dosage."

Kendra's expression looked haunted. "Kendra, is Micah addicted to pills or drugs?"

She shook her head.

"Then why can't the bottle—"

"I wasn't an addict before I was one either. I've read that addictive personality disorder is genetic. I don't want to learn firsthand if that is true."

"I understand," and couldn't fault her. Mothers would do weird things to protect their children. I respected her for that. "But aren't you worried that I am pre-disposed of that disorder too?"

"No. Your mother's story is different." She didn't elaborate and I forced the curiosity of my mother's past down deep.

"Ok. You can trust me then."

Kendra left after handing it to me promising to check in tomorrow. I went into the kitchen and poured a glass of water. I read the bottle searching for directions. It was best to be taken with food, so I warmed up the dinner from last night. I took the food up and set the tray down beside him on the nightstand.

"What is all of this?"

"Dinner leftovers."

Micah cocked his head back and raised a bold eyebrow. "What nigga you had in my house serving food to?"

Cracking up, I picked up the plate. "It was for you. A gesture of appreciation, but you want to be out getting your ribs broken."

He curled his lip unconvinced. I bit mine to keep from laughing at his unfounded need to guard his territory.

"Aight now. I better not find no dudes up in here wearing my drawers and eating my peanut butter cookies."

I rolled my eyes and handed him the plate. "He has his own drawers and prefers Snickerdoodles."

He shook his head and refused the plate. "I'll eat later, but thank you." He looked exhausted so I didn't force him to take it. He nestled his head in his pillow trying to get comfortable. His eyelids were heavy and his blinks slow. "Snickerdoodles? That nigga soft."

I cracked up.

"Just saying the word Snickerdoodles makes me feel like a punk. What real man would ever admit to a woman he likes Snickerdoodles? A soft-ass nigga that's who."

Micah kept talking about cookies until his eyes remained closed and his words were just murmurings. I took the plate downstairs and stuck it back in the fridge. I made another batch of cookies for him. If he refused to eat food, maybe he could take his medication with cookies and milk. A while later I woke up startled, my face stuck to the pages of my study guide. I didn't even remember nodding off.

I heard movement upstairs and a crash to the floor. I rushed up and into Micah's dark bedroom. I reached for the light switch but nothing illuminated when I flipped it.

"I accidentally knocked the lamp over when I tried to turn it on," he said.

"Why didn't you call for me? I would have turned it on." Using the soft moonlight and streetlights casting in through the blinds, I found my way over to the nightstand.

"I did but you didn't answer."

"I'm sorry. I nodded off studying." I crouched down looking for the lamp. I picked it up and turned the knob but it didn't work. "I think the bulb blew. Do you have any more?"

"Try in the cabinet under the—" Micah groaned, "sink."

I stood and walked over to him. "What's wrong? Do you need your pain medication?"

"Yes, please."

In a flash, I brought him some cookies, milk, and pain meds. "I didn't find any bulbs, but I'll go buy one tomorrow." I set everything down and sat on the edge of the bed. "Can you sit up just a little? I brought you some milk and cookies to take with your meds."

"Just the milk and meds,' he pleaded his voice strained. He sat up a little and tried to hold in the moan but did a poor job at it. Instead, I gave him the meds and held the cup as he sipped the milk.

He rested his head back again and closed his eyes. I set the glass and moved to stand when he grabbed my arm. "Stay. Please."

I stayed until he fell asleep. The next day I went out and bought a bulb and replaced it. Jaya spent a good part of the day in Micah's bedroom. After lunch, I cleaned the kitchen and headed upstairs to put her down for her nap. I found her asleep beside Micah. He soothed her hair absentmindedly while he was engrossed in a movie. The sight of them together arrested my heart. I watched them from the door for a bit until he finally noticed me standing there then turned back to the TV.

"You gonna stand there all day or you gonna come watch a movie with me?"

Heat crawled up my neck but I wouldn't let him see me blush. He smirked but I pretended I didn't see it. "I have to study. I was checking in on Jaya. How long has she been asleep?"

"Awhile. She fell asleep trying to stick her finger in my ear." He shook his head as if he were bothered but I could tell he was playing it off.

I giggled. "At least it wasn't your nostrils." I winked and escaped his gaze. Later we ate dinner and laughed at Jah preferring to eat her food like she was bobbing for apples instead of using her hands. After I put her to bed, I took Micah his meds.

"Are you hurting?" He nodded and I could see the pain in his expression as he tried to sit up. "Hold on, hold on. Let me help you. I sat beside him leaned forward and slid both my hands behind his back. "Ok. Now I'm gonna bring you forward a little at a time. You scoot back a little at a time. Then I will fix the pillows."

I waited for Micah to respond but it was as if he had stopped breathing. I looked up into his bruised-covered face less than a few inches from mine and he was staring at me. His eyes bore into mine, I shuttered within. Goose pimples rose on my arms and my stomach flip-flopped.

I broke eye contact before I did something stupid. "You ready?" I asked, my words coming out in a raspy whisper. The man done made my mouth dry.

"Are you?" He asked softly.

I nodded, leaned in so he could brace himself against me, and began to pull him forward but he didn't budge. "You gotta scoot back a little as I pull."

"My bad."

I felt his breath on my neck and I had to check myself. "Ummm. Ready?"

"Mmmm hmmm."

I pulled him forward again and this time he was able to sit up a little. "Ok, just a little bit more." I pulled again and this time he wrapped his arm around me and pulled himself up enough to be propped against the pillows. I released him but he held onto me.

I felt his lips on my neck and I froze in place. When they began to roam I tried to move but he held me tight. Micah intensified the kisses and I began to tingle everywhere. His hand traveled up my back as his lips found their way to mine. He buried his hand into my hair and the nape of my neck and I got lost in his intimate attention matching his intensity. I couldn't remember the last time a man had kissed me like this. And then suddenly I did.

I jumped back remembering where I was, with who and why. Sex that led to pregnancy that led to running away from Ace that led to living in Micah's house. A man that was not my husband. He wasn't even my boyfriend. Hell, we were barely even friends. I covered my mouth embarrassed.

Micah waved me over to him his speech relaxed. "Where are you going? Come back."

"No. We shouldn't have done that."

"Like hell, we shouldn't have." Micah raised his eyebrow appalled. I smiled despite myself. He rested his head against the pillow and stared at me. There was something about the way he looked at me that unnerved me. Like he could see right down to my soul past all the dirtiness, guilt, and shame and just see the real me and the Sharmayne I aspired to be. He held his hand out to me calling me to him and so help me I went to him like a fish being reeled in.

He patted the mattress and I sat down beside him nervous. "Take your pain pills," I blurted out. I grabbed the bottle and twisted the cap. I needed to justify why I was sitting beside this man caught up in all these feelings. He opened his mouth wide like Jaya would and I popped the pill in before I handed him the glass. He took a sip of water, watching me over the rim.

"What? Why do you keep staring at me like that?"

He set the cup down and grinned. "Because you are beautiful. And because you finally let me kiss you."

"You stole it."

"You let me. And I'll do it again."

He took my hand and intertwined it with his. He tried to sit up a little and grumbled, pinching his eyes shut trying to manage the pain from moving.

I waited for him to get situated before I decided to pry. "What happened to you, Micah?"

Micah rubbed his thumb against my hand, gazing at them. He smiled. "I was helping out my family and it got ugly. It's ok. Everything is cool for now."

"For now? You aren't in some kind of trouble are you?" I pulled my hand free from his. I suddenly remembered who Micah really was. A drug dealer that fixed houses but still a drug dealer.

His smile faded as he shook his head slowly. "No. Not at all." He rested his head against the pillow and closed his eyes.

I took that as a sign that our conversation was over and went back to my bedroom. Jaya was fussing so I checked in on her. She'd been sleeping a lot lately and new teeth were cutting through. She felt warm and I was hoping she wasn't getting sick again. The last thing I needed was two patients in the house. I gave Jaya some Tylenol and after a while, she felt cooler to the touch and fell asleep.

I lay in bed thinking about Micah. My overactive brain wanted to pick apart his life and know what happened to him. He didn't have much family that I knew of so I couldn't imagine why he was helping. Something nudged in the back of my mind. At the supermarket, Micah had mentioned making sure me and the baby were good, and I found it strange. Now I was pretty sure he voluntarily walked into something knowing he'd get hurt. But why? I don't know why but I felt like it had something to do with me.

My heart sank. I got up and went into his bedroom. He was awake and looked at me as if he expected me. "Can't sleep?"

"Tell me."

"Nothing to tell Shar. Let it go." He shifted his head and turned his attention back to the television.

I approached the bed and sat beside him. Tears formed. "Please."

Micah turned to me and cradled my face with the hand from his good side. A tear escaped and he wiped it away from my cheek. "You are free beautiful. That's all that matters."

I broke down a mess of mixed emotions. Who was this man that continuously sacrificed for me and loved on a baby that was not his?

This man that brought me into his house and cared for me? I felt shame wanting to shove him in a single box titled dope dealer. He was more than that. I was torn. I couldn't give up my and Jaya's future for a man who lived a dangerous life. But how could I just walk away from a man who nearly gave up his for me and mine?

I cuddled up beside him on the bed and laid my head on his good shoulder. "There are so many things I want to say to you."

He leaned his cheek on my head. "The only one I want to hear is that you aren't going anywhere."

I inhaled and mounted my courage. "Only if you stop dealing drugs."

"Done," he said without hesitation.

I snapped my head up. "Just like that?"

"Yep."

"Well damn. I was expecting you to send me to hell."

"Nah. I stopped dealing a while ago. I'm fully legit. I have a plan Shar and death ain't it. Doing time ain't it either. But I damn sure want you and Jaya to be part of it."

"I have a plan too, Micah. And I think it just upgraded." I rested my head on his shoulder again and breathed.

EIGHTEEN
Tianna

3 Months Later

After the school year ended, I began using errands as an excuse to go search for Sabrina and Tay, using different rental cars. I had purchased some wigs and hats to try and change my appearance. I never parked in the same place twice in a row or drove the same route.

One late afternoon, as I was about to head home, I slowed down when the traffic light turned yellow, rather than try to beat it. Whether it was God intervening or coincidence, I doubt I'll ever know, but I spotted Sabrina's grandmother adjacent to me, struggling with several grocery bags. I watched her carefully to see which house she walked into, but instead, she turned the corner and continued her trek.

The car behind me honked alerting me that the light had changed. I needed to follow her but where she'd turned was a one-way street in the opposite direction.

Damn it.

I sped down the road I was on and made an illegal u-turn. I turned down the street she had and slowed down. She'd disappeared. I crept slowly hoping she'd turned on a side street. I found her in the middle of the street climbing a few stairs into a row home. I parked in the first open spot I found and watched. She set a bag down and opened up the screen door, holding it open with her hip. A girl stepped out of the house grabbed a bag and held the door open. I quickly positioned my camera and began to take photos. Through the focus lens, I was able to zoom in on her face. Although she resembled Sabrina, it wasn't her. This girl was younger and had her hair braided back in long cornrows like Alicia Keys.

After they went inside and closed the door I kept surveillance for another hour but Sabrina nor Tay ever made an appearance. I had already stayed out much longer than I planned, and El was probably wondering where I was. On the drive back home, I tried to calm my anxiety. With everything in me, I wanted to wait there until Sabrina showed her face. All night if I had to, but then what? I had to play this smart and curb my impulsivity. I had Sabrina's address. The realization made me grin. I was still a ways away from getting justice, but one thing was for sure, I'd leave with my family on a week vacation glad I had finally caught a break. School would be back in session in two weeks and I could pick up where I'd left off.

It's funny how your attention and drive could be so hell-bent on one thing and in no time at all, somewhere else entirely. Throughout our family vacation, I had allowed myself to decompress and not have all of my struggles compound my head and heart at full force. Allowing myself to enjoy life was not a crime. I watched as Jay ran out of the water and sat down in the sand collecting buckets full to erect a new sandcastle. El collapsed beside me winded.

"That boy is non-stop. Future athlete."

I laughed. El was preaching to the choir. "Wonder where he gets it from cause the only thing I'm running after is the ice-cream truck."

El ignored my joke, focused on energizer bunny Jay. "What do you mean? Abe is athletic." He dusted the sand off his body and reached for the cooler.

"I'm pretty sure Abe gets that from Pop, and I share no DNA with my dad no matter how much I used to wish he was my real father."

"Well, what about Jay's biological father? Justin? Wasn't he athletic?"

It was strange that I had been with Elijah for years and we didn't discuss Jay's biological father much. I supposed he knew losing Justin was still a painful memory and he respected that. But I also knew I needed to be more intentional in my child knowing his true roots and me getting to a better place of healing. Ever since Jay's paternal grandmother had moved down south, he hadn't had much contact with his biological father's side of the family. His uncle, Jordi, had grown distant in the last year and I didn't push the relationship mostly because Jordi lived a troubled and dangerous lifestyle.

"Justin liked sports and played for fun. He was more scholar than athlete. Jordi, Justin's younger brother was the true athlete. His real name is actually Michael, like Jay's grandfather, but Justin said he earned the nickname Jordi after he dunked on all the neighborhood kids, and they nicknamed him Michael Jordan. It ended up, Jordi."

"Ok. So Jay does have that sportsman DNA in him. Good. We can channel that energy somewhere productive rather than having to tie him down. I ain't old enough to be feeling this old, Ti."

I smiled at my husband. "You are a good father, Elijah. I am blessed you love me and my son. Jay is blessed to have you as his Daddy."

"Woman, you just earned yourself an ice cream cone."

"You stay spoiling me." I feigned blushing and batted my eyelashes before I reached for my wallet and slipped my wrap on. "But you deserve the ice cream. What flavor ya want big daddy?"

Elijah sat back in his beach chair and folded his arms behind his head. The ideal picture of relaxation. "Oh, I can get used to this. Surprise me, Sugar Momma."

When I returned twenty minutes and a mile-long line later, a family had settled beside us, and Jay must have convinced El to take him back out into the water. I waved them over and we all sat together eating our ice cream. The volleyball the neighboring family had been playing with rolled onto Jay's towel and a kid close to his age ran over to retrieve it. He took one look at Jay and made a friend.

"Wanna play?"

Jay looked over at me. "Mom, can I?"

"Don't you want to finish your ice cream first?"

"I'll eat it later."

Elijah laughed as he stuffed another spoonful of mint chocolate chip into his mouth.

"Sure handsome. If you want to." Jay handed me his ice cream that had already half-melted then darted off kicking the ball with the other children. I disposed of it and our trash then sat beside Elijah who'd been in a daze. I followed his line of vision to a woman breastfeeding a baby. I smacked his arm. "Seriously?"

"What was that for?" He held his arm as if it were falling off.

I pointed to the mom like he was stupid.

"She's a cutie right?'

My nostrils flared and I was close to punching the glassy look out of my husband's eyes.

"She's gotta be what, Babe? Maybe three or four months old. That's a good age to hold them. I'd be scared to hold a newborn though. They always talking about 'hold the head' like it's going to fall off or something."

I looked back and forth between El and the woman with her child. He was sincerely staring at the baby. For some reason, that hurt more than had he been eyeing the mom. It was a reminder of both of my miscarriages. Both times, my fault for being careless. I could see the yearning in his eyes for a baby of his own. It's not like we hadn't been trying. We were screwing like jackrabbits and every month I cried when my cycle came on. Elijah never brought it up but whenever I told him we couldn't make love because I was on, I saw the hurt in his eyes and felt the failure in my heart.

I had scheduled a visit with my gynecologist concerned that I couldn't conceive. Blessedly, there had been nothing wrong with me physically, other than putting too much pressure on myself. She had counseled me to let things happen naturally and give it a year of trying before we explored more invasive testing. But admittedly, my patience was as fortified as Jay's dry sandcastles.

I rubbed El's arm. "She's beautiful. And a little porker too. Look at her chubby legs!"

El smiled then turned to me. "Speaking of pork, I was thinking we could stop at Florida Avenue Grill in DC on the way home."

His abrupt change of subject caught me off guard. He moved on from the baby as if we hadn't even seen her. It settled my heart and I happily entertained whatever weirdness El was talking about. "Florida what now?"

"Florida Avenue Grill you uncultured woman. It's the oldest Soul Food Restaurant in the world." He sat back practically drooling. "They serve chitlins and pig feet."

"You do remember that I'm half Puerto Rican, right? I only have half a black card and it don't include the pig feet and chitlin membership benefits. Thankfully."

"Ricans eat pig feet too, *Boricua*, so I guess you are a disgrace to both of your races."

"Me? You're the one that doesn't know how to play Spades. Or dominos. I can live with myself. I don't even know how you sleep at night."

El narrowed his gaze at me, his hands folded on his bare midsection. "Oh. That's we what doing, wife? We firing flaming arrows, huh?"

117

I chuckled. That man could dish it but could never take it. I laid back on my towel and closed my eyes. "Only arrows being fired are cupid's, Babe. Right to my heart."

"Cupid, my ass. I just had to fall in love with a Puerto Rican woman." El's private rant, tickled me right to sleep, my stomach full of ice cream and my heart full of laughter. And for the first time in a long time, I wasn't worried that I had failed my husband.

The next afternoon we drove into DC for lunch at Florida Avenue Grill. El ordered his pig feet and chitlins. Jay insisted on hotcakes although it was lunchtime and I opted for pan-fried chicken while avoiding eyeing El's plates altogether. Being true to who he is, he told everyone in the small restaurant how much his lunch choices made me want to hurl and that he would personally make sure my black card would be revoked. Of course, they all laughed. I kicked him under the table. He told them that too. I couldn't help but laugh until I took one whiff of his food and my stomach rumbled and my mouth began to salivate.

Unfortunately, my husband wasn't lying about my sudden need to vomit. I excused myself from the table and approached the counter. "Could you point me to the women's restroom, please?" The older woman at the counter directed me and before I knew it, I was hunched over the toilet tossing up my coffee and bagel from breakfast. Then I tossed up some more for good measure. By the third stomach convulsion, acidic greenish bile burned my esophagus and I wanted to kick my husband again for cursing me. I finally got myself together and rinsed my mouth before I rejoined my family at the table.

"You ok, Babe?" El burrowed his brows, concerned.

I nodded and kept my mouth shut and kept my vomit breath locked behind lips and teeth. I ordered some toast and nibbled on that, afraid I was going to get sick again had I eaten anything heavy, although my chicken smelled divine. Jay and Elijah thought so too as they picked until it was nothing left but a bone.

When we arrived home, Jay ran straight to his bedroom to play with his toys as if he hadn't seen them in months. "Justin Junior, it's bath time, not playtime!" My shout followed him up the stairs.

"In a minute mom!"

"Jay, if I climb these stairs and your butt isn't the bathroom, guess what's coming to you?" I rested one foot on the bottom step, looking up, waiting for his understanding and consent. I was tired and did not feel like following through on my threat.

"A timeout?" He earnestly yelled back.

I had a mini adult tantrum before I began to climb the stairs. The child didn't share a single strand of DNA with Elijah, but I'll be damned, he loved to test my patience just like his Dad. "A *chancleta, nene!*" I threatened an old-school spanking.

I heard Elijah chuckle before he intervened. "Champ! You better get in the shower quick! Your mom is talking in Spanish like Mom-Mom!"

Before I made it up the stairs, the sound of small feet hurrying across hardwood floors, followed by a door being quickly slammed and locked meant Jay had taken heed to his father's warning. Knowing full well he hadn't taken a fresh pair of undies or pajamas, I made my way into his bedroom.

Just barely through the door I stepped on a small toy and let out an exaggerated F-Bomb like I owned the word. Hobbling over to Jay's bed, I sat down on the corner and checked the bottom of my foot for any wounds. With no punctures, I crossed my foot on my lap and massaged the ache away.

"Action figure or Mattel Car?" Elijah leaned up against the doorjamb observing me, his arms crossed over his chest.

"The print on my foot says lego."

"Ouch."

"Tell me about it. Speaking of ouch, Jay locked the bathroom door again."

El pushed his shoulder off the doorjamb. "I guess it's my turn," he whined.

"Yep."

"Where's the small flathead?"

"Top drawer of my nightstand."

After ten minutes of fiddling with the lock and not getting the bathroom door, I held out my hand and waited for El to hand me the screwdriver from the eyeglasses kit. He stood from his kneeling position and handed it over frustrated. I took his place and stuck the screwdriver straight back.

"I don't know why you tell me to unlock it, knowing my big hands can maneuver that small ass screwdriver and when you can get it unlocked in—" he pointed to the open door annoyed, "ten seconds."

"Cause I gotta keep you humble." I rose and kissed his cheek, an Okie-Dokie grin on my face.

"Says who?"

"I'm pretty sure it's in our vows."

"Obey is in there. Humiliate? Definitely not."

I chuckled and rested my fisted hands on my hips. "No? Really? Then it must be in the official wife manual they hand out to girls the day they get their first period."

El walked away shaking his head and mumbling to himself. "I just had to fall in love with a smart-mouth black woman."

After getting Jay showered and in bed, I opted for a long hot bubble bath. I was so relaxed I began to fall asleep when El brought me a glass of wine and massaged my shoulders.

"Can I join you?"

I nodded and within a minute, he slipped in behind me and I rested against his chest as I sipped my wine. Sex with my husband was great but it was our intimacy that I cherished. He massaged my shoulders, and I was overwhelmed by the love my husband had for me. He was a nurturer, provider, and my best friend. We had an unspoken bond. So many times throughout our relationship he'd known what to do or say without me saying a word. When he came back into my life, my life was stable and content but now I didn't even want to think of my life without him in it. I felt inadequate in not being able to give him the one thing he wanted. A child. Yet he'd never once faulted me. It was my own insecurities that made me feel deficient. My husband was everything God had called him to be. He was far from perfect, but he was perfect for me.

"I love you, Elijah."

He kissed the top of my head. "I love you too, baby."

El was a blessing and my best friend. A few days into our vacation I began to let go of the obsession I had with Sabrina and Tay paying for my loss. My family was beautiful and I needed to begin living life instead of grief. Every day that passed staked out looking for evidence was time I was losing with my family and my only child and most likely the only child I would ever have. I didn't want to wake up one day when Jay was going off to college regretting lost time.

On the drive home from vacation, I had decided to finally let it all go rather than just feeling bad about my covert activities. I wanted to return home and start fresh. Ending my first day on a new road, soaking in a relaxing bath with my husband was more than I could have hoped for. I sipped my wine and rested my head on El's shoulder.

We sat in our bliss of steaming hot water in silence for a few minutes before he spoke again. "Ti, if we can never have a baby together, I would still be a happy man. You and Jay are more than enough."

Tears eased down my face slowly. Once again, he was in tune with me and said what only he could to help ease the self-inflicted pain. "I'm sorry, Elijah." I tried to keep my voice from cracking, but my emotions were on high. "If I wouldn't have gotten out—"

"Babe, please don't." I felt him straighten up behind me and his voice softened. "I shouldn't have blamed you. You didn't know. It wasn't your fault. I'm sorry."

I waited until I got ahold of myself before I replied. "You had every right to be upset. Honestly, it will never trump how upset I am with myself, so I don't fault you for blaming me. I am not ready to forgive myself yet but thank you for your forgiveness. My soul needed it."

Wrapping his arms around me, he continued to comfort my body, heart, and mind. "There is nothing to forgive. It was a tragic accident. I don't want you beating yourself up anymore. Ok?" He kissed me on the top of my head, and I promised to try and forgive myself.

As long as we face everything together, we can get through anything."

And he was right. What God had joined together, no one had the authority to separate.

NINETEEN
Shamayne

2 Months Later

E very day I checked the mail waiting for my bar exam results and every day I walked away from the mailbox disappointed and a little more anxious than the day before. Today was no exception. I climbed the porch stairs and went back into the house. Jaya had been laying on the couch with the sniffles. The fall allergies had kicked all our butts, but we were starting to feel better. Jaya had spent the past two days quiet and raw-faced from wiping her snot on her sleeves. Whenever I tried to clean her nose she'd cry and hide under Micah. He'd take the tissue and hand it to her to do it herself. Needless to say, her sleeve had done a more thorough job.

I kissed her cheek and squeezed her afro puff, but she kept focused on Dora The Explorer. I'd allow her more television time than I normally would because she didn't have the energy to explore life in the house and backyard as she usually did. For two days she'd been living vicariously through Dora.

The oven timer went off in the kitchen and I went in to check on Micah's birthday cake. I set it out to cool and kept busy online researching firms in South Jersey. I had been in contact with some of my old schoolmates and a few had already passed the exam from the last test date and were already employed. Some were waiting for results like me and building connections.

A few hours and a frosted cake later, Kendra arrived with some of Micah's favorite side dishes.

"Hey, baby." Kendra walked in out of breath and I rushed over to help her. She set the bags down with a sigh. "Girl! The temperature really dropped out there today. It's cold." Kendra removed her coat and rubbed her hands together before she picked up the bags she had set down. Jaya sat up groggily and stared at her. "I see you, baby girl. But you gotta give me a minute to warm up before I come to snatch you up," Kendra cooed. Jaya just blinked.

"She hasn't been feeling well these past two days. Micah had some allergies and was the same way. I'm prone to them too but I didn't get it so bad this season."

"Allergies? Micah don't got no allergies. Let him tell it, everything is allergies. He probably had a cold and now Jaya has it. Lord knows she can't stay out of his face. You'd think she was his wife instead of you." Kendra looked back at Jah and made a funny face but Jaya just stared unamused, her blinks slow and long as her mouth hung open to help her breathe.

A wife. I could hardly believe it. My brain told me that it was too fast to get married but my heart admonished me for waiting so long. There was no doubt that Micah loved me, and I knew I loved him. Over the past few months, he'd spent so much time at home recuperating from his injuries, we'd spent a lot of time together. He'd become my best friend and safe place. When he made a ring out of a bandage and proposed, I thought he was joking. I played along and accepted.

A week later, Micah was well enough to go back out into the world and returned the same day with an actual engagement ring. I was speechless but it felt right as had a simple ceremony in City Hall a few weeks later. I was officially Mrs. Payne and he jokingly called me that daily. 'You are definitely Mrs. Payne in the ass,' he'd say.

A month of being a blushing bride had done me good. I couldn't remember the last time I had felt this safe and content in life. Perhaps as a little girl, although I couldn't truly recall then, either. Even my mother-in-law's side comments had lost a bit of their sting. She still needed to back off sometimes, but I was too blissful to let it get on my nerves most times. Including today.

"Ok. Even if it's a cold, she's too young for all the over-the-counter cold syrups. I'll just keep the humidifier on and keep giving her orange juice." I was polite but firm.

Kendra picked Jaya up and the baby laid her head on Nana's shoulder. Kendra changed her tone as if she were talking to the baby. "No, no, no. Take this baby to the doctor. Right, Baby Girl?" Kendra rocked her as she walked around the living room. "Tell Mommy, you don't feel good and need medication."

I inwardly rolled my eyes. "I have children's Tylenol if she needs it."

I carried the side dishes to the kitchen just to put some space between us. I got along with my new mother-in-law for the most part. She loved Jaya just as much as Micah did, but I was a good mother and her comments made me feel like she was insinuating I wasn't. I tried not to get offended, but I failed more times than I wanted to admit.

While in the kitchen I checked on the ribs. I had never made ribs for Micah before, so I hoped he liked them. Cooking had become an adventure. Mostly for him. We learned the hard way that he wasn't fond of grits with sugar after he spit them out after trying them. We literally had an entire debate about sugar or cheese grits. The man didn't want sugar in his grits but argued that it belonged in spaghetti. I still can't figure that shit out. Today he was getting ribs currently being broiled so that the barbecue sauce was sticky and a little charred, exactly as I preferred it.

I heard a commotion in the living room and heard Jaya crying. I peeked out and saw Micah taking off his jacket, a big smile plastered on his face. Jaya held out her arms, reaching for him. "Hey Moochie," he laughed and took her off his mother's hands, smothering her cheeks with kisses.

I went back to getting his birthday dinner ready and opened the oven to check on the ribs. I felt a hand on my ass but that was the one thing I had gotten used to quickly. My husband's hand connected to my backside like a magnet.

"What smells so good?"

"Your birthday dinner." I closed the oven then turned it off before wiping my hands on a towel. I turned around and kissed the birthday boy on his lips. "Happy birthday honey." He kissed me again and prolonged it until Jaya grunted and pushed our faces apart.

"Hey," Micah said to her pretending to be upset. "That's my birthday present you messing wit' little girl," Jaya whined and he kissed her cheek. "You daddy's baby girl," he whispered in her ear. He done had that girl spoiled.

I smacked Micah on the butt. "I'm about to serve you. Go get cleaned up." He disappeared out of the kitchen and I loaded his plate. When I brought the plates to the dinner table, Kendra was strapping Jaya in her highchair. Jaya rubbed her eyes and rested her head against the seat. I hated seeing my baby so melancholy.

124

Micah returned and kissed her on the top of her head before he sat down and bust a grub. Afterward, he rubbed his stomach and stretched. "That was so good. Thank y'all. My mom's ribs are still the best in the world, but baby yours are a close second," a stupid smirk on his face. Why he found it amusing to irk me was beyond me, but I kicked him under the table to let him know he succeeded. He winked discreetly and I nearly blushed, but I didn't give his smart-ass the satisfaction.

We sang happy birthday and I sliced him a big piece of cake. He tasted it and moaned overdramatically. "Yo! This is good as hell. Mom, you put yo foot in this."

"Boy, stop being so damn overdramatic. It's just chocolate cake."

It didn't escape my notice that she failed to tell him she didn't bake it. It was petty to make a fuss that I had, but I was feeling especially petty today. "I baked your birthday cake, honey. I'm glad you love it."

"Mmm-hmmm," was all he replied as I cleared the table.

Kendra wasn't worried about me being petty. She was focused on trying to feed Jaya some cake, but the baby shook her head and pushed the spoon away. Kendra sat back and studied the baby for a few moments. "Is it me or does Jaya look pale? I hope she's not anemic."

Here we go again. Jaya was much lighter than I was, but she was by no means pale.

"Sharmayne, I really think you should schedule an appointment for the baby. I'm a bit concerned."

I eyed Micah who was also studying Jaya. He didn't say anything, and I choose to keep the peace. I took the dishes into the kitchen and placed them in the sink before I returned to the dining room.

"Babe, Jaya does look a little off. Maybe my mom is right."

I bit the inside of my cheek and swallowed what I wanted to say. I wiped down the table with a rag and tried to take on a more mature perspective. *Compromise Shar. Compromise. Marriage is a compromise and they are only looking out for Jaya.* "If she wakes up tomorrow, not feeling better, I will call the pediatrician and schedule a sick visit."

"Ok, that's good to hear. Shar why don't you let me finish cleaning up? If you want, you can take the baby and do what you need to with her. Ain't nothing like a momma's care when one of her babies is sick." Kendra stood up and began putting the cake away. I instantly felt bad for being quick to judge her.

"Thank you, Kendra. I would like to give her a lavender vapor bath and then give her a nice massage." I unstrapped Jaya from the highchair and picked her up.

"That sounds nice. She'll like that," she said as she carried the cake into the kitchen.

"Do I get a bath and massage too?" Micah slapped my butt as I walked past him toward the stairs and I chuckled.

"I have a few more gifts for the birthday boy." I winked and climbed the stairs listening to my husband grunt his approval like a caveman.

After Kendra left and Jaya was asleep, Micah and I enjoyed alone time together. While he was in bed, I brought him an envelope and placed it on his lap.

"What's this?"

"A birthday present. Open it."

Micah nodded and flipped the envelope to the backside. He flipped the metal clasp and slipped a packet of paperwork out of the manila envelope.

He began to read the paperwork then looked up at me confused. "Is this what I think it is?"

"What do you think it is?"

He grinned so wide all I saw were teeth. "You for real Shar? Adoption papers for Moochie?"

I smiled and nodded.

"Awww man." Micah ran a palm down his face and laughed. "Moochie's gonna have my last name?"

"Yep. A Payne just like you."

Micah let the slick comment slide as he beamed at the paperwork stunned, his eyes glassy. "She's my daughter no matter if she has my last name or not, but damn, this amazing. Thank you, baby."

"Wait, I have one more gift for you."

"More? I don't need nothing else, baby. For real."

I placed a long jewelry box on his lap. He looked at it strangely. "You got me jewelry?"

"Nothing but treasure for my king."

"Oh, I'm your king?"

"Yep," I said gushing. "Go ahead and open it."

Micah removed the lid from the box and frowned. "What in the hell is this Shar?" He removed it from the box and stared at it. I watched as it took him nearly a minute to figure it out. "Is this a pregnancy test? Wait, are you—" He paused and looked at me then at the test, then back at me. "Shar? Two lines mean you pregnant?"

"That's what the box says. And the other box. And the other, other box."

Micah laughed. "We're having a baby?"

"We're having a baby," I confirmed calmly.

Micah slapped both hands on his head. "A daddy twice in one day." He looked at me and laughed. He went to sleep well pleased with himself and well pleased with me. If I hadn't have already been pregnant, I would have been that night.

In the middle of the night, Jaya's cries woke me up. I could hear her congestion and I wanted nothing more than to suck it all out of her. There was nothing worse than a sick baby. I felt helpless and bad for her. I stayed up most of the night soothing her, not wanting to wake Micah. He had been trying to play catch up since his injuries and was working from dawn to after dusk every day. He needed his sleep.

Micah's alarm went off and I heard him get out of bed. Jaya had slept for five minutes before she woke up fussing again. That had been my whole night. Minutes of sound sleep in between bouts of tears and coughs.

His voice raspy, Micah stood at Jaya's bedroom door, rubbing his head. "Hey, baby. What's wrong with Moochie?"

I soothed her back as I rocked her back and forth trying to comfort her. "She's been up all night fussing. I'm gonna call the pediatrician as soon as the office opens to schedule a sick visit."

"You been up all night?" He looked upset.

"Since three. I'm ok."

He stepped in and kissed the top of her head. "Ok. I'll go in a little later so I can drop you off at the doctor's."

"No, its ok. I know you have work to catch up on. I'll take a cab."

He refused. "Nah. She's sick. I don't want her in no cab. Matter of fact, drop me off and keep the car." He didn't wait for a reply and headed off to the bathroom. He came back washed up and took over. "Go get some rest. You look tired. I'll sit with her."

I didn't know how to respond to his care. It was so unfamiliar to me I had trouble processing it. I did as he asked and handed her over. Rather than get some sleep, I went downstairs and made him and Jaya some breakfast. An hour later Micah began to yell, panic in his tone. "Shar! Shar!"

I run up the stairs my heart pounding. "What? What's wrong?"

"Something's wrong with Moochie." I see blood dripping from her nose and I panic as Micah is talking at warp speed. "She's burning up. She was awake and her eyes looked like they were rolling to the back of her head. What the fuck, Shar?"

I looked at her with the daylight now shining through her bedroom window and she's pale as a ghost. My panic intensified. "Let's take her to the emergency room. Right now."

I quickly bundled her up as Micah threw on some sweats and went outside to warm up the car. I grabbed her backpack and shove diapers and her insurance card inside. I quickly change into some jeans and a hoodie and took her to the car.

The emergency room at Cooper is the worst and it felt like days before she was called back to be seen. The anxiety only worsened when the doctor called for more testing when they couldn't immediately determine what was wrong. After some time the doctor came behind the curtain and stuffed his hands in his pockets.

"We ran a complete CBC and her levels showed some abnormalities."

"What's wrong? Is my baby ok?" I was on the edge of my seat ready to jump out of my skin."

"I'm sorry but it's Leukemia."

The walls around me closed in. I saw the doctor's lips moving but I could not hear a word he said. Yet, at the same time, every sound was magnified to deafening levels. Micah rocked Jaya on his knee and soothed her back and I could hear the flesh of his palm against her coat. I could hear the drip of her runny nose being sucked back up into her nostrils every time she sniffed them back up. I could hear the tap of the doctor's hand on his stethoscope as he spoke. I could hear the ticking of the clock. I could hear my heart pounding in my ears. And then I tuned it all out. I refused to let that be her future.

Not. My. Child.

We drove home quietly, on information overload with all the steps we needed to take next for Jaya's care. We immediately had her tested to determine the type of Leukemia that had invaded my daughter's helpless little body. Two weeks of waiting for test results had caused me to lose a few pounds. My bouts of morning sickness weren't helping. I was in the kitchen staring into my cup of coffee when the phone rang. I slowly walked over to it and picked up the cordless receiver.

"Hello."

"Can I speak with Sharmayne Payne?"

I hadn't gotten used to my new last name and how ridiculous my name sounded. "Uh, um, yes. This is she."

"Mrs. Payne, this is Dr. Gellar."

I felt my stomach flip-flop and my hands began to shake. A part of me longed to know which Leukemia Jaya had so we could hurry and move on to treating it as soon as possible. Another part of me wanted to remain ignorant. The more detailed her diagnosis became the more I had to accept that this wasn't a mistake or a dream. It was a living nightmare. It was still a shock to me that my baby had cancer.

Over the two weeks, I had had a million questions for Dr. Gellar and he was patient and informative. He'd informed me that some types of Leukemia had had a much better prognosis and survival rates for children her age and that Leukemia wasn't a guaranteed death sentence. Depending on the type of cancer would determine her course of treatment and the outlook of survival.

"Good morning doctor."

"We received the results back from Jaya's bone marrow testing. It's Acute Myeloid Leukemia also known as AML."

"Is that bad?"

"Well, no Leukemia is good, but I'm afraid AML is an aggressive form of cancer that progresses rapidly. As I've mentioned before, there are various forms of Leukemia and AML has several subtypes. Treatment can vary from subtype to subtype. Jaya has AML with the subtype Undifferentiated Acute Myeloblastic Leukemia or simply M0."

I was anxious and just wanted him to get to the point. "Doctor, I don't know what any of that means. Please just tell me how bad it is and is Jaya going to survive?"

He was silent for a moment before he granted my request. "Unfortunately, Jaya's form of cancer has had an inferior survival outcome than the other subtypes."

I wanted to yell and scream and tell him he didn't know what the hell he was talking about with all of his advanced medical jargon. My baby was not going to die! I didn't care what his studies showed. I would not accept it. "But there have been children with this type of cancer that Jaya has who've survived right?"

"Yes," he replied solemnly.

"That's good then! That's good."

"Mrs. Payne, we are going to do everything in our power to treat Jaya but I must be honest, however. It's a very difficult and uphill battle we're facing. No one is ever really prepared for this, but I encourage you to be as ready as you can. Jaya's going to need you to be strong."

"I understand that. I do. But there's hope! If other children have survived, Jaya can too! She's a tough little girl." Hell, she was Camden born. The strength to survive this life was in her genes.

"I believe she is too."

Damn right she was.

"We will need to begin chemotherapy as soon as possible. She will undergo about five months of treatment. The first treatment is intensive and the subsequent treatments will be within weeks of each other. I will have the treatment center call you for scheduling and how to prepare."

"Ok. I will await their call. Thank you for calling, Doctor." I hung up half hope and half dread. My daughter had Leukemia. Never would I have imagined I'd be discussing chemotherapy for my child. That was something you saw in the movies or news with other people's kids, not little black girls from the hood.

There was no use in denying it anymore and wishing it was just a nightmare. My daughter needed me to be strong. Suddenly I wondered if all I had been through up to this point in my life was preparing me for the biggest battle of my life. Micah walked into the kitchen carrying Jaya, her head on his shoulders and I knew my husband had come into my life just when I needed him most. He was one the strongest people I knew and together we would help our daughter through the battle for her life.

He handed me a letter, a smile on his face. "It's here."

I was confused until I saw the sender was the New Jersey Bar Association. I opened it nonchalantly and read it. "I passed," I said casually and stuffed it back into the envelope before I kissed my daughter's cheek. "Hey, beautiful girl." She stared at me before she cracked a smile and my heart was a tornado of swirling joy and anguish.

"That's it? That's all you're going to say? Shar you studied your ass off for this exam and you passed it. Why aren't you more excited?"

"Nothing but Jaya going into remission will excite me. I don't care about anything else. Everything with the power to bring me joy and excitement is standing right in front of me. Right now, nothing else is my priority."

Micah looked at me strangely but didn't argue. "Ok. I understand. But what about dinner? Is making dinner a priority? 'Cause we hungry. Right, Moochie?" Micah looked down at Jaya and shrugged his shoulder to get her attention. She smiled so he did it again. She laughed and I nearly cried. No matter what happened, I would do everything in my power to make sure I saw that beautiful smile until the day of my death, not hers.

1 Month Later

I rubbed my still flat belly in an attempt to calm my anxiety. After Jaya had gone through the first intensive induction chemotherapy with no response, she underwent another round of treatment. The doctor had performed another bone marrow biopsy to test her response to the second treatment and today he was going to give us the results.

Jaya sat on Kendra's lap drinking from a sippy cup as I paced back and forth in the examination room.

"Sharmayne, you are going to wear a hole into the floor. Calm down, baby."

Kendra meant well but until her baby was dying of cancer, she wouldn't understand and therefore had no right to ask me to calm down. I ignored her and walked to the frosted window and stared out into the blurred street before me.

The sound of the doorknob turning and the door creaking open lassoed my attention. I quickly turned around to see Dr. Gellar entering the room. My heart rate doubled, and my hands began to shake. "Good morning doctor."

He closed the door behind him and entered the room with a chart in his hand. "Good morning. How is Jaya feeling today?" He set the chart down and sat down on the rolling stool, turning to face us.

"She's had more energy and holding down food better."

Please tell me my baby is improving.

"That's good to hear." He stared at Jaya for a few moments before he smiled solemnly and turned to grab the chart. "The results from the biopsy came in."

Dr. Gellar began spewing out white cell counts and red blood cell counts and none of it made sense to me no matter how many times I had researched AML and tried to understand it. The closest to medical science I understood was the case of Re A or Roe v. Wade. Yet, I listened intently for something that would answer the one thing I needed to know. Was she responding to treatment?

And then he said, "Unfortunately." The word made me want to vomit but I said nothing and listened.

"Jaya's condition is proving to be chemotherapy-resistant."

My heart sank to the floor between my feet, but I refused to give up. "What happens now? Is there something else we can do?"

The doctor nodded. "The next course would usually be an Autologous Stem Cell Transplant which means using her own cells to transplant back into her body. However, the stem cells we harvested do not contain enough healthy cells due to her cancer being extremely aggressive. The next best option is an Allogeneic Stem Cell Transplant."

I hadn't had a clear idea of what that was exactly but it had been a hot topic of debate amongst law school students discussing current events while I had been more focused on my full-time job and caring for Jaya while in law school. "I've heard a little about stem cell transplants but it was always discussed as controversial. Is it safe for Jaya? I don't want her being tested for trials that can be dangerous."

He nodded as if he knew I'd ask. "The procedure in itself isn't controversial. The lack of donors and who receives the cord stem cell is what has made it a topic of hot debate. For seniors and older patients who tend to have an overall lower survival rate, they require two umbilical cord stem transplants. Because cord stem cells are a limited resource, many argue allocating one, let alone two to patients with a lower chance of survival is considered a waste. Then there are many parents of newborns choosing to store the cord stem cells for themselves, in the event that in the future a loved one would need it if ever diagnosed with Leukemia."

My law-trained brain began to dissect all the doctor had explained and I instantly turned it off. I needed to focus on Jaya's immediate care, not contemplate the stances I'd argue in debates. "So for Jaya, are there stem cells available?"

"As I've said before, donations are a limited resource and there has to be a match, further downsizing viable options. Unfortunately, as of today, there are no suitable matches for Jaya in the registry."

"Well, I'm her birth mother. Maybe I'm a match."

"We can certainly try, but parents are usually not a match. Siblings tend to match the closest."

I looked down at my belly and knew immediately that I would donate my baby's umbilical cord. "I would like to donate my baby's cord."

The doctor looked at my belly confused. "Your baby?"

"I'm pregnant."

He smiled at me sadly. "How far along are you Mrs. Payne?"

"Three months."

He nodded. "I see and that is certainly an option but I'm afraid the speed at which Jaya's AML is progressing, we may not be able to wait that long."

"But Jaya doesn't have any other sibl—" I choked on my words and refused to finish the statement.

"Mrs. Payne are you alright?"

I nodded and listened as the doctor explained the process of stem cell transplant whether from an umbilical cord or through the bone marrow of a donor. I volunteered to donate and understood when Kendra expressed she didn't feel comfortable due to her past history of drug abuse. Later that night I explained to Micah what the doctor had explained to me.

"So, I'll donate too. The doctor said non-blood relatives could be a match right?"

I nodded in response but a corner of my mind had been in constant thought since Jaya's check-up. "The doctor said the best match is usually a sibling."

"Well, we can use the baby's umbilical cord, right? Wasn't that an option?"

I loved that my husband had shared the same ideas I had and was as anxious to find a resolution as I was to save our daughter. "Yeah, but Jaya's condition is deteriorating fast, and waiting almost five more months is not an option. We can't risk waiting that long."

"So what are we going to do Shar? We can't just sit around hoping a match pops up."

I exhaled knowing I had no choice but to do this for the sake of my daughter's life. "Micah, the doctor said Jaya's siblings are her best chance of survival."

"I know, Shar. But you said she can't wait until the baby is—."

I interrupted him. "Jaya has a sibling."

Micah looked at me confused. "Do you have another child?"

I shook my head irritated at the nonsense he was thinking. "No. Of course not. But her father does."

I could see the emotions play out all over Micah's face. "You can't be serious Shar." He stood up abruptly and began to pace rubbing his head in exasperation.

"I don't have a choice."

"We always have a choice!" He yelled. "You are not going anywhere near that man."

I stood up and hugged my husband. "I love you, Micah. I don't ask you for much, but I need you to trust me to do this."

"Sharmayne how could you ask that of me? I can't let you and won't let you and that is final!" He pushed me off him and left the bedroom upset. I sat down on the edge of our bed and exhaled.

No matter what Micah said, I'd risk his wrath and anyone else's to save my daughter. Pride was a luxury I could not afford.

TWENTY

Tianna

T hanksgiving break was approaching and I was excited to host Thanksgiving dinner this year. I sat at the kitchen table after dinner writing out my grocery list when El walked in.

"Whatchu doin' woman? The men of this house are craving some ice cream."

"I think your momma dropped you on your head one time too many Mr. Townsend. You better talk to me like you have some sense."

"Oh! I see last night's spanking wasn't enough and somebody needs another round."

I popped my head up to see if Jay was within earshot. I heard him call out to El to hurry and was relieved he wasn't nearby. I glared at El, shook my head, then went back to my list. I heard him chuckling at me as he opened the freezer. A few seconds later he had a man-trum. "We're out of ice cream? Who ate the last of the ice cream? And why is this freezer stocked like we are hibernating for the winter."

Sometimes it felt as if I were raising two sons. I got up and closed the freezer that he'd been staring into as if ice cream would just magically appear. "You ate the last of the ice cream. You always eat the last of the ice cream." I opened the snack cabinet and handed him some cookies before I took out two tumblers from the cabinet. "Pour some milk for you and Jay and eat the cookies. I'm making a shopping list for the rest of my Thanksgiving list. I forgot a few things. I'll add ice cream."

El opened the fridge and poured some milk. "Thanksgiving list? What for?"

"What do you mean what for? Thanksgiving. We're hosting dinner this year, remember? *Mami* hosted last year so we said we'd do it this year and give her a break."

"We did?"

I looked up at El irritated. "Don't tell me you forgot. You were supposed to invite Liam and Katrina."

El twisted the cap back on the gallon of milk looking confused. "Babe, yeah I did, but to the dinner at the fire hall."

"The dinner at the where?" I eyed my husband as if he had lost his mind.

"Ti, remember my mom is flying up and arranged a catered dinner at the fire hall for all of my family. I figured since my whole family knows Liam and we were going to be there, to invite them to my mom's dinner. Ti, we spoke about this."

I crossed my arms pissed. "We most certainly did not talk about this. El, we have about fifteen people coming to dinner here, including my parents, Abe and his flavor of the month, Pastor Levy, and Brandy—"

"Levy's coming?" El closed the refrigerator door looking lost in sauce before he sobered. "Babe, I don't think Levy and Brandy are coming."

"And why not?"

"Because I told him we were going to the fire hall." El grimaced. "Maybe that's why he looked so agitated." My nostrils flared and I could kick my husband. "Damn, babe. I'm sorry."

"Well, you better fix this. Call them and tell them dinner is here."

"I can't. I already promised my mom we'd go to her dinner. We can't just flake out on her."

"Like hell, I can't. I can't just flake out on my family either. Besides I have a refrigerator and freezer full of food for Thanksgiving that I am not wasting." I went back to my list. "A catered dinner." I shook my head.

"Ti, for real. We need to discuss this. I'm not going to embarrass my mom as her oldest child and not show up. We have to go. It's not like she was trying to be malicious. She had no idea you were planning a dinner."

"And what am I supposed to tell our guests four days before Thanksgiving, Elijah?"

"They can come to the catered dinner too. I'm sure my mother wouldn't mind."

"I mind. I have all of this food that will go to waste. No. I'm cooking Thanksgiving dinner. You can go to your mother's event if you want to." I sat back down and went over my list again. Elijah walked out of the kitchen with the cookies and milk, not uttering another word.

An hour later my mother called me. "*Bendicion.*"

"*Dios te bendiga.* What are you doing?"

"I just took the turkey out to thaw."

"Ok good. I was calling to remind you and I wanted to make sure you still needed me to bring the rice."

"Yes, please. Thanks, mom. I have everything else covered."

"Ok, well I'm going to bring some *patitas* for El."

I wanted to gag. "Mom, pig feet are not on the Thanksgiving menu, but thanks for offering. And El won't be here for Thanksgiving dinner anyway."

"*De que tu hablas?*"

"*Mami,* exactly what I said. El's mother is flying up for Thanksgiving and she set up an event for his family. They are having Thanksgiving at a fire hall somewhere."

"And you weren't invited?"

"Well, yes, but I had already invited people here for Thanksgiving. And I don't want to go to a fire hall for Thanksgiving."

"*Mija,* you go where your husband goes."

"*Mami,* please don't start. He and I already settled this."

"You mean you had a tantrum and told him you weren't going. And trust me, his mother and I have gotten into some disputes, so I understand why you don't want to be around her."

"*Mami,* she hates me. Of course, I don't want to be around her."

"But you love your husband, and he comes first."

"Well, he should have put me first."

"Really Tianna? Does your husband ever not put you first? There is nothing wrong with him wanting to spend Thanksgiving with his family once in a blue moon. And his mother is coming all the way from the east like the wicked witch that she is, I mean Florida." I laughed at my mother's smart mouth. "I'll cook here for Daddy and Abe's eleventh girlfriend this year. Honestly, I don't even try to remember their names anymore."

My mom's slick talk got worse with age. I huffed like a spoiled child. "Fine, I'll go but you are all invited too. Misery loves company mother. And if you say no, I'll tell Jay you didn't want to go."

"That's a low blow but my grandson will learn to get over disappointments in his life. But I'll go just to annoy her and so I don't have to cook."

I laughed as El walked into the kitchen with two empty tumblers of milk. "Ok good. Mom, let me call my other guests and tell them the plans changed. I will call you with the address and time after I talk to El."

He came up behind me and kissed me on the cheek before he spoke into the receiver as I was about to hang up. "Thanks, Ma."

"Why you sneaky son of a —"

"Ah ah ah ah ah. You kiss your mother with that mouth?"

"You told my mother on me? You a snitch now El? That's how we living?"

El chuckled so hard I could feel his body shaking as he held me from behind, my arms pinned down. "Sure didn't. But I did tell her that I saw a frozen turkey in the freezer and asked how long it took to thaw? She said something like it was her fault for not being a better teacher in the kitchen and said she'd call me back. You just so happened to answer the phone."

"Elijah Townsend that was sneaky and underhanded."

"It was genius. And whatever your mother said to convince you to change the plans, she's right."

I removed myself from my husband's backward bear hug and headed for the living room. "She said that even wicked witches from the East deserve a little love now and then."

"See? Your mom knows what she's— Wait! What?"

It was my turn to crack up as I exited the kitchen.

Unfortunately, Thanksgiving Day arrived faster than I had hoped. With any luck, I'd blink and it would be black Friday. I had gotten up early and cooked an oven roaster just in case we had to leave Thanksgiving early or possibly still hungry. I couldn't wrap my mind around Thanksgiving being catered. That was the one holiday you cooked the food yourself to make sure everything was right.

For the tenth time that week, I waved it off trying not to be annoyed by it all. At least I didn't have to slave away in the kitchen for two days. But if the food was nasty there was going to be a hangry woman wearing my shoes.

When we arrived at the fire hall, there were at least twenty cars already parked in the lot. "Damn babe, how many people did your mom invite?"

"Ti, I told you it was my whole family. The parking lot is kind of empty but you know black folk always late."

Empty? I grabbed Jay's hand nervously. Good grief what had I agreed to? We walked in and for fifteen minutes I met cousins upon cousins I had never seen or heard of, with the few faces I knew sprinkled about. Jay was off with the other kids whether he knew them or not.

"El how many cousins do you have and why don't I know most of them?"

He laughed. "Most of them are not my first-generation cousins. Some of them are my cousin's cousins or people my family just adopted as family. Kids my cousins grew up with. I was a military kid so I wasn't here long before we started moving around. I would come for the summer sometimes and hang out with my grandmother and my uncle Alonzo but when I left to go live with my dad during high school, we grew up and went about our lives. He got into the street life, like my grandfather and I wasn't about that. So we are still cool, but we respect each other's lives."

"He's the one you used to talk about in high school?"

"Yeah. We used to say we were cousins because having an uncle my age made people ask too many questions."

I could imagine. I had a million questions about his family myself. "I remember you saying he couldn't come to our wedding."

"He doesn't like flying. Plus, the whole point of us doing the destination wedding was to avoid all of this, wasn't it?"

"Yeah, but I was trying to avoid my family coming, not yours. And it worked."

El laughed. "For mine too."

"But if you two were so close, why hasn't he ever come around the house? Since we've been married, you've never mentioned him or hung out with him, if I can recall correctly."

Elijah's expression hardened before he looked away and avoided looking at me. It was odd behavior for him, but I let it go.

Just then a loud older gentleman, in an even louder suit, strutted up to us looking like a cross between a deacon on Easter Sunday and an old school pimp at the Player's Ball. "Oh! Kay! Neph-ew! This you?" He pointed at me as he surveyed me from head to toe.

"Charles! Hey! How are you fam?" El gave him a bro hug, all smiles.

"I'm cool bro. You know how I do."

The entire time he was in conversation with El, he was chewing on a toothpick and sizing me up like I was a steak, and he was hungry.

"Charlie, this is my wife Christianna. Ti, this is a long-time family friend, Charles. We call him Charlie."

"Family friend?" Charlie broke his gaze from my boobs and eyed El very much offended. "Boy, I was almost your great uncle." He looked both ways before he stepped in a little closer and whispered, "Or your granddaddy, but keep that between us. Your Aunt Lucille won't like that."

El coughed into his fist and I could swear he was a touch uncomfortable, not that I blamed him. Who wanted to hear from Pimp Daddy that he was cheating on your aunt with her sister, that was your grandmother? I sure as hell didn't need that mental picture. I tried to end the awkwardness and get back to the introduction. "It was very nice to meet you, Charlie." I shook his hand and had to literally yank it free from his grasp.

"Pleasure is definitely all mine."

I tried especially hard not to grimace and put on a smile. I'm not sure I pulled it off. I turned away not wanting to see him staring at my breasts again and saw Pop walk in. "Oh honey, look. My parents are here." *Thank God.* "Excuse us. It was nice meeting you, Charlie."

Between leaving Charlie and reaching my parents, I met another two cousins and an actual great Aunt. She was as sweet as but very focused on making sure no one snatched her purse. I was strangely amused by the grip she had on it. So tickled with her I stayed and talk to her for a minute longer after El had moved on to a table of people who had all greeted him loudly.

I hugged Great Aunt Reba and expressed my pleasure in meeting her, heading toward my parents when I saw a woman lean in El's ear and whisper something that just looked inappropriate. He moved his head back almost shocked and look into her face. She sipped from her cup as El shook his head laughing then waved a finger at her before he walked away smiling like a fool. She watched him walk away then said something to two women standing by. They high-fived each other and burst into uproarious laughter.

I regretted wearing heels and my hair out. But who was I kidding? I was not the fighting type. Instead, I strutted by them in my cute outfit and smiled at them. "Happy Thanksgiving," I said sweetly trying to catch up to Elijah. He turned and saw me then waited for me. When I reached him, I knew they were staring so I kissed him on the lips. He was confused for a second before he placed his hands on my waist and returned it.

"What was that for?" He asked smiling.

I ignored the question and walked on. He wasn't exactly on my favorite person's list at the moment. When we finally reached my parents, Charlie had already introduced himself to my mother much to my father's amusement. My mother not so much. *"Que fresco ese viejo!"* The look of disgust on *Mami's* face was priceless.

"I see you've met Charlie." I kept my laughter to myself as we walked toward our table.

My father did not offer my mother the same courtesy. "Relax, honey. He didn't mean any harm. He appreciates a beautiful woman when he sees one. No big deal. It's a compliment." Pop plucked a handful of cheese and crackers from a tray and tossed one in his mouth as he chuckled.

"No big deal, my ass."

I hushed my mom and looked around to see if anyone had overheard her. *"Mami,* please." I urged her to lower her voice. El scratched his forehead looking as if he wanted to disappear. Maybe next time he'd think before he thought our families being together for a holiday was a grand idea.

"Mami, please, nothing. That fresh old man tried to grab my ass."

My father, mouth full of cheese and crackers, nearly choked trying to chime in. *Mami* patted him on the back. "What?" He tried to ask his eyes wide, scowling.

"Tommy, you ok?" *Mami* patted his back trying to help the choking.

El came back with a drink and offered it to my dad. "Here Tommy. Wash it down with this."

Pop took a gulp and began coughing. "What the fuck is this?" He practically shouted as he picked up the cup and stared at its contents. Everyone turned in our direction and I wanted to melt on the spot.

El grabbed the cup and sniffed it. "Damn it. I grabbed the wrong one. I asked the bartender for a little water. I must've picked up my cousin Ruben's cup by accident. He only drinks vodka. I got distracted. I'll be right back."

Pop snatched the cup back. "Nah, nah, nah. I already put my lips to it. Ain't no sense in wasting it. Give it here." He motioned for El to hand the cup back.

El and I looked at each other. My parents weren't big drinkers but were known to drink on social occasions and I supposed today qualified. I shrugged my shoulders at my husband. If Pop wanted to drink, he was a grown man who was entitled to that decision.

"I've only been here five minutes and I need a drink too. El could you please bring me a mixed drink?" *Mami* removed her coat and hung it on the back of the chair. I closed my eyes slowly. My mother and alcohol was a different matter altogether.

"Honey, you sure you want a drink. We aren't home. You can't be out here acting a fool. You know how you get when you drink. You can't hold your liquor, Tanya."

Mami raised a stern eyebrow and blinked intentionally slowly to show her ire. "I most certainly can hold my liquor, Thomas Jefferson Leonard. Thank you very much." She sat down and turned her full attention to Elijah, now all smiles and a saintly expression. "Son, a mixed drink please." *Mami* was a force to be reckoned with and she still could put the fear of God in me. El nodded looking like he wasn't sure what to do before he walked to the bar.

"I'm telling you right now Tianna, if that pervert tries to touch me again, it's gonna get really ugly in here. I am a Christian woman of class and dignity. I will not be disrespected. I can be ghetto if I have to. You rarely see that side of me, but trust me it's deep down in here. *Soy de Camden. Conmigo no jodas.*"

I rarely see that side of her? If anything, I rarely saw the classy, dignified Christian woman but I kept that thought to myself. "*Mami*, please don't make a scene. I will have El talk to him."

Abe appeared beside us in a dress shirt, slacks, and a wool coat looking like a GQ model, while his newest conquest reminded me of a shorter version of Kimora Lee Simmons. "Talk to who?"

"Well, Happy Thanksgiving baby bro. No one," I replied to his question. "*Mami* was just being *Mami*."

142

"I'm not surprised." He hugged me and kissed my cheek before doing the same to *Mami's* and shaking Pop's hand. "Everyone, this is my friend Kakalina or Lina for short."

"Kaka *que*?" *Mami* asked, her voice pitching and looking like she had bitten into something tart the way she scrunched up her face. "*Que clase de nombre es eso?*"

"Lina, Mom. Her name is Lina. She's part Hawaiian." Abe had a higher level of tolerance for *Mami's* crudeness than I had ever had. The woman had been easily embarrassing me regularly since elementary school. Abe was more like Pop and ignored it for the most part.

As I had done since I was a young girl, I set out to pacify the awkwardness. "Hi, Lina. It's very nice to meet you. I'm Christianna, Abe's sister, but you can call me Tianna."

She smiled politely. "It's nice to meet you."

Other introductions soon went around just as Jay crashed into Abe, hugging him around the waist. "*Tio! Tio!*"

Abe was as ecstatic as always whenever Jay idol worshipped him. "Hey, bud. You know you shouldn't be running around. Martial Arts masters are disciplined."

Jay looked at him incredulously. "But *Tio*, it's a party and I'm just playing with the other kids. I don't want to be disalind."

Abe gave him a stern look, trying not to laugh. "You mean disciplined. And ok. But only because today is a holiday. Don't you get into any trouble, you hear me?"

"I won't *Tio*. I mean Sensei. I promise." Jay saluted Abe as his teacher.

"Ok good. Now say hi to my friend, Lina."

"Hi, Lina. Are you *Tio's* girlfriend?"

My child had obviously inherited some of his grandmother's personality. "Jay, hush. And did you say hi to your grandparents?" As uncouth as his grandmother, he shrugged off my correction and greeted *Mami* and Pop.

"Hi, *Papito*." *Mami* kissed his cheeks then checked out his attire, tucking in his shirt. "But Mom-Mom, I don't like it like that." Jay pulled his shirt free."

"No grandson of mine is going to walk around looking sloppy. Tuck it back in and tie your shoes." She smacked a kiss on his cheek and patted his butt when he walked past her.

143

"Pop-Pop, I don't want to put my shirt in. And could you tie my shoe?" Jay lifted his foot, landing it on Pop's lap.

I wanted to snatch that boy up but my father put a palm up to *Mami* and me before we could utter a disciplinary word. He tied Jay's shoe, singing a song that explained how to loop the laces. Jay laughed and asked him to do it again. Much to Jay's amusement, Pop did it again, before he placed Jay's foot on the floor and dusted his lap. "Now Jay, I know you don't want to tuck in your shirt but do you know what happens to little boys who walk around looking frumpy?"

Jay shook his head intrigued.

Pop pointed to Charlie. "When they get older, they start looking like that." Jay took a good look at Charlie. His eyes opened wide like a cartoon's before he stuffed his shirt in his pants so deep, it probably reached his ankles. "Good job," Pop said before he palmed the top of Jay's head and playfully shook it like a rattle.

Everyone was laughing as El returned and handed *Mami* her drink. "Here ya go, Ma. I got you gin and juice since you straight gangsta."

El had a weird relationship with *Mami* and only he could say something like that to her and she'd not find it the least bit disrespectful but would even crack up. "Thank you, son. And don't forget it," *Mami* said pleased as punch. Pop and I looked at each other with that knowing glance as we always had whenever El and *Mami* had a strange interaction.

Elijah noticed Abe and greeted him. "Hey bro. Glad you could make it." They man-hugged before Abe introduced his date.

"Thanks for the invite. Let me introduce you. El, this is Lina. Lina, this is my brother-in-law, Elijah."

Lina stuck out her hand. "Very nice to meet you," she said with a hint of sultry in her tone.

Did this hussy just sexify her voice?

El shook her hand and for the life of me, I swear she held it after he tried to let go. "Uhh, um, yes, nice to meet you too. Have you met my wife already?" He asked her taking a step closer to me.

Her smile widened. "Yes. I've met everyone."

Abe, oblivious to this homewrecker's flirtatious glare, took her coat and hung it on an empty chair. "I'm going to get a drink. Lina, do you want to come?"

"No, I'm good here," she said sweetly. "But could you bring me a Long Island Ice Tea?"

Abe nodded and set off to the bar as his friend kept discreetly eyeing my husband. I turned to my mother to see if she'd noticed but she'd been sipping her drink through the stirrer like a kid at a malt shop enjoying a root beer float. Good grief my family was a hot mess. "*Mami*, that's a stirrer, not a straw."

"Says who? Are you the straw police, Tianna?"

I ignored her smart comment and watched her sip as if she'd run a marathon in the desert and this was her first drink. "*Mami*, you haven't eaten yet. Maybe slow down with the drink until after dinner."

She stopped sipping. "*Christianna.*"

Shit. She pronounced my name in Spanish and with an attitude. That was never a good thing.

"*Desde cuando eres madre mia?*"

Double damn. Whenever *Mami* spoke to me in Spanish, she was irritated but if she asked 'how long have I been her mother?' I know I stepped out of bounds.

El touched my elbow and winked before he leaned in and whispered in my ear. "Let her enjoy herself."

My husband must have seriously forgotten who he was talking about, but I decided right then and there not to police anyone. Other than my son, everyone else was an adult and could govern themselves. And just at that most opportune moment, Marvette graced our table with her presence.

"Happy Thanksgiving, Elijah," she said right before she embraced him gleaming.

"Happy Thanksgiving, Mom." Elijah hugged her then stepped to her side to face everyone. "Mom, do you remember Tianna's family?"

"Vaguely." She waved quickly then said, "Hello," barely glancing at the table.

"I know she remembers me," *Mami* said before she laughed and took another sip through the stirrer.

"Tanya," Pop said in warning.

"Don't Tanya me. She didn't even greet our daughter. Just rude," *Mami* said in a loud enough whisper.

I cut off her rant. "Happy Thanksgiving, Marvette. Thank you for the extended invitation to my family. We are grateful."

She gave me a forced smile. "Anything for my Elijah."

I grinned widely not letting her get under my skin with her undercover remark. "Yes. *My* Elijah certainly does have a way with women."

Elijah furrowed his brow. "What does that mean?"

Not that I had any intention of answering his question, but had I wanted to I wouldn't have had the chance.

"Hi, Grandma!" Jay yelled excitedly. "Where's Uncle Mac?" He rushed over to her and half hugged her, searching behind her for her son.

"Grandma?" *Mami* practically yelled appalled. I looked over at my mother and pretended to scratch an itch on my face, I put my finger to my lips, gesturing to please be quiet and not make a scene. She rolled her eyes at me like a child, picked up her cup, and dramatically sipped through the stirrer, making sure the slurp was loud and obnoxious.

"Uhh, hello Justin," Marvette said uncomfortably first at my mom and then back at Justin, not bothering to return the hug. "Mackenzie is not here. He is with his father for the holiday."

"Aww, man. I wanted to play with him." Jay turned to El already over it. "Daddy, can I go play with the other kids then?"

"Uhh yeah Champ, but stay out of trouble." Jay had already started running away excited before El finished issuing his warning.

"We are about to get dinner started. Elijah, would you mind escorting me to the microphone and saying grace over the food?"

"Give me just a minute mom. I need to speak with Tianna first."

"Elijah, everyone would like to eat dinner. You should go with your mother and say grace." I sat down in between my mother and Abe's empty seat and gave him the biggest, phoniest smile I could muster.

Abe came back and sat beside me, setting Lina's drink down before her. I could feel Elijah burning a hole in me, but I turned to *Mami* and started small talk. After a few moments, he walked away.

It was almost dinnertime and the fire hall had doubled in attendance. Marvette gave her speech and everyone clapped. She announced Elijah as if he were the second coming, and some clapped louder than others. No surprise or shame there. He said grace and afterward everyone lined up for the buffet-style service.

I served Jay and sat him down to eat. He complained about most of the food choices and picked at his food before he darted off to go play.

"The turkey is dry, but everything else is ok," *Mami* commented.

"Those candied yams are something else. Baby, can you go get me some more?" Pop chomped into his turkey leg. *Mami* nodded before she got up to do his bidding. He then got up and went to the bar returning with a second round of drinks for them just as she returned with a plate full of a few extras of everything for him. "Here. I got you another drink." She nodded, sat down, and continued her meal.

I smiled at their easy existence. They served each other as equals. No complaining. No fighting for authority. They just co-existed. Of course, I'd known their history and their bouts of separation and restoration; their fights and make-ups, but they'd survived it all. Marriage was never easy, but when two people chose to never give up, they could overcome anything. My husband's words echoed in my head and I regretted acting childish.

He returned and loosened his tie before he sat down to eat, looking exhausted. I got up from the table and went to the bar. I ordered him a drink and got a ginger ale for myself. I took it to him and set it before him, then walked around the table, back to my seat, the only unoccupied one at the table. Admittedly, I'd intentionally chosen a seat where he couldn't sit beside me, and now I felt bad about it. Especially because he was sitting beside, Lina and her bedroom eyes. If she wasn't careful, she was gonna get the Kaka beat out of her.

I tried to catch El's eye, but he avoided me, even looked past me. I suppose he was irritated with me for blowing him off. I had been a little petty and jealous but I shouldn't have been bothered with him. Technically he hadn't done anything wrong but be fine and he hadn't had much control over that.

Lina picked at her food, while Abe scarfed his down as if he hadn't eaten in months. He went back up for a second helping and Lina couldn't wait to take the opportunity to lean forward to talk to El over the loud music, her titties peeking out. With the music in the background and everyone chattering, I couldn't make out what they were talking about. El leaned in to try and hear her better, moving his ear closer to her mouth. He'd nod while she did most of the talking. He continued to eat and every now and then he'd chime in and say a word or two. He never looked her in the face or breasts during their entire exchange. She, however, kept vigil over his profile as if she needed to recall it later from memory.

Abe returned and tore into plate number two as he did plate number one. He barely gave Lina a sideways glance and I found it odd. They seemed more like strangers than a couple on a date. Abe met my eye and smiled before he leaned over into my ear. "Don't worry. El is used to this and he would never entertain it or disrespect you."

I looked at Abe shocked. So he wasn't as oblivious as I thought. "So you see it too? Don't you mind? She is the one being disrespectful."

"The minute I introduced them I saw her attraction. I'm not bothered because I already discarded her so I am not being disrespected at all. I just haven't taken her home yet because it's all the way in Marlton and I ain't driving all the way over there to drive all the way back here. I'm leaving after dessert though. Drop her skank ass off, then meeting some of my friends at a Sports Bar in Audubon." Abe sat back, patted his stomach then burped. "That food was aiight. I ain't gonna lie. I'd go for another plate, but I can't fit anymore."

"Mine would have been better." I squinted my eyes and dared him to say otherwise.

"As long as I didn't have to cook it and it's free, it's good to me." He and I laughed out loud. "I guess that's true." I looked over and saw Elijah staring at me. When my gaze met his, he quickly turned away, stood up, and grabbed his drink before walking away from the table. He stayed clear of me for a while after that.

At the bar, a group of men were watching a football game on a TV mounted to the wall, the volume muted. I had no idea what they were talking about; defense this, and rumbles and fumbles that. Football never made sense to me.

The bartender asked for my order and I stuck to ginger ale, especially because somebody nearby was eating chitlins and the stench was making me queasy again. My stomach felt like it was rumbling and fumbling. Then again it could've been the mac and cheese. I was beginning to wonder if I was lactose intolerant. For all I know, all this catered food could've been spoiled. That's the kind of foolishness that happened when you catered Thanksgiving. *That damn Marvette.*

As the bartender was filling up my cup, I scanned the room looking for Jay. He was in the same corner he had been in all night entranced, watching a kid play a handheld video game. The bartender set my ginger ale down on a napkin and I thanked her. As I took a sip, a male voice grabbed my attention.

"You must be El's lady."

I set my cup down and looked over to the man who had approached me. A nice-looking gentleman. Right away I could see the family resemblance. He was a few shades lighter than El and a tad shorter but shared the same distinctive nose, deep eyes, and thick eyebrows. I nodded politely and turned away my gaze. I didn't want him mistaking my interest in his features as flirtation. "Yes, I am."

He was silent for a long moment, so I checked to see if he was still standing there and he was, a slight smile and a deep dimple that probably made him dangerously attractive to most women. I, however, was not one of them. Perhaps I was biased, but whatever relation this was to El, my husband was more appealing.

"It is nice to finally make your acquaintance. I've heard a lot about you." He held out his and looked at it for a bit before I accepted it then quickly released it. "I'm Alonzo, Elijah's uncle. My friends call me Ace."

At the realization that it was El's cousin slash uncle, my anxiety calmed a little and I relaxed my shoulders. "Oh, Alonzo. I can finally put a face to a name. I am Tianna. El's told me so much about you."

"I can't even imagine what, but you probably shouldn't believe half of it," he laughed and called the bartender over.

"Likewise. Tell ya what. If you don't believe most of what you've heard about me, I'll repay you the favor." I instantly imagined Marvette whispering in his ear calling me all kinds of witches then laughing out loud like an evil villain. I shook the thought out of my head and sniffed the contents of my cup wondering if it contained alcohol.

"Everything ok? Would you like me to get you another drink?" He looked at me concerned.

"Oh, no. I'm good, thanks."

He nodded and leaned in closer to the bartender to be heard over the music. "Lottie, my usual and another of whatever she is having." The bartender nodded and walked to the other end of the bar.

"First name basis with the bartender. Smooth," I joked.

His smile was easy and relaxed but there was something about the depth of his eyes as if he wanted to plunge head-first into my soul. His gaze made me feel naked yet he hadn't done anything but look directly me. I turned from him feeling uneasy and electrified at the same time. I couldn't ever remember a man's gaze so effortlessly penetrating. He pulled me from my runaway thoughts and spoke.

"Lotti works for me. I own a bar and a club. She's one of my bartenders," he said before he sipped from a cup, his gaze still on me over the rim of his cup.

I looked down into my cup to avoid his stare. "Oh right. El did say you owned a few businesses."

He set the cup down and placed an elbow on the bar, his voice tender. "What else did my nephew tell you about me?"

I shook my head not wanting to repeat all El had said. "Nothing much. You two used to say you were cousins when you were younger."

I halted still when he stepped closer and lifted his hand toward my face. Instead, he touched my hair. "You have a feather in your hair." He removed it and showed it to me, standing too close for comfort for a moment too long. "Were you out catching the turkey for dinner?" He laughed out loud and I smiled not wanting to be rude but feeling awkward as his proximity. I could feel his breath on my face. I tilted my head back and turned away only to lock gazes with Marvette. If looks could kill, I'da been dead.

Ace stepped back and chuckled. "Anyway, yeah. Cousins. We hated when people would start asking us how we were around the same age and be uncle and nephew. Then they'd start teasing us. I remember when I was like ten years old, El was like seven or eight at the time. We had gone to the playground to go compete on the monkey bars. Back then he was shorter than me, but he was always fast. All the neighborhood kids had been there, and we were sporting our new stopwatches." Ace laughed reminiscing about his youth. "I went first. I can't remember my time but I was confident El wouldn't top it. Man, he got on those bars and smoked me. They shoulda been named Elijah Bars the way he would climb those things fearlessly. His agility was crazy. The kids started teasing me. Saying I lost because Uncles are old and slow although I was faster than all of them. El started defending me and a fight broke out. We were both sporting busted lips. After that, we figured it was easier to just lie."

"That's when we were young and dumb." Elijah walked up and stood stoic beside me facing his uncle, his expression unreadable.

Unlike Elijah's, Ace's face lit up. "El!" He pushed off the bar and hugged Elijah, who in turn one-armed him. "How you been nephew? I haven't seen you in like what? Two, three years. I'm surprised you're even here Then again this was your mom's affair so of course, you'd be here. I suppose married life keeping you busy." Ace patted him on the chest then bit his bottom lip, strangely calm and relaxed before he sat on the edge of a barstool. He either hadn't noticed Elijah's demeanor or simply didn't care.

El's shoulders were stiff, his stance rigid. "Yeah. Something like that. Just trying my best to keep my word to my wife. That whole honorable man type thing."

Ace's smile widened. "Honorable man. Right." In Ace's tone, I thought I detected a hint of sarcasm. He and El stared at each other for a few long moments, and I knew something was being communicated between them without words. I could feel the tension mounting.

Ace finally broke the awkward energy and stood. "Well, I should go mingle. It's been a long time since the whole family has been together for something other than a funeral. I see some faces I haven't seen in a while and even some new ones." Ace pointed behind El and me. "Whose little boy is that? He doesn't look like Graham kin. Got his shirt tucked in and all."

We turned to see a group of kids running around, Jay among them. El faced Ace and proudly announced, "That's my son. He may not look like a Graham or even a Townsend, but he's mine all the same."

Ace nodded. "I hear you, Nephew. That whole honorable man type thing again, right?" El didn't even bother to reply and I felt caught up in a war zone with invisible ammunition. "One day soon, I'm gonna introduce my daughter to the fam. My little Princess." He chuckled. "Who knows? Maybe I'll pick up on some of that honorable man stuff."

"Highly doubtful." Marvette walked into the crossfire firing, an ally to her son.

As undisturbed and polite as ever, Ace greeted her. "Happy Thanksgiving Big Sis. This is a nice gathering you put together for the family."

"Funny, I do not recall inviting you." Marvette clasped her hands in front of her, the model of a distinguished woman in her earth-tone woman's suit and infinity scarf, her fashion as sharp as her tongue. An outfit suitable for Sunday Service or Monday business, yet I knew the true person her attire could never disguise.

"Some of our relations extended the invitation and I graciously accepted. And since I contributed to some of the food, the bar, and the wait staff, I thought it only right, to enjoy what I helped pay for. I was glad to help. I'm sure our father is looking down on all of us together, celebrating and giving thanks, and is smiling."

Never one to back down, Marvette reloaded, aimed, then fired. "You must mean up from hell and hopefully burning in it."

"Mom." Elijah looked at her shocked and shook his head at her disappointedly. "Don't. My grandfather wasn't perfect, but he was good to me. And you. He put us both through school."

She softened her expression and faced her son. "His filthy money didn't put you through school. Your father and I did that. That man never did anything from the kindness of his heart for you or for me. Paying for my education was a business deal and nothing more. Don't ever think otherwise. He was never good to my mother and therefore was never good to me. It took me a very long time to realize that and for the rest of my life I will never forget it." She turned back to Ace, standing there mild-mannered and the picture of serenity and politeness. He hadn't even flinched when his sister cursed and decimated his father's character. "You can get the hell out of here. Take your food, alcohol, and staff with you."

Elijah relaxed his shoulders. "This is not the time, nor the place for this. And no one is leaving. Whether we like it or not, we are family and we are going to act like it."

"Because I love my family, I will not disrupt their holiday and make a scene." Marvette pointed a finger in Ace's face. He tilted his head back to keep her from poking him. "And you better keep your ghetto, hood nonsense, trouble out of here."

Ace lifted his hands in mock surrender. "I came here in peace to spend time with my family. Including you, Sis. I don't want any trouble."

"Your act may fool her," Marvette pointed at me, "but it sure as hell doesn't fool me." She walked away in her passive, aggressive manner suddenly laughing with family members that had greeted her with hugs and kisses.

No matter when, where, or why, my mother-in-law never ceased to drag me through the mud, even when the situation had nothing to do with me. I looked over to Elijah who hadn't looked at me once since he'd come over.

"The family is just trying to have a good time so, although Mom didn't deliver her message in the best way, she's still right."

Throughout the entire exchange, Ace had kept an exemplary level of cool, until now. His brows dipped, a look of hurting crossing his face before he masked it. "I'm here for the same reason you are. I just want to spend time with my family. I know our relationship has changed but you will always be my nephew. No. My brother. And Marv may have been right about a lot of things, but she was definitely wrong about one. Pop loved you like no one else. He always said that you were the one good thing that came from him and until the day he died, he made me promise to look after you."

Elijah, turned his face, his eyes glassy. "We aren't kids anymore Alonzo. I don't need anyone to look after me. And whatever happened between us is, in the past. Water under the bridge. But the fact remains that we live different lives and that ain't gonna change. We family, but we ain't friends. Respectfully "

Ace lowered his face and looked to the floor for a moment. He raised his head and nodded at Elijah. "I hear you. And I can respect that. I wish you the best." He turned to me with a soft smile and I felt bad for him. "It was very nice to meet you, Mrs. Townsend." He walked away and I turned my attention to Elijah but he'd walked away in the opposite direction without a word.

Already at the bar, I called the bartender over and order a rum and coke. Abe and Lina walked over and said goodbye. Abe walked ahead of her as if he were alone. That was a disaster if I ever saw one. Every now and then I'd check in on Jay. He was getting sleepy and Mommy was drunk so Pop took them both home. I walked around looking for Elijah. He was at a table with some men in deep conversation so I returned to the bar. After another rum and coke, I was a little tipsy and walked outside for a breath of fresh air.

"You shouldn't be out here alone?"

I jumped startled at the unexpected voice. Ace was sitting on a cement ledge wearing a trench coat and smoking a cigar.

"I just needed a breath of fresh air." I wrapped my arms around myself and turned from him. I just wanted one minute alone in the dark.

"My nephew is a stubborn man, just as he was a stubborn kid and a stubborn teen, but eventually he gets over it. You two will be back to wedded bliss soon."

I closed my eyes and pretended not to understand his very astute assessment. I honestly just didn't want to think about anything but the buzz that had had my thoughts blessedly fuzzy. After a few minutes, the warmth of the alcohol had lost its strength and I began to shiver in the cold November night air but I wasn't ready to leave the tranquility of the silence. The smell of cigar smoke intensified and suddenly I felt warmth on my shoulders.

As soon as I realized Ace had draped his coat over me, I removed it and handed it back to him. "No, thank you."

"Don't be crazy. It's cold out here." He tried again but I sidestepped him. The odor of the cigar wafted in my face and made my stomach churn. I rushed to the bushes, bent over, and vomited. My head was spinning as was my vision. How many drinks had I had? Well, the truth was I was never a drinker and one drink would have been enough but I was certain I had had more. Maybe. I couldn't think straight.

"Tianna, you ok?"

I felt a hand on my back and I straightened. I wanted to go back inside but I felt dizzy and I couldn't get my legs to cooperate. I dropped to my butt and started laughing. "Oops."

"Let me help you up." I felt a hand on my arm helping me stand.

Elijah was standing in front of me. I threw my arms around him and kissed his neck. He wrapped his coat around me but the odor of the cigar kept assaulting my nose. I turned and vomited again. I stood and wiped my mouth with my sleeve. "I want to go home," I pleaded, wrapping my arms around his waist. I rested my head on his shoulder and nuzzled my face into his neck, kissing him. "Can we please go home?"

"Tianna?"

"Behind me, I heard El call my name. I looked toward the voice but everything was fuzzy. I looked up at Elijah, he was smoking a cigar. But Elijah didn't smoke cigars. But he was smoking now. My head was spinning again and I just wanted to sit down.

"Tianna, what are you doing?" The hallucination of El walked toward me as I let myself fall to the ledge and sit. He knelt before and stared. "Baby, what's wrong?"

I smiled tripping over the realness of an illusion. I waved my hand at the apparition wondering if it would disappear but instead it grabbed my hand. "Whoa. This is crazy," I muttered.

"Let's go home," the hallucination said before I fell asleep on the cold ledge.

TWENTY-ONE

Micah

The whispers of a housing market crash had started to become shouts and there wasn't a worse time for it to happen. Jaya's medical expenses were beginning to pile and the profit from my last two flips had been divided between reinvesting into the next house and taking care of my house. That nest egg was dwindling quickly. I'd barely gotten requests to come see my listed property, let alone any offers and I was beginning to worry.

Shar cautiously entered the bedroom, her hair brushed into a high ponytail, tight curls formed into a bun, surprised to see me. "Oh, hey. What, what are you doing here? I thought you were going to go work on a property." She walked over to the bureau and began to put on some earrings.

"Manny cut his hand on the wet saw and had to go get it checked out. The other two brothers don't know how to cut tile, so we called it a day. We can't do anything until we lay the tile down. Are you going somewhere?"

"Oh wow, is he ok? Oh, by the way, the realtor, what's her name? Umm.."

"Nora."

"Yeah, that's it. Nora. She called. I told her I'd have you call her back."

"Yeah, I just got off the phone with her."

I watched my wife walk to the closet and pull out a pair of sneakers and she still hadn't answered my question."

"Everything ok with the house for sale?" She asked as she bent over to tie her sneaker.

I wouldn't lie to her, but the last thing she needed on her mind was money issues. I had always made sure she was never in need and I'd continue to provide for her and Jaya, one way or another. "Just the realtor doing what she does, and updating me. Where you going?"

"Still haven't sold it?"

Now I knew she was dodging the questions. "Nah. She thinks we should lower the price a little bit." She faced me pretending to be fully invested in this bullshit conversation. It kinda stung that my wife thought I was this stupid and gullible, but I'd play the game.

"Well, what do you think? Did she suggest how low to go?"

"I don't want to go too low. I still need to make a profit."

She shrugged her shoulders. "You can't make any profit if it keeps sitting. Maybe you should take her advice. This is what she does."

I knew Shar was right but it was a mental step I wasn't ready to take. Of all the houses I'd sold, I'd never had to decrease the price to any of them and this one was just as nice as the previous ones. Agreeing to her strategy was the first step in admitting that the housing market was on a downslope. I had another one that wasn't done flipping and one I hadn't even begun renovating yet.

Granted I was going to keep the latter two flips very basic, but at this point, I didn't have the money to do anything at all. I needed to sell quickly otherwise I'd have to rent out to pay the mortgage on all four properties. My absolute last resort was renting the houses out and I would avoid that for as long as I could.

I wanted to smack myself. Shar almost had me believing we were engrossed in actual conversation and not playing cat and mouse, but I was back on track now. "I'll run the numbers and see. So where you going?" She stood and went back to the closet as if she hadn't heard me. "Shar? Where you going? Baby, got another appointment?" I asked a little louder.

She walked to the basket of laundry that had been sitting there for three days and began to sort it. At this point, it was becoming insulting. My wife wasn't a lazy woman and tended the house well, but laundry would sit for two weeks before I put it away or she needed something from it.

"Uh, nah. Your mom is on her way over to stay with her for a little while, though."

"Why does my mom have to stay with her for a while? Where is you going, Shar?" I had had enough of the games.

156

She raised her eyebrow and pursed her lips with an attitude as if that was supposed to scare me. "Why are you talking to me like you my dad, though?"

I took a step closer to her, annoyed. "And why you are avoiding the question? What's going on? Where are you going and why are you trying to keep it a secret. What? You cheating on me? Don't let me find out, you out here messing around, Shar."

Straight faced, she grabbed her coat and walked out of the room without saying another word. I followed behind her and snatched her by her arm. "You ain't gonna just walk away and not tell me where you going. Don't piss me off."

She shook her arm free, now pissed herself. "First of all, you are not going to treat me any which way and then expect me to respond to you because I sure as hell won't. I am a grown-ass woman, Micah. I am your wife but I am not your child. And lastly, when have I ever given you a reason to believe I am disloyal and untrustworthy, coming at me like I'm a whore."

"Hey, you were a stripper. How do I know you weren't a prostitute too?"

As soon as the words left my mouth, I wanted to snatch them back and swallow them whole. My arrow hit the bullseye and I saw hurt flash across Sharmayne's face before she masked it with indifference. "I suppose you don't."

She walked out of the house and I didn't bother to go after her. I'd said enough already. I picked up the remote and threw it across the room. It crashed against the wall before landing on the floor in pieces. Jaya began to cry and I mentally smacked myself for scaring her awake.

I went to her bedroom to check in on her and she was sitting up in her Disney Princess toddler bed, lost in a princess blanket. She held up her arms wanting me to pick her up. "Hey, Moochie." I picked her up and as always she laid her head on my shoulder. I kissed the back of her head and rubbed her back. "How you feeling today?"

She lifted her head and kissed me on the cheek. "Dad."

"Yes?"

"Dad."

I chuckled softly. "Yes?"

"Eat, eat."

I headed for the stairs. "I'm hungry too."

Downstairs, my mom knocked on the door before she let herself in. "Hey! What are you doing here? Shar said you were at work and she needed me to stay with the baby." My mom smiled big and opened her arms. "Hey, baby girl! Come here and give me some sweet kisses." Jaya went into my mother's arms and let my mom kiss her.

"There was an accident with one of the workers so we called it a day. Shar just left."

"Oh ok, great. You should have waited for me to get here that way you two could have gone together."

I turned to my mother surprised. "She told you where she was going?"

My mother shook her head. "No. She didn't tell me y'all business Mike. Relax. She just said it was important. It was about a donor for Jaya, so I said, say no more. And here I am."

I nodded pretending that I already knew where Shar was headed. And then it dawned on me that Shar was going to go talk to Jaya's father. When would she learn that Ace was not a man to rely on for help.

TWENTY-TWO
Sharmayne

I took Micah's car without telling him. I was so upset I hadn't been in the mood to be a gracious wife. His words cut me deep. I had had many men say vulgar things to me because I took my clothes off for money. Drunk men who thought because I danced naked for money that they owned my body and when I refused their advances for sex, I was a dirty whore or a slut. A prostitute. I always found it funny that the same men that paid money to see a woman naked and would have paid for sex, were the same ones trying to shame me for not prostituting myself.

Ace had tried to convince me to be one of his high-class call girls. He promised only well-off clients that kept their personal lives discreet. I would decide who I slept with and when. He'd only had two other women he'd given that privilege to, but he'd sampled them first to make sure "his merchandise" was of caliber quality. On the surface, Asia and Seana were making really good money and were well taken care of, but I just couldn't bring myself to go that far.

Ace understood and kept me for himself. If a man wasn't paying to have me, no one could have me for free. I thought it was cute at first. Then one day he asked me to do him a favor. He had a special client that he could only entrust to me. To repay him for taking such good care of me and sparing me prostitution, I agreed.

I closed my eyes, trying not to think about the life I once lived and the man I'd left behind. But how could I? Jaya was a product of my life with Ace. And now she was sick and I had to once again revisit my past for the sake of my daughter. This time, it wasn't about rent money or my mother. My daughter's life was at stake. Time was of the essence. I couldn't wait around and hope for a donor.

I sat outside in the car for a few minutes trying to find the courage to do this. I reminded myself that I didn't have a choice. Jaya's life was

159

what mattered most. I exited the car and walked out into the cold. I inhaled, exhaled, then rang the doorbell. *God help me find the words.*

TWENTY-THREE

Elijah

The coffee wasn't as good as Tianna's, but it was strong and that was all that mattered. I sat at the kitchen table and sipped trying to forget the worst Thanksgiving I had ever had, and I'd had some shitty ones. I heard Tianna puking again and I rubbed my forehead agitated at her and her hangover. She could hold her liquor as well as a bucket with a hole in it. What the hell was she thinking? She wasn't and that was the problem. Ever since she'd lost the baby, she'd become impulsive and irrational. I regretted not just staying home for Thanksgiving as she had wanted. But what was done was done and now all that was left to do was reap what we sowed. She'd have to endure her hangover and I'd have to deal with my frustration.

The phone rang and I dreaded answering it, knowing only two people, had the audacity to call this early in the day; my mother or my mother-in-law, and I wanted to speak to neither. Thomas Leonard appeared on my caller ID, and I guess if I had to talk to either of them right now, my mother-in-law was the lesser of two evils. "Good morning, Tanya."

"They do say that after being married so long, couples begin to look alike, but I don't ever think I will be as attractive as my wife. Not in Charlie's eyes anyway but thank you for the compliment."

I wasn't in the mood for humor, but I'd take that over Tanya's meddling. "Sorry, Tommy. I'm just having a hell of a morning. How are you?"

"Better than you, that's for sure. What's going on? I was just calling to tell you I'd be taking my grandson out for breakfast and do some Christmas shopping. Drop him off later if that's ok?"

"Oh, yeah, that's fine. Tianna is not feeling so well, so that's actually helpful. Thanks."

"What's wrong with my daughter?"

"Being that I don't hear Tanya and she isn't the one who called, I'd say the same thing wrong with your wife."

Tommy chuckled. "My wife is in bed cursing both gin and juice, so I doubt it. What's going on with Ti?"

"She's making out with the porcelain bowl."

Tommy chuckled. "Get outta town! Ti? She's not a drinker."

"Exactly." Upstairs I heard the toilet flush and Ti whining. "I better see if she needs anything. She's really sick. We'll be home, so you can drop Jay off anytime."

"Maybe, I'll keep him for a little longer. Let Tianna recuperate."

I had half a mind to have Tommy bring Jay home now so she could really regret her irresponsible drinking but decided against it. "I'm sure she'd appreciate the quiet."

"You got it. Tell Ti I said to hang in there. Like mother, like daughter." Tommy chuckled again before we disconnected.

I boiled some water and grabbed a teabag. By the time I made it upstairs, Tianna was back in bed in a darkened bedroom, the blinds closed, and curtains drawn. I sat on the side of her bed and set her tea down on the night table.

Sounding like she was dying she called out to me. "El?"

"Yeah Ti. I'm here. I brought you some tea and aspirin." A part of me was annoyed with her, but a bigger part felt bad for her. Whenever I thought about her hugging up on Alonzo, her face in his neck, I wanted to punch a wall. But she was too drunk to know what she was doing. Had I not gone looking for her, I can't imagine what kind of trouble she would have gotten into. I'd already decided that if she didn't remember, I wouldn't bring up last night. No sense in adding to her misery. No harm, no foul.

"Thank you, but I feel horrible. I don't want anything."

I pulled the blanket from over her face. "Gotta at least take the aspirin. It'll help with the headache."

She groaned as she sat up. "Ok." I handed her the tablets and the glass of room temp water I had brought up earlier that she hadn't even touched. "Thank you." She placed them in her mouth and sipped slowly. "I just want the room to stop spinning. Maybe then I will stop feeling dizzy and throwing up."

I didn't respond. I didn't have anything helpful to say. Ti was the one usually tending to us. My nursing skills were grossly inadequate.

I'd have to step up in that department. "Get some rest." That's all the sound advice I had to offer. "By the way, Tommy is keeping Jay for the day. Your mom is not feeling well either, so I doubt she's gonna call. You should have a quiet day."

Tianna giggled before she handed me the glass, put a palm to her head, and groaned. "Please don't make me laugh."

I set the glass down and rose to my feet. "I was being honest, not trying to make you laugh. Now get some rest." I closed the door behind me and went down into the basement pulling out the storage bins of Christmas decorations. If Tianna was feeling better tonight or tomorrow, we could take Jay to pick out a tree. Bin after bin, I dragged them into the living room and spent a half-hour trying to untangle lights to hang outside, before I gave up and drove to buy more. I forgot it was Black Friday and spent an hour trying to find a store with parking, then another in the checkout line.

Last year I told myself that I was going to go through this headache again, yet here I was. I don't know when I became the suburban dad with the white picket fence that complained about Christmas lights, but I was, and I cherished it. I loved my wife and my son. I had a good life. Yeah, Ti and I had our fights, but which marriages didn't? I had everything I needed and if God chose to never bless me with more, I already had enough. Although getting through this line faster would be great.

While I was out, I stopped at Dunkin' Donuts for a drinkable cup of coffee then returned home, ready to throw away Christmas and just watch basketball all day. I tossed the new lights on a bin and decided to do just that. A hoagie and some wings sounded good. A nice cold beer. I headed to the kitchen to find a pizzeria menu. The phone rang twice before it stopped. I looked at the caller ID and saw Tommy Leonard flash on the Caller ID again. I guess I underestimated Tanya's tenacity. Although, honestly, she meddled more like a best friend as opposed to a mother hen, and Ti didn't entertain her mother past a certain point. Thank goodness.

A half-hour later I heard the shower running and was relieved Ti was now able to get out of bed. I made her some toast and boiled some more water for tea. Hopefully, she'd be able to stomach it if she ate a little at a time.

The doorbell rang as I dropped the teabag in the mug. I wiped my hands on a dishtowel and headed for the door curious who would stop by for a visit without notice. I done already told these people that I did not want satellite cable. It rang again just as I turned the doorknob and pulled it.

I was stuck on stupid for a minute. Of all the people that could have knocked on my door. "How do you know where I live?" was all I could think to ask. He had his back turned to the door then spun on his heel to face me, looking dapper as always. I had no idea why my uncle was here and I was sure I'd live to regret this visit. I didn't want to be rude, but I sure as hell did not want him in my house. "What are you doing here?" I tried to sound casual although I owed him no pleasantries. "You are the last person I'd expect knocking on my door."

He stuffed his gloved hands into his peacoat and smiled. All my life I'd been told we looked like brothers and for the first time, I saw a version of me when he smiled. I didn't like it.

"Uhh yeah. Sorry, I didn't call first. Truthfully, I didn't think you'd take my call."

"And you thought I'd welcome a visit?"

Alonzo looked at me before facing the ground, kicking a pebble with his toe. "I was hoping, but I understand if I'm not welcome. I actually had two reasons for my visit."

"What's the second?"

"Your wife was wearing my coat when you left last night. I don't care about the coat, but I need what was in the pocket."

I looked behind me at the coat rack and didn't see it hanging there. I vaguely recollected Ti draped in it, wiping her mouth on the sleeve but I couldn't remember where she'd put it. I held the storm door open. "I have to go look for it. Come inside and get out of the cold." He was letting the heat out. Alonzo stepped inside and stood by the door.

The tea kettle began to whistle so I tended to that first. I checked the kitchen for the coat but still hadn't found it. I was about to head upstairs when I saw the coat haphazardly tossed on a dining room chair, falling to the floor. I grabbed it and the odor of vomit assaulted me. I thought about having it dry-cleaned but that nigga could afford it. He was standing where he could see me so I didn't check the pocket, although I was curious to see what dragged the city-slicker out into the burbs.

"Here it is. It smells like vomit." I tossed it at him and it smacked him in the face. That was unintentional but I wasn't sorry. He pulled his face back and scrunched up his nose before he covered it with his bejeweled hand. He wore two gaudy rings on his index and middle fingers. The true mark of a drug-dealing pimp.

Suddenly I remembered Tianna hugging him, her face in his neck and I wanted to slam him against the wall and punch him in the face endlessly. Not just for taking advantage of my wife in her inebriated state but for what he'd done to me in the past. For a long time, I harbored animosity toward the man who I once considered a brother. I had lost all true respect for him. Over the years I'd let it go or so I thought. But seeing him smoking a cigar, his arm around my wife like he was in a rap video made me want to pound on him and all my feelings of disgust for him rose from deep.

Alonzo stepped further into the living room and began to fumble with the coat, searching for the pockets. He tried the first one, but it was empty. He searched the second and pulled free a wad of money. He tossed the coat on the coffee table and began to count his money.

"Get the hell out my house and go count your money somewhere else." This nigga was one bold son-of-a-bitch. Alonzo continued to count as if he hadn't heard me and I began to walk toward him when I heard Tianna.

"El?"

I turned around and saw her coming down the stairs slowly wearing just a towel. I rushed up the stairs and cut her off the rest of her descent. "Go back upstairs, babe."

"I have to talk to you," she said drowsily.

"Ok, I'll come back up in a minute. Go back to the bedroom."

She pinched her brows and looked down the stairs past me. "What's going on? Why are acting weird?' She inhaled deeply before exhaling a breath. "That shower exhausted me."

"Go get some rest. I'll bring you some toast and tea." I looked back to check on Alonzo quickly before practically pushing her up the stairs.

She nodded. "Ok. Thank you, baby."

After Tianna closed the bedroom door, I made my way back to the living room. Alonzo was sitting on the couch, leaning forward. "How's Tianna feeling?" He asked casually.

"I told you to leave."

He looked at me and smiled. "I will. But first, we need to talk."

"We don't have anything to discuss."

"Fine. Then you can just listen. It's not a long story." Alonzo sat back and motioned to the chair across from him, inviting me to sit down in my own house as if he were the king of this castle. I was now actively controlling my anger. My fists began to ball up and I clenched my jaw to keep from raging out. "Suit yourself," he said then began his story.

"My first memory of you was when I was about five years old. You were only about two at the time. It was Father's Day. My mom had taken me to visit my dad. Or so I had thought. Pop told me much later, she was there for money and to leave me with him because she couldn't trick with a five-year-old watching." Alonzo laughed humorlessly. "I sat in the corner and stayed out of trouble as I was told. I think I sat there with no one saying a word to me for hours as if I didn't exist. And then your mom walked in with you. You were a loud and goofy kid. Pop took one look at you and gushed. 'There's my grandson,' he said before he sat in his chair and watched you play."

My anger began to subside and I'll be damned my curiosity increased as I watched Alonzo lose himself in his story as if he were reliving it.

"Back then, Marvette felt bad for me. She offered me food and gave me a little attention. I instantly liked her. Still kinda do, but don't tell her that. I watched you wondering why Pop was so intrigued by you but didn't give his own son an ounce of attention. After a few years, the lack of attention didn't bother me. It actually helped me learn to live without love or company and whenever you came around, I would study you. The well-mannered apple of my father's eye and I began to emulate you. Although Pop still ignored me, everyone else, took a liking to me. I learned real fast how to manipulate emotions and situations for people to like me. But never Pop. I put on every mask I could to win his approval and none of them worked. Then you began to come for the summers. Your Mom and Dad started having problems. She was drinking so heavily back then. Dad made her go to rehab."

Since Alonzo had begun talking, it was the first time we'd looked at each other. He smirked at my subtle reaction to my mother's addiction to alcohol. Back then I had found it strange when she told me I'd spend the summer with my grandfather. She wasn't particularly close to him. I had never known it was because she was in rehab.

"Ah. I see you didn't know your mother was an alcoholic. She's clean now, but once an alcoholic, well you know the rest." He shrugged his shoulders nonchalantly as if we were having small talk about the weather.

I balled my fists up again but remained still.

"Yeah, she was. Is. Was. Anyway, your dad had cheated on her with a Hispanic woman. Maybe that's why she can't stand your wife. She don't care for the *mamis* too much.

After she found them together she wanted to leave him, but she didn't have any money or any place to go. So, Pop took pity on her for your sake and also because he had treated her mom like shit and this was his way of recompense. He told her that if she sent you to him for a few summers, he'd pay for her to return to school and her living expenses until she got on her feet.

"Marvette hadn't been in her right mind when she made a deal with the devil. She was smart enough to enter rehab though. Of course, after she was clean, sober, and of sound mind, she realized the environment in which you were spending your formative years was poison. But she'd already become financially dependent on Pop, and it took her a few more years before she was able to break free from him. By then you had gotten not one girl, but two girls pregnant."

Alonzo began to laugh. My rage began to bubble to the surface. I had driven myself crazy wondering if God was punishing me with no children for being so careless with my seed. Although I had loved Tianna as a teen, I had no business having unprotected sex with her. Had I been more responsible, she wouldn't have gotten pregnant or miscarried at seventeen years old. My mom wouldn't have sent me away to live with my dad and torn us apart.

"But here's where the story kinda takes a bit of a turn. See? Pop was extremely angry that your mom sent you to go live with your dad. He was depressed for a while. One night, he saw me sitting at the table eating dinner and for the first time in my life, my father hugged me. He cried on my shoulder and kissed my cheek. He looked me in my eyes as he cried. I cried too. I told myself, it took him losing you to realize what he had had all along; a son that wanted to make him proud. I had even started hustling without him knowing it so I could show him I knew how to earn money and be street smart, just like him. So, I cried, finally ready to have a bond with my father."

Alonzo sat forward and looked me dead in my eyes, his mouth tight and eyes narrowed. He was getting angry, and I didn't know what to expect next, so I kept my guard up.

"Pop looked me in my face and said, 'Elijah, when did you get back? Your mom brought you back.' Then he hugged me and said, 'You are the son I wish I had always had.'"

Growing up, I had always known my grandfather loved me. I never could see the person everyone had known him to be because I never saw that side of him. Or maybe I just didn't want to see it. Even hearing Alonzo's heart cry didn't taint him in my heart. Perhaps that was wrong, but I couldn't bring myself to ever feel sorry for my supposed uncle who had been careless with my life.

Alonzo calmed himself and sat back and crossed his legs as if he hadn't just tight-rope walked between rage and serenity. "Ironic, that I was the one that ended up taking care of him and taking over the family business. And doing it better than he or his father ever had, if I do say so myself. Don't get me wrong. I loved Pop. Well, the best way I knew how to anyway, but he was single-handedly responsible for creating the heartless man you see before you."

He grinned, then slapped his lap, uncrossed his legs, and rose to his feet. "You are probably wondering why I just told you all of this. Well, that's simple. I hate you. I think I've always hated you on some level. All my life, you've gotten everything I've always wanted. Except for one thing. A child. Flesh of my flesh. Blood of my blood." He clapped his hands and laughed out loud. "I didn't even have to intervene again to make your life as miserable as mine had been. God is handling all that. I don't even need to dirty my hands."

He began to walk to the door and I was undecided if I wanted to choke him until he couldn't breathe anymore or let him walk out of the door. My mind kept faltering between being an honorable man and the man born into a bloodline of criminals, evil men, and wicked heritage. It was true that a curse carried down for generations. Who was I to believe I was free from it?

"Did I tell you, I had a daughter? I did, didn't I? I'll make sure I bring her to the next family function and introduce her to your bastard son. Of course, they aren't related but they can still be friends I suppose. Oh, before I forget," Alonzo removed a wad of cash from his pocket and tossed a few hundred-dollar bills on the floor, "that's for your wife. She earned it. The look on your face when you saw her sucking on my neck with her soft ass lips. Whew! I'd pay to see that again. Maybe next time, you can watch her suck my—"

I didn't wait for him to finish his statement before I grabbed him by the throat, pushed him against the wall, and began to ram my fist into his mouth. Jay's school pictures crashed to the floor. I lost control. I saw red and wanted to see more. He punched me in my jaw and my head snapped back. But I didn't feel anything. I began to punch him with both fists as if he were a punching bag and I were a boxer in training. After a cycle of blows, he fell to one knee and spit blood out onto the hardwood floor before I kicked him in the face.

Falling over, he held his mouth and began to laugh. "You are just like us Elijah. A violent, vicious, no-good, heathen." His laughter echoed in my head and I wanted to kill him, but the worse thing I could do was be who he wanted me to be. He stood up and positioned himself into a boxing stance. "That's all you got, Nephew?"

"Get out."

He ran toward me and wrapped his arms around my waist in a tight grip, ramming me into the end table, knocking over a lamp before my back collided with the wall. He pulled back and rammed me into the wall again. Tianna's large, prized mirror came down, shattering when it fell face forward. I clasped my hands together and began to pound on his back. His hold on me loosened so I hammered into his back harder, After several hits, he fell to his knees and I kneed him in the face. He felt backward groaning.

I kicked his foot as he writhed in pain. "Get the fuck outta my house. Stay away from me and my family. All of my family."

A knock on the door heightened my adrenaline. I should have known that Alonzo never traveled alone, everywhere he went, Huggie wasn't too far behind. So be it. Right now, my only goal was to make sure Tianna remained safe in our home. Even if it cost me my life.

TWENTY-FOUR

Tianna

I rested in my bed, upset with myself again, for getting drunk. I didn't remember anything. Not even how I got home. Elijah was probably pissed at me. *Crap.* Marvette was probably dragging my name through the mud. As if she needed another reason to hate me.

When the phone rang, I instinctively knew it was *Mami* and answered before El could. "Hello."

"Hello. It's your mother."

"You know you don't have to say that every time you call, right? I know it's you."

"Is that how we were taught to greet our mothers? I raised you better than that."

I sat up as best as I could before I responded. "*Bendicion*, mother. How are you feeling?"

"*Dios te bendiga.* I feel like crap."

I held my head as I tried not to laugh. "Hangover?"

"Hangover, hang under, hangman. Only thing I don't have hanging, is a pair of—"

"*Mami*! You are supposed to be a God-fearing woman. Your mouth is something else."

"God created me. He knows more than anybody how much of a mess I am, so don't lecture me."

I needed to change the subject because there were topics of conversation never to be had with a parent, and this one was dangerously close to crossing a boundary. "Did you like the food yesterday? It was actually better than I thought it was going to be but I still did miss the Spanish food."

"From what I remember, everything was good."

Unable to resist, I had to tease her. "Was the company good too? A little birdie told me you have a new secret admirer." I covered my mouth so she wouldn't hear my amusement.

"I don't know what you are talking about. Tommy liked the candied yams. He went up the buffet three times just to get more."

Her bypassing the topic made me giggle harder. "You know what else happened three times? Charlie asking me if you are happily married." That hadn't actually happened, but I knew it would get a reaction from her.

"*Viejo sucio,*" she said disgustedly.

I laughed so hard my head began to pound. "Oh, my head. I gotta stop laughing. The room is spinning again." The violent urge to vomit caught me off guard. I dropped the phone and ran to the bathroom. After emptying the bile from my stomach, I sat on the floor trying to catch my bearings. I was tired of being sick and I promised I'd never drink rum and coke ever again. I called my mom back after I made it back to my bed. She answered without a hello because apparently phone etiquette only applied to how my mother raised me and not how hers raised her.

"Why are you throwing up? I heard you." Sheesh. She got straight to the point.

"Rum and coke are gin and juice's first cousins."

"Smartass. You aren't too old for *fuete* you know?"

The way I was feeling, I wanted to be smothered with sympathy, not mothered with threats. "I'm too sick to get whipped right now, *Mami.*"

"Too sick to come over for dinner later? That's why I was calling. Since we didn't cook, I have no Thanksgiving leftovers. Tommy put our ham to cook for me this morning before he left. Figured we could do a small Thanksgiving."

"I don't even want to think about food."

She tsked like she always did when I didn't jump on her invitations. "*Pero nena.* How much did you drink? I threw up a little bit last night and once this morning. It's already noon though. You should be feeling a little bit better by now. Did you take some aspirin?"

I had to think to recollect what I had drunk, but it hurt to think. "I only remember having two drinks and I really don't want to think about it. But you know I'm not a drinker. And everyone gets over hangovers differently."

"*Chacho.* I'm your mother. I know a lot more than you think. Now go take a pregnancy test."

Here we go. I turned over in my bed and closed my eyes. Why did she have to be like this? "Why is it every time I get sick you tell me to take a pregnancy test? I'm hungover, *Mami*. Not pregnant."

"Why is it every time I tell you to take a pregnancy test, you're pregnant? *Fijate. Hija fuiste, madre sera.*"

I stuffed my face in the pillow ready to fall back asleep. "I'm already a mother, *Mami*?" I responded groggily. "What does that have to do with anything?"

"But you haven't been a mother to a girl. Very different. And I know my daughter very well. Now go buy a test and call me when you get the results. I'm praying for a granddaughter. Her middle name can be Tanya. *Aye virgen, que chuleria.* Then in twenty-five years after raising her, if I'm still alive, you can tell me I was right. A mother knows her daughter better than her daughter knows herself."

I was too old to roll my eyes in secret, but I couldn't help myself. "Goodbye, mother. I'm going back to sleep."

"Tianna, you've already had several miscarriages. And you were drinking yesterday. You need to start taking care of yourself and my granddaughter. Take a test and schedule an OB/GYN appointment as soon as possible. I'll talk to you later. *Dios te bendiga.*"

Mami hung up before I could respond. All of my life I'd known her to be a bit dramatic, but she'd never purposely say something so insensitive to me knowing of my past health history. She'd always been incapable of telling a joke because she simply didn't speak the language of nonsense. Suddenly I was anxious. What if she was right? Now I couldn't just ignore it. I dragged myself out of the bed and into the bathroom. I pulled out a pregnancy test from my hiding place under the towels. I had become obsessed with getting pregnant, I'd bought enough pregnancy tests to service a small OB/GYN clinic. I tore the box open and didn't bother reading the instructions. Testing had become second nature to me.

After I was done, I set the test stick atop the box on the sink and undressed. I decided on a warm shower to help calm my nerves. After five minutes, I had to turn off the water and get out, it had drained me so immensely. I stepped out onto the rug and picked up the test. Two lines. I set it down not wanting to believe it. I picked it up again and stared at it to make sure I wasn't hallucinating. Still two lines. I grabbed another test and retested. You weren't supposed to read the test after three minutes because it could be inaccurate after that time frame. And yet again; two lines. Tears began to stream down my face. I was pregnant. I. Was. Pregnant.

I dried myself off then sat on the toilet lid to rest and detangle my hair. My hands were shaking so badly. I was filled with joy and I knew El would be too. But I had been drinking and I wondered if that had hurt the baby. I needed to talk to Elijah. I opened the bathroom door and thought I heard voices. I began to walk down the stairs.

"El?"

He rushed up the stairs and stopped me from going down. "Go back upstairs, babe."

I was beginning to feel faint from moving around too much but I needed to tell him. "I have to talk to you," I said drowsily.

"Ok, I'll come back up in a minute. Go back to the bedroom."

He was acting strangely. I looked down the stairs past him and saw the Christmas storage bins on the floor. "What's going on? Why are acting weird?' I asked breathlessly. "That shower exhausted me."

"Go get some rest. I'll bring you some toast and tea." El looked behind him quickly before practically pushing me up the stairs.

I consented not wanting to ruin his surprise of decorating for Christmas because boy did I have a gift for him. "Ok. Thank you, baby."

I returned upstairs and called *Mami* back. She wasn't the least bit surprised but she was excited. I swore her to secrecy. I wanted to surprise everyone on my own terms and she agreed to hold in her enthusiasm. I decided that a Thanksgiving do-over would be a good idea and when El came upstairs I'd run it by him. *Mami* cut the call short to prepare convinced we'd make it.

I slipped on some tights and a tee not wanting to get back in bed. Instead, I sat in my lounge chair, turned on the radio, then pulled my sketchbook and pencils free from the side table drawer. I'd have to ask the OB/GYN how paint fumes would affect the growth of the baby, once I had my visit. Painting was my passion but it could not hold a candle to the well-being of my baby. I beamed with joy. Already thinking about how to protect my child. I still couldn't believe I was pregnant.

I began to sketch a teddy bear when I heard a commotion downstairs. I stopped and listened. I shook my head. Only God knew what El was doing. Who would have thought putting up Christmas decorations would be so chaotic. Another loud crash and this time I heard glass shatter. "Oh no. Not my beautiful mirror. If El broke my mirror, he is going to have more than seven years of bad luck." I set my sketchbook and pencil down before I slid my feet into my house slippers, and headed downstairs.

I wanted to cry already. I loved that mirror. It had been my paternal grandmother's, bequeathed to me when she died. I hadn't had much history with my biological father or his family until a few years ago when he died. I'd finally gotten a chance to meet my grandmother and I instantly fell in love with her, and she with me. She didn't survive long after that but I cherished the time I had with her. I had commented on her mirror during a visit and she just smiled. The fact that she remembered and left it to me, meant more to me than I could ever say. It was simply irreplaceable.

Elijah Townsend I am going to murder you dead. Then revive you and strangle you.

Two steps down the staircase and I felt lightheaded. I heard Elijah cursing and telling someone to leave. I eased down the stairs and heard a knock on the door. I stopped and waited on the stairs where I couldn't be seen. I had no idea who was in my house, who Elijah was talking to, or who was knocking. A part of me wanted to rush into the living room and come to his aide if he needed it, but this time before I reacted impulsively, I remembered my baby.

I battled helping Elijah and possibly bringing harm to the baby or protecting the baby. *Lord, what do I do?* I suddenly remembered Elijah acting strangely. Now it made sense. He had told me to wait upstairs because he was protecting me from whoever had been here. He hadn't even known I was pregnant. If I risked his baby again, he'd never forgive me. It took all of me to stay hidden. But rather than go back upstairs, I waited close by because as much as I already loved my child, no one was going to just hurt my husband in our home. In the meantime, I'd listen to my husband.

Now decided on what to do, I waited patiently. A second knock on the door caused me to peek as I saw Elijah walking to the front door. I had no idea who could be at our door but I felt foreboding in my spirit. I heard the creak of its opening, then eery silence.

TWENTY-FIVE
Sharmayne

Words failed to form in my thoughts let alone be verbalized when he answered the door. He looked angry and that wasn't helping. I reminded myself why I was there and pushed aside all fear.

However, he beat me to the punch. "Who are you?" He asked.

"I used to work for your uncle, Ace. Alonzo, I mean."

He turned his face and yelled to someone in the house. "Who did you bring to my house?" I heard no response.

I was confused. I had no idea who he was talking to. "I'm sorry. I know you have no idea who I am, but I have to talk to you. In private. It's important."

Elijah looked at me as if he was about to rip my head off, raising my anxiety, but no matter how rude, angry, or mean he was, Jaya needed a donor and I couldn't leave until I knew if her biological could help.

"I don't know who you are or why you are knocking at my door, but get the hell off my property and take him with you."

"Take who with me?" I asked not understanding what he was talking about. I tried to look inside the house to see who he was referring to but he pushed me back. "I don't know what you are talking about. Elijah, look. I am here alone and have something extremely important to talk to you about? Can I come in?"

"Alone?" He asked suspiciously.

"Yes. I swear." I handed him my purse and raised my arms. "You can check my wallet. My name is Sharmayne."

Elijah checked my wallet then eyed me suspiciously. "Payne? I don't know anyone with that last name. Who are you?"

175

"That's my married last name. My husband is Micah Payne. Can I please come in? I can explain why I am here and answer any questions you have."

He hesitated but then moved aside. "Come in," he said matter-of-factly.

I walked in afraid of what I was getting myself into, but I'd always known Elijah hadn't been like Alonzo or his grandfather and that truth helped settle my nerves. I remained rooted by the door not daring to go where I hadn't been invited. Shards of a shattered mirror littered the floor and crunched beneath my feet. Elijah pulled me by my elbow bringing me further into the house before he looked out the door, then quickly slammed it closed.

I saw a man lying on the floor unconscious and my eyes darted to Elijah. He was staring at me half-crazed, with a curiosity in his eye. He shoved my purse back at me. "Start talking."

I nodded, trying to find the words. "Um, yes. Right. My name is Sharmayne."

"You already said that. How do you know my name and where I live?"

"Right. Well, I, I, I used to work for Ace."

Elijah looked over to the unconscious body, then back at me and I froze in fear.

God, please, don't let that be who I think it is. I pointed at the body. "Is that—?" I couldn't form my lips to say his name. Elijah neither confirmed nor denied it. "Is he dead?" I asked, my hands beginning to shake. Elijah's face softened before he shook his head.

He ran a palm over his head his rage beginning to wane. "What do you want?" He asked cantankerously.

I never thought the day would come that I'd share my biggest secret but for my daughter's well-being, I'd announce it to the world if I had to. "I know you don't remember me, but we've met before. A few times, actually." Elijah looked at me with a blank expression, so I continued. "I used to live with Alonzo and I helped take care of your grandfather during the last few weeks of his life."

Elijah's gaze narrowed before he shook his head confused. "I vaguely remember Alonzo saying something about a woman helping but what does that have to do with me?"

Ace began to groan as he struggled to sit up. He spat out a mouthful of blood before he held his jaw presumably from it being in pain. He looked over at me stupefied. "What are you doing here?" He struggled with his words but he managed to get them out.

I swallowed the lump in my throat. Confessing to the world was probably easier than sharing my secret in front of Alonzo. He was the one person in the whole world I was too afraid to share this with. I contemplated leaving but I stopped myself. Jaya's welfare was more important than my fear. I turned back to Elijah and continued.

"When I was younger, I was in and out of foster care. My mother was a drug addict. When I was a teenager, Alonzo took me and took care of me and he gave me an opportunity to earn money."

Ace began to laugh. Elijah and both looked over at him and he met my gaze. "Sharmayne, you make me sound so noble and you so innocent. Tell him what you did Sharmayne."

I ignored him and returned my attention to Elijah who now seemed intrigued and looked between Ace and me. "At first, I washed dishes and helped the cook, and Ace paid me under the table. Once I had finished high school and started attending, college, majoring in law, Alonzo offered me the chance to earn more to help me pay for school." I lowered my face, a bit ashamed of continuing the story. "I became a dancer. I stripped at his club and performed at private parties."

Elijah's gaze darted to Ace's before returning to mine. "Was she there?" He asked Ace. Ace leaned his head back against the couch and closed his eyes, ignoring Elijah's question, a smile on his face.

"If you are asking, was I one of the strippers at your bachelor party, yes. I was." Elijah covered his face with his hand. "Alonzo had hired me specifically to entertain you, while the other girls entertained your friends. I am the woman you had sex with that night."

Elijah rushed closer to me, his voice in an aggravated whisper. "I don't know why you are here telling me this now but that was the past and the biggest mistake of my life. My wife is upstairs sick. Leave. Now." He tried to push me out the door.

I shook my head no, pleading for him to finish hearing me out. "No, please. I need to finish talking to you. It's a matter of life and death."

A soft voice from behind him startled me. "Please don't go. I'd like to hear the rest of your story."

Elijah's eyes closed slowly, and I could feel his distress. I felt guilty for bringing this to his home, but I was desperate for a solution, and if this was what I had to do, so be it. Over the years, I'd not bothered him once regarding Jaya. I had kept my promise to never tell a soul about that night and had Jaya not been terminally ill, I never would have. But I would not stand by and watch my daughter die to save Elijah's distress. I looked behind him and saw a pale-faced, slender woman, her eyes glassy, straggling toward us.

"What do you need to tell my husband that is so important?"

I stepped out from in front of Elijah and made her my audience. At this point, I didn't care who heard it, but someone needed to. "I am so sorry to bring this news to you. I know it seems like I'm here to cause you trouble but I'm not. I have a daughter. She'll be two years old in a few months and she is sick. She has an aggressive form of Leukemia. The chemotherapy she received did not help so she needs a bone marrow transplant. There are currently no donor matches for her." I began to cry vocalizing the severity of Jaya's situation. "She's the most beautiful and sweet little girl."

Elijah, now angry again, practically shouted, "What does that have to do with me?"

"The best donor match is a sibling. I saw you with your son at the Crown Plaza and wanted to beg for your help."

Elijah shook his head at me frustrated. "My son? What does my son have to do with your daughter?"

Alonzo rose to his feet and interrupted me. He grabbed me by the arm, shaking me as if I were his troublemaking child. "What do you mean my daughter is sick. Bitch, why didn't you tell me! You should have told me!"

I pushed Ace off me, and in his battered state, he fell back then tumbled over. "She is not your daughter, Ace." I looked at Elijah, facing him with a truth I wanted to take to the grave. "She's Elijah's."

"Elijah's?" His wife asked breathlessly.

Elijah grabbed my arms and began to shake me furiously. "What is wrong with you? Why are you coming here and lying? Did my uncle put you up to this?"

He released me, then grabbed Ace by his coat and pulled him up to his feet. "Why? Why did you put her up to this?"

Ace swung on Elijah, catching his jaw. Elijah stumbled to the floor. "Everything that is mine, you always have to have it," Ace said as he towered over his nephew and I could see the hatred in his eyes. "I hate you." Ace pointed at me. "And I hate her." As Elijah tried to stand, Ace kicked him back down. "See?" He chuckled. "God hates you too. He will never let your seed multiply. Here's another one of yours that won't survive because you are cursed. Just as I was cursed and my father was cursed. You aren't any better than me in your suburban house with your white neighbors and sweater vests. You a hood nigga just like me."

Elijah didn't combat his uncle in words or flesh. Ace looked down on him and spat in his hair. He then turned to me and approached me slowly. He grabbed me by the throat and squeezed. "I was the one who looked out for you when your mom abandoned your raggedy ass. I was the one who loved you and fed you and took care of you. Even when you stole my money, I didn't kill you. You deserve every bad thing that happens to you, you fucking whore." He pushed me so hard, I fell into a side table nearby. "This ain't over," he threatened before he swung the door open and walked out.

Elijah's wife stood nearby looking shellshocked before she fell to her knees and broke down. Elijah was in his own state of disillusion before he looked over at his wife sobbing in the quietude. He made his way over to her on his knees and tried to console her. "Tianna, baby. Please, it's not what you think."

She pushed him away and tried to stand before she stumbled back down. I watched her and she seemed off to me. I'd seen women in this state before but I didn't want to assume or get myself more involved in their lives. I'd already thrown a bomb into their house and my only business here revolved around Jaya.

I wrote my phone number on a piece of paper. "I know this is all a shock to you, but please believe me that I wouldn't have come if it wasn't urgent. My daughter is dying. Please consider having your son tested to see if he is a match."

Elijah's wife began to laugh hysterically. "His son? You came here with your sob story, not caring who's home you wrecked. Not caring whose fiancée you fucked, and whose marriage you destroyed, all for my son. Well bitch, it was all in vain. My son, yes my son, is not Elijah's biological son." She laughed again before she began weeping.

My heart shattered. "Not his son?" I turned to Elijah. "What does she mean, not your son?" I lowered myself to the floor and looked him in the face. He shook his head at me. "But I saw you with him with you at the Crowne Plaza. He was wearing a soccer uniform. That's how I found him. And you." I grabbed Elijah by his shirt and began to shake him, crying uncontrollably. "He has to be your son! Jaya needs a bone marrow transplant! My baby can't die!"

Elijah gripped my wrists and yanked me free from his shirt, angry tears streaming down his face. "He is not my biological son. Please leave."

His voice was barely above a whisper but his words resounded in my ears. I let my hands fall to my knees in a heap.

I looked around me feeling defeated. Three adults all sat weeping, on a bed of broken glass and a shattered mirror, an ironic reflection of our hearts.

TWENTY-SIX

Elijah

The rollercoaster of emotions I found myself on was making me dizzy. I didn't know what to process first. I had a daughter. She was dying. My wife just found out I cheated on her. My mother was an alcoholic in recovery. My uncle harbored hate for me for most of my life. It sounded ridiculous in my head and yet here I sat on my living floor between two women who had equally held all I ever wanted in this world and with the aftertaste of a sad past in my mouth.

I needed to man up and do what I had to do. Right now Tianna was my immediate priority. She didn't look well and with her history of depression and anxiety, I needed to make sure my wife was ok. I neared her and dusted off the shards of glass and mirror on her hands. She was bleeding but didn't seem to care. "Ti, baby. Stand up. You are cutting yourself." I took her hand to help her up, but she pushed it away.

"Don't touch me." Her voice was weak and strained. I could hear her anguish and my heart broke knowing how much I'd hurt her.

I'd explain everything to her, but first I needed to get her off the floor. "I know you hate me right now. I understand that, but please just let me take you upstairs so you can rest. You look exhausted."

Silently, she began to crawl to the stairs over the broken mirror, not even wincing from the pain the shards should cause. I'd seen this side of her before. It was the beginning of her shutting down and going numb. She'd become a zombie to protect herself and avoid feeling pain. The problem was, she'd shut down so completely, she wouldn't feel anything at all. Not love or joy. Not hunger. Not physical pain. Nothing.

At the bottom of the stairs, she fell over to the side and just lay there. I rushed to her side. "Tianna?" I rolled her over. She was still conscious but pale and weak.

"I'm very tired." She promptly passed out.

I tried to wake her. "Tianna? Tianna?" The woman who'd claimed I was the father of her child, made her way over to us, her face streaked with dry tears and her expression grief-stricken, but I couldn't find it in me to feel bad for her. I looked up at her too mentally exhausted to deal with her. "I told you to leave."

"She was probably drugged. You should take her to the emergency room."

Was anything that ever came out of this woman's mouth, not gloom and doom? I didn't know whether to believe her or not. "What do you mean she was drugged?"

"When I was a dancer, I saw it all the time."

I looked at Tianna trying not to panic at her state of disorientation. "That's not possible. The only place she's been is at my family's Thanksgiving dinner. She wouldn't have gotten drugged there."

The woman chuckled humorlessly. "You still don't get it, do you? Your uncle is an evil man. I wouldn't be surprised if he came here just to personally see if she was ok."

No matter how much Alonzo hated me, I couldn't accept that he'd intentionally try to hurt Tianna. "He wouldn't drug my wife." I tried to revive her again. "Tianna? Ti? Wake up, baby."

"He drugged you."

There was nothing crazier in the world that she could have said to me. And yet I did not dismiss it. "What the hell are you talking about?"

"Ace had specifically asked me to be your dancer." She hesitated and I could see her struggling to say what she wanted to. She began to speak again but didn't meet her eyes. "He asked me to drug you and sleep with you. He said if I did this for him, he would never prostitute me again and I could just be his girl. I did not want to be a prostitute so I agreed."

As the rage inside of me rose, so did I. I stood before her, only mere inches from her person. "Did you just say you drugged me?" She didn't respond and fortified her stance although I could see her trying to hide her trembling. I began to laugh, the humiliation too much to withstand. "You drugged and raped me." I clapped and laughed harder.

"I didn't rape you," she said now facing me. "I was drunk too. I did take you into your hotel room but you were the one all over me. You kept calling me by a woman's name. I am not a prostitute! I left the money because, a one-night stand I could live with, but prostitution, I couldn't. I told Ace that I did what he asked but didn't tell him that I left the money. And I didn't take the pictures he wanted either. I told him someone stole the camera before I had a chance to get the photos. I left you a note hoping you wouldn't say anything to him. I didn't expect to get pregnant. As soon as I found out, I ran away from Ace and have raised my daughter the best way I could. I promised you I would keep your secret and I held to that." She wrapped her arms around herself looking pathetic and sad.

"Am I supposed to thank you for that? Am I supposed to thank you for trying to frame me? For not even having the decency to protect me with a damn condom, knowing I wasn't in the right state of my mind? For having my child and not telling me about her? For only coming to tell me because now she is sick? For robbing me of the small amount of time, she has been alive? Am I supposed to thank you for any of that?" I roared my emotions overflowing like an unwatched boiling pot. I unleashed and unleashed some more, yelling every word. "Am I supposed to feel sorry for you? I don't feel sorry for you! Get the fuck out of my house!"

She shook in fear before she began to cry and fled from the house. Tianna began to groan. I quickly dried my tears, picked her up, and drove her to the emergency room hoping she was okay and thinking of how I was going to deal with my uncle. But first, I had to get my wife some medical attention. I didn't want to even think about my marriage being in critical condition with a small chance of survival.

TWENTY-SEVEN

Tianna

After assuring *Mami* I was ok in the emergency room, I hung up with her. She had agreed to keep Jay overnight and to save me some Thanksgiving redo leftovers. I said ok to appease her, but I had had no appetite and the mention of food make my stomach churn.

I stared up at the emergency room ceiling trying not to fall apart. Every time Elijah walked in, I pretended to be asleep. It was immature and cowardly even, but I felt like I was on the verge of erupting so I suppressed it. I didn't want to cry another tear, or ask why, or talk about it. I heard footsteps and peeked to see if Elijah had returned, but instead, it was the doctor.

"How's the patient feeling?" She picked up my chart and began to read so I didn't offer a response. Why ask me a question you wouldn't even give me the courtesy to listen to? I turned and faced the blood pressure stand beside me. "Christianna?" She called. I faced her giving her my attention but remained silent. "The results of some of your tests came back."

Elijah walked in as she was speaking. He looked at me, anguish written all over his face but it didn't move me. Seeing him started my hamster wheel of emotions. I was heartbroken by his betrayal and astonished at his deceit for years. And although he didn't know he had a child, I was embittered toward him for having a child with someone else. It wasn't logical. It wasn't fair. It was selfish. It was immature. Yet, I couldn't and wouldn't talk myself into being reasonable because no matter who, where, when, or why, Elijah slept with another woman. My husband fathered a child that wasn't mine.

I was not ok. I wasn't going to pretend to be ok. I didn't want to see or talk to him. I hated him. I was mad at myself for loving him. In front of me, I saw nothing but a lie. Everything I thought we had was a lie.

My entire marriage was a lie built upon a faulty foundation and truth came and rammed a wrecking ball into it.

The doctor followed my gaze and turned in his direction. She stopped discussing my results. "Christianna is ok to discuss your results now?"

Elijah spoke up, just when I had. "Yes, I am her husband.

"No, I'd like privacy."

Elijah's eyes pleaded on his behalf as his words failed him when all he could do was utter my name. "Tianna."

"I don't want you here. And when I get home, I don't want you there either. Get out." He shook his head in understanding before he walked out from my curtained-off area.

The doctor walked him out from my sanctioned area then returned confirming he'd left the emergency room. She didn't waste any time getting back to task. "Your results came back. There were no traces of any narcotic drugs."

I was relieved but still lost. "Then what is wrong with me?"

"It seems to be a combination of food poisoning and pregnancy. And perhaps a little too much to drink last night?"

Embarrassing. "I am not a drinker and did have a few drinks last night."

"That would do it. I would urge you to refrain from alcohol while you are pregnant. Excessive consumption has been linked to birth defects."

"I didn't know I was pregnant until earlier today." Just saying it aloud broke my heart but I was going to try to fight the urge to go to the dark side that was calling out to me. I wanted to drag myself into inner hibernation and close off everything and everyone to dwell in numbness. Yet, I'd known all too well that being so severely depressed was a scary and lonely place. As ironic as it seemed, I preferred to feel pain with the hope that I'd one day again feel joy, rather than feel nothing.

I needed to feel love for my son. He needed his mother's love. It wasn't enough to know I was supposed to love him or that memory served to remind me that I did. No. I needed to feel every ounce of love for him. People often feel lonely when they don't feel loved, but nothing is worse than not feeling love for anyone at all. If hell was a feeling, that was it. It was after many doubts of suffering those numbing episodes that I learned that God is love and an existence without God was hell; no flames, fire, torture, or Satan needed.

When I returned home, Elijah's car was in the driveway. I paid the cab driver and entered the house quietly. The voices of NBA commentators greeted my ears. I guess my request for him to leave went in one and out the other. I had planned on cleaning up the mess, but it had already been done so I headed for the stairs.

"Tianna."

He startled me. I was hoping he hadn't noticed I was home but I kept walking pretending he wasn't.

"Tianna."

He was closer this time and I began to ascend the stairs quickly. I made it to the bedroom and almost had the door closed before he unexpectedly pushed it open.

"Tianna. We have to talk."

"I have already heard more than enough. But thank you."

"Stop it. I didn't do it intentionally."

I about-faced, angrily. "So your penis just fell into her vagina without your participation? Let me guess. She cut open your balls and scooped out some semen and got herself pregnant."

"You are being ridiculous! I'm telling you the truth. I don't even remember any of it. I only remember waking up the next morning to a note and very fuzzy memories."

"So you knew you slept with someone that wasn't me and you didn't tell me. You kept that from me for years."

"I never planned that and I didn't tell you because I didn't want to hurt you over someone who meant nothing, and who I didn't even know."

"Well, your unplanned cheating got a woman pregnant with your child. So you had unprotected sex with her?"

He couldn't even look at me at this point. "Yes," he said barely above a whisper. "But you are making it sound like I looked for it. I didn't."

I ignored his pleading. "You then have the audacity to come and have unprotected sex with the wife after having unprotected sex with a prostitute." I let out a humorless laugh. "Honorable man, my ass."

"Tianna, stop it. Please believe me. It's not like it seems. I have always been honest with you. Since you have been my wife, I have never done anything but honor you and be a good husband."

"Honest with me? A good husband?" I took a step back to control myself. "Honest with me," I repeated and laughed. "You have been lying to me for years. How could you look me in the face and even dare to call yourself honest? I don't believe anything you say now. I trust none of it and none of you. You are a liar and a cheater. You disgust me. Now leave."

He shook his head and tightened his lips, his fisted hands on his hips as he looked down at the floor before him. "I'm not going anywhere and we are going to work this out because that's what married couples do. We work through our problems. There is no quitting, Tianna."

"Ok. You aren't leaving? That's fine. Jay and I will."

"Like hell you are. You are not going anywhere and you are not taking my son anywhere."

My killswitch was activated and I found myself extremely calm. I took one step closer to him and looked him in the eyes. "You made the bed, but I don't have to sleep in it. It seems you are doing a great job finding someone else to do that already. And Jay is *my* son. Mine. You have the child you always wanted. Congratulations, Daddy."

I disappeared into Jay's bedroom despite Elijah's protest to be heard. I locked the door behind me. No tears. No hurt. I felt nothing. And for the moment, I wanted to feel nothing. I rested in his twin bed and thought out my immediate plan for my future. That was interrupted by a few rounds of vomiting. Once that nausea subsided, I felt a little rejuvenated and began to pack Jay's clothes.

After an hour I emerged from Jay's bedroom and found mine empty. I packed my clothes and made a few phone calls before I sat at my computer and found two one-way airline tickets leaving the following afternoon. After Elijah had fallen asleep, I snuck our luggage into the car. The following morning I dressed for Sunday service as usual and left before Elijah had. I grabbed Jay before *Mami* had set out for her church service. I made Jay give her lots of hugs and kisses before we left. She had no idea we were leaving. No one had.

Every five minutes Jay would ask a question. His excitement was cute at first and then I began wondering if I was about to lose my mind.

"Mommy, are we getting on a plane?"

"Yes, we are."

"Mommy, where are we going?"

"Away."

"Mommy, are we going to see Mickey Mouse?"

I laughed. "No. But we are going to see someone better."

"Who?"

"You'll see."

"Mommy, where is Daddy?"

"At home."

"Is he coming?"

"No."

"Mommy, I miss Daddy. I want him to come. Can we call him?"

"Not right now."

"Later?"

"Jay. Enough with asking me a million questions."

"But Mommy—"

"Jay. I said 'Enough'.

He pouted and sat his rear end in the terminal seat, quiet for a while. Once we boarded the plane, he looked out the window and started the questions all over again. I pulled out a coloring book and crayons that entertained him for a while before he fell asleep for a while on the long flight. By the time we landed, it was still evening in California.

We got our luggage at baggage claim and walked outside. It took only thirty seconds before I heard shrieking.

"Ti! Ti! Ti! Ahhh!"

Jay slid his little hand into mine and pressed closer to me. "Mommy who is screaming like that?"

I saw a petite woman with a large, red bun of curls atop her head waving her hands in the air as if she belonged on the tarmac instead out here. She looked both ways before she crossed, heading directly toward us still waving and screaming.

"No. That can't be—"

"Momma B!" Jay dropped my hand and dashed ahead of me into the arms of the redhead. She picked him up, smothering him with kisses. Jay laughed and hugged her, equally excited as she was.

Tears came to my eyes seeing my best friend and sister of the heart. I walked toward them and allowed them their reunion uninterrupted. She finally set him down on his feet and faced me.

"Red hair. You could've warned me."

"Coming all the way to Cali on one day's notice. Now we're even," she grinned.

I tried to be happy at the moment of seeing Bianca after so long, but I was an emotional wreck and I couldn't hold back the tears for another minute. A six-hour flight with nothing to do but think and vomit had taken its toll on me.

We hugged. "Whatever it is, we'll figure it out," she assured me.

Once we got to her house she warmed up the spaghetti she had made Jay. Bianca's spaghetti was his favorite and after a bowl of ice cream, he was fast asleep.

"I'm sorry we barged in on you but I didn't know where else to go." With Jay being up Bianca's butt since we'd arrived, she and I hadn't gotten around to discussing why I was seeking refuge. I feared if I would've told her over the phone she would not have welcomed me and more than anything I needed to leave Jersey.

She looked over at me offering me a sad smile as she dried the dishes and put them away. "Why did you need to go anywhere other than home?"

On the flight, I thought about how I'd tell her and decided to be completely honest. And so I did. She remained quiet as I spoke. Until I got quiet.

"So no one knows you are pregnant or that you are here?"

I shook my head caught between feeling ashamed and feeling justified. Bianca picked up the phone and handed it to me. "Call El and tell him you are here. You don't have to tell him you are pregnant tonight but don't make your family worry sick over you."

I shook my head, tears brimming my eyes.

"Yes." She insisted. "I'm going to go shower and put my pajamas on, then we can talk some more if you want."

I dialed the house number and it rang twice before El answered it. "Hello." His voice was alert although it was past midnight.

"I'm in California with Bianca. Jay and I are safe."

"I have been worried sick about you. I thought you were at your mother's but she called to speak with you and said she hadn't seen you since you picked up Jay."

"We're fine. Goodbye."

"Tianna, please wait."

I hung up. I had no desire to speak with him. The phone rang a few seconds later. "Hello."

"Please come home."

I hung up again. He didn't call back and I was glad for it. I just needed time and space to think. I got comfortable on the couch and Bianca emerged from her bedroom. "Did you call?"

"Yes."

"And?"

"I don't want to talk to him, B."

"Ok. I understand. It's all very fresh and you must be overwhelmed. I'm gonna pour me a drink and you are getting a glass of water." I laughed for the first time in days.

We talked all night. Not just about Elijah and my marital problems but also about Sabrina and Tay. Bianca threatened to beat their asses more times than I could count and she meant it every time. We talked about Jay and reminisced about Justin. My mom and her dad.

"How's Abe?"

"He's good. Still doing martial arts. Still dating flavors of the month." Bianca cracked up. "If I told him I was here, I could guarantee you that he'd make a slick flirty remark that he wouldn't dare say to your face." I smiled thinking of the dorky look on my brother's face when he was trying to be smooth.

"Did I ever tell you he asked me out?"

My face turned red on Abe's behalf. "Uh, no! When the hell did that happen and why didn't I know about it?"

"At the party after Lil Man's Christening. I think he was drunk."

I vaguely remembered Abe drunk and *Mami* threatening his life. Pop saved him. "*Mami* almost choked him when he told Pastor Carstarphen that he was 'cool as hell' and asked him if he wanted to take a shot."

Bianca cracked up. "I figured he wasn't in his right state of mind."

"Not at all. I will say though that my baby brother has grown up. Jay loves him so much. He's closer to his uncle than anyone else."

Bianca's smile waned. "Have you seen Jordi? How is he with Lil Man?"

I shook my head. "He hasn't seen him in two years. Ever since Mrs. Saunders moved away, he stopped taking my calls. Jay still talks to his grandmother every Saturday morning though.

"That's good." She spun her glass, fidgeting with it and I could tell she was in deep thought. "Justin would be so sad to know that Jordi isn't in his son's life."

"I've tried B. I really have."

She shook her head and assured me she understood. "Jordi is an adult and he knows what he promised his brother. I know you don't hinder their relationship. He shouldn't let anything stop him from keeping his brother's memory alive and carrying on the legacy of their namesake."

It saddened me to think about Justin's family. He was considered the good son and tragically lost his life for simply being a black man in a white neighborhood. It had been a long time since I'd allowed myself to grieve the injustice of Justin's life being taken from him. I supposed being pregnant elevated my hormones because all of my emotions were at the surface and I could cry without much prompting.

Bianca saw the tears streaming down my face and quickly wiped hers away. I knew she still grieved the loss of her fiancee but had found happiness again. I wiped my tears as she wiped hers. "You're such a prego," she joked.

"Well, what's your excuse?"

She lifted her cup. "Alcohol."

We laughed and laughed. "So where's your boyfriend?"

"San Francisco visiting his parents. His mother sprained her ankle, so he went to help for a week or two."

"Why didn't you go?"

"Because it wasn't a planned trip and I'm on shift. Plus, I don't want to spend a few weeks with his mother," she joked. "Speaking of mothers."

"Oh, we are not going to talk about Marvette. I feel sick enough."

For another hour we laughed and joked before we went to bed. One night turned into a week. Bianca's boyfriend returned so she stayed with him and let Jay and I stay at her place. A week turned into two, then three, and I began mentally planning to move to San Diego permanently.

TWENTY-EIGHT

Micah

After Sharmayne finished her phone call, I eyed her waiting for an explanation of what was going on. Ever since she had confessed she had gone off that day in search of Jaya's biological father, that was not Ace, as she had let me believe, I looked at her differently. I didn't trust my wife and I questioned everything she did and everywhere she went. What else hadn't I known about? What other secrets was she keeping?

She had admitted that Ace had wanted her to be a high-class call girl but other than Jaya's sperm donor, she had never taken any clients; as if I could really believe that. What the hell were the chances of her getting pregnant by her one and only time prostituting herself? She tried to run that game on me about not getting paid meant not technically selling yourself for money. I wasn't buying that bullshit though. If a man intended to shoot another man to death, but the man didn't die after being shot, that doesn't change the fact that he intended to kill him.

She walked into the living room with her hands on her hips. "That was Elijah, Jaya's biological father. He wants to visit her."

"Absolutely not." I stood to my feet and walked past her like she had lost her damn mind.

"Micah. Be reasonable."

I spun on my heel ready to explode. "Reasonable? How I am being unreasonable? I do not want a strange man in my house around my daughter. How do I even know that this man is her real father?" She raised an eyebrow and I knew she was about to go off.

"That is now the second and the last time you will refer to me as a whore, prostitute, gold-digger, or anything other than your wife. You knew who I was when I was younger and before we got married. And I already told you I was never a hooker. You will respect who you

192

married. Not once, have I ever thrown in your face what you did before you went legit. And since marrying you, I have given you the respect you have earned. And not because you are legit now, but because you are a good father, husband, and provider."

I knew she was right but my pride wouldn't let go. I couldn't help but think she played me. The fool who turned a hoe into a housewife, and now pregnant. Even if I wanted to leave, I'd be tied to her forever. I ran my hands up and down over my face in frustration. Rather than get into an argument I left, checked in on one of my properties then stopped by my mother's place. She was prepping dinner for Auntie Rose.

"Hey. I wasn't expecting you. How's my beautiful girl?"

"Past few days she's been good. You wouldn't even know she is sick."

"That's good. Real good." My mom opened her cabinet in search of a storage container. She found a few but none of the lids matched. She summoned me over and pointed to the top shelf she didn't reach. "Grab those up there for me."

"Why do you put them up there if you can't reach them?" I complained but brought them down. She ignored me after I handed them over. "And Sharmayne? How's she holding up?" She found a lid and began ladling soup into a storage bowl.

"Your guess is as good as mine." I sat at the kitchen table and fiddled with the small, fat chef salt and pepper shakers.

"What's that supposed to mean?"

I began to think about how much I didn't know my wife. Truthfully, how much neither one of us didn't really know each other. We'd gotten married way too fast but what was done was done. I wasn't going to leave her but I'd be damned if she thought I was just going to sit in my own house and watch as she and whoever Jaya's clown biological played happy family.

My mom snatched the salt shaker out of my hands. I hadn't even realized I had been gripping it so tightly. "Stop molesting my salt and pepper shakers.' She moved them to the counter next to the sink.

"I'm sorry. I was just thinking about something."

"Clearly. Wanna share what had you looking like you want to punch someone?" She put a lid over the soup left in the pot and sat in the chair across from me, drying her hands with a hand towel.

I shook my head. I didn't want my mom to know my business. It was embarrassing enough.

"I've never been married so I can't give you advice about that, but I am a mother I can tell you that a good mother would do anything for their kids. I don't expect you to understand that, but think about how much you love Jaya. Wouldn't you do anything to save and protect her?"

"Of course, I would. Why would you even ask me that?"

"So then, how much more do you think her mother, who carried her for nine months and has been with her every day of her life would do to save her?"

I knew my mom was right logically but my pride wouldn't let me support my wife's decisions, especially because of how she'd gone about it all. She should have told me before she went to a man's house to ask him for anything for our daughter. The day she agreed to be my wife and since, we became a family. Jaya became my daughter in all the ways that mattered. Yet when shit hit the fan I wasn't even included in the decisions that affected our family. And because some clown paid to have sex with Shar, not even having the decency to wear a condom, he got to play a role in her life with one phone call? He got to decide what happened to my daughter? Every time I thought about it, it pissed me off.

"Son, cut her some slack. She is doing what she thinks is best."

"As my mother, how could you sit there and think my wife clowning me is ok? That's bullshit!" I stood up frustrated, ready to bolt. The last thing I needed was my mom choosing my wife's side.

"Sit down, and don't you talk to me like that." My mom looked up at me, her eyes narrowed.

"No. I'm a grown-ass man. Not some little boy."

She stood and approached me. "A grown-ass man in my house, won't ever disrespect his mother in her house."

"This is my house! This is my building! I let you live here! Don't get that twisted!" I felt the slap to my face and it stung.

"I don't care if you own the entire earth, don't you ever disrespect or raise your voice at me like that again. How dare you throw in my face all the things you've done for me as if I'd asked you for any of it? You asked me to live here. That was a favor to you. And if you are keeping score of who's done what for who, let me remind you that I wiped the shit off your ass when you were a baby and the blood off your face when you were a man. I've fed you baby food as a child and made you ribs as an adult. I've held your hand as a little boy walking to school and that same hand on your way into the emergency room just several months ago. I am your mother, so to me, all of that is what I am supposed to do. I don't tally it up as a bill and then toss it in your face when you get on my nerves, asking you to pay up or acknowledge me.

"I don't need to get in your marital business because that is between you and the wife you chose. No one chose her but you. You reap what you sow. But may I remind you, she was the woman by your side when you couldn't even lift your arms to feed yourself. She was the woman that refused your help because she wanted to pay her bills on her own. She didn't ask you to invite her into your life. You moved her into your house. You put yourself on this path. You so steady talking about owning this building, how bout you own your decisions. That woman even went as far as to ask that piece of shit Ace, for help so she could pay the rent she owed you."

My eyes darted to my mother's.

"Yeah, I know all about that. Don't nothing stay secret long in these streets. And I know what you did to help her. You so steady worried about looking like this and people talking about you like that, while your wife is thinking of how to save her child's life. She doesn't give a fuck what anyone thinks about her. She ain't got time for it. And I respect her for that. I'm not saying I agree with how she handled certain things, but all she knows is how to take care of herself and Jaya, no matter what. Rather than sit here moping, go show her you are someone she can rely on. Go be the daddy you always bragging you are. Son, right now there are things more important than who Sharmayne had sex with two, three, five years ago. Go home and be with your family because you don't know how long you will have that privilege. Time is precious." She gave me her back and put the lid on the soup she's ladled before placing it in a plastic bag. "Please drop this off at Auntie's on your way home."

I remained quiet and took the soup she gave me. What could I say? She served herself some soup and sat down to eat it. I kissed her on the top of her head and left without a word. She was right but in my stubbornness and pride, I couldn't bring myself to tell her.

I stopped at Auntie's house and gave her the soup. She talked my ear off for twenty minutes before she chewed me out for not coming to visit her more often. I kissed her on the head too and bounced. The women in my life were causing me too much stress. I spent the rest of the day and long into the evening working in my third flip property alone. The way my money was looking, I had to take on a lot of the labor myself and only call the Mendez boys in on specific jobs that required more than one person or was beyond my scope of skill.

By the time I made it home, Shar was in bed and Jaya was asleep. I showered and found a plate of food in the microwave for me. I warmed it up and ate. I stayed at the dining table in deep thought about my finances. Medical bills had started to come in. I was able to pay the first few with no issues. Shar had started a payment plan with the ones that were too high to pay in full. I hadn't told her how low the account was and she never asked.

She took whatever I gave her to make the household run and wouldn't ask for a dime more. Sometimes, she'd even stretch it farther than I had anticipated. She was used to making pennies stretch. I felt anxiety welling up inside of me. I didn't want her to have to stretch pennies. I felt incompetent and like I was failing my family.

I heard her before I saw her. She held onto the railing as she descended the staircase, her feet encased in fuzzy slippers. She got to the bottom step and retied her robe. "What are you doing down here all alone?"

"I just got home a little while ago. Showered and ate dinner. Thank you for leaving a plate aside for me."

"There are leftovers in the fridge. Do you want some more?"

I shook my head. All I wanted was my happy family back. Shar walked over to me and stood in front of me. She ran her hands over my head and tilted my chin up to look at her.

"You are my husband and I am your wife. Jaya is our daughter. No one comes before that. No one."

I untied her robe, lifted her shirt, and kissed her belly which had begun to protrude. My child was in there. I needed to remember that when I chose to become a husband, I chose to make Shar and Jaya my world and I was responsible for them, even in Shar's mistakes. I was their keeper. If she messed up, it was my job to help her fix it and provide the safe boundaries in which she was to operate. I didn't want to control her. She was her own person, but I needed to keep her safe, even from herself. Sometimes that would require her to be still, stay put, and rely on me as her partner. We were supposed to be a team.

"Shar, I need you to remember that too. Y'all are my family. It is my job to provide and protect. You are not living your life alone anymore. You can't go off making decisions for our family on your own."

"I will do whatever I have to do for Jaya, Micah."

"And you need to trust that I will too. We will together. I love that little girl as if she were my own, Shar. I want to do whatever we can for her. But we gotta be a team. We got enough going on as is without us being at odds."

She nodded but I could see the fear of relinquishing control of her independence and it saddened me. After all this time, she still didn't trust me to do what was best for her and Jaya. I ignored my intuition and took her nod as confirmation that she was on board with us tackling life together. For now, that would have to do.

"Elijah will be here the day after tomorrow to meet Jaya. He donated bone marrow. I doubt it's a match, but it's worth a try."

I nodded and avoided an argument about not agreeing before she invited a man into my house. It was about Jaya, not me. But that nigga had another thing coming if he thought he was coming to claim a daddy position that was already filled. No matter what, Moochie was my baby girl.

TWENTY-NINE

Elijah

I wrapped Tianna and Champ's gifts and placed them under the tree. She'd be back for Christmas. There was no way she'd not be home to spend Christmas with her parents. I told myself that every time I purchased her a gift. I needed to stay positive.

I slipped on my coat and picked up the large, wrapped box I'd left by the door. I don't know why I was nervous to meet a two-year-old, but by the time I'd arrived at Sharmayne's door, my hands were shaking. I knocked and exhaled before she answered the door. She looked as uncomfortable as I felt.

"Hey. Please come in," she said. "I just finished bathing her. She had a spaghetti mishap."

I grinned. "Does she like spaghetti?"

"She likes to play in spaghetti if that's what you mean?"

I stepped aside as she closed the door. "My son loves spaghetti." I had a quick mental picture of Jay telling Ti that Bianca's spaghetti was better but still eating every bite. My heart ached. I missed him so much it made me choke up. I changed the subject for my sake as much as hers. She eyed me as if she knew I was dying inside. I handed her the gift. "Thank you for letting me meet Jaya. I hope you don't mind, but I bought her a gift."

Sharmayne accepted the gift. "You didn't have to do that."

"Of course I did. I have two years of catching up to do with her." Sharmayne looked at me and I could tell she was embarrassed but I had no intention of adding to her guilt no matter how much she deserved it. After being without Tianna and Jay for a week, I had learned to let go of all my strife. Life was too precious to waste. I made amends with Sharmayne and asked to meet my daughter. I had donated my bone marrow and as Sharmayne had warned me was possible, I wasn't a match. But that didn't mean I was going to just fall to the wayside. I had a child that I didn't know I needed to fix that.

A bearded and fierce-looking man came down the stairs presumably with Jaya in his arm. She wore a red and gold outfit, her head resting on his shoulder. Sharmayne introduced us.

"Micah this is Elijah Townsend, Jaya's biological father. Elijah, this is my husband, Micah." Sharmayne tugged at Jaya's shirt that had gotten stuck under Micah's arm, exposing her belly, smoothing out her top, and covering her up. He nodded at me but said nothing.

"Nice to meet you," I replied but when I looked upon her, I lost all interest in who else was in the room. She had lost all of her hair due to treatment but it had begun to grow back. Despite her baldness, I saw my face in hers. She had Sharmayne's eyes but everything else was Townsend. I was fascinated with her. Sharmayne cleared her throat and I realized I had been staring.

"Jah Jah. Look. A present for you."

She looked at her mother and didn't budge. I could tell right away she was a daddy's girl. I felt a tinge of jealousy I wasn't that particular daddy. I had been cheated out of that privilege but what was done, was done and now I could only use the time that I had as best as I could. My focus was on my daughter and I wouldn't spend the limited time in her presence angry and bitter. Micah passed Jaya to Sharmayne. "I gotta go check in on the house. I'll be back in an hour."

"Oh. I thought you had already gone this morning." Shar received Jaya and put her down on the floor, eyeing her husband, unspoken words being communicated between them. If I had to guess, Shar didn't want to be alone with just the baby and me, and Micah didn't want to be here with the baby and me. He'd given me an hour to be up out of his house if I was reading the situation correctly.

I wasn't going to overstay my welcome. I wanted to ease into the transition for Jaya's sake. Yet, I also knew time wasn't working in my favor. I hated thinking she wasn't going to live much longer, but I couldn't ignore the fact that her prognosis hadn't been good and her options were very limited.

I lost focus of the married couple and paid attention to the beautiful little girl on the floor fussing for Micah to pick her back up. He had said a few words to Shar that I hadn't been paying attention to but when he bent down to kiss Jaya goodbye, I could see he wasn't in a good mood. I pretended not to notice when he disappeared out the front door and Shar huffed.

Jaya began to cry and Shar tried to calm her. She sat on the floor and brought the box closer to her. Jah-Jah, come look. Let's see what Elijah bought for you. Jaya whined a little more before she sat on Shar's lap and laid back against her. I sat on the couch nearby and watched her. It didn't matter if she opened the gift or not. I just wanted to be near her.

Shar tore the corner of the wrapping paper urging Jaya to tear the rest, but she whined, not wanting to open the gift. "I'm sorry. She is feeling sick today. She was doing well for a few days but this morning she woke up with a fever. She's been a little cranky."

"That's understandable." I didn't want to force her to do anything except beat cancer. I wish I had had the authority to do that.

Shar opened the gift and Jaya just stared at the box. It was a pink ride-on car, she could scoot herself around on. Now that I thought about it, that was probably the worst gift. I had no idea how much energy she had or if she shouldn't be scooting. Tianna would have known the perfect gift to buy her. But then again asking my wife to purchase for an illegitimate child born while we were married was selfish and inconsiderate.

Jaya eyed the box and I wondered if she was intrigued. "Do you mind if I put it together for her?" I asked, needing something to do to feel useful.

"Yeah, sure," she said probably just as relieved that she wouldn't have to entertain me.

I sat on the floor, opened the box, and assembled it. It took all of ten minutes. Aligning the little stickers that looked like headlights and the windshield had been the hardest part. The left tail light was a little crooked but it wasn't too bad for my first time. Jaya had watched me the entire time I was pimping her ride. After I was done, I pushed the car toward her. "Hop on. Take her for a spin. Stay under the speed limit though."

She looked at me as if I were crazy. A two-year-old was doing a banged-up job of making me feel mad stupid. Sharmayne turned around so I wouldn't see her laughing at me.

She took Jaya off her lap and tried to motivate her. "Come on Jah-Jah! Let's take a ride." Shar stood up and pulled the car closer. She picked Jaya up and sat her atop of it. Jaya just looked down at it confused. Shar put a hand to her back to steady her and began pushing her slowly. At first, Jaya just sat there like a bump on a log. Shar stopped pushing and stood erect holding her back. "That's a backbreaker," she joked.

"I'm sorry. I didn't think this out. I should have bought her something a little easier."

"Oh no, it's fine. She likes it. I'm a few months pregnant and for some reason, this pregnancy makes my back hurt."

"Congratulations."

"Thank you."

Our awkward interactions made me uncomfortable. I didn't want to pry or try to engage Jaya too soon and scare her so I just watched and spoke when engaged.

Sharmayne must have sensed me at ill-ease and filled the silence. "When I was pregnant with Jaya, I had the worst heartburn my entire pregnancy."

I suddenly found myself intrigued by her pregnancy with my child. "Was she born with a lot of hair?"

"Boy, was she! She had a head full of slick, dark hair. Within three months it was a full-blown afro."

I laughed picturing her. I looked over at her. She was intrigued with all of the buttons and began to push on them. The dashboard begins to light up and play music. Jaya looks up at us surprised. "Dance," she said and we both laughed. When the music and the lights stopped, she started them all over again.

I was pleased she liked the car but I owed her so much more than that. After a few minutes of watching her, Shar offered me a drink but I declined. She excused herself and returned with a few photo albums. "Would you like to see some pictures of Jaya?"

I lit up with anticipation as she handed me the photo albums. From her newborn picture to Easter to Christmas, page after page were filled with memories of a daughter I never knew existed. Trying to absorb everything from each photo, I wondered where were they taken, what time of year, how she was felt, and where was I when all of this was going on? I asked a few questions and Shar sat beside me happy to share the details she remembered. I could imagine this was as hard for her as it was for me, if not harder.

Jaya walked over to us and climbed on Shar's lap, looking at the photos with us. A picture of Micah holding her snatched her attention and it was the liveliest I'd seen her. She pointed to the picture. "That Daddy."

Sharmayne chuckled. "Yes, it is. And who is this?" She asked pointing to Jaya. Jaya pointed to herself and Shar laughed. "Yes, that's you. Very good." She tickled Jaya's stomach and the giggling that erupted from her frail body, warmed me up inside. I had never heard a sound as beautiful as my daughter giggling. I began to tear up and quickly reeled back in.

"Thank you for showing me these."

"Of course. If you like, I can make you some copies."

I was taken aback by her suggestion. "If it's not too much trouble. I don't want to burden you. I know you have a lot going on."

"It's no burden at all. I'd be happy to."

I was grateful for her willingness to make this easy. I could have been raising hell and threatening to fight for my parental rights, but I was hoping we could come to an amicable agreement once Jaya was in remission. Her being treated was the priority but I still needed to do my part. "I was going to wait to bring this up, but now seems like a good time. I'd like to pay for Jaya's medical expenses."

"Like hell, you will." Micah unexpectedly appeared and closed the door behind him, pointing at me. "Listen here partner, we don't need ya money. Jaya is well taken care of. Believe that."

"Micah, calm down." Shar put Jaya down on the floor and walked over to her husband and something to him in a whispered tone. I supposed my hour was up and I didn't want to cause trouble. I'd keep the peace for my daughter's sake. But not Sharmayne, Micah, or even Tianna were going to keep me from being a father to my child.

"Daddy," Jaya said excitedly and ran over to him. For the first time since I'd been there, she smiled and I saw the dimple on her cheek, similar to mine and Alonzo's. It made my heart yearn for my child and I did not want to leave her, but I'd had no choice.

"I'm going to go. Thank you for welcoming me into your home." I knelt and kissed Jaya on her forehead. "I'll see you soon beautiful girl. You be a good girl." She gripped Micah's leg not paying me any attention. I smiled at her before I walked out. Once I got home, I sat in the car for a few minutes before I made my way inside. I now dreaded going home to an empty house. I grabbed a beer from the refrigerator and plopped myself on the couch, channel surfing. Christmas Specials played at nauseum. I clicked the TV off, tossed the remotes aside, climbed the stairs to my bedroom, and thought about my wife. I missed her so much.

I hadn't cried since my dad had passed several years ago until that moment. Everything I loved and wanted in life was far from me. My wife. My son. My daughter. I had tried to be a good man and a good husband and yet here I was lonely at the mercy of others. Part of me was angry with Tianna for not trusting my love for her. All of these years, loving her and Jay, how could she not know she was the love of my life? Why was she so damn stubborn and quick to shut down and run? Of all the times I needed her in my life, it was now. I was becoming a shell of a man lost in grief and yearning.

I wanted to be close to my wife but didn't know how to. I picked up her robe and smelled it, but her scent had been gone from it for days now. It wasn't until two days after she'd left that I'd realized she'd taken a large amount of her and Jay's clothing. It was heartbreak all over again. She had left intending to stay gone. I sat down at the desk in our bedroom and turned on the computer.

Tianna,

I miss you. I need you. I'm sorry. Please come home.

Love,
El

I stared at the email for an hour before I got the courage to send it. After that, I began to send her emails daily. I had no idea if she was reading them or not and she'd never respond but after the first few emails, it didn't matter. It was my way of feeling close to her and it helped me get through the days without my family. I refused to give up on her, my son, or my marriage.

THIRTY
Tianna

I went back to the apartment to search for a job after finishing Jay's homeschooling for the day and visiting Bianca's dad in his nursing facility. I felt bad for burdening Bianca with my unexpected and extended stay, not that she minded. She loved seeing Jay almost daily and had begun to tell him stories about Justin that I had never heard and had made a copy of a few photos of Justin as a teen that she had had.

Jay had asked me about Elijah more times than I wanted to count and I didn't know what to do. I had no intentions of ever reconciling with Elijah and wondered if it would do Jay more harm than good to allow him to have a relationship with a man who would no longer be in his life. Then I rubbed my belly and remembered that no matter, Elijah would be connected to me for the rest of my life.

I had finally allowed Jay to call him, with Bianca sitting nearby as I took a shower. I didn't want to hear the conversation and when he asked Jay where I was, Jay could be honest and say I wasn't available. Because I know El so well, Bianca confirmed that was exactly what happened. Every few days Jay would call and we'd go through the same routine.

A part of me felt like a baby mama that kept a child from his father, not telling Elijah I was pregnant. Yet, I had to do what I thought was best for me for the time being. Elijah was an adult that had made his own decisions and now had to pay the consequences for his actions. I couldn't allow myself to feel sorry for the man that betrayed me and lied to me.

I exited the rabbit hole I had chased my runaway thoughts into and got back to rebuilding my life. I opened my email to draft an email to a school a few miles down the road and was shocked to see a bunch of emails from Elijah. The first one was short and to the point. He wanted me to go back to New Jersey. I almost laughed at it, instead I deleted it, then returned to sending my resume.

Later that evening, I found myself wondering what El could possibly have to say with so many emails. Curiosity getting the better of me I opened up my email and began to read through them. The first few were more of the same as the first, asking me to return and telling me he loved me. And then I read one quite different.

Dear Tianna,

It's crazy how the only person I want to share this with is the last person who would want to know or even care, but I met my daughter a few days ago. Her name is Jaya. She looks like me. Even has my dimple. She lives with her mother and father and they both seem to really love her. That brings me comfort on some level. She's sick and was mostly quiet while I was there but I'm glad I was able to spend time with her. Anyway, I just needed to tell someone. I pray you and Champ are doing well. He seems to love California. I miss him. If we ever become a family again, I won't ever complain about how active he is. The house is so quiet without him, I find myself missing the noise. I miss your laughter. I miss my best friend.

I love you,

El

I didn't know what to do with that information. I wanted to punch him in the face for talking about what had brought me so much pain, yet I also felt bad for him. I closed my email and called my mom. If anyone could take my mind off my sorrows, my mother could. Pop answered, instead.

"Hey, Pop."

"Hey, Ti. Could you at least pretend you are happy to hear my voice?"

I snickered. "I'm sorry, Pop. I'm always glad to hear your voice. I was just expecting *Mami* to answer."

"She's visiting your grandmother."

"And you didn't go?"

"I was there last weekend. I met my quota for this quarter." I laughed. I didn't blame my father for not wanting to be there often. Growing up, I had avoided her family for many reasons. "Ever since you up and left, she's over there more often. I think she misses you but doesn't want to admit it."

I felt bad, but *Mami* would be ok. She had Abe, Pop, and her entire family to keep her company. "Well, I guess that means I'm meant to talk to you. How are you feeling? Are you following your diet?"

"I just ate a row of Oreos. You're Mom's gonna be pissed when she gets home, but I enjoyed the experience."

"Yeah. You're a dead man."

"Enough about me. How's Cali?"

"It's beautiful here."

"That sounds like you don't plan on coming back East."

I didn't have the heart to tell him that I was already making plans to stay. "Would that be such a bad thing?"

"Tianna, you are an adult and need to decide what is best for you. I don't know what's going on with you and Elijah, but running away is never the solution to anything. You stay and work it out or you stay and decide to end it. Either way, you face it, baby girl. Then if you want to move out west, so be it."

He was right, but I wasn't ready to face Elijah yet. It occurred to me that my parents could relate to my situation and had survived over twenty years of marriage with their trials of infidelity. "Pop, can I ask you a question?"

"You just did, but feel free to ask another." My father never let an opportunity pass to be clever with his words or generous with his wisdom.

"What made you want to fight for *Mami* when you two split up?"

"I realized something after I cheated on your mother. Something I took for granted. I could replace my lover, but I could never replace my best friend. Her fine ass was what attracted me to her, but her friendship is what made me stay, and what made me come back after I messed up."

My dad's words choked me up. Elijah had said he missed his best friend. I felt myself longing to lay in my bed and laugh as we used to. Laughter turned into love-making. I closed my eyes and let the tears stream down my face.

"Mommy?"

I quickly wiped them away so Jay wouldn't see me cry. "Come here handsome. Come say hi to Pop. He's on the phone."

Jay rushed over and for several minutes they discussed the usual nonsense they did: Jay asking for the most ridiculous of things while Pop promising to try to fly him to the moon.

We ended the phone call and Jay and I watched a movie before his bath time then bed. I had taken a warm shower and laid in bed staring at the ceiling. I had yet to tell Jay he was going to be a big brother. I was worried he'd tell Elijah and I wouldn't ask my son to keep a secret on my behalf, but I was running out of time. My clothes were getting tighter and soon my slender frame wouldn't be able to hide my baby bump.

I prayed for God to lead me because the further I drove with tunnel vision away from hurt, the more lost I became. *Lord, please take over and lead me where I need to go.*

The next morning I received a response to a private school I had applied to, extending an invitation for an interview. After that more responses came in during the week and I was excited. God worked fast.

I arrived at my fourth interview in ten days, my top a little tighter than I wanted. I had begun to burst out of my work attire and seriously needed maternity clothes. For today, I'd have to bust a gut through this top and ride with it.

I met with the director who'd I caught eyeing my swelling belly then avoided looking there. Two minutes in and I was already uncomfortable. After answering several questions related to my education and experience, she asked why I moved to California.

I subconsciously touched my belly trying to find the best way to respond. She looked at my hand before she quickly turned away. I was beginning to think she was uncomfortable with my pregnancy. I set my hand down on my lap and avoided the habit of caressing my abdomen and focused on the interview. "It was a personal decision. My best friend lives here and I thought it would be a great move for my family and me?"

She smiled nervously. "My husband and I moved here early in our marriage and it's been wonderful. Has your husband found the transition to be an easy one?"

I tripped over her question. "My husband?" I hadn't remembered mentioning being married and I wasn't wearing a ring. The last thing I wanted to think about was my failing marriage or Elijah.

Director Chen's face turned ten shades of red. "I'm sorry. I shouldn't have assumed. I meant your spouse. Has your spouse found the move to be an easy one?"

She looked at me as if she wanted to faint and now I was the one embarrassed. She thought I was offended because she assumed I was married to a man. Which meant, she now thought I was married to a woman. I had two options: embarrass her again and correct her or tell her the truth. I considered myself an honest person. Then again, it was probably easier for her to think that I was a lesbian rather than explain that I was a woman headed for divorce from her husband because he cheated with a stripper who had his baby secretly and, who was now dying of leukemia.

"Yes. My wife is a nurse. She took a job at U C San Diego Health and it has been great," I said. *Lord, please forgive me for lying.*

"You told her you were a lesbian?" Bianca yelled as I added the cheese sauce to the cooked shell noodles.

"I didn't think I could explain the truth and still get the job."

"So you told the director of a private Christian school that I was your wife? I bet she was jumping up at the chance to hire you after that, Ti."

"And I'm pretty sure she knew I was pregnant. She looked at my belly a few times."

"There's nothing wrong with being pregnant by your husband Tianna. You should have told her the truth."

I mixed the cheese sauce then scooped it into a bowl. Of all the things in the world I had to crave, macaroni and shells were my addiction. "Yeah, sure. Director Chen, I ran away from my cheating husband who sleeps with prostitutes and I'm carrying a child he doesn't know about."

Bianca winced. "I guess that does sound a little scandalous." She sat down on the stool. "But I guess that means that that wasn't what God had planned for you."

"Apparently, none of these jobs have been." I devoured my mac and cheese and tried not to let anything disrupt the satisfaction.

Later that night I opened my email. Elijah had been consistent in sending them daily although I'd go a few days before reading them. This time, however, I read each one, and with the last one he sent, I cried myself to sleep.

THIRTY-ONE

Sharmayne

Two Months Later

Elijah had come every week, once a week. Then he began to visit twice a week. Every time he was due to arrive, Micah would leave the house. At first, it bothered me that my husband was ok to leave me alone with a man twice a week for an hour or two, but the more it became the norm, the more I thought it was for the best. I wasn't proud that I had kept Jaya from a man who obviously wanted to be active in her life. At the time I thought I was doing what was best for everyone but I had been wrong and it was very evident to me now.

She had begun to warm up to Elijah and he continued to spoil her. I had to practically threaten him to stop buying her toys. He insisted on making up for missed time and I assured him that his presence was all she required. Another person loving my daughter was the best gift she could receive.

Every visit they'd play together and he'd forget I was in the room. Eventually, I got comfortable enough to sit in the kitchen while he spent time with her alone. Once I even ran to the market because I needed an onion for dinner and the ones I had, had gone bad. The further along in my pregnancy I made it to, the more difficult it was becoming to carry Jaya when she was feeling weak or care for her as best as I could. Elijah began stepping in to let me take much-needed naps or to run errands.

One Saturday afternoon I was in the middle of scrubbing some potatoes I wanted to bake when I heard Elijah calling for me frantically. "Sharmayne! Sharmayne!"

I ran to the living room as fast as I could. Jaya was laying in his lap, eyes closed and he looked like he'd seen a ghost. "What's wrong?"

"I was reading her a story. She climbed onto my lap. At first, I thought she'd fallen asleep but she was out too fast. I tried waking her up and she won't respond."

I knelt before them in a panic and checked her small chest to see it rose and fell. She was still breathing and I relaxed a little bit. "She's breathing."

I saw Elijah's shoulders relax a little. "Ok. That's good," he said relieved.

I shook her a little. "Jaya? Hey baby girl." She didn't respond. "Jaya?" Still nothing. She was unconscious and that set my alarms ringing once again. We rushed her to the emergency room where she was admitted. She regained consciousness a while later but was very weak.

I called Micah from the hospital and he rushed over. Jaya saw him and smiled. "Daddy."

"Hey. Moochie," he said sweetly as he sat bedside, holding her hand. "You feeling a little tired beautiful girl?" Jaya blinked up at him with her big brown eyes and said nothing. We took turns holding her hand as she was in and out of sleep.

Elijah kept vigil for a few hours that night, keeping himself confined to the corner of her hospital room. He'd refused to sit at her bedside and I couldn't pretend to understand why but I let him be.

As I had dared not believe, the doctor told us that she didn't have much time left and there wasn't anything more they could do but keep her comfortable and arranged for her in-home hospice care.

The days passed quickly. Like a cowgirl, I tried to wrangle time and get it to slow down. Every moment that passed was one day, hour, minute, second closer to my daughter leaving me. Every time I thought about it I had the urge to vomit and had suffered a few panic attacks. I refused to leave her side or even discuss arrangements for her burial. My child was not going to die and I was not going to pick out a casket, clothes, or anything for it. When Micah brought it up, I banned him from her bedroom. How dare he give up on her like that?

He pulled me close and hugged me against my will. I broke down in his arms and cried until I could barely breathe. I pounded on his chest and screamed. And he took it. He let me cry. He let me pound on him. He let me scream. And then he took me in his arms again and let me sob.

One late morning a few days later, Elijah arrived with a teddy bear, looking like he hadn't slept in days. Had I not witnessed it myself I wouldn't have believed it when Micah rose from the chair by Jaya's bed and offered it to Elijah. This time Elijah came near and thanked Micah. Jaya saw him and she called out to him, "Lijah."

He broke down in tears before he addressed her. "Hey, baby girl."

"You not baby. No cry Lijah."

He quickly wiped them away before he laid the teddy bear beside her.

She looked at the teddy bear for a few moments before she looked back at him. "Mommy say no toys."

We all laughed and Elijah nodded. "You remember that huh? Let's ask Mommy if one more is ok." Elijah turned to me and put on a show for Jaya's entertainment. "Mommy, is it ok if Jaya has this toy?"

I pretended to think about it before I shook my head. "Yes, Jah-Jah. You can have anything you want my love."

Elijah nodded and picked up the teddy bear. "Good, because my friend wants to meet you." Jaya looked at him not understanding. He picked up the pair. "Jaya, this is Elijah-jah."

She looked at the bear and smiled. "Jah-Jah," she repeated weakly.

"Yep. Elijah-jah." Jaya smiled again, so naturally, every chance he got, Elijah repeated the bear's name. Although I hadn't done it intentionally, when I realized that her nickname was a part of Elijah's name, I chose to ignore it and chalked it up to coincidence. Yet, I think it was destined for this moment.

Elijah entertained Jaya until she fell asleep. As her pain progressed, the medicine increased, causing her to sleep for longer periods. Sometimes she'd wake up delusional and not recognize us. Today had been a good day. She had stayed up longer than she had been. She was alert and the nurse was pleasantly surprised at her responsiveness.

My family and friends began to arrive and see her one last time to say goodbye and it bothered me that they'd show up for her goodbye but not for her hello into this world. Yet, I was too preoccupied with making sure she wasn't in pain or in need that I lost interest in that matter altogether. And then my mother showed up crying and carrying on.

I pulled her into the kitchen. "Stop putting on a show. Nobody wants to see it."

"What you mean Shar? That's my grandbaby." She bawled and I was unsure if she was drunk or high or what but she wouldn't stop crying.

Micah stepped into the kitchen and gestured for me to keep calm and let her grieve. He was right. I did not have time to babysit my mother. So long as she kept the show in the kitchen and away from Jaya, I wasn't going to waste my energy on her.

Micah rubbed my back and handled my mother. "Hey Felicia, you can sit in here for a few minutes, ok? We don't want the baby to see us cry. It scares her."

She shook her head up and down as she wiped her tears and snot on the sleeve of her jacket, two sizes too big. "Thank you, Brownie. I just love that little girl. That's my grandbaby you know? I used to babysit her. She was a good baby. A real good baby."

My mother began to sob again and it annoyed me. I looked at Micah to give him the eye roll he always knew how to interpret but he was staring at my mother like he was looking at a ghost. "Mike? You ok?" I touched his forearm trying to snap him out of his trance. "Micah?"

He looked at me strangely. "Yeah, I'm good. I'm gonna go check on my mom. She wasn't looking good."

I nodded and agreed. Kendra had been here day and night for the past few days, helping with visitors and trying to give me a break. She was more of a mother to me than Felicia had ever been. She was grieving while still helping us and taking care of Auntie. Micah eyed my mother again before he walked out of the kitchen. I didn't know what that was about, but right now I could only focus on Jaya.

"I'm going to go spend time with my daughter. Don't make a scene or I'll ask you to leave." She began to weep again and I left her in the kitchen. I hadn't noticed when she'd left, nor had I cared.

Kendra managed to get everyone out early and Micah and I spent a quiet night alone with Jaya. Every night I was scared to fall asleep and I'd wake up and she wouldn't. It had begun to take its toll on my mental and physical health. Micah constantly reminded me that I was carrying a baby and that I needed to be healthy. I felt guilty for not having a happy and attentive pregnancy. I strongly believed that babies could feel their mother's joy and pain. Yet, I had been more pain than joy for most of my pregnancy.

I nodded off by Jaya's bed and jumped up startled in my own. I rushed to Jaya's room and found Micah watching over her weeping quietly. I tip-toed back to my bedroom and lamented over my family. I didn't understand why this was happening to us. A short while later, Micah came back into the bedroom.

With swollen eyes, he looked upon me. "Thank you."

I instinctively knew that he saw me enter and exit Jaya's bedroom and was appreciative that I gave him privacy. I didn't need to vocalize it. I went to my husband and embraced him. "Thank you for choosing to be her Daddy."Micah began to cry again and I joined him.

My husband had shared many things on many levels in our short life together, but nothing had brought us as close as this moment no matter what other issues had been coming against us.

The next morning the nurse arrived for her daily visit and informed us to prepare ourselves as best as we could because Jaya probably wouldn't make it through the night. We stood vigil by her side for two days with Elijah spending a great deal of time with us. She was unconscious most of the time. On the second night, Micah picked her up and we walked around the house singing her lullabies. Then Micah sang her her favorite.

"Where's my Moochie? Where's my Moochie? And then you sing, *"Here I am, Here I am.* Ok. I know you're going to get it right this time. You ready?"

I smiled at this game they always played. No matter how many times, Micah had taught her to respond, she'd always say 'Here Daddy' and he'd pretend to be upset that she sang the wrong lyrics before she'd laugh so hard her stomach shook.

He sang it a few times and we just watched her sleep. We sat in her room and he held her on his lap. My stomach had been pretty big and it was hard on me to hold her for long periods of time.

"Where's my Moochie? Where's my Moochie?"

Jay looked up at us and smiled. "Here Daddy," she whispered before she rested her head on his shoulder for the last time.

THIRTY-TWO

Elijah

The man staring back at me in the mirror did a passable job concealing his grief. My heart was a wreck and I wanted to lay down, close my eyes and never wake up. I looped my black, silk tie over and under as my dad had taught me years ago, making sure the result of a well-tied tie was 'a nice size knot.' I gripped the cuff of the sleeves of my black button-down shirt as I slid my arms into my suit jacket. I straightened my tie as I looked in the mirror one last time before heading out. I didn't want to attend my daughter's funeral. I didn't want my daughter to be gone. I didn't want to have on funeral clothes. I wanted to scream and cry, but I was a black man, and a black man didn't behave in that manner. We bore hurt and grief, and we manned up. Having tantrums was for children and I had put away childish things long ago. Right now, I had to straighten up, be strong and be a man and that's exactly what I would do.

I arrived at the wake and went to speak with the director. I had taken care of all of the funeral arrangements and wanted to make sure everything was set. Micah had given me some direction in what he thought Sharmayne would approve of, and I kept to it as best as I could with the limited details provided. Afterward, I sat in the back, for many reasons. I had no place of significance in Jaya's life, and I did not want to impose or be seen. I did not want the millions of questions as to who I was and why I was sitting up front.

But to be honest, it was mostly because I was a coward, afraid to see my daughter laying in a casket and still be able to keep it together. I was there a half-hour before the funeral home was filled with people I had never met in my life. Sharmayne and Micah arrived and sat by the casket. She was a wreck as I imagined she would be. My heart went out to her. I couldn't pretend to know her grief, but I suffered my own kind of mourning. I had lost Jaya twice in my lifetime.

215

I kept to myself and waited for the service to begin. I wanted to get it all done and over with, but a large part of me didn't want the service to end because once it did, it was time to pay final respects and head to the cemetery. For three nights I had had nightmares of seeing Jaya's casket lowered into the ground. I'd wake up in cold sweats, gasping for air. I knew that Jaya was in heaven healthy and whole, but the devil was running rampant in my head causing me anxiety regarding her mortal body. I began to chase my thoughts down a rabbit hole and began shaking my leg to release my anxious energy.

I felt a hand go across my shoulders and rub me sympathetically. "I know this is hard, but you'll get through it."

The source of comfort surprised me. "What are you doing here?" I rose from my chair and hugged her, relieved I wouldn't have to face this alone.

"Where else would I be but by your side?"

She hugged me tightly and I almost lost it. "Thank you for flying in. It means a lot." I hadn't expected her to come but I was grateful for my mother's support.

"You don't need to thank me. That's what mothers do." Looking like the well-put-together woman she always presented herself to be, she sat down beside me and set her purse down. "The casket is so small. It's very sad."

I knew she was trying to fill the silence and didn't mean any harm, but her words were only adding salt to an open wound. I didn't respond, hoping she'd take the hint. Gratefully, she did, and she kept me company, quietly, until a woman who appeared high stumbled in and made a scene at Jaya's casket. She was wailing and incoherent. Micah walked over to the woman and tried to settle her but she refused to be calmed. Suddenly Sharmayne was in front of her, and the woman quieted down. I don't know what Sharmayne said to her, but the woman barreled out of the funeral home in anger, spewing curse words in a rage.

"How ghetto," my mother whispered. I ignored her comment. Grief did things to people others wouldn't understand.

After the sympathetic words from the clergyman, Sharmayne had a complete meltdown. She lamented so loudly it was as if she were grieving for her and on my behalf, letting out all I couldn't. Seeing her so distraught nearly broke me. Micah calmed her and took her outside to get some air. In her pregnant condition, I could only assume Micah was caring for her in ways she wasn't thinking of; not that I blamed her.

A while later, they returned, and Sharmayne made eye contact with me. She approached looking exhausted and broken. Sniffling, she wiped her nose and exhaled before she spoke. "Why are you sitting all the way back here?"

I rose and hugged her. "Lots of reasons, but I'm more concerned about you. Are you ok?"

She shook her head and began to cry. "Our baby is gone."

I swallowed the lump in my throat and fought the tears that had begun to brim my eyes. I side-arm hugged her. "She is in a better place, not hurting or sick." As cliché as it sounded, it was the only thought that had brought me an ounce of comfort.

"I'm selfish. I want her here. With me."

I nodded in understanding because I felt the same way. Three months with Jaya hadn't been nearly enough. If I could give anything to have her back, I would. But that's not how it worked, and I had to accept that God worked in a way I'd never understand. At least, that was what I had been telling myself over and over again whenever I tried to make sense of it all.

My mother rose and offered her condolences to Sharmayne. "I'm very sorry for your loss." Sharmayne looked at her blankly.

I removed my hand from my pocket and introduced them. "My apologies. Sharmayne, this is my mother Marvette. Mom, this is Sharmayne, Jaya's mother, and her husband, Micah."

Micah stuck his hand out, but my mother bypassed it and waved before crossing her hands in front of her. "My deepest condolences to you both. I know this must be an extremely difficult time for you, just as it is for Elijah. He didn't have a lot of time with her, but I can see his deep grief."

I felt awkward and ashamed. Of all times my mom chose to be passive-aggressive, this had to have been the worse. "Mom, I could not even begin to understand the grief of Jaya's parents." I turned to them humbly and offered my deepest condolences. Sharmayne ignored my mother, mostly because she was distraught and most likely didn't catch on to the implication of being denied rights to my daughter, but Micah had not. His stance was rigid, and I hoped he wouldn't escalate the situation. While I understood my mother stepped out of line, she was still my mother. I would check her at a more appropriate time, but I wouldn't allow her to be disrespected. "Mom, they are ready to pay final respects. Why don't you go wait for me in the car while I say goodbye?"

She tensed up but nodded quickly before she offered condolences once more and headed out the door. I knew she was embarrassed and upset that I had sent her to sit in the car like a scolded child, but I could not stress about my grown mother's feelings of offense when she had clearly been wrong to begin with. Micah eyed me curiously but relaxed. I was glad that was de-escalated but truthfully, it wasn't what had my full attention. The anxiety of saying my final goodbye to my daughter was rearing its ugly head and everything was falling to the wayside fleetingly.

As people began to file out of the funeral home, they stopped and offered personal condolences to Sharmayne. Although not intentionally rude, she didn't give any of them a response. She looked lost in space and time. Micah put an arm around her. "Baby, it's time."

She began to sob and shook her head furiously. "No. Please, no."

He slipped his hand in hers and reassured her. "You can do this, Shar."

I understood her struggle. I don't know what made me do it, but I took her other hand. "You were strong for her in life. Be strong for her now."

She hesitated before she nodded. Micah put an arm around her and together we walked toward Jaya's small, pink casket. Once we were within a few feet, my feet found it hard to move. Sharmayne kept a grip on my hand I had no choice but to continue forward. When I made it to her casket and saw Elijah-jah gripped underarm, the dam holding back my emotions broke. The attempts to keep my sorrow at bay failed and my grief poured out like a flood around me. I was drowning in my own anguish and heartache.

I collapsed to my knees seeing my baby girl lying still as if she were Sleepy Beauty. How could she look so peaceful when my whole world felt like chaos? I wanted to hear her call me 'Lijah.' I wanted her to chastise me for buying her more toys. I wanted her to giggle when I pretended to be in pain. I wanted her to crawl on my lap again and dig her finger up my nose.

Why God? Why? I yelled at God internally. Why would He bring her into my life just to snatch her away? I would have been better off not knowing she ever lived. I immediately took that back. I was grateful for having three months with her. I wanted to smack myself for not snatching Sharmayne by the arm and leading me to Jaya the minute I knew she existed. Instead, I was so caught up in Tianna leaving me, I waited weeks before I even reached out. Weeks I wasted. And now she was gone. Why God? I wanted to roar out. Instead, I wept like a child. I couldn't remember the last time I had cried so hard. Not even for my father had I felt such despair. The love of a child was like no other.

I hadn't realized Micah was picking me up off the floor. I looked up at him and grabbed ahold of myself. How dare I fall apart, when he was Jaya's true daddy. I apologized and he shook his head at me. "Don't apologize, man. I get it. Trust me, I get it."

I straightened myself up, looked at Jaya one last time before I kissed her forehead, and made my way to the side. I hadn't even dared to look at Sharmayne. I could not fall apart again, nor could I see her distraught again. I was hanging on to my sanity by a thread.

I heard her wailing and I exhaled to keep from doing the same. A few minutes later, Micah found me. He had put Sharmayne in the limo and he and I would serve as the pallbearers. I zoned out and don't even remember getting to my car.

My mom opened my passenger side door and got in. I'd forgotten she was even here. She was quiet and I could tell she was upset about me sending her outside. I didn't care. I ignored her attitude and waited to fall in line with the funeral procession. One of the funeral attendants began to hand out the orange stickers for the windshields.

"Are you family?" He asked.

"I don't mind riding in the back of the—"

My mom leaned over toward my window and interrupted, "He is the father and paid for the funeral. Thank you."

I went to tell him that my placement in the procession did not matter. What did I care if I got there first or last? I didn't want to get there at all. But it was too late. He'd already stuck the sticker on my windshield and directed me behind the hearse and limo, cutting off all other cars.

"You really need to learn how to speak up sometimes, Elijah. It's only right that you are in the front."

I was too emotionally raw to deal with any of it. I did as he instructed then waited quietly in line, lost in thought. Jaya's sweet face frozen in time arrested my cognizance of the present. She was just a baby. Round and round my thoughts went until my mother tapped my arm then pointed out the window as the limo had gotten a healthy lead on me. Cars began to honk, and I eased my way forward.

The burial was a blur and I only remember snatches of sight and sound: a teddy bear arrangement made of pink roses, a dove being released, the sniffles of attendees, the screams of Sharmayne begging to not put her child in the ground to suffocate. The screams. The screams. The screams. I didn't know where her external ones ended and my internal ones began.

Being the first to arrive at the cemetery meant being stuck between all of the cars behind me and the hearse and limo in front of me. Sharmayne stayed until Micah carried her away limp and unconscious. I couldn't stomach another minute of anything and longed to get home and medicate and drink myself to sleep. I wanted to sleep for days.

As we began to leave the cemetery my mom started in again. "That was a very lovely service. Other than the few ghetto mishaps. But you can't really expect too much from people from Camden."

"You're from Camden."

"Correction. I was born there but I did not grow up there. My mother had the good sense to move us to Glassboro."

She came home with me and for a while, I tuned out whatever she was going on about after that. Then she mentioned Jaya and I was suddenly attentive.

"It's a shame I didn't get to meet her. I was waiting for the DNA results." She ruffled through her purse nonchalantly as if we were discussing bingo at church.

"DNA test? What are you talking about?"

She chuckled. "What do you mean what do I mean? The DNA test Elijah. To prove she was your daughter." She stopped looking through her purse and I could feel her eyes on me. I quickly turned and could feel the hole she was burning in my face. "You did get a DNA test, didn't you?"

For the life of me, I couldn't understand her. "Are you serious right now?"

"I most certainly am serious. You mean to tell me that you paid for this entire funeral and that I flew all the way up here and you don't even know for certain she was your daughter?" She huffed a humorless laugh, dumbfounded. "Boy, have I failed as a mother." She shook her head, removed a mint from her purse, unwrapped it, and placed it in her mouth.

"My sentiments, exactly." My entire upbringing my mother had said and done some questionable things, but the love of a child endures much. I'd learned that even children abused physically and sexually by a parent, still wanted to be in the care of their parent. And after my father cheated on my mother, I pitied her and vowed to always take care of her. I had never wondered if she took that vow for granted until now because what kind of mother would chastise her adult son minutes after burying his only biological child? What kind of mother insisted on always having her way in her child's life? A narcissistic and selfish one.

"Elijah Townsend. How dare you? Ever since you married that woman, you have broken your vow to me to be good to me and take care of me and I have remained quiet just allowing the disrespect. Now, another woman tells you you are a father and you're so gullible you believed her too. Pretty women need simply to bat their eyes at you and you play right into their hands. Just like your father."

I went over the edge. "Shut up! Just shut up! I am not anything like my father. I love my wife! She is a good woman and that's more than I could ever say about you! My father left you because you're coldhearted and mean as hell! I didn't understand then, but I see it so clearly now!"

She began to cry. "I can't believe that you are treating me this way over a woman that moved across the country and left you like a piece of shit. Yes! Your beloved wife is more loyal to her tantrums than she is to you. Even a baby that you don't even know is yours comes before your mother. That woman is a stripper and a prostitute and used you to pay for the medical bills and funeral and you are sitting here in mourning. Pathetic. But I'm glad I got to see all of this. I can learn from my mistakes for Mac's sake. Take me to my hotel. Immediately."

I laughed at her audacity. "You are such a hypocrite. You've been an alcoholic. You married my father for advantage, not love, and when that backfired you ran away from him. Just as Tianna did. The only difference is I love my wife and did not intentionally cheat on her. I don't want anyone but her, and I am always going to want her. I have loved her since I was seventeen years old and that is never going to change.

And as for Jaya. She is my daughter because I say she is. I don't need you, DNA, or anyone to prove anything to me. Not that I need to explain it to you, but let me extend you the courtesy of some knowledge and what a real father does for his children. I volunteered to pay for her medical expenses and her funeral because that is what a man does for his family and children. Not everyone is your father, the extortioner. You've lived such an embittered life for so long you think everyone is like the people that have hurt you. My wife is nothing like you or them. I am not your father. My heart goes out to my brother, but I pray that his father has a bigger influence on his life than you do because a toxic parent is worse than an absent one."

"Be careful not to be so quick to speak about others, without looking at your own life son. Funny, how you were daddy of the year when you were taking care of her son, and now you have no rights to him at all because that was never your son. And I'm sure you being the 'toxic' parent is exactly why your wife is keeping him from you and is on the other side of the country."

"Actually, I'm right here Marvette. Nice to see you still have the sweetest things to say about me." Tianna looked at me and raised her eyebrows sarcastically.

My mother began to argue.

"Leave." I didn't care what she had to say. I only wanted to see my wife.

"Elijah, we are not—"

"Now."

She stopped talking, snatched her purse from the table, and left. I took a step toward Tianna, ready to embrace her, but her expression changed.

"No. I came back to New Jersey, not to you. I am here to offer my deepest condolences and understanding. No matter what has happened between us because I know how devastating the loss of a child can be and I wouldn't wish it on my worst enemy.

I nodded. Her words hurt, but she was here, and for now, that was enough.

THIRTY-THREE

Micah

For two weeks, I gave Sharmayne her space to grieve and stayed out of her way, but at today's doctor's appointment, the doctor expressed his concern regarding the amount of weight she had been losing. She was already on the smaller side, to begin with.

"Shar, you gotta eat. C'mon on now! I miss Jaya too! But you gotta be a mother to this one too, baby. Please eat something."

She nodded her head in her zombie state as she had been since the funeral. She slept in Jaya's room every night and cried herself to sleep. I didn't know what to do but let her be. How could I tell a mother to stop grieving for her child? But how could I be her husband and a father to our baby and let her make herself sick and put the baby at risk?

I went out for a walk needing to clear my head. As if Shar's health and grief weren't enough, something that had been bothering me for weeks but I couldn't move it on yet because some puzzle pieces were still missing. When Shar's mom had come to visit Jaya, she had called me Brownie. The only time someone had ever called me that was when Huggie almost killed me at Ace's place. The more I thought about everything that had gone down, the more I was convinced that Felicia was behind a whole lot of shit that Shar didn't know about.

I could bet that she'd assumed as I had, that Jaya was Ace's baby and had told him all of Shar's business in exchange for drugs or money. I wouldn't be surprised if Ace had Felicia steal the money back he'd loaned to Shar, just to put Shar in his debt.

I slammed my fist on the table, thinking how I paid that motherfucka ten thousand dollars and how he'd been playing us for a long time. The value of my properties had gone upside down and were worth less than what I owed on them. Ten thousand dollars would go a long way right now.

I decided right then and there that I needed to step up for my family and my livelihood. My baby girl was gone, but I was still responsible for my family that was still here. I needed to take care of Jaya's mother and baby brother or sister.

A week later, I went home, took a hot shower, and made Shar an omelet. I brought her into the kitchen and sat her at the table as I had done a year ago.

"Sit and eat it."

"I'm not hungry, Micah."

I looked at my wife and rather than get angry, I picked her up, sat her on my lap, and rubbed her belly. "There is a precious baby in here. God put you in charge of caring for him or her. Know why?" She shook her head sadly. "Because he knew if He could trust you with Jaya, He could trust you with her sibling. The best way to honor our daughter is by being the same parents we were to her, to this one, and any other ones that come along."

Tears streamed down her face before she nodded. "Ok." A few minutes later she took a few bites and smiled at me. "It's good. Thank you."

I was grateful she was trying but I knew her grief ran deep and a few bites of an omelet wasn't going to solve everything but it was a start. I needed my wife, the feisty woman, intelligent lawyer, fighter, and strong woman to find her way back so together we could rise from all of that buried us.

THIRTY-FOUR
Tianna

W ithin two weeks I managed to get my teaching job back in Camden. I suppose it's where I belonged the entire time. Pop's words played in my head on repeat. He was right. Running away was never the answer. Yet now that I was back, I was still stuck in limbo and didn't know how to move forward with my life. I needed to tell Elijah I was pregnant, but it never seemed like the right time. I had no desire to talk to him, yet at the same time, I felt the need to be by his side during his grief. I understood the impact the loss of a child had on a parent. The loss of three children, that had never had the chance to be born had broken my heart in ways I'd never felt before, so I could only imagine the grief of losing a child you've held in your arms and showered with kisses.

For the time being, I was covering as a substitute, dealing with teenagers that I wanted to strangle. I wasn't fond of being a sub, but I was reaping what I'd sown when I left town and my job in a hurry. Yet, it was still better than sitting home overthinking life. On my first day back, Coach Edelson didn't waste time overstepping boundaries.

"Look at what the cat dragged in!"

I smiled. "Good morning, John."

He sat on a student's desk, one leg on the floor for stability. "Back to Camden, huh?" He chuckled. "You know what they say: 'Once you go black, you never go back.'"

I opened my bag, half-paying attention to his nonsense. "Newsflash: You're white, John." I teased.

"What?" He asked offended. "Woman, my momma, black. That makes me black."

I stopped shuffling through paperwork and looked up at him confused. "I thought it was, 'You are whatever your father is.'"

"Who the hell said that?" John's eyebrow damn now peaked near his hairline.

"Oh, I don't know? Only billions of people around the world who carry their father's last name, legacy, and bloodline?"

"That's BS. I am whatever *I* say I am. And I am a black man." He pursed his lips together and strutted around like George Jefferson.

"Cool. I agree. Don't let anyone shove you in a box. So is Edelson your mother's last name?" I asked knowing damn well that wasn't his black momma's last name.

The firs-period bell rang and he walked to the door sour. "Shut up, Christianna. That's why you're a sub now." For the first time since I'd been back to Jersey, I genuinely laughed and I needed it.

During lunch, I sat outside, not entirely comfortable around my peers again. I wasn't ready for anyone to know I was pregnant, so I kept my distance from people. I kept hearing *Mami* telling me to be careful of '*mal de ojo*,' because apparently, Puerto Ricans believe someone giving you the evil eye has the power to curse you, your baby, your house, your car, your hair, your toenails, and everything associated with you.

Superstitions aside, I walked to the lower floor of the main building to cover the culinary arts teacher, Mrs. Wright, for the afternoon, who'd gone home, sick. I walked into her class and sat at her desk. I reread the lesson plan and her notes for the day's assignment. The good Lord knew I'd come a long way in the kitchen but teaching a class was not something I was confident I'd excel in so I'd explain the classwork and let them do their thing.

The students began to trickle in, asking if I was subbing, then excited that their teacher wasn't in today. I began taking attendance and calling out names.

"Marissa," I said. I looked up and made eye contact with the young girl I'd seen open the door for Sabrina's grandmother, the day I'd followed her home.

"Here," she replied as she raised her hand.

I tried to play off my surprise but she seemed the least bit affected by me. I wondered if she had even known who I was. She began to laugh at a joke from a classmate and paid me no mind. Throughout the class, I avoided looking at her. After the bell rang, I was relieved that class was over and that I only had to deal with that today as the cooking teacher would be in the next day.

Or so I thought. The following day, I was told I'd be covering her schedule for an undisclosed amount of time. I sat in my car for lunch with the sole intent of unbuttoning my pants to let my abdomen breathe. I seriously needed maternity clothes.

I don't know why I was surprised when John jumped in my car uninvited. "Here." He handed me an ice cream sandwich. "Better eat it fast, before it gets messy."

I didn't even question him and enjoyed the gift. We began talking about the students and how a few of the seniors had tried a time or two to kick game, their corny lines, and how I'd reject them. John laughed.

"Well damn. I've used a few of those lines on a few women myself. Shit. Maybe that's why I'm still single."

I cracked up so hard. Yeah, I could see John had no game at all.

He interrupted my amusement. "It's good to see you laugh again. I missed your smile and I missed you when you were gone," he admitted.

I looked over at him and could see he was sincere. I didn't know what to say. I hadn't thought about him at all but I was sure that was rude to admit, so I smiled awkwardly.

"I made you uncomfortable, didn't I?"

Yep. I shook my head. "No, not at all. That's kind. Thank you for saying that." *Forgive me, Lord.*

"Chris, I know you're separated and aren't thinking about a new relationship right now, but when you are, I'd like the opportunity to take you out. On a real date. With real food."

He could have turned into an ice cream sandwich and I wouldn't have been more shocked. "Umm, John. I'm extremely flattered. I had no idea you felt that way but I'm still married and until I'm not, I won't even think of or discuss seeing another man. I am still in love with my husband. I don't know if we can get past our problems, but that doesn't change that I am still married and will live my life as such. I'm sorry."

He smiled sadly. "I'm not surprised. Just makes me like you more." He drummed my dashboard. "Well, lunchtime is ova Rover! Get your ass to class."

We exited my car and walked beside each other laughing. "That was so corny! And did you just call me a dog?"

"Never!" He said then barked.

I laughed and headed toward my classroom while he headed in the opposite direction. I was anxious about possible drama but after a week, I saw that Marissa was not at all like Sabrina, so I managed to disassociate her from her kin. I was even grateful she didn't seem to know me either.

When I arrived home at my parent's house one evening, Elijah had left a message with my mom saying he had to fly out of town for an urgent business meeting and couldn't pick up Jay for school in the morning. After thinking about it, I took the plunge. With Elijah gone for a few nights, I decided to return to the house and sleep in my old bed. I had missed the comfort of it.

The next morning I put Jay on the bus and went to work. The arrangement had worked well and I'd slept like a baby. We'd do it again tonight as it proved to be convenient. Selfishly I thought to myself. I'd be sorry when Elijah returned.

During sixth period, Marissa walked into the class and smiled as she walked past me to her desk. I returned a half-smile and didn't give it much credit as genuine or not. As long as she wasn't starting trouble it didn't much matter if she spoke, smiled, or cartwheeled her way inside.

I'd begun to get into class and told the students we'd play a game like the Food Network and I'd judge everyone's dish. They got into it and partners presented a sample of their assignment. The idea had seemed better in my head cuz I now had to taste six samples of dry-ass cornbread made from scratch. By sample three, I was choking and Marissa gave me a glass of water.

"Sorry. That was ours."

I looked up at her looking pathetic and cracked up. "It's still better than mine so I'd be a complete hypocrite if I failed you yet still fed mine to my family.

She looked at her partners and shrugged. "Does that mean that we failed?"

I sipped the water. "No. That means we aren't going to ever talk about this again and I retire Food Network games for the rest of my time in this class."

She laughed. "Ok. Cool."

That night I made it home and went through the usual family rituals with Jay. Homework. Dinner. Bath. Bedtime. Afterward, I showered then got into bed in one of Elijah's tees. I'd launder it before he got back so he wouldn't know I'd worn it. I'd managed to hide my small belly well with loose-fitting blouses and sweaters. At home, I just wanted to be free of anything restrictive. Especially at night. I'd gotten so hot, I'd start sweating and stripped to my undies.

It was two am when I got up for a glass of water and thought I was sitting in an inferno. I began to worry that something was wrong with my pregnancy. I had never had this experience with Jay or any prior pregnancy. I felt my anxiety climbing and did my breathing exercises to calm myself. I'd call the OB in the morning.

A few hours later, I felt the heat of a body pressed up against mine. My exposed breasts were being fondled. I was half-asleep but felt the touch moving slowly down to my abdomen before the touch lost its sensuality and felt more probing. Before I knew it, I was being spun on my back and the bedroom light being flicked on.

I squinted my eyes against the light and saw Elijah standing over me looking like he'd seen a ghost, his hands on his head and his eyes on my stomach. It was slow registering but it soon hit me like a freight train. I didn't know what to say.

"Are you— Are, are you—"

He couldn't even get the words out.

"Yes, I'm pregnant."

He shook his head and placed a palm over his mouth before he spoke again. "How far— Is it mine?" He was angry.

I sat up in bed, suddenly cognizant that I was topless. I looked for my t-shirt and slipped it on. Elijah looked at the tee. "Is that my tee, Ti?"

I stood up and walked over to him, ready to let him have a piece of my mind. "First of all, yes this is your stupid t-shirt. Second, and oh my God, yes this is your baby. And lastly, you're a dick." I slipped my shoes on and headed for the stairs. I turned back around. "I'm going back to my mother's. It's late and I don't want to wake Jay up, so you can put him on the bus tomorrow."

What an asshole.

I walked down the stairs holding on to the railing before I heard his footsteps behind me. "You gonna run every time you hear something you don't like?"

I turned around. "I'm not running. I'm just not addressing your bullshit and nonsense."

"Know what Tianna? Just go. I'm sick of your hypocrisy. You are pregnant and didn't even tell me. What kind of shit is that? You left and didn't tell me where you went. I was fucking worried sick! You took my son and kept him from me. And then to top it all off, I go to surprise you at work with lunch and find you sitting in your car on a lunch date." He let out a humorless laugh. "I come home and find you in the bed half-naked and for a moment I thought you came home, but you were just here to serve your own need. So go on to your mother's house. My son can always sleep here because this is his house, but I am not your lackey. So get your ass back here in the morning and *you* put him on the bus." Elijah marched back into his bedroom, closed the door, and left me standing there ten kinds of stupid.

The following day at work, I kept my distance from John and ate in the teacher's lounge with a few colleagues. I avoided where I usually ran into him.

During cooking class, Marissa brought me one of her chocolate chip cookies. "To make up for the cornbread."

I graciously accepted it. "Thank you. I never met a chocolate chip cookie I didn't like."

"Huh?"

I snickered then ate it. "It was very good. Thank you for sharing."

"So, I get an A for today, right?"

"A-plus."

"Good. I need to pass tenth grade. I can't get left back again."

"Are you in trouble of failing now?"

She shook her head. "Yeah. My grandma kept me home for a while after Sabrina got jumped. You were the teacher that tried to help her right?"

I looked up at her stunned. So she did know who I was but she kept talking as if she didn't care.

"Anyway, so my grandma didn't want me walking to school by myself. I missed a lot of time his year. I do Saturday school now trying to make up for my truancy."

I shook my head intrigued. "How are you doing in your core subjects?"

"What's that?"

"English. Math. Science."

"Oh! All the boring shit you mean." She covered her mouth. "My bad. All the boring stuff. All Ds. I got a C in science though. I like science."

"Not great, but still passing." I tried not to make it seem so hopeless.

"Yeah. I did a lot of work to get my grades from F to Ds. I don't want to fail no class. This class is my best grade. I want to have at least one B on my report card. I know I'm not real smart like Sabrina, but that's ok. I just want to go to the next grade, you know?"

I nodded. "Yeah. I do know."

Class ended and our exchange stayed at the forefront of my thoughts. I dissected everything she'd said and yet I couldn't tell if she was being genuine or not. For her to compliment Sabrina to me, felt insensitive yet, she did not say anything directly offensive. Perhaps I was reading too much into it. I got home and Jay was already there. Elijah was in the kitchen talking to Pop.

"Mommy! You're here!" Jay ran up to me and wrapped his arms around my waist. "Daddy said we can have pizza for dinner tonight."

I set my purse down on the couch. "Well, that's up to Mom-Mom baby. This is her house."

"But we're going to our house like yesterday. Mommy I don't want to stay here again. I want to play in my room and Daddy said we could go with him."

Moments later, Elijah stepped out of the kitchen, all smiles. "Hey Ti. Champ wants to go home with me. Do you mind? I'll put him on the bus."

"Um—"

"Please Mommy," Jay begged.

I was hesitant but one night away to give my parents alone time was a good thing. I nodded. "Ok. One night won't hurt." I could just sleep in the guest bedroom downstairs. The bed was comfortable enough.

"Awesome. Go grab your stuff Champ."

Jay pulled his arm in and raised his knee. "Yes!" He ran off and came right back, dragging his backpack and jacket. Jay began to pull my hand. "Let's go! I want some pizza."

"Whoa Champ, slow down. I'm taking you to buy pizza. Mommy said she wants to stay here." Elijah looked at me, his expression full of passive-aggressive sarcasm.

Jay looked up at me. "Mommy, you want to stay here?"

Elijah's stare bore into me. I bit the inside of my cheek and nodded. "Yes, baby. I do."

Elijah picked up Jay's backpack. "Ready?"

Jay let go of my hand and nodded excitedly as they walked out. "Daddy, can we go to King of Pizza? And can we get pepperoni on it?"

I heard the echoes of their conversation until the door closed behind them. A part of me felt left out. My family leaving me behind.

"You, ok?" I turned and saw Pop standing at the bottom of the staircase. I smiled and my eyes began to tear up unintentionally. He came over and hugged me. "What's wrong?"

I wiped the tears. "Just feels like my family just left me behind."

"Tianna, I love you but don't hate me for saying this. Maybe you can understand a little of how Elijah felt when you left him. You moved across the country and took his son. Didn't even tell him."

Guilt and anger struck me at the same time. I stepped back from my father's embrace. "Pop, he cheated on me! And fathered a child outside of our marriage! I had a right to leave him."

Pop nodded and waited for me to finish speaking, but that was all that needed to be said. "Tianna, have you spoken to Elijah about this at all?"

"Spoken to him about what? I don't need to hear more than I already heard."

"Ti, sometimes you get in these moods and only see what you want to see. You did this to me and your mother as well. You should really talk to your husband."

I was getting frustrated that my own father was siding with the man that cheated on his daughter. Then again, men always stuck together. "I take it you've spoken to him." He nodded. "Did he tell you he slept with a stripper?" My father was about to start making excuses for him and I cut him off and I waved my hand at him. "No Pop. A simple question only requires a simple answer. Yes or no."

Pop nodded. "Yes, Ti, but—"

"And did he tell you that this same stripper had his child?"

My father was getting frustrated. "Yes, Ti, but you don't know—"

"Pop, I don't mean to be disrespectful, but I don't need to know anything else. Excuse me. I've had a very long day. I'm going to go shower."

I made it up one step when *Mami* called out to me. "*Hija*." Something in her tone shook me. "I know how you feel, and I don't blame you for being upset, but you have to talk to Elijah."

I hadn't been too surprised when Pop defended Elijah, but my mother had too, and I felt as if I had been living in an alternate dimension where nothing and no one made sense. My mother would cut someone who dared look at her children wrong and she was defending my adulterous husband. "Not you too. Of all people, *Mami* you are taking Elijah's side? Or does Pop have you brainwashed?"

My mother's eyebrows elevated to the heavens, and she cocked her head to the side. I knew I had gone too far, but I wasn't a child anymore. I was a grown woman, and I did not need my parents meddling in my marriage. "I'm going to bed. Good night."

"*Christianna Fe!*"

I kept going. What could she do, beat me?

"Oh no she didn't." I heard my mother storm off.

"Christianna Faith Townsend Leonard."

This time I halted because in my entire life my father had only called me by full name once and I vividly remember being disrespectful in return and then disowning him. The hurt I'd seen in his eyes that day scarred me and was one of my biggest regrets. I promised I'd never hurt him that way again. And although I wasn't going to let my parents run my life, I would not be respectful. Especially in their home.

"First and foremost, don't ever talk to your mother that way again. I don't even understand how you grew up with her and you think you could get away with that." He looked at me like I had lost my mind. "I don't know where she went off to, but I promise you, it ain't good for you. Second, you know damn well your mother would never allow a man to hurt you. She beat her own brother within an inch of his life, what would she not do to someone else?"

"I'm sorry. I didn't mean to be disrespectful. I'm sorry. But I'm not a little girl or a teenage girl anymore. I can make my own decisions and my marriage is between Elijah and me."

"Nobody wants to get in your business, Ti! Your mother and I finally got you and your brother out of our house. We ain't tryna bring y'all nonsense back up in here, girl."

A commotion drew our attention. My mother, huffing and puffing, appeared dragging Jay's duffle bag of clothing and my suitcase. She stood upright, hands on her waist, and caught her breath before she lifted a finger and wagged it at me. "Take your kid and get out," she said between breaths.

My father clapped his hands and cracked up. "I hate to tell you I told you so, but I told you so."

I walked back down the stairs annoyed. "What do you mean? You are kicking us out?"

"That's what I said," she replied as she nodded.

"*Mami*! Where am I supposed to go?" Parts of my clothes were hanging free through the zipper that she hadn't even zipped fully closed. "You ain't got to go home, but you gots to get the hell up out of here. You and your babies."

Between *Mami* beginning to walk away and Pop laughing hysterically, I got angry. "You are kicking your pregnant daughter and your grandson out with no place to go?"

My mother turned back toward me, not an ounce of remorse on her face. "My grandson is with his father and is going home like you need to do. You are so steady claiming you are grown but Tianna, you still behave immaturely. Your husband slept with another woman, and she had his child. Yes, that's true, and had you stabbed him—"

"Tanya," Pop interrupted shaking his head. "Come on now. Don't encourage that nonsense."

Mami rolled her eyes and addressed Pop as if I weren't standing in front of them. "I forgot she's a softy and was raised in the suburbs."

"And, she's only half Puerto Rican so she didn't inherit that whole crazy gene you have," Pop added.

Mami shrugged as if that were a disappointment to her. I shook my head in disbelief. This all had to be a weird dream. "I am standing right here."

"You need to be standing in your own house and go talk to your husband. That stripper drugged him, and he didn't even know he was having sex with her. You so steady going jumping on planes taking my grandbabies across the country when all you had to do was talk to your man. Scream, shout, cry, get it out, but talk, Tianna. You didn't have to forgive him. But how can you make such life-altering decisions without even hearing the whole story? That woman came into your house, said some words and you fell apart. You ain't supposed to allow anyone on the outside to break up your home. You are supposed to be for each other. Partners. Teamwork. You gave that woman all of your power. Now had you spoken to him and heard his side and still decided to walk away, then that's different, because you made a fully informed decision, baby."

The truth slapped me in the face so hard, I stumbled back emotionally and mentally. I didn't even know what to say.

"Go home, Tianna."

I began to cry, and she hugged me.

"Go. You can pick up your bags later."

I thanked her and left, suddenly in the mood for King of Pizza. Within twenty minutes I was parked beside him in the parking lot. It took me a full ten minutes to find the courage to go inside. I locked my doors and walked in. I saw Elijah sitting at our usual table and Jay playing the pinball machine. I walked over to the counter to ask what they'd ordered so I could add mine to it. Two women were chatting, not minding the counter. One finally noticed me and walked over laughing at what the other had said. "Right. Single dads are your kryptonite. And he is really cute." My ears perked up and my radar began to beep. The woman at the counter turned to me, her hand on the register. "Hello, how can I help you?"

"Do you have macaroni and cheese?"

The woman looked at the waitress quickly, then back at me. "Um, no we don't. Sorry. We're a pizzeria so we have pizza, hoagies, cheesesteaks, wings. Things like that." She pointed up to the menu. "You can see everything we serve up here."

"Oh ok. Let me take a look. Give me a minute." Dumb ass women. Of course, they didn't sell mac and cheese. I just needed a minute and a reason to listen to their conversation a little.

Just as I thought, she went right back to continue the conversation with the waitress. "Did you see if he's wearing a wedding ring?"

The waitress stood off to the side. "Not yet. I'm about to go see if they need anything. I'll check now." She headed toward El's table.

Oh, is that right? "I'll have a cheesesteak with fried onions, salt, pepper, ketchup, and mayonnaise. For here."

The woman nodded and invited me to take a seat as they had plenty of open tables available. I headed straight toward the guys and found the waitress all smiles and giggles. "Yes, my son plays for the township in the little league. If your little guy wants to join, let me know. I'll give you my phone number before you leave so you can call me. The kids love it. The program is really great."

Elijah, ever the gentleman, entertained her. "That's really cool but we already have a full schedule with karate and our township's soccer team. But thanks for the offer."

She nodded. "Oh, no problem. So, what township does he play for?"

I raised an eyebrow at the audacity of this hussy and interrupted their conversation. "Hi. I placed my order at the counter. Could you bring it to this table? I prefer the company here."

She looked at me like I had lost my mind. "Oh. Ma'am, this table is already occupied but there are plenty of other tables you can choose from that are available." She eyed Elijah as if they were best friends. He looked at me as if he had no idea who I was.

"I see that. You aren't too busy today. Which makes me wonder why that gentleman over there has been waving you down for a few minutes and you haven't paid him any attention."

She straightened and eyed him. "Excuse me ma'am but I am helping a customer. You do not need to tell me how to do my job. If you find a table, I will deliver your food when it is ready." She looked and Elijah and shook her head. 'Wow,' she mouthed to him. He shrugged.

He tried to hide his amusement. I wanted to knock him upside the head. I had something for his ass. I bent over and kissed him on the lips. At first, he resisted me, then he gave in before the waitress yanked me back.

"Ma'am! What do you think you are doing?" She looked at Elijah, annoyed. "I am so sorry."

"What you sorry for? He's not. Did you see him fighting me?" I shook my head at her stupidity. Before I knew it, she bent over and put her lips on my husband's. He jumped up and back away from her, hand over his mouth. I yanked her by her ponytail and snatched her back. "What the hell are you doing?"

"Crazy bitch!" She yelled at me as she tried to fix her hair.

"This is my husband, so the only crazy one is you."

The waitress looked at Elijah stupefied. "This is your wife?"

Elijah eyed me like I was a complete stranger, didn't respond to her question, and asked one of his own. "Can I please just get my pizza to go?"

Her supervisor came over and asked the waitress to go wait in the back. She rushed and got Elijah's pizza just as the customer that had been trying to flag the waitress, yelled. "Excuse me! I've been waiting for fifteen minutes!

"I'll be there in a minute sir," she promised. "Sir, it's on the house. We are sorry for any inconvenience. Ma'am, your order is ready. We prefer you pay at the counter and take your food to go."

Elijah laughed and walked toward the door. "Champ. Pizza's ready. Let's go."

Jay left the game and when he saw me, he ran toward me. "Mommy! You came to have pizza with us?"

The entire restaurant looked at me, then back at Elijah shocked. He noticed and addressed the room. "Oh, no. We're not together anymore." He waved Jay over. "Let's go, Jay."

I stormed out after them completely mortified. That damn Elijah. He was strapping Jay's seatbelt in, so I waited for him to close the back seat door, so I could get to my driver's door. I didn't even want to look at him, nor him, me. He slammed the door and then walked around to his driver's side. I rushed to my door and opened it. I felt the door slip from his hand and me being spun around. Elijah got in my face and held it between his hands as he bore into my eyes. He looked angry and his touch was rough.

"Get your hands off me!" I yelled and yanked his hands off my face. "Leave me alone."

He snatched me up again and pushed up against the car, his body flush to mine, his face in mine. "You were wrong, and you know it," he said angrily. "You were wrong." The storm brewing in his expression saddened me. My husband would never hurt me, but he was furious enough his emotions were overflowing from his usually well-sealed reservoir. Angry tears filled his eyes, but he wouldn't let them escape. "You left me. You took my son, and you left me like I meant nothing to you." Elijah pushed away from me and walked to the driver's side of his car.

This time I snatched him back. He pushed my hands off him and continued forward, enraged. I hadn't the strength to get him to stay physically, but maybe my heart could do what my hands could not. "I'm sorry. I was wrong." And I knew it. And I meant it.

Elijah got in his car and drove off. I drove to a park and sat in the parking lot for a few hours contemplating everything before I went home. I unlocked the door and set my purse at the entrance.

"What are you doing here?" Elijah's angry voice greeted me. I wasn't going to argue with him. I picked up my purse and headed to the guest bedroom. He pulled at my arm. "Tianna. Don't walk away from me."

I removed my arm from his hold. "Only you get to storm off Elijah?"

"We've both done enough leaving, Tianna. Not just me."

"I tried to come back and you embarrassed me in public!"

"You embarrassed yourself."

Oh! I was getting ready to shut down or blow up. "That woman was flirting with you and you were flirting right back."

He massaged his forehead with his thumb and index finger. "I don't know what conversation you heard, but she tried to give me her phone number and I refused it. Ti, that happens to me more often than you think, and I can tell you right now, I have never even entertained a woman on that level, let alone had a lunch date with her in my car."

I knew that was coming. "Neither have I. John Edelson was just trying to be nice and he did admit to me that he liked me. I immediately shut him down and I have avoided him since. There was no date. So if you are done, excuse me." I walked around him and entered the guest bedroom.

The door closed behind me and before I knew it Elijah had me pinned up against it. "Stop walking away from me." His face was so close to mine, I could feel his breath on my face.

I turned away from him. "I don't want to argue with you." With his thumb, he guided my chin back to front.

"It's not just about you. You hurt me too! I should be grieving my child but I don't want to make you uncomfortable so I keep it to myself. But you walk around like you are the only one hurting."

My heart, soul, and pride stung all at once. I was looking in the mirror of ugly once again and I wanted to bolt. I reached for the doorknob and he brought me back, shaking his head in frustration. "You need to face this of you're gonna want to run again. Tianna, please don't leave me again. A third time will time break us for good."

I thought about what he said and it saddened me. This hadn't been the first time we'd faced this. When we dated in high school, his mother had said some things that made me walk away from him without giving him the chance to explain. Oddly enough, I was pregnant then too but lost the baby.

I rubbed my belly this time and knew I didn't want to go without El for years again. This time around, I wasn't a scared teenage girl. I was a wife that had been longing to give my husband a child. Elijah looked down at my belly and then backed off.

"I love you, Ti but you gotta show me you love me back. I need to know you are as committed as I am."

He left the bedroom and I fell asleep with his words weighing heavy on my heart.

THIRTY-FIVE
Sharmayne

One Month Later

My contractions had come hard and fast and I'd wondered how much of my back pain had been true labor. Micah sat vigil beside me, fretting over me every time I had a contraction. I needed a needle poked in my spine on the double.

"Breathe through it, baby," he encouraged as I squeezed the pillow.

Twenty minutes later I was on my way to relieving the pain and only feeling the infamous 'pressure.' My labor had been much faster and a lot easier the second time around. I'd delivered another girl. With all that had gone on with Jaya, I hadn't given this pregnancy the TLC it had needed and that was most evident when I didn't have a name picked out yet. Micah had fallen in love with her at first.

He cried and went through all of the excitement of having your first child. I found myself resenting him for being able to be happy for a new baby when I'd just buried my first one. How quickly he seemed to forget about Jaya. But I kept my thoughts to myself.

The second day after delivering, Micah had thought of a name and I was fine with whatever he chose to name her. Until he named her Destiny and I took offense to that too. His daughter was his destiny and my daughter was dead. Still, I kept quiet.

Once we got home, things quickly got worse. Within half an hour of being home, I found solace in Jaya's bedroom. The minute I had entered into it, I snuggled up in the day bed we had bought her when she'd gotten sick so that I could lay down with her. I hugged her blankets that had long since lost her scent and wept. An hour later Micah entered the room with the baby.

"Hey. We came to visit."

I watched them as if they were trespassers. Micah sat in Jaya's rocking chair holding the baby and I felt the momma bear in me beginning to growl. I remained quiet knowing on some level he hadn't done anything wrong. Until he laid the baby in Jaya's old crib. I roared on her behalf defending her territory.

"What are you doing? No. She has a bassinet in your bedroom. Go lay her in there."

Micah looked taken aback. "Ok, Shar. I'll take her to our bedroom. I didn't mean to upset you."

"Well you did, so please leave."

He did and I felt myself calm down. "See baby? Mommy didn't forget you. You're still mommy's girl."

Later that day Kendra had arrived and had been just as smitten as her son had been. The more she cared for the baby, the further I detached and retreated into my grief.

"Are you going to try and breastfeed, Shar?" She'd asked one of the rare times I left Jaya's bedroom. "It's healthy for the baby and will help you get your shape back," she teased.

"I don't care about my shape. I'm still not lactating so just stick to formula." The truth was I was glad I was not lactating. I hadn't held the baby since the hospital and didn't want to. I didn't want anything to do with her. I wanted my baby back. God was trying to replace *my* Jaya for a Destiny that I did not want.

THIRTY-SIX

Elijah

Tianna and I had taken some small steps forward trying to save our crumbling marriage. She'd remained in the guest bedroom at my suggestion. I missed her body as much as her heart, and soul but I needed her to understand that our issues weren't just going to go away with sex and intimacy. I needed to acknowledge that our physical relationship had always been beyond amazing but it wasn't enough to sustain a marriage. We needed trust and partnership. But I know myself and I'd be right back stuck on stupid for her if we were intimate. A few times I had to practice self-control to focus on the big picture and the long-term goal instead of the short-term satisfaction. It was what was best for us as a couple and I planned to see it through. I was glad we had begun to heal those wounds.

Other wounds weren't so easy to heal. I parked outside of Sharmayne's house and choked up. I hadn't been here since the night before Jaya died. As crazy as it sounded, all of the issues with Tianna had distracted me a little from my mourning. Ever since Tianna had found a level of common ground to build upon, grief had rushed back into the emotional and mental spaces, my stress and anxiety had vacated.

After letting me in, Micah walked me upstairs. "Thanks for coming. I don't know what else to do. I was hoping maybe you could talk to her. You and her share a common bond over Jaya."

I didn't know what expectations Micah had but I'd agreed to try. I knocked on Jaya's bedroom door. "Sharmayne? It's Elijah. Can I come in?" After no response, I knocked again. "Please?" Still nothing. "I miss her too," I said and headed for the stairs.

I heard the door creak open. I walked back toward it and found it ajar. I entered and left it open for propriety's sake. Sharmayne was lying in Jaya's bed, quiet, and seemingly despondent. The TV was on, but I had the feeling it was watching her more than she was watching it.

The memories of Jaya sick in her bedroom smacked upside the head like an entertainment wrestler. I was overcome with so much heartbreak I'd nearly choked on anguish. I swallowed the lump in my throat and fought back the tears. I walked over to her crib and saw the book she'd had me read to her over and over again. I picked it up and opened it. This time the tears refused to be held back. I quickly put it back and wiped my tears. When I turned and faced Sharmayne, she was sitting up in the bed staring at me as if she were ready to maul my face. Her expression was fierce, almost psychotic. It was also worn and pale.

Her appearance had changed drastically. She was extremely thin, her cheeks sunken in. My heart instantly went out to her. "How are you?"

She eyed me for a moment. "Micah asked you to come."

It was a statement more than a question. I nodded once. "I'm glad he did. I've been wanting to come but I didn't want to intrude." She remained quiet. "He is extremely worried about you."

Still, she said nothing. I knew I was going to have to stop trying to handle her and just be her friend.

I sat down on the floor and rested my head against the wall and closed my eyes. "I can't stop hearing her call me Lijah. I can't get her laughter out of my head or my heart."

I heard her sniffling and after a while, she finally spoke. "I am extremely sorry I did not tell you about her and that I robbed you of your place as her father. I see no silver linings in this black cloud but I am glad she had one more person love her while she was here. And she loved you too."

By this point, the tears were streaming down my face but I never once looked at her. It was my turn to remain quiet for a while.

"My wife is pregnant. She has had three miscarriages and she is finally pregnant. She hid it from me for months. For so long I prayed for a child to carry my bloodline and you come along and give me the most precious gift. Please don't get me wrong, I love my son. I will always love my son, but Jaya was my flesh and blood.

"After so many years of praying, God has answered my prayers, but I feel guilty for being mad at God. I can't help but wonder if he is trying to replace Jaya." I stopped talking, fearing I said too much. I'd never thought I'd accept that I felt that way, let alone say it aloud.

Sharmayne let out a humorless laugh. "You had the courage to say what I couldn't. I resent Micah and Kendra for moving on so fast. I resent the baby. I can't even say her name. And I know in my head I am supposed to love her, but there is a disconnect. My heart is fully occupied with love for Jaya and grief for Jaya. I have no space left for anything else." She began to sob. "I want my see my Jah-Jah. I want to be with her and her with me."

I cried again understanding how she felt. It was strange that I felt a level of comfort that someone understood me. Yet, my heart broke that someone understood me. I got up from the floor and sat by her on the bed and wrapped an arm around her. She began to wail, and I sat there and let her cry it out. She fell asleep and I tucked her into the bed with Jaya's blankets. I found a bottle of pills by the bed and assumed she's been taking them to avoid hurting.

On my way out, I told Micah about the pills. "She is still in deep grief. I don't think I was much help, to be honest. I'm really worried about her."

Micah nodded. "Thanks, man. You are the only person she's talked to since we got home from the hospital, and I didn't know about the pills, so you helped more than you know. I'm going to call her doctor. Thank you."

I nodded. "No problem. Anything I can do to help, I will. Oh, and congratulations on the baby. She's beautiful."

Micah's face beamed proudly. "Like her momma," he replied, and jealousy reared its ugly head. I had longed for that S on my chest feeling of Fatherhood for years and now it was closer than I'd ever had it and still seemed out of arm and heart's reach.

THIRTY-SEVEN

Tianna

The new normal of life was beginning to settle in. John had taken the hint of me avoiding him and had backed off and I appreciated that. I was the permanent teacher for the Culinary Arts Class for the remainder of the year due to Mrs. Wright being out on disability. I had found a groove with the students and the class had flowed well. Ironically, I had formed an attachment to Marissa. She was a kind-hearted girl, but a victim of her circumstances.

One afternoon I was walking to my car after school when I heard someone screaming for help. I saw Marissa hysterical and rushed over to her. Her hands were soaked in blood.

"Oh my God, Mrs. Townsend! Please, help me! Please!" Tears were streaming down her face.

I began to follow her, asking where the blood had come from when I spotted Sabrina, covered in blood, sitting on the corner of the street where Marissa's house was located, a body unconscious lying in front of her. I stopped dead in my tracks and put my hands to my belly.

Marissa realized I stopped and turned back, trying to pull me toward her. "Please Mrs. Townsend. I need your help."

I looked into her eyes and I saw despair and terror in her eyes I wanted to help her, but I couldn't make the same mistake twice and risk my baby's safety.

Marissa released my hand and began to scream out for someone to help her. A car is approached, and she rushed toward it seeking help. They slowed down and looked at the scene before driving off, ignoring her pleas for help.

God, please protect my baby.

My heart broke for her. I began to head across the street before I got snatched back. "Go call an ambulance," John commanded. "Hurry." He rushed over to the corner, while I returned inside the school and placed the emergency call.

245

When I ran back out, I saw John pushing down on the stomach of the person lying down on the ground. I headed toward him wanting to help but he yelled for me to stay back. Marissa and Sabrina were nowhere to be found. The sirens I'd heard in the distance had gotten louder the closer they came before suddenly police and ambulance were on the scene. The body lying on the ground was placed on a gurney quickly and gone before I could begin to understand what was going on.

I gave an officer my statement and waited for John to finish giving his before I approached him. He had been wiping his blood-stained hands on towels provided by a neighbor. "Don't come too close," he warned me.

"What in the hell happened?" I asked from where I stood. "Best I can tell, that girl Sabrina, stabbed the other girl lying on the ground and I don't think she's going to make it Chris. She lost a lot of blood."

I was shocked. "Were Marissa or Sabrina hurt?"

"I don't know. I was too busy trying to stop the other girl from bleeding out. An older woman snatched them up then they all ran down the street. I don't know where they went."

A few days later Marissa returned to school. She remained quiet for a few days. One afternoon I found her leaning against my car after school.

"Thank you for not snitching on us."

I shook my head. "Please don't thank me. I had nothing to tell. I didn't intentionally keep your sister's secret." I unlocked my car door.

Marissa nodded. "Sabrina turned herself in."

That intrigued me. "Good."

"Mrs. Townsend, you don't even know the whole story."

"Marissa, I think you are a kind young lady, but your sister—"

"My sister never laid a hand on you. And the only reason she joined that gang was because of me. She was protecting me. I had gotten mixed up with them and then I backed out not wanting to be in a gang. Well, there is no backing out of a gang. Those girls threatened to initiate me in or kill me, and my sister took my place. We were supposed to move to Florida next month with my dad and she was going to go finish high school there and go to college. She is the smart one and had good grades. I was the one always in trouble."

"Marissa, I know you love your sister—"

"Yes! I love my sister. Yesterday I was walking home from school and Tay saw me and told Sabrina that they still planned to deal with me because I had made their gang look soft. Sabrina reminded her that she had taken my place and they said that that didn't matter. Sabrina blacked out and stabbed Tay."

I couldn't believe what I was hearing. "That was Tay? Is she dead?"

Marissa looked at me afraid and shook her head, no. She's in a coma. "Please don't tell anybody all of this. I didn't think you'd snitch."

I looked around worried for Marissa's safety. "Why are you out here?"

She looked at me earnestly. "I can't fail school. I can't let Sabrina down. After all she did for me, I have to do good. I have to. I already missed a lot of school. I can't fail, Mrs. Townsend. I can't."

I sent her home immediately. I went back into the school and arranged for her to be home-schooled for her safety. Two days later, Marissa and her grandmother moved to Florida after Tay succumbed to her injuries.

THIRTY-EIGHT

Micah

It had been several months since Sharmayne had had Destiny and she hadn't been any better. I called her doctor but Sharmayne refused to talk to her or seek treatment. She insisted she had been fine.

An early Saturday afternoon, Sharmayne had come downstairs to the living room, showered, and wearing a spring dress. It had been so long since I had seen her up and looking alive.

"Wow, babe. You look beautiful."

She looked at me and tears filled her eyes. "Thank you for always being good to me. You are the best husband any woman could be blessed to have." She kissed me on my lips and hugged me.

"I love you Shar."

"I love you, Micah." She smiled at me. It wasn't the bright smile I had come to love but it was a smile and I thanked God for small steps forward. She walked over to Destiny and looked down at her. "She's gotten so big. She looks like you," she added. She tugged at Destiny's foot then ran a finger down her cheek. "You be good for daddy."

"Are you going somewhere?"

This time she beamed a smile so bright it warmed me. "Yes."

I laughed. "Ok. Want to tell me where? It's beautiful outside. Maybe we can take the baby for a walk."

"This is a walk I need to take alone. I'll be ok," she promised me. It was the happiest I'd seen her in a year.

I smiled at her relieved. "Ok, baby. Enjoy your walk."

She kissed me again and walked out the door singing, *'Where is Moochie? Where is Moochie?'* It saddened me but if that's what Shar needed to feel close to Jaya, I supposed that was ok.

I changed the baby's diaper then fed her. As usual, she fell asleep after her bottle. I stared at her and smiled. She did look like me a little bit. I put her in her bassinet and called my Mom seeing what we were going to do for Mother's Day, the following day, now that Sharmayne was coming around, I wanted to celebrate her but be sensitive to her grief. My mom suggested just a small lunch or dinner at home as not to pressure her. I would go buy her some flowers too. Not a big celebration but healing took time, and we'd take it one step at a time.

An hour turned to two, then three and by the time it was dark outside and Shar hadn't returned home, I began to worry. I took the baby to my mom's and went out searching for her.

I returned home to see if she'd been back, but she hadn't. I don't know why, but I went into Jaya's room. On Jaya's bed, propped up on the pillow was an envelope with my name on it. I snatched it and tore it open.

Dear Micah,

I am so blessed to have received all the love you have given me and Jaya. I used to think that she loved you more than me, she was so stuck to you like glue. I don't blame her. You were and still are an amazing father. I know I haven't been a good mother to Destiny and I am sorry about that. But to be honest, she was better off not being exposed to me. You and Kendra have been great with her.

I need to tell you a few things:

First, please tell Elijah, that God has blessed him no matter what it may look like. Second chances are beautiful, and time is too precious to waste. Love well. He'll know what I am talking about.

Second, I know my mother was linked to Ace for years but I never dared believe it. Please keep her away from Destiny. No matter what.

Third, I don't know if this will mean anything to you, but please know I never stole the money Ace accused me of. That money was buried in his grandfather's recliner and if I had to guess, it was his cousin, Wesley that stole it.

And last, by the time you find me, I'll already be with Jaya. Please don't be sad for me. With her is the only place I want to be. The only place I'll be happy. Please bury me next to her, in the dress, I am wearing. It was the dress that taught her the color pink and that she loved.

Here is Jaya's life insurance policy check. I didn't cash it because it meant accepting that my baby was gone and I didn't want to be paid for her death. I offered it to Elijah to repay the funeral and medical expenses but he refused it. Please use it to help pay for your houses. I know you tried to keep that from it but not much got past me.

I love you Micah Payne. Keeping living, loving and learning.

Love Always,

Sharmayne

I drove to the cemetery, hopped the fence, and found my wife's body, laying beside Jaya's grave. She was gone, her body cold and stiff. I fell to my knees, and in disbelief. She'd overdosed on my prescription pain pills. My mom blamed herself remembering that Shar had once mentioned abusing pills and my mom dismissing her concern. But I knew it wasn't my mom's fault. I'd seen the signs of depression and didn't protect my wife from herself. A lesson learned at a very high price. I later learned Shar had probably also suffered from severe post-partum depression. My ignorance of such a condition didn't rid me of my guilt but I was relieved to know there was a deeper reason for her distance from Destiny and had she received proper treatment, she would have come to love Destiny as much as she loved Jaya.

After a few weeks of my own grieving, I shared Shar's letter with Elijah and my mom. I had cut out the portion of the letter that spoke about Ace and mailed it anonymously to his house. Both he and Wesley disappeared for a while. Ace popped back up months later. It was rumored he'd killed Wesley and had taken time away from Jersey, distraught over Sharmayne's death. He'd asked for her entire letter, but I denied his request. I hadn't protected my wife in life as I should have, but I would in death.

As she requested, I buried her beside Jaya and visited them daily. Many nights, I'd sneak in after dark and mourn my family until daybreak, my tears soaking their plots. I missed them so much I ached inside, but I had a daughter who needed me more than the plots of Shar and Moochie. I couldn't do anything for them except keep them alive in my heart and in Destiny's. That became my focus. I made sure Destiny knew how special her mother and sister were.

THIRTY-NINE

Elijah

D eath had surrounded me like a plague and I couldn't take anymore. After learning about Sharmayne, I battled guilt for not doing more to help her rather than cry and telling her how I understood her pain. For the rest of my life, I would struggle with the unknown if I'd helped pushed her to the decision to take her own life.

I kept a copy of the passage she'd left to me in her goodbye letter in my wallet and read it daily. I wanted to honor her in some way and take the advice she couldn't take herself. I had asked Tianna if I could come to her OB visit with her. She looked surprised.

"Of course, you can." She smiled warmly. "I do have to stop somewhere else afterward though but you can tag along."

I nodded not caring where we went. I just felt the overwhelming need to be with my family and not waste time, make up for lost time and not take for granted that we had time.

At the appointment I was amazed by the rapid heartbeat of the baby and all that the doctor had said was going on. He did a vaginal check that I didn't like but I stayed quiet. On the way out Tianna made an appointment for a week and I promised I come to that one too. "Is the doctor going to check your hot spot again, because I was this close to knocking him on his ass?"

Tianna laughed then smirked. "From now on, he'll probably to check to see if I'm dilated."

"If you dying what?" The word set me on edge.

She smiled sadly at me. "Not dying. Dilated. That means how much my cervix has opened up."

"Your circus? Tianna, what the hell? What is with all these crazy terms?"

This time she laughed. "Only circus is this car 'cause you acting like a clown."

"You the one talking about the circus like I know what the hell you talking about."

She rolled her eyes. "The doctor has to check my vagina hole every week to see if it's pliable enough for your baby's big ass head to come out of. The more pliable it becomes, the closer I am to labor."

I didn't even have a vagina but my groin tensed up imagining that experience. "I'm so glad I was born a man. Y'all bleed every month. Gotta buy tampads. That's disgusting."

I hadn't heard my wife laugh so hard she snorted in ages. I wanted to laugh with her but I was pretty sure she was laughing at me.

"What's so funny?"

She snorted again before she caught her breath. "You are so stupid. Tampons or Maxipads, or pads, but not tampads. Just mixing and matching and making up your own words."

"Whatever. You know what I'm talking about. The sticks or the pillows that y'all use to soak up y'all nasty ass blood." She kept laughing and after a minute it became contagious.

We pulled into a parking lot and I had no idea where we were. "So what's the mystery place Ti?"

"It's not a mystery place, but I didn't tell you about it because I needed to work this out on my own."

That left me with more questions than answers as we walked into a building that looked like it was a recreational center. We went down a flight of stairs and into a large space with chairs set up in a circle and then some rows behind. We sat down in the rows behind. People began filing in and filling in random seats. The seats in the circle filled up quickly. "Ti, where are we?"

Before she could answer a man address the group and thanked everyone for coming. He mentioned seeing a few new faces and welcomed them.

"Last month, we had some great dialogue and share time. I'd like to continue along that path but first, let's see if anyone has anything positive to share about their journey.

A woman raised her hand and a baton was passed down to her. When she received it she talked about a foundation she had founded had gotten its first sizable charitable donation to help fund the funeral expenses for families who had lost a child and couldn't afford them.

I looked over at Ti, but she clapped and was genuinely engaged in the group, not paying attention to me. After a few minutes, the session began to intensify I realized that every person in the group had lost a child. Some had been battling grief for years.

To hear them share their feelings of all that I had been feeling was surprising. I wasn't ready to share my trauma but hearing people who have been where I am and seeing how far they've come was crucial for me. Grief was different for everyone and there was no set timetable to get to a place of healing.

I thought about Sharmayne and wondered if a place like this could have helped her. I suppose I'd never know but it made me that much more determined to not take advantage of my blessings and my family.

After we'd left the group session I drove and let Ti relax. She was tiring out a lot faster. I took her home and stuffed her face with mac and cheese. She went to the guest bedroom to lay down and I followed her.

"You ok?"

I nodded. "Yeah, but I have so many thoughts spinning in my head. I had no idea you were grieving so deeply. I'm sorry I wasn't more supportive. Thinking about Sharmayne and the last time I saw her, I thought she was losing her mind. Then I remember when you were chasing down gang members and thinking the same about you, that scared me. Grief doesn't care what you look like or where you grew up or if you are a schoolteacher or a stripper or a lawyer, it has the potential to drown anyone. Me included."

Tianna rested and listened, rubbing my back as I sat on the bed. I had had enough of living apart from my wife. I laid down beside her. "I love you Ti. And Champ. And this one too. For the first time since she'd been pregnant, I intentionally touched her belly. I know I haven't been as receptive as I should have been but I will be from now on. All in."

"Me too. All in. And I'm not ever going anywhere again. But I'm warning you, you asked for it."

I rubbed her belly and kissed her forehead as she fell fast asleep. "No, baby. I prayed for it."

EPILOGUE

Tianna

Eleven Years Later

My husband pulled me into his arms and kissed my lips before pressing his lips to my forehead.

"Gross. Can you guys please stop kissing?"

Elijah snatched Josiah by his hoodie when he walked past and put him in a headlock. "You got about four more years before you'll change your mind about what's gross."

"Nope. Girls are annoying."

I crossed my arms offended, "Hello. I'm standing right here."

My son smirked. "You're not a girl. You're a mom. That's different."

Elijah snickered quietly as he slipped his jacket on. "He's got a point."

I smacked Elijah on his butt as I walked behind him to grab my jacket. "You complaining?"

"Depends. Can I watch ESPN in the UK, once we move?"

"I'm pretty sure the internet is also known as the World Wide Web, emphasis on World. You'll figure it out how to keep up with American sports."

Elijah picked up his keys from the hall table. "That wasn't a yes, Christianna."

I chuckled. "If they don't, just become Rugby fan. It's their version of football."

"Negative."

"You can complain later. Let's go. I don't want to be late."

We made it to Jay's first football game of the season a little early expecting it to get crowded and we were right. "Jay had had a great Junior year on the Varsity Team and was one of the star players of the team. As we walked to find seats in the bleachers, a few of the team parents greeted us as well as some fans that praised Jay's athletic skills.

Seeing him out there warming up, made me emotional. My son had nearly outgrown me and *Mami* had to look up at him. The facial hair and the giddy girls vying for his attention was all too much. I couldn't believe he was almost eighteen years old.

The hardest part of moving to England for school was leaving Jay behind. He had started his senior year of high school, and playing football was his life. After much prayer and thought, Elijah and I had decided to allow him to stay in New Jersey to finish his high school years and start college in the fall. He had been working hard to excel athletically but was hoping to win some academic scholarships. I couldn't disrupt his future to follow my dreams across the ocean.

It was close to game time when Micah arrived with Destiny. As usual, she and Josiah sat next to each playing their hand-held video games, unexpected best friends. Elijah and Micah had gotten closer over the years. Micah had done a good job raising Destiny as a single father. He had recently found a girlfriend. Hopefully, he'd finally let himself be happy.

Destiny was content for the most part. She was a bit shy and a tomboy like you wouldn't believe, but she was sweet and well-mannered. The only time she'd ever spoken back to me was when I offered to buy her some cute dresses for spring and summer. She'd had a meltdown and I never brought it up again. I knew it had something to do with her mother and I felt bad for triggering her. After that I was more mindful to just let her be who she was.

Mami and Pop arrived a few minutes later, her arrival overdramatic as always wearing custom gear in support of Jay. "*Mami*, you are so extra."

"Or maybe you are just too boring, Tianna. My grandson is the star of this football team and I am going to represent because if there is one thing *Boricuas* know how to do, it's represent. *Wepa mija. Wepa.*"

Crossing the Atlantic suddenly didn't seem like enough distance between my mother and I. I let *Mami*, be *Mami* and turned my attention to the field. The teams were announced as the players ran out onto the field, much to the delight of the fans. The starters were then called by name and an eager group of female classmates cheered a little too excitedly for my son. Little fast-ass girls. *Mami* noticed too. Where I frowned upon their behavior Mami encouraged it.

"That's my grandson! Isn't he handsome girls?" They giggled.

I leaned over to Elijah. "I don't think we should leave Jay behind."

Elijah, paying me half-mind, yelled encouragement to our son. "He'll be fine, Ti. We raised a good kid." I began to get emotional. "Besides, Abe is on him more than we are. Speaking of which, where is Abe?" Elijah looked around quickly before his focus was back on the field. "That defensive line grew since last year. Champ needs to pay attention. This isn't the same team as last year." Micah agreed and chimed in something about someone being a beast.

I had no idea what they were talking about. "Abe's running late, and hopefully he'll be the one keeping Jay in line 'cause my mother is trying to pimp our son."

Elijah gave me his full attention and stared at me confused. "What?"

I shook my head. "Never mind."

He rubbed my back, then turned back to the game. "Ti, stop worrying. God's plans never fail, baby."

That was the best truth. I settled my heart and cheered my baby on. By game's end, Jay had caught a majority of the completions and had scored a touchdown. After the game, he ran up to the gate to greet El and Abe as he did after every game. El grabbed his helmet mask and brought their faces together while Abe tapped the top as a congratulatory gesture.

As Jay walked to the locker room, fans and coaches are offered congratulations and praise. It settled my heart even more. This was where my son belonged and I had to trust God more than my brother or even Jay himself, to make sure he was good.

After the game, Jay met us out in the parking lot. He kissed me on the cheek, and I congratulated him on a great game. "Thanks, Mom." He was all smiles as fans walked past and complimented him, gracious and courteous, he thanked them all and remained humbled, unlike his grandmother. She sashayed up hooting and hollering.

"That's my baby!"

Jay shook Pop's hand and kissed Mami on her cheek and smiled. "Thanks, Mom-Mom." Their exchange was short and my parents left promising to be present for the next home game.

I was ready to go too. "You hungry baby? Let's go eat."

"I'm tired but there's a party at Jonathan's house. Just a few guys from the football team and a few friends. Can I go? I won't stay long.

I want to make an appearance though. Last year when I would go home, they started saying I was being cocky. Coach encouraged us to spend time together outside of school and practice to build up team comradery."

I nodded. "As long as Daddy says it's ok with him." El came over after talking to the father of another player and went through the same conversation with Jay as I had.

"No drugs. No sex. No booze. Be home by midnight. We are leaving early in the morning."

Jay chuckled. "I know Dad. I'll be home by eleven. I just want to make an appearance."

I watched my son walk away and began to cry. I still saw my baby boy in the body of a young man. To think I had almost given him up as a baby to now not wanting to let him go.

"Stop crying, Ti. He'll be fine." El put an arm around my shoulder.

"Yeah, Mom. He'll be fine. He's probably kissing girls like Dad said."

I elbowed El in the stomach and he chuckled. He made a grab for Josiah who had sidestepped him. El began to chase him and I shook my head. One child on his was to maturity, two still to go. I rolled my eyes and laughed. I thanked God for surviving the up and down journey of motherhood. Not all women had. My husband finally caught Josiah and put him in a headlock and threatened him. Josiah laughed then got free and ran to the car. Elijah, out of breath, grabbed my hand and held it.

"You know wife, we have some pretty great kids."

I smiled and agreed. "I also have an amazing husband." I rested my head on his shoulder as we walked.

"And I have a hood wife and a good wife."

I cracked up. "And don't you forget it."

The End

HOOD BOY, GOOD BOY
PROLOGUE

Jordi

H e left the liquor store, pulled the bottle out of the black plastic bag, and took a swig of whatever cheap pint of liquor he'd bought. He'd been out of jail for three months and I'd been watching him. He lived a miserable existence; drinking every time I saw him. No family. No friends. No job. Hustling doing small, odd favors like washing cars for spare change or panhandling, begging people for money. He was very much pitiful, but I wasn't in the habit of pitying the people responsible for taking my family from me.

My father had been dead for over twenty years. My brother, Justin had been gone for over fifteen. Yet, the pain was as fresh as the day they died. I took a long drink from my own bottle, crossed the street to my car, and drove to my lonely ass Tamarack Apartment off Ferry Avenue. I'd been living Eddie's life far longer than he had so I knew what he was thinking when he went to the liquor store every day. I knew what he was feeling when he went home to loneliness every night. I knew how he regretted decisions that had changed his life and cost others theirs.

But even still, that changed nothing. That man robbed me of my father. My whole world changed when he stabbed my father in his rage toward someone. As far as I was concerned, Eddie Pena's life was a walking death sentence the second I learned who I would make pay for all the loss I'd endured. Now that I had a face to match a name, it was only a matter of time before he'd get what he deserved.

Thank You so much for reading Hood Girl, Good Girl

If you enjoyed this book, please consider leaving a review on Amazon or any of the major bookstore retailers.
Be sure to check out these other books you may enjoy.

Released August 2021   Releases June 2022

 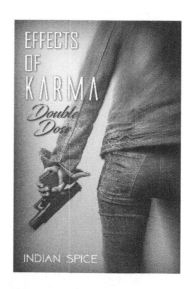

AVAILABLE NOW

ACKNOWLEDGEMENTS

Of all the books I have written, this one has been the most difficult by far. A string of non-writing-related issues resulting in delayed and postponed deadlines, writing, release, and whatever else you could think.

With Jaya having Leukemia it was extremely important to me to make it as accurately and believable as possible and not give my readers a lot of fluff. I spent countless hours researching diagnosis, prognosis, and treatment plans of Leukemia. Of course, I could not learn everything but before including anything I verified that Jaya's condition, treatment, remission rate, symptoms, probability of mortality versus survival was actually possible. This novel is based in 2005/2006 when stem cell therapy had been extremely controversial, and the donor banks were not as stocked as they are today. I pray I was able to capture a realistic scenario from a medical standpoint.

Although I did not go into detail, I aimed at Sharmayne suffering from grief and postpartum depression simultaneously. I researched mothers who suffered from both grief and postpartum depression and discovered that suicide was the second-highest cause of postpartum deaths at a rate of twenty percent. Coupled with the statistics that parents who committed suicide after the loss of a child usually did so if the child was between the ages of 1-6 and most often took their own lives within a month after the loss of their child, it was fairly probable that in real life Sharmayne was indeed a high risk-factor for suicide.

I cried many times writing the death scenes. I had spent an enormous amount of time in research that both Jaya and Sharmayne were in my thoughts for months and although they are fictitious, their research used to bring accuracy to their stories were based off actual statistics of many young children and mothers who indeed suffered these real fates.

If you know anyone who is suffering from depression, suicidal thoughts or postpartum depression, please say something or call for guidance and help.

First, I always give honor and glory to my Lord Jesus Christ, for without him I have nothing and am nothing.

To Stephen Lester, RN, you are a doll! While it is much easier to research and find information regarding diagnosis, prognosis, and treatments of cancer online, finding information on what a typical day for a patient looked like was not as readily available. Then I remembered my friend Stephen was a brilliant RN who works specifically with terminally ill patients. He was a vast wealth of knowledge regarding the specific and general care these patients received daily. He was able to provide how care was administered from a nursing/caregiver standpoint. I sorta, kinda bothered him a lot, but he was always generous with his knowledge and patient with my million follow-up questions. Basically, I got on his nerves, but he endured and for that, I am eternally grateful! Thank you, my newest Bestie...lol!

Indian Spice, thank you so much for reading in advance and giving me encouragement and feedback from a writer's standpoint! You cheer for me as much as I cheer for you. My life has become more enriched and blessed with you in it! I love ya Sis!

To my children, family, and friends that I ignored, cut off phone calls, canceled plans, and generally put you on hold so I could finish on time, not only were you all so understanding, you all encouraged me to keep writing! I love you all bunches and bunches!

Cynthia Marcano

About The Author

Cynthia Marcano is a native Jersey girl enamored of Jesus, reading, and cake, born and raised in Southern New Jersey to Puerto Rican parents. She loves to incorporate South Jersey culture with life as a Christian and Hispanic woman into her fiction writing. She founded Feeding Thousands Publishing in 2015 and launched Urban House Publishing in 2019. She currently lives in Dallas, Texas.

When her nose isn't stuck in her laptop designing graphics or a book reading, you can probably find her listening to music, avoiding the dishes, and spending time with her three beloved children.

She Will Rise, a brand devoted to encouraging others through heartbreak and loss was launched in 2019 to empower women into business, inner and outer beauty, and self-love. Through her organization, Cynthia leads women on self-discovery and self-love "journeys."

www.CynthiaMarcano.com
Facebook - @AuthorCynthiaMarcano
Instagram -

Made in the USA
Monee, IL
20 May 2022